COLUMBUS: DEMETER
Project Columbus, Book 3

By J.C. Rainier

Columbus: Demeter
Project Columbus, Book 3
Copyright © 2013 by J.C. Rainier
Published: 10 September 2013
ISBN: 978-0-9882482-8-1
Publisher: J.C. Rainier

Please follow J. C. on Facebook or Twitter (@JCRainier), or check http://jcrainier.com periodically for blog updates and a sneak preview of the fourth and fifth books in the Project Columbus series, scheduled for release in Spring 2014:

Columbus: Winter (Kindle Exclusive)

Columbus: Deluge

Currently Available by J.C. Rainier:

Columbus: Flight

Columbus: Ashes

Columbus: Demeter

>BEGIN PLAYBACK|

Gabrielle Serrano
Civilian
25 March, Year of Landing, late morning
Camp Eight
>|

Dr. Petrovsky's feet made a muffled scraping noise as he shuffled them across the packed dirt floor of the modest hut. His body was clothed in a clean blue coverall suit like those that the colony's soldiers wore, every detail immaculate, right down to the American flag sewn into the left shoulder. He lowered his frame onto a stout chunk of palm trunk that Gabi liked to use as a table, though he had scolded her several times and told her it was his chair. His eyes were half open, and he groaned as he took the weight off of his legs. Gabi popped up from her woven play mat – a gift from Jeanette Vandemark – and skipped over to the doctor with a sweet grin on her face, dragging her dusty, matted stuffed cat, Pelusina, with her. She flung her arms around his belly and squeezed.

"Oof. Good morning, Gabi," he grunted.

"Good morning! Have you seen Mama?"

Dr. Petrovsky nodded as he yawned.

"Where?"

"She's here, but she just woke up, dear. Give her a minute."

"Why won't she hurry? I'm hungry," she whined.

Petrovsky let out a long sigh and scratched at his stomach with one hand. His belly had shrunk a lot since Gabi had met him, and his eyes seemed to get sadder with every passing day. At one time, Gabi thought that he looked a lot like Santa Claus. When his beard first grew in, he had ruddy cheeks and a laugh that would shake his belly. The beard he sported then was not white, but she did not care. He used to make her laugh with his jokes. Now his long shaggy beard was marred with streaks of white and gray, his face had taken on the color of ash, and he no longer laughed. All Gabi ever saw him do was tend to her mother, as well as the other colonists who came to the clinic when they were hurt or sick.

"You're not the only one." He looked down at her with a gaze that suddenly flared with intensity. "You promise me you'll stay here while I get breakfast, okay? You don't leave the clinic without me or your mom, got it?"

"I promise."

Dr. Petrovsky rose to his feet and walked to a short partition in the back of the hut where her mother slept. He muttered something around the corner, and then headed across the room, past rows of woven frond beds, and through the curtain that served as a door. As he drew the thick shade across the entryway, the room was engulfed in silence and near darkness. Only a faint glow from the sun penetrated the thick woven roof above her head.

Gabi knelt down in the dirt and placed Pelusina on her now vacated "table". She cooed at the cat and stroked its crusty fur. She snuggled with it, and carried it around the silent hut with her. Gabi tried to occupy her time, but as the minutes passed in eerie silence, she began to feel a knot of loneliness deep inside.

"Mama?"

Silence answered her. Her skin began to crawl as she slowly crept toward the partition wall.

"Mama?" she whispered.

Again there was no response from her mother. Gabi squeezed Pelusina tight against her chest and walked up to the partition. She poked her head around and saw her mother, curled up under an unzipped sleeping bag, with an arm thrown across her eyes to block out the light.

"Mama?"

Without moving a muscle, she replied, "What is it, Gabi?"

Her mother's voice, though soft and cold, washed away her anxiety. "Mama, when are you going to get up?"

"In a bit."

"I'm hungry."

"Dr. Petrovsky went to go get you breakfast."

"I want you to make me breakfast, Mama."

Her mom rolled over and curled into a tight ball. Her eyes opened, but stared off at the wall.

"I can't, honey."

"Why not?" A pout began to form on Gabi's lips.

"I'm not feeling well."

"Awww. I'm sorry, Mama."

Gabi marched around the corner and knelt next to her mom, then flopped on top of her with both arms outstretched in a giant hug. Her mom shrugged a shoulder free and pushed Gabi backwards, and she rolled off of the edge of the low bed.

"Not now, Gabi," she growled.

Gabi's lip quivered. She grabbed Pelusina and scurried back around the corner, sniffing and wiping away a tear. She was about to burst out crying when she heard the door curtain slide to the side, and light flooded in from outside. Gabi caught a flash of dark blue as her eyes struggled to adjust to the light.

"Good morning, sweetie," called a light, feminine voice. "I've missed you."

"Haruka!" she shouted and bounded up, flinging her arms around her friend's leg. Warm arms wrapped around her sides, and soothing hands patted her on the back. "I missed you too. I missed you *so* much!"

"How's your kitty?"

"Pelusina?" she asked. She backed out of the embrace and proudly held up her stuffed cat. "She missed you too."

Haruka smiled and gave Pelusina a quick pat on the head. Gabi giggled and rocked as she cradled the cat in her arms.

"Gabi?" her mother called. "Come here, please."

Gabi looked over her shoulder and saw her mom leaning against the partition wall. Her hair was a disheveled black mess, her eyes seemed puffy, and she wore a thin red robe that ended just past her knees. Gabi complied with the request, marching quietly over to her and giving her a hug. She received a quick pat on the head, and her mom squatted down to be at eye level with her.

"Gabi, can you go make my bed and then play with Pelusina back there for a bit?"

The smile on her face quickly waned. "Aww. Can't I play with Haruka for a bit?"

"Now, Gabi," huffed her mother.

Gabi stomped her feet and crossed her arms, but was met with a look that meant she was only one step away from getting in deep trouble. She trudged around the corner behind the partition, dragging her feet in a dramatic show of reluctance. A glance back revealed that her mother was not watching her, but had disappeared on the other side of the wall.

Frustrated, she threw her tiny body on the bed. It was raised only a couple inches off the floor, and was filled primarily with sawdust and sand. Two layers of interwoven palm leaves lay on top, keeping anyone sleeping in it from getting too dirty. Gabi grabbed one corner of the dark blue sleeping bag that her mother had scavenged from one of the sleeper pods and tugged it neatly to one of the corners of the bed. She repeated this process three more times, and then lay her back on the bed, holding Pelusina above her and making the cat fly through the air like a furry superhero.

She finished her game and curled up with the animal for a moment. She then heard her mother's voice shriek out clearly from the other side of the wall.

"Gabi's doing fine, okay? I'm fine too, not that you really care."

"That's not fair," Haruka retorted, her voice ringing sharply through the air. "I was trying to help you."

"You abandoned me when I needed you the most. How was that helping?"

"Abandoned you? You pushed me away. You wouldn't let me near. And you say I abandoned you?"

Gabi lifted herself off of the bed and walked to the edge of the partition wall. She squeezed her stuffed companion tight to her chest as she poked her head around the corner. Her mother and Haruka stood in the middle of the clinic floor. Her mother was gesturing wildly as she shouted at Gabi's friend.

"Oh please. Don't try playing the saint with me. You gave me nothing. You couldn't even catch the son of a bitch that did this to us."

Haruka closed her eyes and tilted her head slightly. "It's not that easy, Maria. He didn't just stand around and wait for us to come get him. When he came back to steal food, he could have killed Doctor Petrovsky."

"But he didn't," her mother snarled impatiently. "And you and your lackeys couldn't find him afterwards, either. God, can't you do anything right? What are we even doing with you in charge?"

"I know you're angry, I'm still here for you. Anything you need, I will…"

"It's too late," her mother sobbed as her voice dropped. "Just leave me alone."

Haruka's shoulders slumped. "Maria, don't do this."

"Get the hell out, you bitch!" her mom's voice shot up an octave as she screamed through her tears.

"Mama, that's a bad word," Gabi shouted.

Haruka's eyes shot open and both women glanced over at Gabi. Her mother had tears flowing down both cheeks, and her eyes were bloodshot. Haruka's expression twisted, her eyebrows arched upward, and her jaw slacked.

"Get back in bed," her mother yelled. "Now!"

Gabi's heart dropped and her lip trembled.

"Maria, don't yell at her. She didn't do anything."

Gabi's mother turned back to face Haruka. She swung her right hand repeatedly at her, raining blows down on the woman's arm. Haruka barely flinched, taking only one step back.

"Don't ever tell me what to do with my daughter. Get out. Get out!"

Haruka's hand shot up and caught the wrist that was pummeling her. Instantly, her mother began flailing at Haruka with her free wrist, which Haruka caught after the second blow. Her eyes darted between Gabi and her mother. Haruka shook her head, released her grip on Maria's wrists, and then walked out of the clinic without another word.

Gabi's mother turned to face her. Tears rolled down her cheeks while a snarl formed on her face. Her finger shot up like an arrow and pointed toward the bed.

"Back to bed. Now. Don't come out until I tell you to."

Gabi could not hold back her fear any longer. Her mother was clearly angry with her, and she hadn't the slightest idea why. She scurried back to the bed and fell face first on it, sobbing uncontrollably. She clutched Pelusina, but the little comfort that the cat gave her was overwhelmed by her mom's vicious snarl playing over and over in her head as her stomach growled from a missed meal.

Dada, why aren't you here?

Darius Owens
Ex-USAF
25 March, Year of Landing, 09:12
Gabriel landing site
>|

A pair of brightly colored birds with four wings dipped and wove through the gray skies above. Darius took a bite of eggs from his ration pouch and washed it down with a swig of coffee. The hot liquid spread a wave of warmth through his core that cut through the crisp chill of the morning. From all around came the din of the tent city that had sprung up on the river side of the massive sleeper ship.

Gabriel's crew had spent the previous day working with the civilians to organize and erect the camp, as well as distribute the first meals to the families. Darius had done the latter, moving from tent to tent, handing out two meal packets for every person at a given tent, and then moving on as swiftly as he could. It was also a job that he felt he could do without running into Colonel Eriksen.

The last time he had seen *Gabriel's* commanding officer, he was beet red and grinding his teeth together so loudly that he was afraid the entire crew pod had heard.

A technicality, he thought. *I'm staking my career on a technicality. Maybe even my life.*

Darius flicked three dashes of hot sauce from the miniature bottle included in the ration onto his eggs and took another bite. His gaze shifted to the bridge, high atop the bow of the ship. He calculated the odds that the colonel would be on the bridge at that moment, reviewing the situation from his command chair.

Has he even set foot on Demeter yet?

He finished his breakfast, stowed the waste in the outer pouch, and methodically rolled it up, as he had done dozens of times over the course of their journey. He found a waste collection point near the base of the ship and threw the trash into the large metal bin. Darius leaned on the bin and looked back at the camp. He could make out crew members in their blue flight suits making their way through the camp, giving orders to the civilians. Many men and women followed them and began to form in a large semicircle at the end of camp.

Darius nearly jumped out of his skin as a hand slapped down on his shoulder. He turned to face a grim-looking Captain Quinn, accompanied by Sergeant Marks. A quick glance revealed the grip of a Taser protruding from the holster on each man's belt.

"You need to come with me. Colonel Eriksen wants to see you."

Darius felt his heart jump in his chest. The palms of his hands began to moisten, and he had to remind himself to take a deep breath. Without a word, Darius nodded, and fell in behind Quinn. Marks brought up the rear, and a few minutes later, the three men marched around the stern of *Gabriel* and onto the wide loading ramp. Distant mechanical echoes from within the belly of the ship confirmed that her unload process had begun.

At the top of the ramp stood Colonel Eriksen. His square jaw seemed to unlock, shift, and lock again as he saw Darius approach. He dismissed two airmen who had been taking orders from him just seconds earlier. Eriksen folded his hands behind his back and walked swiftly down the ramp to meet them.

"Thank you, Captain, Sergeant," he nodded to Quinn and Marks. "Go help with the civilian duty assignment."

The men saluted and jogged off toward the gathering crowd at the camp. Darius wanted to give a sigh of relief, but he dared not to do so in front of the colonel. Instead, he took in a deep breath through his nose, and spoke with in a soft, measured tone.

"You wanted to see me, Colonel?"

Eriksen bobbed his head. There was an uncomfortable pause as he glared at Darius. His skin began to tingle, and he bit his tongue to keep from breaking the silence by speaking out of turn.

"I've thought about what you said during your little spat of... insubordination," Eriksen said. The lack of inflection in his voice stunned Darius, and a shiver went down his spine. "Trust me, I thought a lot about it. I even thought about sending Captain Quinn down to the camp yesterday to drag your ass up here and lock you in a sleeper berth for it. I didn't even care if all the colonists saw it."

"T-thank you for not doing that, Colonel."

"Shut up. I'm not done," Eriksen growled. He tugged at his cuffs and cleared his throat, and the eerily calm voice returned. "I will acknowledge that I have ordered you to do some rather unpleasant things recently, but that doesn't make up for questioning my authority in front of the crew. I see another problem here, and that problem is that you're completely right about your tour having expired. Now, I could stop gap you, but then we'd get into legal proceedings, and then you might just incite the rest of the crew with your nonsense, and the whole damn thing would fall apart."

"The whole what, sir?"

Eriksen paused for a moment and his eyes narrowed. His gaze then moved to the tent city, and he began to pace slowly. "That's the last time you have to call me sir, Mr. Owens. I'm giving you what you want, for the sake of the colony."

"What I want, sir?"

"Yes. You're relieved of your duties. I'm giving you a general discharge as of now. There are two conditions, though. Violate either one and so help me I'll make you wish you hadn't left Earth."

That's not what I want, Colonel, and you know it.

Darius nodded and asked, "What are the conditions?"

"First, you never mention to anyone, not even a civilian, that the crew's tour of duty has expired. We need the crew intact. Second, you stay out of all colonial affairs. You do not speak to me unless I seek you out, and you do not interfere with how the colony is set up and run. You find yourself a job, you keep your head down, and you stick to it. Do you understand, Mr. Owens?"

More than you understand. He nodded. "Understood. Am I to understand that job assignments are being made right now?"

"Correct. Now if you please," Eriksen swept his hand toward the gathered colonists. "Go make yourself useful."

Darius turned away from the ship and jogged toward the crowd. Colorful insults came to mind as he replayed the colonel's words in his head, followed by a slew of comments that he briefly wished that he had said to his former CO.

Sweeping me under the rug, aren't you, Colonel? He reached the end of the crowd and waited as Marks, Quinn, Garza, and Smith interviewed colonists and assigned them tasks. *Fine with me. I'm done playing your games. It's time to build a new world, and I'm ready to do my part.*

Anonymity was something he hoped the crowd would give him, though it was only a matter of a couple minutes before he found himself answering questions about what he did on the ship. It didn't take longer than the second such question to figure out that he needed a new wardrobe if he was going to shed his former life; the blue flight suit made the colonists believe that he was part of the crew, and even telling a little white lie about the crew giving him the uniform because his original clothes were torn up just didn't sit well with Darius.

After receiving a somewhat merciful assignment of unloading camp supplies from Airman Garza, Darius stole away into the cargo pods of the ship, seeking the textiles pod. He knew that a store of durable civilian clothes would be stored within, and though it was a little on the early side for anyone to be distributing the contents of the neatly stacked crated from that pod, Darius procured a pair of jeans and a shirt that would make him look the part of a civilian. This was the guise that both he and Eriksen wanted. Though procured under distasteful circumstances, the new threads made Darius feel a little more at ease with his new position.

This feeling passed quickly as Captain Quinn approached him only a few short seconds after Darius stepped back into the lower gallery. His heart raced, wondering if the captain had seen him taking colonial assets for himself without permission.

"We need to talk, Lieutenant," Quinn spoke, his brow furrowed.

Shit.

"Yes, Captain?"

Quinn took him by the elbow and gently steered him a few pods deeper into the belly, looking over his shoulder every few seconds, as if they were being followed. When they came to their destination, the captain locked his gaze with Darius, and his expression took on grave concern.

"Look, whatever it is between you and Eriksen, you've got to stop it."

"What?" Darius retorted, almost fumbling over the single word.

"I know this has something to do with his decision to land on this side of the river, but you've got to stop it. Just let him be for a while, and everything will be okay."

Oh, it goes so much deeper than you think, Captain.

"Doesn't it bug you what he's done? I mean, think of the Operational Guidelines. What part of it says that the commanding officer of any ship may deviate from an accepted landing site?"

"Section five, subsection seven, article A," the confident reply came back.

"Article A?" Darius almost choked. "Article A deals with cases of crew mutiny."

A scowl hardened on Quinn's face. "Convenient. He had one. Not a big one, but by a legal technicality you gave him that right."

"That wasn't mutiny. That was me asking a question," Darius growled. "That was *after* he changed course, and you know it. Besides, why should you care?"

J.C. Rainier

"I don't want you to do anything that will fuck up Brandon's chances when the time comes."

"When the time comes for what? Eriksen's going to have to thaw him out, then he's going to have to figure out what to do with him. If he's got any brains at all, he's going to let him go. Maybe not buck wild, but some job close by in the colony."

"That's the idea," Quinn nodded. "But after the little outburst between you two, I'm not sure I can trust that. At least not if you keep riling him up. I swear, since we came into the atmo, he's turned red and that damn vein in his forehead keeps popping out every time he talks to you. So will you knock it off so he can calm down and think straight?"

Darius's upper lip twitched for a moment, but he sighed and relented. "Fine, whatever. I'm done with him anyway. Find me something to do outside these damn walls, and you'll never have to worry about me crossing paths with him again."

"Good," Quinn nodded. "Tomorrow you'll start with the power crews."

Stringing poles and power lines for the eventual city. That should be far enough away.

"Fine," Darius agreed. Quinn left him a moment later, and after a few minutes to calm himself, Darius turned his attention to his original task of unloading the hundreds of canvas tents borne deep in the ship's belly.

Capt Haruka Kimura
USAF
25 March, Year of Landing, midday
Camp Eight
>|

A well worn line on the dirt floor of the Palm Palace marked the strip along which Haruka paced back and forth. Her legs throbbed and her feet complained with every step she took. Nearly an hour had passed since she first began her nervous compulsion. Colonists cycled in and out of the Palace, filling the air with the buzz of life. She ignored them all, lost in her own problems.

Damn it, I know I can still be there for her. She doesn't have to shut me out.

Maria Serrano had made it clear that she was still upset at Haruka. She had tried to apologize, but Maria would have nothing of it. Their argument had picked open a festering wound between the two women.

Damn Leight. She's right. He should have caught Carney by now. The fact that the little bastard is still running around isn't helping anyone, and it's driving Maria mad.

Haruka had considered it a victory when Leight had officially handed over the duty of tending to his group of survivors. His claim was that he couldn't effectively manage them while pursing Carney, though after the fact she realized that it wasn't worth the struggle—either with her or the survivors—and that relinquishing his flock to the unified command of Haruka would ease everyone's burdens.

So why hasn't it all gone smoothly?

She spun around and shuffled in the opposite direction, glancing up briefly at Charlotte as she released her class for lunch. Stares from the children fell upon her, followed by whispers. Their eyes seemed to judge her, but she shook her head and continued on. The cuffs of her flight suit chafed on her purple-blotched wrist, so she rolled them up. There was a noticeable lull in the whispers and mutters in the gathering hall. Her eyes came up and caught those of Karina, a fifteen year old survivor of pod ten. Karina's eyes grew wide and she quickly averted her stare.

Haruka sighed. *Maybe it's just me. Maybe everyone just thinks that I'm a monster. I know my disease isn't pretty, but it doesn't change a thing about me. I'm here to lead them, to protect them.*

Even still, the walls seemed to close in on her, and the urge to find

J.C. Rainier

something to occupy her time overwhelmed her. The farther away from the rest of the village the better, as far as she was concerned. The storm curtain made an unmistakable scratching sound as she pulled it back, and her eyes took a moment to adjust to the high noon sun.

With the children pouring out of the palace, the open town square was humming with activity. Parents and caretakers portioned out meals of grilled fish, pepperines, and greens from the banks of the river. Haruka turned away from this spark of vitality, choosing instead the path down the hill. Her grumbling stomach stopped her after only a few hundred feet, and she turned back to collect a small lunch, mentally berating herself for skipping breakfast earlier.

She picked a spot along the wall of the palace where the short overhang of the roof cast a miniscule shadow, then sat with her back to the wall, partially to maximize the shadow's coverage of her body, and partially to give her tense muscles a chance to relax. She closed her eyes as she chewed the first bite of her fish.

So many things have gone wrong. So many things can still go wrong. Luis. Maria. Carney. Leight. Even James has been rattled lately. If I can't get this under control, how can I even think about keeping the whole village under control?

"No napping," James chirped, forcing her alert.

He slid his rear down the wall, taking a seat next to her, a dented metal plate heaped with food balanced precariously on his left hand.

"Not napping," she retorted.

"Not eating either, apparently."

Haruka speared some greens from her plate, deliberately drawing them slowly to her mouth as she returned a caustic glare as she chewed.

"Bad day?" he asked, his tone flat, unreactive.

"No one's died today. Must be a good day."

"Setting the bar as high as ever, I see." He paused for a moment as Haruka took another bite. "So what is it this time?"

"Maria." She barely had time to let the name escape her lips before sinking her teeth into her pepperine, as if casual conversation and a piece of fruit could stop James from interrogating her.

"What this time?"

"Oh, the usual. Carney's a son of a bitch. I'm an incompetent bitch. You're all incompetent idiots. Oh, and apparently telling her not to yell at Gabi for no reason is a bad thing, too."

James groaned and set his plate on the ground next to him, then pinched the bridge of his nose. "What did you do?"

"Huh?" She was caught off guard, and it took a moment for her to relay the scene from earlier in the day to the level of detail that he required. He looked at her intently as she retold the morning's incident. A few more moment passed, and the corners of his mouth twitched upward, and then he burst out laughing. "What? It's not funny!"

"No, it's not. That's why I'm laughing."

"Have you gone off the deep end?" she growled.

James wiped the corners of his eyes as he regained control. "No. It's just that in the middle of fighting with her you go and push the one button that every parent has. You might have pissed her off less if you had just smacked her."

"Don't tempt me. No matter what I do I can't get through to her, and it's frustrating the hell out of me."

"Just let it go. She'll come around."

"I'll believe it when I see it," Haruka muttered under her breath.

She finished eating her pepperine and picked at her fish, though the latter she barely ate as it cooled and her appetite waned. Instead she took a few minutes to watch the spectacle of the communal lunch, something that she had taken for granted. She realized in that moment that a few people from amongst the survivors took it upon themselves, with no commands or intervention, to prepare meals for everyone and make sure that the villagers were fed. They came from all walks of life.

Among them, Haruka recognized Mike Tran, who was a recent high school graduate who came to Demeter with his family. He worked alongside his mother, who had held various odd jobs on Earth to support her children. Even Charlotte lent a hand organizing the school children during their lunch breaks. There was also an ebb and flow to this caretaking position, with a half dozen or more other villagers who would work the lines two, three, or four days a week, volunteering when there was a lull in their assigned work.

Something seemed out of place to Haruka. She checked her surroundings to confirm her suspicions, and it took a minute for her to figure it out. In line, waiting for food, was a scraggly youth, dressed in tattered blue jeans and a long leather jacket that covered his sweaty, grimy tank top. His forehead seemed drenched in sweat, yet Haruka couldn't figure out why he didn't remove his coat.

She rose up and walked toward him. Instinct told her to go for her weapon; she unsnapped the catch on her holster and firmly placed her hand on the grip of the nine-millimeter pistol at her side.

"Captain?" James asked quizzically, scrambling to his feet.

"Hey," she shouted at the young man. He didn't react, so she doubled her pace. "Hey, you!"

As she was nearly on top of him, he wheeled around and reached behind him, into the concealment that the thick jacket provided. Time seemed to slow, and Haruka saw the wild fire burning within the youngster's eyes. His beard was patchy and thin in places, but a birthmark on the man's neck made Haruka's heart stop cold, and for a split second she felt panic and fear burst forth, and her hand fell away from her M9.

Shit, it's him!

Lon Carney's arm clutched at a weapon behind him. Haruka lunged forward just in time to keep him from bringing Luis's stolen M4 carbine to bear; its stock had been removed, allowing Carney to hide it in the bulky clothing. Though she was able to prevent him from aiming the weapon, her grip on his forearm did not keep him from discharging it. Three loud booms erupted from the rifle, and in unison the villagers screamed and bolted, scrambling for any cover they could find.

Carney brought up his left elbow, catching Haruka in the ear. Her head was ringing, and she reeled from the blow, losing her grip on Carney's arm. He then planted a solid kick to the small of her back, sending her sprawling face first onto the ground. She knew she was defenseless against the murderer. At first she shouted a denial in her mind, as if that would stop him from killing her in cold blood. Her next thought was whether or not she would hear the fatal round being fired.

Three more cracks burst forth. More screams ensued. Haruka didn't feel a thing. She was aware she was alive, because she could still hear the terror expressed by the children, as well as a muttered, desperate prayer coming from Charlotte. She bolted to her feet and wheeled around.

Carney and James were locked in a deadly dance, each man with his hands around the other's neck, squeezing. Carney's rifle had been knocked aside, presumably by Haruka's savior. But James was losing. Though Carney was not a large man, he was still much younger and stronger than James. Haruka could tell that he had little time left before losing consciousness; his knees were starting to buckle, and his grip on Carney's throat was shaky.

Haruka drew her pistol and flipped off the safety in one swift motion. She leveled her aim at Carney, but the erratic movements of the fighting men kept her from getting a clean shot. She circled to her left, hoping to get clear of her operations chief. She then planted her feet, lowered her aim a little, and cycled two deep breaths as she watched James slip out of consciousness and drop to the ground as his legs gave out. She forced aside the panic and anger that accompanied watching her friend collapse, Carney's fingers still ringed tightly around his throat. The distraction that James served was all she needed as Haruka took two steps to her left and zeroed in on her mark.

Three shots rang out from the barrel of her pistol. The recoil of the pistol took her by surprise with each subsequent squeeze of the trigger, and she found flesh only with her last two shots. The first caught Carney far lower than she had anticipated, and his right knee exploded in a geyser of blood and bone fragments. The second strike took him in the thigh. He collapsed to the ground, howling in pain and clutching at his lame leg as a torrent of blood mixed with the parched and packed dirt beneath him. Haruka wasted no time in closing the gap to just ten feet, training her Beretta on Carney's head.

"Don't you twitch," she barked. Haruka glanced around at the terrified villagers who were still trembling behind whatever cover they could find. "Someone get James to the doctor, *now!*"

A few moments of hesitation passed, but Mike and his mother eventually emerged, grabbed James under the arms, and dragged him away to safety. Carney spotted his weapon in the dirt, just beyond his reach, on the other side where Haruka couldn't reach it. He flailed one hand toward it, but Haruka fired a warning shot into the sky before again leveling the weapon at his head.

"Last warning. Don't move."

"Just fucking do it," he snarled back, his voice full of pain and hatred.

"No. You answer my questions," she shot back sternly. "Then we'll see about your punishment."

Carney let out a pained grunt, then started panting. He looked down at his shattered knee, then back up at the woman who had inflicted the damage. "I'm not saying anything, bitch."

"You *will* answer for the crimes you've committed."

"Crimes I've committed? Crimes *I've* committed?" Through his pain, she could hear the indignity in his voice, as if she had the audacity to commit some sort of affront to him.

"That's right. Murder. Rape. Assault. What you've been running from for the past two months."

Haruka glanced up and saw that the villagers had now moved away from the area behind Carney, and were filtering to the safety in her periphery and behind her. She could not see them, but she was keenly aware of their presence, watching every move and listening to every word.

"No," he spat. "I was fixing *your* crime. I had to leave my dad at home. I watched my sister drown right after the crash. And what the fuck did I find when they dragged my ass ashore? God damned families of illegals on the new planet."

Haruka was stunned by his words. "What the hell did you say?"

"I thought these ships were supposed to be for us. For the real Americans. Not filled up with a bunch of Mexicans and their dirty chink bitch leader."

She ground her teeth for a second as the momentary urge to end his racist drivel made her trigger finger itch. She took a quick breath and growled, "If you're going to insult me, use the right term." She waited for him to react, but he only continued to snarl and wince. "I'm not Chinese, kid. My father is Japanese, and my mother is whiter than you. Besides, you're wrong."

"Yeah? Prove it."

"I don't need to. You just didn't care to find out. Your ignorance blinded you to what was real. Your claim is that illegal immigrants were placed on board. Not true."

Carney's eyes narrowed. "What about the one I beat to a pulp? Or his pretty little wife?"

There's the confession. Disgusting, but there.

"Luis Serrano was a seventh generation Tejano. His grandfather was a Texas Ranger. Not that you'd care, since you're not interested in facts."

"Bullshit."

"How would you know?" Haruka snapped back. "Did you ever take the time to talk to him? Did you ever sit by the fire and have a meal with him and his family? Of course not. Because if you had, you wouldn't have killed him, you little prick."

Haruka bit her tongue immediately after the insult flew from her mouth. She regretted it at once, wishing that she could take it back and show a more even demeanor. But Carney's obstinate zeal infuriated her, as did his utter lack of empathy for the Serranos. She took a deep breath and calmed herself, then continued.

"Everyone who set foot on one of those ships was thoroughly screened. All but two of them were American citizens. Both of them crew members. Both of them died on the bridge of *Raphael* when it went down. I'm sorry for the loss of your sister. But your grief and your blind hatred are no excuses for what you did."

"Save it. I'm still breathing," he growled, his voice escalating. "You don't have anywhere to put me. I'm going to be a thorn in your ass as long as I'm still alive, just like I have been for the last two months. So what are you going to do about that, huh? Queen Kimura? Is that what you're going to have people calling you? Well fuck that, and fuck all of you."

Carney rolled to his side and he lunged for his rifle. Haruka squeezed the trigger twice, ending Lon Carney's life in full sight of the gathered throng. Her fingers went numb, and all she could fixate on were the two holes in Carney's back, seeping with the blood of the first person she ever killed. It wasn't until Troy removed the gun from her hands that anything else around her existed.

"J-James," she stuttered.

"He's alright," Troy muttered softly as he gripped her shoulder. "Doc's with him now."

Haruka turned to embrace her friend, to lean on his shoulder and try to make sense of Lon Carney, and to comprehend that she had taken his life. A life that, despite wanting so badly to end for so long, she now felt guilty about taking. Then a tiny, tear filled face stared back at her from the crowd.

Oh God. She saw it. Gabi saw him die.

Gabrielle Serrano
27 March, Year of Landing, pre-dawn
Camp Eight
>|

She stood frozen in place, trembling uncontrollably. Though she tried to will her feet to go, they were as immovable as stone. Wisps of vapor drifted through the air, masking the eyes that coldly stared up from the ground. Gabi whimpered and turned her face away.

Look at him, Mija, her mother's voice echoed from afar.

"No!"

Look!

"No!"

A gentle breeze kicked up and the vapors shrouded her. Gabi's vision was dominated by a grayish-white blur. Chills ran from head to toe, spreading out across every inch of her skin. Her arms wrapped around her body, but they did little to cut through the ice that grew inside her.

"Mama," she croaked.

He took your daddy away, but look at him now, her mom beckoned. *He can't hurt us now.*

The wind shifted, and the browns, greens, and blues of the jungle were all around her. She fixed her gaze at a single leaf on the ground, tracing the pattern of the blue veins over and over in her mind.

Look at him.

"I don't want to!"

LOOK AT HIM!

Even though her mother was nowhere near her, the words struck a deep fear within her. Trembling, she raised her head and looked at the crumpled body lying on its belly in the middle of the village square. Two deep red circles on his back grew little by little, wet and shiny. Her gaze was fixated in terror on the young man's pale face as the one eye she could see slowly melted away into a red, horrific mess, writhing with worms and hideous bugs of all kinds. Gabi shrieked at the top of her lungs.

Everything went dark in an instant, but her lungs still let loose a blood curdling scream. When her lungs had nothing left to push out, she gasped in a quick breath, then coughed and choked for air.

"Gabi? What's wrong?" Dr. Petrovsky called from the darkness.

Gabi was aware that she was sitting upright. She hunched over her knees and clutched them with her arms, sobbing. From her side, she heard a disapproving hiss.

"Are you okay, Gabi?" the doctor asked again.

"Go back to sleep," Gabi's mom growled.

There was a shuffling noise, and Gabi felt a hand on her foot. She jumped back and screamed in alarm.

"Shhh, it's just me," Petrovsky soothed.

"I'm s-scared," Gabi stammered.

"Go to sleep," came a stern warning from her mother.

"She's had a nightmare, Maria," Dr. Petrovsky rebuked. His tone changed as he addressed Gabi. "Come here, honey."

She reached her arms out into the near total darkness. She fumbled for a moment until she found the doctor's arms, and let him pull her into an embrace. Gabi cried into his shoulder as he slowly stood up, cradling her to his chest. He stumbled around very slowly in the darkness for several minutes until he found the front curtain of the clinic and pulled it aside. A dim glow in the night air was visible to the east, along with thousands of stars above their head. The outline of the Palm Palace was visible a few dozen feet away, bathed in a soft light from the bright moon of Persephone.

"Now then," the doctor said, "what's going on?"

"I'm scared."

"Scared of what?"

"The dead man."

Dr. Petrovsky walked a few feet in silence. "Do you mean the man that Haruka shot?"

"Yeah."

"Gabi, honey… he's dead. He can't hurt anyone. Not you or me or your mom."

"But he's really scary," she protested.

"Why?"

"He's in my dreams. He's in my dreams and he has worms and bugs, and he stares at me."

"Dreams can't hurt you. They're not real."

"I know, but it's really scary!"

Dr. Petrovsky sighed and rubbed her back. "Alright, let's make sure you dream of something that's not scary. When we go back inside, let's find Pelusina, okay?"

Gabi sniffed. "Okay."

"Alright, and then when you find Pelusina you're going to go back to bed, but you're going to do something special for me, okay?"

"I don't want to go back to bed!"

"It's okay, dear," he continued, "because here's what you're going to do. You're going to imagine that Pelusina is a princess kitty. Do you think she can be a princess, Gabi?"

"Y-yeah."

"Alright. And the princess kitty gets to play with all the princes and princesses of the realm, right?"

"Right."

"Alright. So what I want you to do is dream about Pelusina playing with one of the princesses and her royal dollhouse. And when you wake up, I want to hear all about what happened in the dollhouse, okay?"

She sniffed again and wiped her cheeks with the back of her hand. "Okay."

"Good," he said as he carried her back into the darkness of the clinic. His voice lowered to a whisper. "Let's find Pelusina now, and you can go back to sleep, okay?"

"Okay," she whispered back.

After another minute or so she was back on her mother's bed. Her mom was snoring gently. Gabi quietly patted her hands around in the dark until she found the overstuffed cat, and then slipped under the opened sleeping bag. She closed her eyes and tried to conjure images of Pelusina dancing under a starlit sky, a tiara wreathing her head just under her ears.

Instead, the stars themselves became the backdrop, and Gabi drifted off to sleep to pictures of constellations dancing around a half moon.

Cal's feet shuffled through the damp grass as the line slowly moved forward. He shivered and rubbed his hands on his arms. The sun was just beginning to peek over the shadowy horizon to the east. Gray tendrils of clouds streaked the blue morning sky like long claw marks. A low din came from all around; families in the line for breakfast held hushed conversations, and other colonists in the encampment were starting their morning routines. Familiar scents taunted his nose as he drew nearer to the camp kitchen. He closed his eyes and breathed in deeply, picking out the single scent of fresh coffee.

A little reward for our work, he thought.

For the past two days, Cal had assisted with unloading cargo from *Michael* and helped set up the sprawling encampment that was nearly as long as the ship, and several times as wide.

Yet what amazed Cal the most about the unloading process was when the crew of *Michael* revived the livestock carried inside a pair of specialized cargo pods. The technology that kept these beasts of Earth in stasis was nearly identical to what was used in the sleeper berths, but on a widely varied scale, based on the animals it served. Cal took a quick look at the camp near the rear loading ramp of *Michael*, where a series of pens had been set up to contain the animals. Armed guards patrolled the perimeter, keeping any possible predators from Demeter at bay.

The breakfast line – one of five such lines – moved again, and Cal caught a glimpse of the kitchen through the few remaining bodies in front of him. A flash of chestnut colored hair made him smile and left a tingle of anticipation in his fingers. His pulse quickened and he swayed from side to side, waiting for his turn. He picked up an enameled plate and cup from the table at the edge of the kitchen, then a fork and butter knife from the basket just beyond. Finally, the family in front of him moved out of the way, and he moved to the head of the line. Alexis greeted him with a shy smile. She wore a grease-stained apron over her jeans and shirt, and her hair was tied back in a bun.

"Good morning, hot stuff," he said, the corners of his mouth tugged tight through his grin.

"Yeah, right," she replied, rolling her eyes. "I look like a mess."

"Come on now. You know I'm glad to see you."

"Of course you are." She leaned slightly across the portable propane griddle in front of her. "Your girlfriend is making breakfast for you and two thousand of your closest friends. What's not to like?"

Cal chortled and handed his plate to her. As he did so, his eyes dropped to the griddle surface, and his heart skipped a beat.

"Is that… is that what I think it is?"

"It is. Colonel Dayton ordered it. I guess he was tired of eating out of food pouches. Or maybe he wanted to remind us all of home."

Cal's eyes darted between the various cuts of fresh pork and bacon that sizzled on her grill. His mouth watered as the smells of freshly cooked meat nearly overwhelmed him.

"Are you serious?"

"Uh huh. Pick one."

"Wow. The last time I had anything fresh was back on Earth. I'll take a slice of ham, please."

Alexis grabbed a thick ham steak with her tongs and slapped it onto Cal's plate. She then topped his cup off with coffee and handed them back.

"There's more down the line. Gail made some pancakes, and Ray thawed out some fruit." She paused for a moment. "So what are you up to today?"

Cal fidgeted, shifting his weight from one foot to another. "I'm not sure. I don't think they're going to need my help unloading today. Most of what's left is supposed to stay on *Michael* until we get some farms or a medical clinic. I'm going to see what kind of work I can scrounge up."

Scrounge, indeed. Because I'm not supposed to be here.

"Well, I hope you find something good. I'll see you later, okay?"

"Yeah. Thanks."

Alexis blew him a kiss and winked as he moved to the next station in the kitchen. Gail was a middle aged woman, heavy set and blonde. She was a kind woman too, at least when she had her coffee. She gave Cal a curt nod and slid two modest pancakes onto his plate. Ray Conyers, Gail's husband, manned the final station in the row. He dipped a ladle in a large bowl of partially frozen strawberries, then liberally smothered the pancakes with them before Cal turned and left the kitchen.

He wandered down the hill toward the river and found a small boulder to perch on. Cal set his coffee cup next to him and set to eating his breakfast. He wasted no time in sampling the fresh ham. He closed his eyes and moaned loudly as he took the first bite. He washed it down with a sip from his fresh, piping hot coffee. The next ten minutes were spent relishing the first non-preserved food he had eaten since Earth.

With his belly full of food, Cal returned briefly to the kitchen to leave his dishes at the wash station. He then began a long walk around the edge of the encampment, looking for signs of forming work parties. As he made his way around the perimeter, he could only see signs of colonists rousing from sleep or securing their tents. Cal walked almost a kilometer around the edges of the encampment, past the animal holding pens, arriving at the rear cargo ramp of *Michael*.

Here he found promising signs; Hunter stood guard on the ramp, armed with a clipboard and pen. A short line of colonists formed in front of him. As each one approached, he asked a few questions, jotted down notes, and relayed instructions back to them. They then proceeded down the ramp and took a spot in one of a half dozen groups around the bottom of the ramp. Several pieces of heavy machinery were also arranged at the bottom of the ramp. Among the equipment he could identify were a front end loader, a backhoe, and a tanker truck. Several more machines that he was unfamiliar with also stood idle. From within the hull of the ship, Cal could hear the unmistakable whine and deep rumble of a turbo-diesel motor.

There's work for sure today. I can feel it.

Cal bounded up the ramp and fell in at the back of the line behind a short, pudgy man in a wrinkled flannel shirt. He glanced back over his shoulder, straightened his glasses with one finger, and smiled.

"Morning," he chirped cheerfully.

"Morning to you too, sir," Cal replied.

"I've been waiting for this ever since we got here."

"For what?"

"A chance to get to work. I was feeling a bit off there for the first couple days, plus I'm not sure how much help I would have been. I mean, this is all a bit much for me."

"What's a bit much?" Cal asked.

"The camp. I mean, I've gone camping before, but the scale of this is awesome. I think I've only seen anything like it in Civil War movies."

Cal nodded. "It did take a bit, but we managed."

"We?" his companion asked his eyes widening. "Did you get to help with it?"

"I did."

"So you're part of the crew?"

"Sort of. It's a long story."

The man extended his hand. Cal grasped it and gave a firm shake. He could not help but notice the soft grip and clean nails of the man's hand. "I'm Neil. Neil Leclair."

"Cal McLaughlin. So what did you do? You know, back on Earth?"

"Well, that whole situation was a mess," he said, rubbing his chin.

"What do you mean?"

"Well, a couple years back, I graduated from UC Davis. I was on track to start with the USGS, when the War broke out. My position was immediately put on hold. While I was trying to figure out what to do, we got invaded, and I bounced from refugee camp to refugee camp. Then one day I get approached by the military, saying I had been selected for something called Project Columbus, and that was pretty much that. They took me to Wyoming. When I saw the rockets, I figured that the project must have been a lot bigger than I thought."

A couple years... forty years... no difference, right?

Cal found himself nodding throughout the conversation. "You're not kidding there."

"Anyway," Neil continued, "The weeks went on and more and more refugees kept pouring in. I figured it was only a matter of time before we were all blasted into space. And, well, you know the rest, I'm sure."

"That I do."

"So what did you do?"

"Nothing," Cal said with a slight sigh.

"Ah. Here with your parents then? What did they do?'

Cal cast his gaze down at the ramp plating. The wound of his father's sacrifice ached as the image of his face came to mind.

"I'm sorry, did I say something wrong?" Neil asked.

"My parents are dead. Dad sacrificed himself to put me here."

The revelation was met with an awkward silence.

"I-I'm sorry," Neil finally said in a hushed tone.

Cal shook his head and looked back up at his companion. "It's okay. You had no way of knowing."

"No, seriously. I feel bad."

"Hey," Cal said, extending his hand and giving a brave smile. "Water under the bridge, my friend."

Neil shook Cal's hand again, and Cal could see the relief on his face. Neil exhaled loudly. "Thanks."

"Hey there, Cal," Hunter interrupted. The grin he wore on his face was wider than the flag emblazoned on the shoulder of his flight suit. "What's cookin'?

"Not much, Hunter. Just looking for a job, as usual. We got any more to unload today?"

"Sadly, no. Just a few heavy machines, and regulations say the crew is supposed to handle that."

"I understand."

"Wait, I thought you said you were part of the crew?" Neil interrupted.

Cal shook his head. "I said it was a long story."

"Cal is officially a civilian advisor," Hunter explained. "There are certain things he's not allowed to do on *Michael*, no matter how much we like him." Hunter playfully jabbed Cal twice in the ribs.

"That's okay. I can wait. Neil here was in front of me, so it's only fair that you assign his work anyway."

"Very well then." Hunter turned to face Neil and brought his clipboard and pen to the ready. "Neil, last name?"

"Leclair."

"Occupation?"

"Refugee."

"No job before we left Earth?"

"I never got to start one."

"College degree?"

"Yes, sir."

"In?"

"Geology," Neil said as he straightened his glasses again.

"Alright. We can definitely use that today. Look down the ramp behind you. Report to group four for further assignment. Count clockwise from the bottom left of the ramp."

"Thanks," Neil said as he waddled down the ramp.

"Alright, let's see what we've got for you here, Cal." Hunter scrutinized the sheet in front of him, then flipped to the next page briefly, and back again. "Damn."

Cal's heart sunk slightly. "What?"

"I just didn't realize how many technical jobs there were in this batch."

"Please tell me you have something for me today."

"I do, but you're not going to like it."

"That's my problem, not yours."

Hunter lowered the hand with the clipboard to his side and looked directly into Cal's eyes. "No, seriously. It's probably going to land you in an expedition group. It's could take you away from camp for a long time."

Cal nodded and sighed, then thought for a moment. "But could you guarantee me work tomorrow?" Hunter's silence was all that Cal needed to make up his mind. "I guess the good news is I won't be bugging you for work every day, right?"

"You're sure about this?"

Cal nodded again.

"Alright," Hunter said. He jotted down some notes on the second sheet of the clipboard. "Report to work group four for further assignment. Good luck, my friend."

Cal got a firm handshake from Hunter before he jogged down the ramp and joined up with his assigned work group. Neil was already in the thick of the group, hard at work making friends with a dozen other colonists. Cal sidled up next to him to listen in.

"So what do you think they're going to have us do?" asked a tall brunette woman standing to Neil's side.

"I'm not really sure," he answered. "Maybe if we go around and say what we all used to do, we can figure it out. I'll start. That guy on the ramp put me here after he found out I was a geologist."

"Forest Service ranger," added the woman.

"I was a botanist," called a man from deep within the group.

Other voices rang out with professions.

"Private security."

"I worked for a resources exploration company."

"Long haul truck driver, here."

I see a pattern here, I think.

A deep rumbling noise accompanied by a high pitched whine caught their attention, and the group turned to face a machine that made its way down the loading ramp and onto the ground. It turned directly for work group four, lumbering slowly.

"What the hell is that?" Neil asked.

The machine wasn't anything that Cal could directly recognize. The body, for the most part, looked like a heavy-duty crew cab pickup. Enough of the sheet metal was recognizable so that Cal knew that was what it started its life as before heavy modification. The turbo-diesel engine revved slightly, and the beast picked up speed before turning to the side and stopping directly in front of the group. Cal had to look up somewhat to see the cab, despite his height.

Underneath the frame of the truck, significant changes had been made. A heavy steel skid plate ran from bumper to bumper. The front suspension contained a number of complex lift components, several of which he remembered from Rob's truck. Massive knobby tires shrouded the front wheels. The factory bumpers had been eschewed in favor of custom protective plates that wrapped around the front, reminding him of the armor on some military vehicles. A spotlight was mounted to the A-pillar on the passenger side, and a massive snorkel intake was secured to the driver's side. Part of the bed was enclosed, and a large tank could be seen under the enclosure. The most dramatic modification, however, was that the rear axle and wheels had been completely replaced by a pair of tracks, almost identical in size and shape to those on the backhoe he had seen earlier.

The engine shut off, and Cal could see the driver's legs as they dropped to the ground below on the far side.

"I know what we're doing," he muttered to Neil.

The driver walked around the front of the machine, and Cal gulped when he recognized the short bobbed haircut and stern scowl of Lieutenant Traci Josephson. She caught him staring, and her brow furrowed for a moment. She then proceeded to a position just in front of the rear passenger door of the truck.

"Good morning, colonists of *Michael*," she belted out. Instantly, all conversation within the group died. "I'm Lieutenant Josephson, and I'm here to give you your work assignment."

Oh, God. I'm screwed. I should have told Hunter to find me something else.

Josephson raised an arm and pointed to the hulking monstrosity behind her. "This is a crawler. This is going to be your home for now. Each of you has been selected for the Expeditionary Forces, or EF, as we are going to refer to them going forward. The EF is here to scout the nearby landscape for the purposes of mapping them out and seeking resources in all forms. This includes material, mineral, biological, and even hydrological sources." She paused and scanned the faces of the crowd. "Some of you don't know what I'm talking about. You don't have to. Your tasks are simple: drive the crawler, and keep your scientists safe."

"Safe?" blurted Neil, drawing Josephson's immediate attention. "We're going to be doing something dangerous?"

"Welcome to Demeter, Pillsbury. We know nothing about this world outside of a roughly five kilometer radius from the ship. We have no idea if there are aggressive animal species on this planet." She marched up to him with a swiftness Cal had never seen from her before. Her eyes scrutinized him from top to bottom. "You're obviously one of the scientists. Remember when you're out there to keep your eyes open and your friends close."

Josephson made a crisp about face and resumed her original position. "For you scientists in the group, we have limited lab equipment for the field. You will have no shortage of sample containers, and when you are here at the base camp, you will have unlimited access to the lab equipment on board *Michael*. Pack up any personal belongings you wish to take with you and meet back here at thirteen hundred hours for your specific squad assignments and directives. You may or may not have had prior military experience, but let me make this clear; these are *orders*, and you are expected to carry them out as if you were a member of the crew. Scientists, *dismissed!*"

Neil, along with half of the crowd, scurried away immediately after Josephson's last word. The remaining men and two women looked at each other with some measure of confusion. Josephson climbed onto the running board on the passenger side and retrieved a rifle from the rear passenger seat, as well as a belt with a holstered pistol. She jumped back down and held the sleek, magazine-fed rifle high in the air with a single hand.

"Can anyone tell me what this is?" she barked.

Timidly, another tall, skinny teenager raised his hand. "A rifle?"

"A rifle," she scoffed. "Jesus, boy. I hope you get eaten before your scientist does."

Cal cleared his throat. "Lieutenant Josephson, ma'am. That's an

AR-15 semi automatic rifle. Five point five six millimeter," he trailed off for a second and squinted at the magazine under the stock. "I believe, thirty round capacity."

"And why the five fifty six and not the two twenty three?"

"Because that's the same round as your military-issued M4."

She nodded and leaned the rifle against the running board. "Good boy. Ever fire one?"

"Not that model, ma'am. I had an old bolt action Remington back home."

"Can you identify this?" she asked, drawing the pistol.

"Of course. Colonel Dayton gave me one three days ago. Beretta M9 semi auto pistol. Nine millimeter."

And Dad had a couple of those too, you crazy bitch.

"That's good enough for me. I don't have time to teach all of you, so you get a pass on the weapons training. Get your gear packed and report back here at twelve hundred hours to get your training on the crawler."

"Yes, Lieutenant," he smiled and saluted, eliciting a sneer from her.

"The rest of you have one hour to get your bags packed and get back here. Move!"

Cal walked swiftly as the group broke up. Josephson called out to him as he passed, "Say goodbye to that pretty little girlfriend of yours. I hope it's not the last time."

He paused for a second as his temper flared quickly. He curled his fists into tight balls and for just a second, he considered attacking her. A quick glance over his shoulder revealed her stroking the Beretta like a stray cat, and thought better of it, instead breaking into a run.

He made it to the camp kitchen in about five minutes, arriving just as they were finishing the dishes and beginning preparation for lunch. Cal huffed his way up to Alexis, threw his arms around her, and then doubled over to catch his breath as soon as he let go.

"Cal? What's going on?" she asked.

He panted hard, unable to respond.

"Did you find work?" He nodded. "That's great! What is it?" Cal stood straight again, but still could only gasp for air. She must have read the look on his face, because her smile changed in a heartbeat to a frown. "What's wrong? Is it something bad?"

"I have to leave," he gasped.

"What?" There was a loud clatter as she dropped a stack of plates that she had just washed. "Why? Where?"

"Only work I could find…"

"Take a minute. Please." She led him to a supply crate and directed him to sit. He did so, and finally caught his breath.

"The only work Hunter could find me was in the Expeditionary Forces. I should have said no. I should have just had him find me something else tomorrow."

"Expeditionary Forces?"

"I'm going to be part of a group that leaves the camp to go explore the nearby area. Mapping, cataloging, finding resources. I… I don't know how long I'll be gone. Oh God, Lexi… what have I gotten myself into?"

"Shh," she soothed and stroked his hand. "It's okay. You'll be back when you're back."

"I don't know. The way Josephson was talking, it sounds like she doesn't expect a lot of us to come back."

"She's just trying to scare you. You'll come back. I know it."

He looked up into her emerald green eyes. "How do you know?"

She smiled and said, "Because I'll be waiting for you."

Darius trudged up a short rise to the camp kitchen. The colonial staff was hard at work feeding the last of the stragglers their breakfasts, and starting the task of dishwashing. He placed his dinnerware on one of the piles awaiting a wash, taking an extra moment to tidy and arrange the haphazardly discarded dishes.

Though they had been specially preserved in near cryogenic conditions, the powdered eggs and pancakes that served as the morning's meal did not sit well with Darius. Even after using a packet of hot sauce that he had managed to squirrel away the previous day, the eggs still made his stomach churn. He made an exit from the back side of the tent, and slowly wandered down the hill behind the kitchen. He cast his gaze north across the river at the camp that dotted the visible landscape between his position and *Michael*. Heavy machinery moved along a hillside far away, toward a stand of trees located near *Gabriel's* intended landing site.

Darius sighed and turned away. Watching the progress of the other encampment was a bittersweet daily reminder of both what Eriksen had inflicted on the colony and what both sides were able to accomplish independently. The civilians on the *Gabriel* side of the river had no idea that the ships were supposed to land side-by-side. He hoped that *Michael's* colonists were similarly in the dark.

He returned to the kitchen. The breakfast lines had all cleared out. Darius picked up a clean cup and went to the first station. Rory Baines, manning the station, did not see Darius approach at first, as his attention was focused on cleaning a coffee pot. The crow's feet at the corners of his eyes were accentuated by the wrinkles on his forehead and his pursed lips as he scrubbed the inside of the pot.

"I hope that wasn't the last of it," Darius said in a low grumble.

Rory jerked back as he startled. "Darius. You scared me."

"Sorry, didn't mean to."

"It's alright. I should have known you'd be back for a second cup." Rory flicked suds from his wrists and wiped his hands off quickly on a dish towel, then reached for another decanter. "I was just about to throw it out."

Darius offered the cup, which was promptly filled. He brought it to his lips and took a drink. It was still warm, though nowhere near the piping hot temperature he preferred.

"Can't waste a perfectly good cup of joe."

"I wouldn't want to." Rory's slight smile disappeared and his lines tightened. "I still don't know how we're going to feed everyone all the time with what I've seen on board. If we don't have a good crop and a plan to save most of it, we're going to blow right through it."

"Have faith, my friend," Darius replied calmly. "Besides, I can't wait 'til we start getting actual fresh food. No offense to you, but I think the stuff we've been eating is going to give us gut rot sooner than later."

"Oh, I can't wait to start cooking something real. Besides, what you fly boys have been bringing us shouldn't even count as food, if you ask me. I'm almost thinking the MRE's they had us all eating were better."

Darius laughed heartily at the former Army staff sergeant. He had told Rory that he had been in the Air Force, but did not feel it prudent to disclose the nature or date of his discharge. Instead, he let his elder believe that they were simply both former military officers chosen for the same program. From what little time they had been able to converse over the past few days, however, Darius knew him to be very honest, amiable, and even humorous.

"So do you have a minute, or are you having a flashback to your fine years on KP duty?" Darius asked.

"Good one," Rory laughed. "I got time to talk if you've got time to help me wash."

"It's a fair trade." Darius gulped down the last of his coffee and stepped around the station. He rolled up the sleeves of his recently procured denim work shirt and grabbed a sponge. "So, what's the buzz this morning?"

"Well, let's see now. I heard they've sent out a few exploration teams to go scout around this area for resources." Rory slowly scrubbed the inside of a large skillet as he thought. "I heard a couple folks talking about how plots for a few farms have been laid out, and they're going to see about plowing them, maybe as soon as tomorrow."

"Plowing, huh? Shouldn't they be using the tractors to bring in timbers so we can build houses or something?"

"Oh, I heard they are. Did you get a chance to see those animals they brought out of the ship a couple days ago?"

"I did."

"Well, someone was smart enough to put a few good old fashioned plow horses in with the mix," Rory continued. "Damn smart right there. Even if we suck every drop of fuel out of that rust bucket we flew in on, we'll still have horses around to help out. How 'bout that, huh?"

Doctor Kimura would be pleased by that. He and Doctor Fairweather came up with that idea.

"Sounds like someone was thinking ahead," Darius replied, downplaying his extensive knowledge of the ship and its cargo.

"Oh," Rory exclaimed as he snapped his fingers. "There was something really weird I heard today, too. It was from a couple of the fly boys talking to each other. They said something about a doctor who's going to be going on trial here real soon."

The pot and sponge slipped from Darius's hands and crashed to the ground. "Wait, what?"

"Whoa!" Rory jumped back, trying to avoid the stream of water that poured out of the fallen cookware. "You okay there, Darius?"

He rinsed out the sponge and picked up the pot. "Yeah, sorry. You just caught me off guard there."

"I know, it's pretty crazy. We've been here all of what, four or five days? And already they've caught someone breaking the law. A doctor, no less. Boy, I don't know what kind of screening the government did on us before we were accepted if something like that happened."

"Do you remember which crewmembers were talking about it?"

"Yeah, why?"

"Call it curiosity. Who was it?"

"I don't remember their names. Just their faces. The first guy probably would have come up to your chest. Dark hair, a little older than you. Kinda Latin looking."

Garza, maybe?

"And the other guy?"

"Big strapping redhead. You couldn't miss him if he was a mile away."

That must be Quinn. Damn it.

"Did they say why he was going to be tried?"

"Oh, I asked when I overheard. They just got this real serious look on their faces and told me he stole from the government." Rory took the pot from Darius's hands and gave it a quick rinse, then dried it off with a towel. "If he's been stealing supplies, I can't blame them for wanting to put an end to it quickly."

"Did they say who was going to represent him?"

"No, man. Why are you so interested in this?"

Darius put his hands on Rory's shoulders and squared him off to face Darius eye to eye. "You have to trust me. This man isn't a thief. He's a good man, and most of us would be dead if it wasn't for him. I need to know absolutely everything you know."

"How do you know?"

Darius released his grip and unrolled his sleeves. "You remember how I told you I was Air Force?" Rory nodded. "My date of discharge was the twenty fifth or March, Year of Landing, on the planet Demeter. I was the computer specialist on *Gabriel* up until then. I can tell you the names of the men you heard that rumor from. Airman Doug Garza, and Captain Tyler Quinn. The accused man is Doctor Tadashi Kimura. And he even admitted himself that he stole government property, but it sure as hell wasn't supplies."

Rory's eyes narrowed slightly as he brushed off his shoulders. "And just what did he steal?"

"Those sleeper ships." He jerked his thumb at *Gabriel*.

The veteran opened his mouth to speak, but paused for a second. Darius could see Rory process the information, and then his eyes widened as if a spark went off in his brain. A look of realization rose on his face.

"Well, I'm not here to judge," he said. "But I'd say you need to go find a guy by the name of Don Abernathy. That is, if Colonel Eriksen hasn't already."

"Attorney?" Darius asked.

"Yes sir."

"Any idea where I can find him?"

"I'm pretty sure he's set up on the far side of camp, pretty much in the shadow of the bridge. He's mentioned that it's quite a walk up here. He's about my height, graying hair, has a wife, a rowdy teenage boy, and a little girl who's as cute as a button."

"Thank you, my friend," Darius smiled. "I owe you one."

"Great. Should I start a tab?"

"If you do, I'll go broke."

Darius turned and hurried down the hill toward the ship.

I hope this Abernathy knows something about what's going on.

Calvin McLaughlin
1 April, Year of Landing, 16:06
Approximately 20 miles west of Michael landing site
>|

Cal popped a handful of trail mix into his mouth. His eyes were cast skyward, watching the soft orange reflection of the campfire's flames reflect off of the boughs of the towering pine trees. The last remnants of light had died off from the night sky, and Cal eagerly anticipated catching sight of an animal that Neil claimed to have seen the night before.

It seemed like a silly prospect, the way that the geologist had described it; a small raptor-like bird, that periodically emitted a faint glow from its body. Cal told him that it was probably just a shooting star, but Neil was insistent that it was a creature.

"Stargazing?" Neil asked.

"Trying to find this bird you're talking about."

"I don't think it's dark enough yet."

"That, or you're making it up," Cal replied, giving his friend a little ribbing.

He finished the last of the trail mix before wadding up his ration pack and throwing it onto the fire. Flames licked at the edges of the brown plastic pouch. It began to sag and deform a few seconds before it was engulfed, smoking and melting into a black puddle. The light from the fire danced in Calvin's eyes, mesmerizing him with its hypnotic dance. The addition of a fresh branch onto the fire added a crackling that was like a thousand tiny firecrackers. The long, blue needles of the pine each curled and then popped in a miniscule final hurrah.

The fire itself was modest, with a diameter of just over a foot. It cast a gentle warmth that kept the infringing cold of the evening at bay. The sun had set, leaving the higher hills and distant mountains to the west as dark silhouettes in the murky sky. The bright moon, Persephone, bathed them in a pale glow. The darker twin, Arion, was low to the eastern horizon, barely visible without the sun's direct light.

A flash of light caught the corner of Cal's eye and he snapped his head to the right to see. His heart skipped a beat from the surprise, but he quickly felt foolish as he found that it was just the crawler. Lieutenant Josephson had opened the door to retrieve something, and the light had reflected off of the mirror on the door. Cal shook his head and threw the last of the empty ration bags on the fire, where they were consumed in seconds.

"So why are we doing this again?" asked Neil, sitting on a rock to his left.

"To make room for more samples, I guess," he replied with a shrug. "It's not like we have a garbage dump to take it to when we get home anyway."

Elaine wrinkled her nose as she stared at him with coal black eyes. "That can't be good, melting plastic in a fire like that."

Elaine Montoya was the second scientist assigned to the exploration crew. She had been selected for Project Columbus for her skill in agricultural science, though Cal had not pressed her for details. During the days, Elaine was Traci Josephson's responsibility. Cal was assigned to look after Neil. As such, and with Josephson's strict adherence to her own militaristic guidelines for the mission, he had not had more than a few minutes to converse with her.

"I don't know," Neil sighed. "It's not like we ate every particle of food in those bags. Sooner or later it would have to start rotting. Maybe this isn't such a bad idea."

Neil, on the other hand, was quite talkative. Cal knew almost as much about him as he knew about Hunter or Alexis. Neil didn't restrict his conversations to his life story, either. Before they had left the camp, Cal had never heard of Rocklin, California. Not only could he now point it out on a map, but he knew where to get the best pizza in Rocklin, how far UC Davis was from Neil's home in Rocklin (which caused Cal to question his sanity in commuting every day in college), and where every fault line within five hundred miles of Rocklin was located.

And the rocks, Cal thought. *He really loves rocks. Maybe a bit too much.*

Elaine rolled her eyes at Neil. "What, you think a little mold's going to hurt you?"

"It might. You never know what mold from this planet can do. We haven't had a chance to study it."

"It's not just mold," Josephson added as she sat down across from Neil and propped her rifle against a log. "We don't know what anything out here can do. That's why we're burning our trash right now. You never know just what might come lurking because it can smell the garbage.

"That's ridiculous," Elaine scoffed. "What, you think some sort of native raccoon is going to jump up into the back of the crawler and go rooting around?"

"Well, those might not be big enough," Cal said as he stretched his hands out to warm in front of the fire. "But a bear sure would. And that's sure as hell something I don't want to wake up and find in the bed."

"Glad to see someone gets it, even if it's just the mooch over there," Josephson said, jerking her thumb at Cal.

Cal rolled his eyes and shook his head. He turned his gaze back to the fire, analyzing the glowing embers deep within that shimmered from bright red to black.

"Well, aside from the smell of burning plastic," Neil chimed in, "I'm glad to be sitting here. Nice warm fire, the stars coming out, and look at that. Two moons. I could get used to this."

"Don't. We're only going to make a fire every few days so we can burn our trash. Otherwise we'd be inside bedding down for the night."

"Aww, come on, Mom," Neil teased. "Let us kids play."

"I'm not here to let you play. I'm here to keep the mission rolling."

"Seriously? Come on, Lieutenant, I'm not saying I want to throw my sleeping bag on the ground out here, but we should at least take advantage of the opportunity. You know, get to know each other. Maybe tell some ghost stories."

"I'm not here to be your friend either, Chubs."

Cal glanced around the fire. Neil looked like a child whose toy had been taken from him, while Elaine seemed lost in thought as she looked up into the inky sky. Josephson poked at the fire with a long, thin stick, stirring around the embers and spreading them out.

His mind went back to the journey on *Michael*, and how Josephson continually demeaned and threatened him. Yet here she sat, just a few feet from him, still casually throwing insults at those around her. He caught sight of the dark barrel of her rifle as the pale light made it dance in and out of the shadows.

She doesn't seem to like Neil either. Maybe it's not just me, he reflected.

"So," Cal said, clearing his throat after his first word. "I wonder. What could possibly be so wrong in one woman's life that she pushes people away and belittles them all the time?"

"Stow it, McLaughlin," growled Josephson.

"Could she be insecure? Nah, with so much confidence, you know

J.C. Rainier

she's the life of the party. The go-to girl for conversation."

"Shut up."

"Or maybe she's sore about something. Hmm. Drew the short end of the stick and got assigned to the same crew as some whacko kid that she can't stand? Doctor Taylor's pet?"

"You're asking for it, numbnuts," she snarled and bolted to her feet. "Knock it off."

"Or what, you'll call me names? Threaten me like you did back on the ship? Jesus, it's no wonder you haven't made captain yet. I'd have thought you would have figured that out by now."

A loud slap pierced the air as Josephson snatched her rifle one-handed by the barrel and hoisted it from the ground. For a moment there was almost dead silence, with only the crackle of the fire to be heard. Cal watched her stern, hardened gaze fixate on him. Her eyes narrowed and her mouth twitched. Her hand shook, rattling the rifle, and her knuckles turned white as if she was trying to strangle the life out of her weapon with her bare hand. Then, without warning, she turned away and walked quickly to the crawler. As she turned, Cal could have sworn he saw a tear on her cheek.

Oh, hell. What have I done now?

"That was rude, Calvin," Elaine said, shattering the silence.

"What? She had it coming," Neil retorted. "It may have been a bit harsh, but Cal did us all a favor there."

"Are you kidding me? I know she's a bit rough around the edges, but that was uncalled for."

"What, like her calling me 'Pudge' or 'Chubs' all the time is alright?"

"Guys," Cal interrupted. "Let it go. I'm sorry that you had to see that, but it was a long time in coming."

"What do you mean?" asked Elaine.

Cal sighed and rolled his shoulders backward. He looked up at the sky, at the myriad of pulsating stars, and the bright, mostly full Persephone. Though the sheer number of stars he could see was far fewer than on *Michael*, the presence of a moon in the sky was something that brought a certain comfort. He took a deep breath, relaxed, and spoke to the scientists.

"I don't know how much you know about me, Elaine, but I'm not supposed to be here. My dad got me onboard the ship, but he wasn't able to come with me. The first time I met Josephson I wasn't exactly…"

"Wasn't exactly what?" she asked after a few seconds.

"Lieutenant Josephson was the one that informed me of my father's death. It was accidental too; she had assumed that I already knew. I didn't react well, and shoved her. I didn't really even mean to, I was just really upset. I knew this was a mistake, and I apologized for it the first chance I got." Cal paused a moment to compose his words. "I've apologized many times, in fact. But every time I've seen her when there wasn't a superior officer around, she has picked on me, bullied me, and threatened me. What you saw tonight was me finally having enough. I don't know, maybe it's because I saw her treating Neil the same way, and it pissed me off."

He brought his gaze back down from the heavens and looked at his companions around the fire. Both were staring into the flames. Neil nodded slightly and adjusted his glasses, while Elaine sat on her hands and shuffled her feet.

"Well," Neil said. "I didn't particularly like all the name calling that she's done over the past few days. For what it's worth, thank you. Thank you for that little part of you that stuck up for me, even though I never asked."

"You're welcome."

"I had no idea that's what it was," Elaine blurted. "I… I just thought she didn't like me. Or Neil."

Cal could see the glint of tears rolling down the botanist's face. "What happened?"

Elaine wiped her hand across her cheeks and took a breath. "I just thought at first she was being a bit of a hardass, like those drill sergeants in the movies that ride their recruits hard. It was starting to get really lonely and quiet up there, which is weird when someone is following you around with a gun. So I tried talking to her, but she'd keep yelling at me to 'stop picking daisies' and to 'hurry up, flower girl.' Then she started in with the names."

Cal slowly rose and walked over to Elaine, jerking his head at Neil on the way over. He got the hint, and followed Cal. They sat down on either side of her, and Cal put an arm around her shoulders.

"Don't take it personally. She's probably more bark than bite, anyway."

"It's not just that," she continued, choking back tears. "I miss Danny and Gloria. I miss Trevor. I want to go back to the ship."

"Are they your family?" Cal asked.

She nodded, resting her head on his shoulder. "Trevor is my husband. Danny and Gloria are my kids. I know it's only been a few days, and we're supposed to be out here for weeks, but I want to go back. I can't be out here that long."

"I know how you feel. I'm missing someone back at the ship, too. It sucks to be out here, but we'll get to make up for lost time when we get home, I'm sure of it," he said, giving her a gentle hug.

Neil threw his arms around both of them, which felt very awkward to Cal. It lasted only a couple seconds, and both Elaine and Cal glowered at him afterward.

"What, no hugs for the guy who *doesn't* have someone back at the ship? I see how this works."

Cal's jaw dropped open and he was at a loss for words. A moment later, Elaine burst into near hysterical laughter, and slapped the portly geologist on his arm. He smiled and gave her a light squeeze across the shoulders.

"Cal's right, though," he continued. "Once we get back to the ship, we get to play with all the lab equipment and see what kinds of fun stuff we brought back from our little trip here. And that means we get to stick around at home for a bit."

Home. Alexis's smile came to his mind, and he thought about how he would fulfill his promise of their first date on the planet.

A streak of blue caught his attention in the branches beyond the fire, followed by the shriek of a raptor. The light flared up along the sides of the bird's body for a mere second as the bird took flight into the woods. Cal's jaw dropped and he gasped.

"See?" Neil beamed. "Did you see it?"

"I did," Elaine replied. "Wow. What the hell was that?"

"I'm not sure," Cal added.

But I wish Lexi was here to see it.

The green mass stretched on the ground started to look more like the heavy storm curtain that adorned the front of the Palm Palace. Haruka smiled and reached for another leaf from a small, domelike pile nearby. She folded it lengthwise between two fingers and slipped the tip into the edge of the weave, then pulled it through and upward. The coarse fibers scratched along her skin like fine sandpaper, and yet her grin widened. For the first time since the band of survivors from pod eight arrived at the beach, she felt a swell of pride from seeing the fruits of her labor.

For the first time in what seemed like months, she was well enough to work on a task that she knew would directly contribute to the growth of the village. The third building to be constructed was nearing completion. In a matter of a day or two, Troy's crews would be ready to put the final touch on the modest hut: its door.

In reality, the "door" that was to be utilized was no different than what the Palace or Dr. Petrovsky's clinic utilized, which was a thick, tightly woven mat of palm. The thin leaves that fanned out like hundreds of feathers from each palm frond were deceptively tough. One of the other colonists had discovered early on that if they were woven tightly enough, they were both waterproof and extremely resistant to wind. For this reason, they were incorporated in not only the doors, but the roofs as well. They had been tested as a matting material for bedding, but because of the rough texture of the final product, the colonists stopped producing the beds after only six were made. All six could be found in the clinic; Dr. Petrovsky insisted that they find use instead of being thrown out.

The doctor was a prudent man, and he had a way of persuasion that Haruka admired, even when it meant that he was forcing her to rest for a day or two. The idea of reusing materials was quickly implemented in the village; it had not even required Dr. Petrovsky's special political skills to enact it. With so few manufactured supplies available, reusing anything that was salvaged was better than trying to make something from scratch.

After weaving a dozen more leaves into the edge of the door, she stood up and stretched. Knots in her back complained as she twisted from one side to the other. She closed her eyes and her hand rose to the back of her neck in a futile attempt to rub away the tension. Haruka then rolled her neck slowly from side to side. She felt two pops, followed by an odd combination of a momentary pain and immense relief.

"Captain Kimura," she heard James say softly.

Haruka opened her eyes and met his gaze. She was taken aback when an unusually clean, baby-faced man looked back at her.

"James?"

"Yeah?" he replied.

Haruka stumbled and stammered as she tried to search for her words. "Your... beard. What happened?"

He ran his hands down his smooth shaven face. "Ah, that. I have some news for you. Will found another cargo pod out in the jungle. Looks like it's mostly toiletries. They brought back a couple crates worth of supplies with them and he's marked the location in case we need to go back."

"Interesting find. I assume they brought back soap?"

"Of course. It felt good to clean up a bit, even if we don't have hot water."

Haruka nodded. She imagined being able to brush her teeth for the first time in ages. She even had a fleeting daydream that a bath would somehow be able to wash away the cruel purple blotches that marred her skin from her neck to her toes.

"Have we had any luck on our project with the workshop pod?" she asked.

"You mean finding a way to power it? No, I'm sorry. Without some sort of a generator, we can't make any juice." A wishful sigh escaped from his lungs. "I haven't come across anything that we could salvage that would be able to make the windmill idea fly. And even if there was, there's a whole chicken-and-the-egg problem. Troy needs a way to make a mast that's both thick and straight enough to support the sails without them binding."

"Well, I'm sure you won't give up. With a little luck, Will and his boys will find one of the equipment pods. I'm sure one of those would have what you'd need."

"Probably. It would be nice to get the machinery in that pod up and running. I never thought I'd be so eager to see nails being manu-factured."

Haruka moved over to a smooth boulder jutting out of the ground a few feet away and slowly lowered herself onto it. She glanced at the curtain that she had been weaving earlier while sitting on the very same boulder and wrung her hands together, making the nearly raw skin on her fingers ache.

"We don't have any iron. You know that."

"True, but I don't need any if that equipment's still in good shape. If we find an equipment pod, a generator's not the only thing I'll be able to strip and reuse. There're others that you've mentioned that I think I can use to set up a crude recycler. It'll be slow, but we could pull apart that hulk on the beach and turn it into usable material."

She leaned back and imagined James unbolting a locker door from the innards of the dead pod. "Wouldn't that be something."

"Well, if it stays this quiet around here, I might just see if I can get the pod's radio working again."

The words were a cruel jab. It had been exactly one week since Haruka had killed Lon Carney, though rumor had it that some colonists felt it was an execution. Those that had been present knew better; Haruka only fired when Carney went for his rifle. Still, there was a small but vocal element that firmly believed it was an execution without trial.

Even so, the focus of the colony was no longer on the threat that Carney created, and the progress that was being made in the silent wake was telling. It was also an indictment of how much damage a single crime did to the colony. Not only when it happened, but for the entire time that it took to bring closure to the matter. Haruka turned away and looked off into the distance at a nearby hill, which each day was being stripped of a little more of its vegetation to make room for a farm. She watched as a palm swayed back and forth much farther than any of the surrounding trees before it toppled a minute later.

"Did I say something wrong?" James asked at last.

"I'm sorry to have taken away your favorite job," she sneered.

James knitted his eyebrows and they shot skyward. "Huh?"

"I'm sorry that you feel you have so much time on your hands since Carney's gone."

"What? Wait, that's not what I meant."

"Then what *did* you mean?"

James waved his hand in a dismissive gesture. "Nothing. I was just saying I'd like another crack at the pod. I think I might be able to get it going long enough to see if there's anyone else out there listening."

"Don't knock yourself out," she retorted. "Lieutenant Marsolek has his orders if something goes wrong. And assuming the other ships landed where *Raphael's* beacon landed, the pod's transmitter isn't strong enough to talk to them. Only *Raphael's* was."

He nodded and gave a weak smile, but Haruka could tell that her response had let a little wind out of his sails. An awkward silence descended. Haruka decided that she didn't want to be smothered by it, so she grabbed another palm leaf and turned the frayed, incomplete bottom edge of the storm curtain to face her.

"Since you brought up Carney," James said, shattering the silence. "We may have a problem with that."

"He's dead," she said coldly, slipping the tip of the twelve inch long leaf into the weave.

"Yes, he is. But I'm afraid the issue's not completely put to bed."

Haruka sighed and her shoulders slumped as she looked up at a single white cloud high in the sky. "What now?"

"I've heard some mumblings about how you handled things too harshly."

I doubt Luis would have agreed.

"Alright. What have you heard?"

"I'll be frank," he replied. "I've heard a rumor that there might be a group of colonists that are going to seek to replace you."

Haruka laughed nervously. "Good. If they want to run the show, let them."

"I'm being serious here."

She looked up and saw the slight frown on his face. His hand picked at his hair, and at once she knew that not only was he telling the truth, there was something more serious going on.

"How serious?"

"I don't know. It might just be forcing an election to be held. But one of the rumors I heard, and I have no idea how reliable the source is, was that they intend to assassinate you."

Assassinate. Well, I guess I'm important enough to someone to be a threat. If his source is reliable, in any case.

"Nothing solid so far though, right?"

"Right."

She nodded. As her fingers wove another strand into the door curtain, she thought about the next move. If there was to be a play for power, she could understand the desire. She wanted to make sure the pieces were in place to protect her against a worst case scenario, even though she didn't believe that anyone left around would actually want to see her dead.

"Alright. Keep your ear to the ground. Make sure Troy does, too. I don't want either of you to do anything right now other than listen and report to me. Understood?"

"Right. Business as usual," he nodded.

"Except the whole keeping me up to date bit. Do that a bit more often, okay?"

"Okay."

"Thank you, James."

"You're welcome." He paused and took a moment to admire her handiwork. "Looks like you're almost done there. Troy will be happy; he's just about ready for it."

Haruka nodded. "Just glad to be doing something again. I'll make as many of these as he wants."

Calvin McLaughlin
3 April, Year of Landing, 14:40
Approximately 31 miles west of Michael landing site
>|

The last rays of sunshine faded from Cal's skin as the sun—dubbed 'Bravo'—dropped below the jagged gray mountains ahead. His skin cooled, prompting goose bumps to rise on his arms. He opened his eyes from a squint, as the light no longer flooded his vision. Green spots danced in his view and he tried to blink them away, to no avail. After a minute, his eyes adjusted and his sight returned to normal.

Cal looked up at the sparse canopy of blue-needled Demeter pines. The dying orange glow of the sun at the tops of the trees gave them an eerie countenance, like fiery sentinels. Except for the more lush undergrowth and cooler temperature, the place where he stood bore strong resemblance to Caney Creek. He cocked his head, took in the scenery, and closed his eyes. A faint memory of the campground in Texas came to mind.

There were more trees back... He caught himself wanting to think the word "home," but corrected himself. *Back on Earth.*

His eyes fluttered open as he heard a splashing noise and a curse. He glanced down at the narrow, rushing stream to find Neil rising from his knees from the shallow water at the bank. One hand clutched a root on the steep bank; the other cradled a plastic sample jar tight against his chest. He slowly slipped his back foot under him and rose as the weight of the jar's contents threatened to plunge it into the creek.

Cal set his rifle on the ground and knelt down, stretching his hand out toward the geologist. As Neil regained his feet, he passed the jar to Cal, who then gently placed it next to him and helped his friend up the bank. Neil plopped onto the dirt and winced.

"You okay?" he asked.

"Yeah," he said as he reached for his right ankle. "Son of a bitch, I think I twisted it. I took a bad step and went face first into the creek."

Cal reached for Neil's ankle but was waved off. His charge heaved forth great breaths as he rubbed the injured leg. His pants were soaked below the knees, as were his socks and shoes. Though not completely soaked through, Neil's shirt and coat were wet on the front and sleeves.

"We're going to need to get you some dry clothes. Can you make it to the crawler?"

"Yeah," Neil said through a grimace. "Just give me a sec. Hey, can you take that jar back to the crawler for me?"

"Sure thing."

Cal rose to his feet and collected his rifle, then hoisted the jar of rocks. It was much heavier than he had anticipated, and he nearly dropped it back to the ground. With a second heave, he raised the jar level to his eyes and swiveled his hand, admiring the grainy, multi-hued stones within. They were rather sharp in places, but generally smooth. Cal guessed that they were part of a larger rock that had been broken.

"What are these?" he asked.

"Samples of sandstone," Neil replied.

"It's taken you two hours to collect these?"

"Not just those. I've already got three smaller jars of other samples I've put back in the crawler."

"Still seems like a lot of time for just a couple samples."

Neil hobbled to his feet, favoring his right foot. "I needed to make sure I got as wide of a variety as I could get. Less chance of missing something important, right?"

"Right."

Cal turned away from the stream and began to walk toward the crawler, which was parked on a slight incline a hundred yards from the stream, where the trees thinned out enough that its body could maneuver through the woods. He startled a small flock of birds, sending them into the sky in a meandering flurry of black and grey streaks. Cal then reached the crawler, hopped up on the running board, and placed the sample jar on the edge of the bed. He then swung over, found the compartment that was set aside for Neil's work, and secured the small round jar in place with a dozen others like it. His task completed, he climbed over the side and lowered himself onto the right side tracks, and then to the ground.

Neil finally caught up, limping slightly. He didn't seem to be too injured, though his wet clothing gave him a certain bedraggled air. Cal opened the rear passenger door and swept his arm upward.

"Welcome home, Doctor Leclair," he grinned.

"I'm not a doctor," Neil groaned. "Stop calling me that."

"Sorry. Just having a little fun."

Neil shook his head and returned a weak smile. He then looked around the cab of the crawler. "Hey, where are the girls?"

"Probably picking flowers again. I'll go get them. Lock yourself in there tight, okay?"

"That's fine. I'm done for the night anyway. Want me to warm up dinner?"

"Give me five minutes before you start."

"Alright," Neil replied.

Cal closed the cab door after Neil's legs were clear. He walked a few feet from the crawler and cocked his head, trying to listen to the sounds carried on the wind. Chattering and singing heralded the birds he had surprised a few minutes earlier. The creek babbled as it rushed by, and a monotonous rustle rose and fell in volume as the wind blew through the tops of the pines. Far off, he could hear the two women talking. He had no hope of knowing what they were saying, as he could only barely determine that they were out in the woods somewhere in front of the crawler.

He picked his course through the shadows in the dying light. The women were ahead of him, but still quite distant.

Damn. How far did they go?

Cal bounded forward in hopes of closing the gap before the light failed entirely. A breeze kicked up, and the swaying of the trees was joined by a symphony of rustling leaves and twigs from the brush below. The din swallowed up all other noises, and he had to stop his progress and try to pick up the voices again. After a minute, the winds calmed, and he was able to distinguish his targets again. They had moved closer, but shifted slightly to the right. Cal corrected his heading and moved again.

His heart leaped into his throat as a terrible, deafening roar pierced the night sky, followed by the sounds of breaking branches. A pair of light brown flashes streaked across his vision. He was barely able to recognize them as a species of elk-like creatures that had been discovered just two days after landing. They were extremely fast, and no colonist had ever gotten within a hundred feet of one. Yet these crossed almost within arm's reach of Cal. They jumped to the base of a nearby tree and then scattered in different directions. Another roar ripped through the air, and a massive, dark brown shape bounded to the spot where the elk had split up. It stood up on its hind feet, and Cal had to crane his head upward to see the terrible, twisted face that again roared through rows of jagged, dagger-like teeth. At the end of each of its short, thick limbs were paws the size of a dog's head, punctuated with multiple long, straight claws.

Oh fuck!

As if it were able to hear the word in his head, the beast dropped to all fours and twisted its head around to face Cal. It glared at him with wide, fiery eyes. Saliva dripped from between its fangs as it let out a breath that smelled of death. It lunged at him sideways, slamming its massive shoulder into Cal's chest. He sailed nearly twenty feet through the air before sliding another ten on his back. The AR-15 clattered to a stop somewhere in the darkness, out of reach. He struggled to draw in a deep breath, trying desperately to regain the wind that had been knocked out of him.

The beast leaped once and covered over half the ground that he had been thrown. Its jaws widened into a sadistic grin, and it howled. Terrible shivers ran down Cal's spine as the beast's call shook him to his very core. His hand clawed at the holster on his hip, and he managed to free the pistol. The beast rose on its hind legs again, then slammed its front legs to the ground, shaking it.

Oh shit.

His fingers trembled as he tried to release the safety, but his fingers had gone numb from fear, and he couldn't feel what he was doing.

A blast echoed through the air, and Cal's hands shot to his ears. The beast wailed, and thrashed to its right side. He heard two more cracks, and then saw the animal lunge in the opposite direction from him. Then, a second later, a long staccato burst poured forth. The massive brown terror lurched and jerked as the rounds found their home. The fire stopped, there was a loud gurgling noise, and the beast collapsed.

Slowly, and shaking in terror, Cal rose to his feet. His chest ached fiercely and he could barely move his right arm. He disabled the safety on his pistol and chambered a round, then walked toward the beast. As he approached, a flashlight shone in his eyes.

"Holy shit," Lieutenant Josephson exclaimed. "Was it trying to eat you?"

"Y-yes," he stammered.

"Are you alright?" he heard Elaine's voice through the darkness.

"Yeah, I guess." He paused. "I.. I've lost my rifle. It... it hit me, and... and I don't know where it landed."

The light lowered to illuminate the head of the animal. Cal cautiously moved around the body and sidled up next to Josephson and her charge, Elaine. He then looked down at the felled beast, keeping the pistol trained on its skull.

Josephson traced the light beam down the length of its body. Its head bore a modest snout, but the powerful jaws were lined with a horrific set of teeth that would put the predatory carnivores on Earth to shame. Its canines were almost four inches long, and had a pronounced curve to them. The shoulders were thick and powerful, as were its short legs. Cal had seen it leap more than its body length despite the stubby limbs. Its paws bore four claws each, about six inches long. As Josephson swept the light from end to end a few times, he realized that the beast was about ten feet in length, and the shape of its skull and its overall shape and muscularity were reminiscent of a giant bear. Its demeanor had certainly been more aggressive than its Terran counterpart.

"That thing was tough," Josephson remarked. "First few shots barely slowed it down." She released the magazine from her weapon and looked at it quickly. "All out. Shit. Okay, let's find Cal's rifle and get the hell back to the crawler."

They spent the next three minutes searching near where Cal had landed on his back. The weapon was found on the ground about twelve feet from where he had come to a rest. Cal had no doubt that if Josephson hadn't come around he would not have been able to find it before the animal killed him.

Oh God. I don't want to be out here any more. Just let me go home. Let me go back to Lexi.

Darius Owens
4 April, Year of Landing, 10:04
Gabriel landing site
>|

"We apologize for the lack of appropriate accommodations for this meeting, Mr. Owens." Fred Hausner greeted him with a smile and an extended hand. Wrinkles on the attorney's forehead accentuated his bespectacled face, and his short, tidy blonde hair had faded to a near platinum shade. The casual dress of such an important man was equally striking, though Darius knew that the man's professional wardrobe, if it still existed, sat more than four light years away.

Darius reached his hand out and shook that of Mr. Hausner, repeating the greeting with Don Abernathy.

"No need to apologize, sir. We haven't built your office yet."

"I think there are more important things that should be built first. That's neither here nor there, however," he replied. "Thank you for coming. Would you prefer to sit or stand?"

"I've been on my feet a lot the past couple days, so I'd like to sit, if you don't mind."

"Please, be my guest. I'd just like to get this done before the loggers finish their lunch break and come stomping through here again."

Darius lowered his body onto the mighty trunk of a felled tree. Drag marks running down the gentle slope and up another short rise marked the path where the logging crews dragged the tree after it had been cut down. Broken bits of bark, shattered limbs, and three other harvested trees marked the staging area where timber sat and awaited processing a few hundred feet away at the ship. Darius glanced across the river to his left, catching his daily glimpse of the life of the other crew.

Fred Hausner took a seat to his left, straddling the trunk. Colonel Eriksen had been very quick to find a prosecutor to handle the trial of Doctor Kimura, and his selection was a man who, despite his clothing, looked every bit the part. Fred's lines hardened and his brow furrowed as he flipped open a sketch pad and clicked his pen to the ready position.

To Darius's right, Don sat down as well. He carried only a Bible with him, but his lack of writing material was offset by his steel-like focus. When Darius had found him in camp and explained the situation, Don had immediately offered his services in defense of Doctor Kimura. Securing representation for his friend was a relief, but hearing of Don

J.C. Rainier

Abernathy's experience affirmed that Rory's recommendation was the right one. After graduating from Harvard, Don had practiced criminal law for nearly two decades in Boston, serving as an assistant district attorney at first, later moving on to a prestigious private firm.

Don cleared his throat. "In the absence of a court officer, I agree to serve in that stead for the purposes of swearing in and party identification. Mr. Hausner will serve in that stead for recording of the particulars, as well as transcription."

"I will be taking shorthand notes in place of a full transcript," Fred added. "As we currently lack the equipment to record a full transcript. Both of us have agreed to these terms ahead of time. Is that alright?"

Darius affirmed with a curt nod. Don stretched out his arm with the Bible face-up on his palm and nodded. Darius placed his hand on the Bible.

"Do you swear to tell the truth, the whole truth, and nothing but the truth, so help you God?" Don asked.

"I do."

"This is a deposition in the matter of the People versus Doctor Tadashi Kimura. The date is the fourth of April, Year of Landing, Demeter colony." Don glanced down at a digital watch that he produced from his sweatshirt pocket. "The local time is ten oh eight. The venue for this proceeding is at the lumber staging point just northwest of the sleeper ship *Gabriel*. Present are prosecuting attorney Fred Hausner, defense attorney Don Abernathy, and the witness, former United States Air Force Lieutenant Darius Owens. Mr. Owens has been sworn in, and we are ready to proceed. Would you like to go first, counselor?"

Fred finished jotting a note on the pad and nodded. "Thank you. Can you please state in what capacity you served while you were with Project Columbus?"

"I held the rank of First Lieutenant. I was assigned to network and computer maintenance on *Gabriel*, with a secondary duty as a communications officer."

"And when were you assigned to the Project?"

"April 2011."

"Thank you. I understand that you were present at the time Doctor Kimura was placed under arrest, correct?"

"Correct, sir."

"And do I understand correctly that Doctor Kimura voluntarily surrendered, and gave a confession?"

"You understand correctly, sir."

"And what did he say in this confession?"

Darius paused for a moment as he examined the prosecutor, who scratched more notes onto the pad of paper. "The confession was recorded on Colonel Eriksen's orders. You can hear exactly what he said, if you like."

"I understand that, but I want to hear it in your words," Fred retorted without skipping a beat.

"Objection," Don interrupted. "Replaying the recording of the confession will give us the exact words as Doctor Kimura spoke them, rather than hearsay as Mr. Owens interprets what the doctor said."

"Objection noted. Please, continue Mr. Owens."

"Huh? Didn't Mr. Abernathy object?"

"I did," Don replied. "But unlike in a court, you still have to answer the question."

"Very well." Darius paused and took a deep breath as he recalled Doctor Kimura's speech on the bridge. "He said that he and the other doctors on the research team modified the computer algorithm that selected passengers for the sleeper ships. He said that they found that the original algorithm that they had sent to Congress for approval had been altered, and that they didn't believe that a colony could survive, given the skill set distribution that happened when the modified program was run. Doctor Kimura pointed out that a very high number of Congressmen and their families ended up on the list. Because of the depletion of critical professions, Doctor Kimura and his colleagues altered percentages of certain other professions, or eliminated them altogether."

"And he said that his family, as well as others involved with the modification and cover up, received spots on the sleeper ships?"

"He did, sir."

That's going to look bad, Doc.

"Did he mention any accomplices?"

"Yes, sir. Doctors Fairweather and Benedict worked together to modify the program, and they had sympathizers in the Air Force that helped them move the replacement passengers to the PCRL compound in Wyoming."

Fred cocked his head and arched his eyebrows skyward. "When did you first meet Doctor Kimura?"

"May 2011, sir."

And no, I didn't have anything to do with this, if that's what you're thinking.

"Did any of the research staff approach you about alteration of the algorithm?"

"No sir."

"Did any of the research staff or any other Air Force personnel approach you about moving passengers into or out of the compound?"

"No sir."

Fred scribbled furiously on the paper for a minute, and then looked up. "He's all yours, counselor."

"Thank you." Don rose from the tree trunk and stretched, then scratched at his chin. "You say you met Doctor Kimura in May of 2011. Did you have any contact whatsoever with him or any of the other Project Columbus research team prior to your assignment in April of that year?"

"No, sir."

"Did Doctor Kimura explain to you why he altered the selection algorithm?"

"Yes, sir," Darius replied. "He made it pretty clear that if the version that Congress approved was used, the chances of a colony surviving were much lower."

Darius caught a movement below on the hill out of the corner of his eye. He glanced down and saw someone moving up the hill quickly toward them.

"Did Doctor Kimura give you any indication that he intended to steal the sleeper ships?" Don asked.

"No, sir. As far as I knew, our mission was going along according to the Project Columbus mission procedure. It wasn't until we had left orbit and Doctor Kimura admitted to his part in the incident that I knew anything was out of the ordinary."

Darius checked the hill again and saw Colonel Eriksen nearing the crest. His face was as red as his beard, and his teeth showed through his snarl. Darius could feel the pit of his stomach rise as Eriksen stormed directly toward him.

"What's the meaning of this?" he bellowed.

Fred Hausner shot up from his seat and moved between Darius and the colonel. With a voice as calm as a summer's night, he said, "Sir, you can't be here right now."

"The hell I can't. He's not supposed to be here," he yelled, pointing a thick finger directly at Darius.

"This is a legal proceeding. You can't be here," Fred repeated.

"Lieutenant Owens is not allowed to be involved in any colonial affairs," Eriksen screamed. Veins throbbed in his neck, threatening to burst at any second.

Darius's fingers scraped along the bark and his teeth grated at hearing his former title.

I'm not in the service any more, Colonel.

Don moved next to his colleague, forming a blockade through which Darius could no longer see his former commanding officer. "You need to leave now, sir. This legal matter supersedes any standing orders you may have given this man. To say otherwise would be countermanding your own order, and would mean that Doctor Kimura's charges would be nullified."

"Bullshit."

"It's true, Colonel," replied Fred, unshaken by the hulking square of a man that faced him. "Now please leave and let us work on the task that you gave us."

A moment of silence fell, then Darius heard the footsteps of Eriksen moving off.

"I'm warning you, Owens, stay out of it," he shouted as he moved down the hill.

The attorneys shook their heads and turned to face Darius. Fred rolled his eyes, but both then walked to Darius.

"My apologies, Mr. Owens," Fred said.

"It's not your fault."

"We can continue this at another time if you wish."

Darius shook his head. "It's alright, we can continue."

Don chimed in. "We're just about done anyway. I only had one more question left for you, if you don't mind."

"Go right ahead."

"Did Doctor Kimura admit his role freely, or was he caught in some action that aroused your suspicion?"

"He just hit me out of the blue with it. He seemed a little off when I was talking to him, but I had no idea what I was in for when he started explaining things."

Don nodded. "Anything else, counselor?"

"I have one more question," Fred replied. "Did you develop a personal relationship with Doctor Kimura or any of the other researchers after your assignment to the Project?"

"Of course, sir. All of them." Darius sighed. "The Kimuras were like a second family to me. Lieutenant Kimura was busy with her training so I didn't get too much time with her. But Doctor K, his wife, and his other daughter…" He trailed off as he took a moment to reflect on the times they had spent together at PCRL Laramie. "We were close."

"And he didn't tell you anything about what he planned?" The question was instantaneous and blunt."

"No sir."

"Why?"

"Because I would have turned him in," he admitted with a heavy heart. "Just like I did on the ship. I would have betrayed his confidence to execute my duty."

Fred finished his notes and flipped the tablet of paper closed. "I think that wraps it up. Thank you for meeting with us, Mr. Owens. We'll let you know if we need you again, or if we set a date for the trial to start."

The two lawyers shook his hand again, and he left from their impromptu meeting place, opting to go down the hill on the river side, opposite of where Colonel Eriksen came from. On his way down, he looked to a distant hill on the *Michael* side of the river where the green hillside slowly changed from lush green to broken stripes of brown over the course of a couple days.

Farming.

For a moment, Darius wished he was with the other crew, far from the troubles of *Gabriel*.

"Good morning, Captain," Troy said cheerfully.

Her head throbbed and a deep shiver wracked her body. She could feel the sweat on her brow even without drawing her hand across it. The smile disappeared from Troy's face and he instead cocked his head and gave her a sympathetic look.

"Are you feeling okay?" he asked.

Haruka waved her hand dismissively. "I'm fine. Your report, please?"

"Are you sure?"

"I'm fine, I swear."

Troy peered at her for a second, and then shrugged. "Alright. We completed another hut yesterday. We can have another two done within the next two weeks, but we have a new problem."

"Alright, give it to me."

"We can't cut down trees and drag them up here fast enough. We can't even start another building until we get more."

"I've thought about that," she replied. "It looks like a big problem, since we don't have any trucks to move them around. Do we have anything else we can build with? Mud maybe?"

Troy scratched at the fresh stubble on his face. "Nothing that I've seen so far. The silt in the river here is more sand than clay, so it's not so hot for building with. Maybe we can come up with something, but it's going to take a bit. I'm running out of options in the meantime."

"It's not the only thing that's making me nervous. But I have an idea. See that low rise over there to the south of us?"

Troy squinted and scanned the horizon where Haruka pointed. "Yeah."

"Think we can clear it and set up a farm?"

"Clearing it's not a problem," he sighed. "We could use the timber over there to build a house or two on the hill. But once we tear it all up, how are we going to irrigate it? Or keep the damn rats from chewing everything up?"

Her head began to spin and she leaned against a tree for support. Troy took a step toward her, but she put up her hand. "We can't solve a problem that we don't even have yet. Let's get it built and then worry about it."

Haruka barely got the words out before a stabbing pain shot through her left side. She twisted and grimaced, and then doubled over. No sooner than she had done so, her stomach revolted, and what little she had eaten came up in two loud, violent retches.

She felt Troy's hand on her back. "Jeez, are you okay?"

She nodded and straightened her back. She spit out an errant chunk from the back of her throat. "I'll be fine. Get to work."

"Are you sure? I can take you to see Doctor Petrovsky."

"Will you stop it already?" she growled. "I know how to get there myself. Just get back to work, please."

"Alright, jeez." She could hear the defeat in his voice, and she glanced over her shoulder and watched him walk away, taking a look over his shoulder every few steps.

Once he was out of sight, she doubled over in pain again, leaving one hand on the bark of the palm. Her mouth burned, and the acrid taste of vomit lingered. Her breakfast lay at her feet, and had landed in a pepperine shrub. Haruka coughed and spat, trying to avoid breathing in the foul stench of bile and acid that made her gag. Another violent shiver washed over her, and her fingers and toes felt like ice.

She trudged her way up the path to the village, clutching her stomach the whole way. She walked between the new huts that Troy's teams were constructing; one was a mere skeleton, the other had four walls and the beginnings of a roof structure. She emerged from between them and made her way past the Palm Palace to Dr. Petrovsky's clinic.

Inside, the doctor was nowhere to be found. Haruka's former Chief of Medicine, Emilia Reiber, walked around the short partition wall at the back and greeted Haruka with a smile, which waned quickly when she sized up Haruka's condition.

"Please, come lie down," she said, grabbing Haruka's arm gently and guiding her to one of the woven palm beds along the wall. Emilia placed a nearly frozen hand to Haruka's forehead. "You're burning up. Lie down; I'm going to get you some water."

Haruka complied. The scratchy leaves of the bed were cold against her skin, and she could feel the chill through her clothes as well. A sharp twinge of pain stabbed at her, and she curled up on her side and closed her eyes.

"Is Doctor Petrovsky in?" she croaked.

"No, he was called away. One of the fishermen cut his foot, so he went to help out. He should be back in a while." Emilia's whispered voice suddenly became very close, and Haruka could feel something hard pressed to her lips. "Here, drink this."

Cool water trickled into Haruka's mouth and down her lips. She swallowed, almost gagging on the first rush. The second swig went down smoothly, and she took a deep breath.

"How long has this been going on?" Emilia asked, doing her best to mimic Dr. Petrovsky's mannerisms of medical inquisition.

"I woke up this morning and couldn't get warm. I threw up a few minutes ago. That's when the pain started."

"Did you eat anything this morning?"

"Ration pouch."

"And last night?"

Haruka paused to recall what she had for dinner the previous evening. "Fried shark, baked bank root, and pepperines."

"Any nausea last night?"

Haruka shook her head.

"Any fatigue?"

"Yeah. Last night was the same as most days. A little worse today."

"Alright. I'm going to keep my eye on you. No running off without me or Ken saying it's okay, got it?"

"Yes ma'am." Haruka tried to smile, but she wasn't sure if she was able to manage anything more than a twitch of her lips. Her head swam and her body shivered all the way to her toes. She felt Emilia place something on top of her. It was cold for a moment, but quickly began to retain her body heat, giving her the first sensation of warmth all day. Haruka opened her eyes for a second to confirm that Emilia had covered her with an unzipped sleeping bag.

Her energy had been sapped by her body attacking whatever affliction with which she was dealing. Sleep soon came to her, though it was fitful. Babbling voices held meaningless conversations while she strained to listen. She would be too warm one moment and then freezing cold the next. The bedding beneath her scratched at her bare skin and caught her hair as she tossed and turned. Still, she forced herself to rest until she could not stand it any longer.

Haruka opened her eyes and sat up. Daylight filtered through the partially open storm curtain. Maria Serrano sat upright on a bed along the far wall. Gabi sat at her feet, playing some sort of game with her stuffed cat. Dr. Petrovsky knelt at Maria's side, speaking with her. Every few seconds, Maria would nod an acknowledgement at the doctor. They finished, and both stood up. As Maria reached her hand for Gabi, her eyes caught Haruka's. Without a word, Maria snatched up her rather surprised daughter, and quickly left the clinic.

Dr. Petrovsky noticed Haruka was up, and walked over to her. He smiled, and spoke in his usual cheerful bedside tone, even as he prodded and examined her.

"Good afternoon, Captain. I hope you're feeling better."

"A little. What was that about?"

"Hmm?" he asked as his eyebrows arched.

"Maria. Is something wrong with her?"

"Oh, she was just checking in."

Bull. Maria would rather be alone than talk to anyone. And she hasn't lived here since the first hut was built and the colonists gave it to her.

"How is she?" Haruka asked.

"She's doing fine, all things considered."

All things considered. Her husband was murdered. She was raped. And I was a terrible friend. All things indeed.

"That's good. How have you been? I hear there was some excitement down on the beach today."

Dr. Petrovsky laughed under his breath. "You could say that. Nick misjudged a roller and got rolled over in the surf a couple times. He got spun around, didn't know where he was, and sliced his foot open on some coral."

Haruka placed her hand on the doctor's. "Nick as in your son, Nick? Oh, I'm sorry, Doctor. Is he okay?"

"Thank you, Captain," he smiled. There was a hint of pain behind it, and sadness in his eyes. "He'll be fine, but he's going to be off his feet for a couple days. I know that's what's going to upset him the most about this."

"Well, I know he'll heal up in no time and be back out there wrangling sharks."

"That's true." He squeezed Haruka's hand slightly. "And you'll be back out there wrangling colonists."

"Ah, haven't you heard? I've found my new calling. Making curtains and roof panels," she said with an impish grin.

"So I've got Troy to thank for you not taking it easy, then?" he jabbed.

"You can thank Troy that I'm only weaving and not trying to lift trees or anything like that. He wouldn't let me work on anything more strenuous."

"Well, if you're not going to run the colony, then it's probably one of the best jobs for you to do."

Haruka nodded. "I was thinking about getting Maria to try it."

The smile vanished from Petrovsky's face and he pursed his lips.

"What?" Haruka asked.

"I know it's hard, and you need every able body to be at work, but she can't be pushed. She needs time to heal."

Haruka could feel her impatience begin to rise. "She's had a couple months to grieve, but she's not getting any better. Not even after she and Gabi watched Carney die."

The color drained from Petrovsky's ruddy cheeks, and he swallowed hard. "That would explain Gabi's behavior, then. I'm sorry, I had no idea she saw that."

"Yeah, well, you can imagine how I'm not exactly thrilled with the so-called 'progress' that is being made with her, Doctor. I've given her space and let you do what you felt is right to let her heal, but if she doesn't do at least something to contribute to the colony soon, we're going to stop doing things your way."

"You know, you've had a hard day. Maybe you should just rest a little bit more and we'll start over tomorrow." He placed his hand on Haruka's shoulder and gently pressed, trying to get her to lie down, but she shrugged off his hand.

"I'll rest because I know I need it, but I'm not changing my mind. Three more days, Doctor. She rejoins the work force, ready or not. Your way or my way."

She settled back into the bed and curled up, facing away from Dr. Petrovsky.

Calvin McLaughlin
12 April, Year of Landing, 05:55
Approximately 42 miles northwest of Michael
landing site
>|

Calvin startled awake as a loud snort filled the cab of the crawler. He flipped around quickly inside his bag and searched for the source of the noise. Stretched across the floor of the rear seat was Neil, snoring erratically. An empty sleeping bag hung part way off the edge of the bench seat, threatening to tickle his nose and set him off again. Cal yawned and then shifted onto his side. Another empty bag sat in the front passenger seat.

The girls are up early this morning.

He closed his eyes for a moment, but the dull throbbing in his head told him that going back to sleep, even for just a minute, was not about to happen. Instead he opened his eyes and stared blankly at the fine white fog that coated the inside of the windshield. His breath reached out in ghostly trails, billowing into a roiling cloud as it touched the glass. A childish whim ran through Cal's mind, and he grinned. He sat up, extended a finger, and began to draw in the condensation.

A rolling squiggle near the bottom of the windshield represented the ground, and he then made several stick-like trees jutting up to the middle. Above, near where the rear view mirror would have been mounted on a regular truck, he drew two crescent moons. Four stick figures were drawn standing on the ground below, all but one with wide smiles. Cal then drew a wide, snaking river down the center of the windshield, and large, rectangular bumps on either side, with small engine bells on the rear. As a finale, he drew arced, dotted lines between the two mock sleeper ships, and rubbed several "explosions" into them. Across the top of the glass he scribbled a single phrase.

BATTLE OF CONCORDIA

Another sharp snort came from the back seat, followed by a long groan.

"Morning, Neil."

After a short pause, Neil asked, "What time is it?"

"Just after six."

Cal heard rustling vinyl in the back seat and felt the crawler sway slightly. Neil's head popped up over the seat back. His hair was a chaotic, tangled mess, and his hands shook slightly as he opened his glasses and put them in place.

"Where are the ladies?"

"Probably at work already. They were gone when I woke up a few minutes ago."

Neil's hands raked through his hair as he attempted to tame the thick mat. His eyes looked forward at the windshield, and a grin crept across his face.

"Are we declaring war on the other ship?"

"It had to happen," Cal replied dryly. "I was getting bored. They were getting too relaxed. It was time for a sneak attack. And soon we shall rule all of Demeter."

"Good for you. Did they have better food over there?"

"More of your favorite." Cal opened the cavernous center console that separated the driver and passenger seat and fished out two brown pouches. "Space rations. Certified nutritious, and oh so delicious."

Neil let out a disappointed groan as he took a meal pack from Cal. "Can't I just eat Elaine's plant samples? I don't care if they're poisonous. At least I'll die a slightly happier man."

"Don't worry, I'm just about there with you." Cal tore open a package of scrambled eggs and dumped the entire packet of hot sauce onto them. "It wouldn't be so bad if there was just a little more variety. Or at least something out there that we knew wouldn't kill us, just to spice it up now and then."

"Better safe than sorry, right?"

"Right. Though the worst of it is the coffee. Now that I've had a taste of the real stuff, it's hard to stomach this pre-brewed pouched crap. I just try not to think about the fact that it's more than forty years old."

Neil cringed and his nose wrinkled. "Why did you have to tell me that? Now I'm going to think of that any time I try to choke one of these damned things down."

"Your choices aren't great. Eat stale eggs or starve."

"Fair enough."

The two men consumed the rest of their meal in silence. After collecting the waste, Cal climbed out onto the running board and stowed the trash in the increasingly full bed.

Not much more room for samples, he thought. *Maybe Josephson will let us turn around soon.*

They had slowly traveled north, where they crossed a stream that

J.C. Rainier

Neil had mucked around in for several days, and followed a bend in the river that passed between the sleeper ships downstream. Both scientists had collected what Cal thought to be an enormous number of samples. Only a few empty jars remained, and Elaine had staked a claim to them, citing her belief that Neil's rock samples would survive whether or not they were sealed. The trees also grew more tightly packed, and every day he had a harder time picking a path deeper into the wilderness. By the looks of the timber growth in the next valley, Cal believed they were as deep as they could go in the crawler.

Maybe if they set up a base camp here and continued on foot they'd get farther, but we're not equipped for a foot expedition.

He reached back into the cab to retrieve his belt and rifle, and then jumped down, found an adequate bush, and relieved himself before going back to the crawler. Neil waited outside, hunching over slightly and breathing into his cupped hands.

"No creeks for you today," Cal joked. "Hypothermia isn't on my list of acceptable injuries."

"No creeks. Just that spring over there."

Cal shook his head. "It's always water with you, isn't it?"

"Hey, give me a coring drill I can play with and I'd be glad to stay away from water. Until then, I've got to look for the easy stuff."

Cal escorted Neil a few hundred feet through the woods to a small spring that formed at the head of a murky pond. The banks near the spring were stained a deep red color, and strange white foam seemed to coalesce where the water slowed farther out.

"This is promising," Neil chirped as he knelt at the water's edge. He pulled a small trowel from the toolbox he carried with him nearly everywhere and plunged it into the dirt. It did not bury far, and rather than a scraping noise, it clanked. "Very promising."

"What is it?" Cal asked, rising up on the tips of his toes to try gain a better vantage point.

"You'll see."

Neil dug for a minute, then retrieved a small steel pick from his box and chipped away at the hard red rock. A chunk fell away and splashed into the spring, and Neil fished it out.

"Yes!" he exclaimed as he held up the rock, no bigger than the palm of his hand.

"What? What is it?"

"It's called bog ore, and it's evidence of iron. We should look around for more springs." He secured the tools and red rock in his kit and bounded away into the woods. Cal followed on his heels and hoped that the scientist wouldn't stumble over his own feet and into another bone-chilling body of water.

"Wait up," Cal called.

He brushed against a low hanging limb. A startled bird shot into the sky, squawking at him in disapproval. Neil pressed on and headed for another small pond just a few feet ahead at the edge of a stand of pines. He reached the water's edge and knelt down. Cal caught up and took a minute to catch his breath.

"I think there's more in here," Neil exclaimed. "I'm definitely marking this on the map."

Cal heard a distant pop, which echoed through the hills. His feet froze in place and he cocked his head. "Shhh," he hissed at Neil.

"What is it?"

A second later, another report rang to his ears. This time he was able to hear a minute difference in the timing, giving him a rough sense of where the shot came from. More than one shot meant that Josephson wasn't dealing with a pest. Cal's fingers began to tingle and he swallowed hard

"Oh shit. The girls. C'mon, let's go!" Cal started into a headlong sprint in the direction of the gunfire.

"Wait! What's going on?" he heard Neil from far behind.

Cal glanced back only once to make sure that the geologist was pursuing. Once he knew that Neil was on the move, he pushed his legs to the limit, jumping over roots and dodging around trees like a halfback in full flight. Another shot rang out, and he adjusted his course slightly to the left to compensate. He knew he was closing in on Josephson's location.

"Josephson! Elaine! Where are you?" he screamed.

In the distance, he could hear Lieutenant Josephson scream out a taunt. "I'm over here, you giant son of a bitch." Another round was fired, and Cal recognized the softer report of her Beretta. "That's right. Get away from her. Take me on, you fucker."

Cal slowed for a moment to prime his AR-15 for combat. The weapon was powerful and accurate, but didn't have the fire rate of Josephson's prized M4 carbine. He contemplated a more cautious approach, but the panic in Josephson's voice as it carried on the wind was escalating. Whatever she faced, Cal knew it was dire, and the lieutenant might not last long enough for a measured approach. Again he charged headlong at the sound of the struggle.

Through the trees, he could make out the outline of the crawler. A flash of blue was quickly blotted out by a hulking, brown creature that jumped and snarled as it danced around the clearing.

Shit, not again.

Cal charged to the edge of the clearing just in time to see the end of Josephson's fight. The giant bear-like creature slammed its shoulder into her side, and then swept its great paw down low to the dirt. Before she hit the ground, it scooped up under her, and she was thrown like a ragdoll about fifteen feet. She skidded on her side until her body slammed into a rock. She did not move.

"No!" Cal screamed.

He brought the rifle to his shoulder and took quick aim down the rear sight. He massaged the trigger three times in quick succession, and the AR-15 belched fire as three rounds traveled the gap in less than the blink of an eye, finding their homes. Two tore into the bear's torso, and a third into its foreleg. It screamed and reared onto its hind legs, and then dropped to a crouch.

Oh shit!

The beast leaped as Cal squeezed off another two rounds, which sailed under it and into the armored bumper of the crawler. Brown fur and thick muscle sailed high into the air. Cal froze for a moment as he waited for the weight and the claws to crash into him. The hulking animal landed just short, but its weight shook the ground so violently that Cal stumbled back a step. The predator took advantage of this momentary drop in Cal's guard, and a second, shorter hop sent Cal skidding on his back. He came to a stop suddenly as a short bush cushioned him from slamming into a thick tree.

Cal's hands were empty. He glanced to his right, but the rifle was nowhere to be found. A terrifying roar filled the air, and Cal watched as the beast prepared for another lunge.

Oh God. This is the end. I love you, Alexis.

His right hand shot to his belt, unsnapped the holster, and drew the Beretta in one motion. He raised it, but realized as the beast's haunches tightened that he didn't have enough time to release the safety and fire a shot before the inevitable attack.

CRACK, CRACK, CRACK.

With a single spasm, the bear collapsed. Blood gushed from two holes in its massive skull.

Cal's ears were ringing, but he was vaguely aware that someone was trying to talk to him. A hand cradled underneath his arm, and he was helped to his feet. Neil stood by him, AR-15 in one hand, and Cal's arm in the other. He had lost his glasses somewhere along the way.

"Are you okay?" Neil's mouth was open wide in a scream, but Cal could barely hear.

He nodded, though his shoulder ached and blood poured from a scratch on his cheek. "The girls," he coughed. "Come on."

Cal picked his way around the fallen beast, keeping his pistol trained on it until he was clear around its backside. He ran to Josephson, who lay crumpled on the ground, bleeding from a gash on her left arm.

"Get the med kit, Neil," he screamed.

Cal heaved her onto her back. Her pistol rolled from her hand and onto the dirt. He could see her chest rise and fall, if not a bit labored.

She's still alive.

Cal gently slapped her cheek. "Come on, wake up."

She groaned and rolled her head, but her eyes didn't open.

Calvin rose to his feet and turned to the crawler. He saw Neil Leclair standing near the front fender of the crawler, frozen. "Neil, I need that med kit. Now."

Neil did not move. Cal covered the thirty feet between them in just a few seconds. When he arrived at Neil's side, he caught the larger man's arm. Both of them dropped to their knees.

Oh God, no. No, no, NO! Oh, fuck... WHY?

The eviscerated corpse of Elaine Montoya gave no answers. It only looked skyward through dead eyes.

Darius Owens
12 April, Year of Landing, 08:13
Gabriel landing site
>|

Miguel Barajas craned his thick neck upward momentarily to assure the pole was not tipping. He then took a step back and lowered his gaze to the hole in the ground. He beckoned to the driver of the crane with one hand, watching as the base of the pole slowly inched towards the hole. When it got close, Darius grabbed it firmly with both hands and guided it to the center of the hole. Miguel made a patting motion and the boom of the crane creaked lower. The pole slid with a scraping sound and then hit bottom.

"Alright, straighten 'er up," Miguel called.

The machine whined and creaked, and the pole edged its way into a vertical position.

"Hold 'er there!"

Darius grabbed a shovel and began pushing the loose dirt into the hole around the edges of the new pole. Miguel joined him doing likewise, his biceps bulging through his shirt every time he pushed or pounded against the growing pile. In less than five minutes, the task was completed, and the strap on the crane slacked.

"Another one down," Miguel remarked. "Eleven more to go."

"Eleven until we branch out," Darius corrected.

He leaned outward from the pole and looked at the half dozen others that stuck out of the ground in a straight line between them and the support section of *Gabriel*. Behind them flowed the river. The line of utility poles was meant to run from the ship to a few hundred feet from the river, where ground was being cleared to erect industrial buildings. Darius ran his gloved hand along the surface of the reddish surface of the pole. His fingers crossed the gnarled bump of a knot. The wood was lighter at this point on the pole; it appeared that the cheap stain that was used to protect the native Demeter lumber had not been properly applied at that point. It was a common flaw in the poles they used, but without access to pressure treating, creosote, or even tar, it was meant as only a temporary measure.

I wonder how many years we'll get out of these before we have to start replacing them.

Darius tamped down the dirt around the base of the pole one more time for good measure before he slid the shovel onto its carrying rack on the side of the small crane. The crane's operator, Ivan Novak, wiped his brow with a filthy red handkerchief before donning his hard hat once more. He noticed Darius looking at him, and gave a thumbs up. Darius returned the gesture, slapped the door twice, stepped onto the side plate, and grabbed a handle just behind the door. He heard a similar thump on the opposite door, and the crane lurched forward.

A muddy track, devoid of all vegetation, roughly marked the line of the telegraph road. Bumps every few feet gave away the presence of rocks hidden in the mud, further buried by the steel tracks of the crane. Darius enjoyed the flow of air over his cheeks as the conveyance carried them forward over the crown of the hill. The far bank was also being similarly cleared by the crew of *Michael*, and the beginnings of a wood structure could be seen in front of the ship's dull, steel mass.

Ivan drove the crane just under three hundred feet to where another pole had been laid out on the ground. Fresh soil flung in a circle around a hole marked where the auger had pierced the earth earlier in the morning by the other work team. The crane slowly moved into position, and Darius and Miguel jumped from the side and cinched the sling around the timber.

"You think we can get all these done today?" Darius asked.

"Shouldn't be a problem," Miguel replied. "If a long day doesn't bug you. I just hope Ali and the boys save me some of the good stuff when they serve up dinner back at camp."

Darius smiled at him as the crane hoisted the top of the pole into the air. "Ah, didn't I tell you? I've got your back. Rory will make sure we're all fed. And you, sir, won't have to worry about your boys sneaking chow from you. I heard a little bird say that you missed out on the strawberry shortcake the night that the colonel allowed a little treat for all of us."

Miguel's mouth twitched. Darius could tell that, despite how much he loved his children, Miguel was irked by the loss of the one treat that Colonel Eriksen had authorized for the colonists. "Naw, man. I did it for my boys."

You don't have to put on the front for me. I know the rationing is wearing on all of us.

Darius and Miguel took their positions on the far side of the hole. Miguel went through a series of hand gestures, telling Ivan to lift the pole off the ground and move it forward. Darius carefully aligned the base into the center of the gaping maw of earth, then Miguel instructed Ivan to lower the boom a few inches at a time until the base of the pole

J.C. Rainier

was six feet deep. Darius stepped to the crane, retrieved both shovels, and handed one to Miguel.

"You sure it's cool, asking your boy to do that for me?" Miguel asked.

Darius thrust his shovel deep into the loose dirt. "Rory's a real good guy. If there's one thing he understands and respects, it's a working man. If you do an honest day's work, he'll do right by you when you need it. He expects the same in return."

"I don't got a problem with that."

"Didn't think you would." Darius paused for a moment and watched Miguel throw four shovels full of dirt into the hole. The words that ran deep from his emotion came out with no thought. "Maybe if we all lived like that back on Earth, the War would never have happened."

Miguel leaned against his shovel and dabbed a cloth across his brow. "The world had a few more problems than respect."

He's right. Darius sighed heavily and threw more dirt around the side of the pole. *Neighbors can get along fine for the most part, but different parts of a city...*

He forced a smile as he tried to shove aside thoughts of a ruined Earth. "Well, getting him to set aside a little of whatever he's whipped up is a small price to pay for you doing the lion's share of the next phase."

"Just remember not to plug the lines into the ship until after I'm done stringing them up, right?"

"Right. I wouldn't want your widow beating my ass with a shoe, now would I?" Darius grinned broadly.

"Hah. Ali wouldn't use a shoe. You'd only wish she did after she was done with you."

Ivan's smoky voice cut through their conversation. "Are you ladies done gossiping? We have work to do, you know."

"Ah, go back to your throne, Princess," Miguel taunted playfully.

"It's a hundred fricking degrees inside that beast. You can call me Princess when you make a fan and put those arms to work cooling me down."

Darius chortled at the exchange between his crewmates. "Managers, right?"

Metal rasped as Miguel scraped another layer of dirt into the hole.

"Can't get his hands dirty, right? Just gotta bitch and moan while another guy sweats. Heaven forbid he breaks a nail."

"I heard that, Barajas," Ivan sneered, though he bore an impish grin on his face.

"Go back to eating your borscht, Novak."

"It'd be better than Private Owens's food packs."

"Hey," Darius protested as he stifled a laugh. "That's Lieutenant to you. I wasn't a grunt, thank you very much. I went to officers' school to learn how to ruin my life."

"Holy shit, they sent you to school?" Novak replied sarcastically.

"I know. Can you believe it? Look! I can dress myself!"

"Wow, man," Miguel interjected. "Who's your designer? Bob Vila?"

Darius could no longer contain himself and he began to laugh almost hysterically. Miguel and Ivan joined in. Darius had to gasp for air when Ivan let loose a particularly ridiculous laugh, and Miguel looked as if he might pass out at any moment.

A low rumbling noise brought the comedy to an abrupt end. Darius glanced around and saw Airman Jake Smith riding up the hill on a pinto gelding that was a little too small for his frame. The trio waited for the Air Force enlistee to arrive and dismount. He walked with a sharp step directly to Darius.

"Lieutenant Owens, sir," he saluted.

"I'm not an officer any more, son. No need to salute," he said, holding back a sneer. Darius knew that the young airman did not mean any offense in addressing him by his former title, though it still stung a little.

"Sorry, sir."

Darius's hand curled and then relaxed. *I said I'm not an officer any more, kid. Don't you listen?*

"What can I do for you?"

"Sir, I have a letter for you, from Colonel Eriksen," he replied as he produced a piece of paper from the pocket of his flight suit. He extended his hand, and Darius took the letter.

"Thank you, Jake."

Smith saluted, but Darius did not give one in return. Instead he unfolded the paper and began to read as Smith walked back to his horse.

MR. DARIUS OWENS

    IT HAS COME TO MY ATTENTION THAT YOU ARE SLATED TO TESTIFY AS A WITNESS FOR THE DEFENSE IN THE UPCOMING TRIAL OF THE PEOPLE VS. DOCTOR TADASHI KIMURA. PLEASE BE AWARE THAT SUCH ACTIONS WOULD BE CONSIDERED MEDDLING IN THE AFFAIRS OF THE DEMETER COLONY, AND WOULD BE IN BREACH OF THE CONDITIONS OF YOUR DISCHARGE. IF YOU SERVE AS A WITNESS YOU MAY BE SUBJECT TO COURT MARTIAL FOR DESERTION. I HOPE THAT I DON'T NEED TO REMIND YOU THAT THIS CRIME IS SEVERE, AND THE PUNISHMENT MAY INCLUDE DEATH.

    CHARLES ERIKSEN
    COLONEL, USAF
    COMMANDING OFFICER
    DEMETER COLONY
    ALPHA CENTAURI B

"What the fuck?" Darius muttered.

"What is it?" asked Miguel.

Darius thrust the paper into his companion's hand and stormed up to Smith, who was firming his grip on the reins.

"Airman Smith," he shouted. "Did you read that letter?"

"No, sir. My orders were simply to deliver it to you."

So he's willing to send out someone as clueless as Smith to deliver a threat?

"Can you please give a response to the colonel?"

"Yes, sir."

Darius's lip curled and his voice lowered an octave. "Compliments of *Mister* Darius Owens, would you kindly inform the colonel that his demands are illegal, and I will see to it that the people's counsel is made aware of the existence of this letter?"

Smith's eyes grew wide and his jaw slacked. He could form no words, instead nodding in acknowledgement as he turned the horse away and galloped back toward *Gabriel.*

"What the hell is this?" asked Miguel.

"A threat," Darius replied.

"Why does Colonel Eriksen need to threaten you over this trial?" Ivan asked.

"Because he wants an innocent man to die."

Gabrielle Serrano
12 April, Year of Landing, midday
Camp Eight
>|

Gabi charged into the surf and thrust her hand out. The tips of her fingers brushed the left arm of Caleb as he tried to twist out of the way.

"You're it," she giggled and staggered back toward the gleaming sand. She lost her footing, throwing her arms out in front of her to catch her fall. The cast on her injured arm flung a spray of water that narrowly missed her eyes as she charged onto the beach.

Caleb pumped his legs and burst forth from the sea. He made a bee line for another young boy with sandy blonde hair. Gabi giggled as Caleb tried to tag the other boy, but missed, and ended up face-first in the sand.

"Gabi!" Kelly Vandemark called out.

She looked around and spotted Kelly farther up the beach, near the empty steel pod. Kelly waved her arm in a circle, beckoning to her. Gabi bounded up as Kelly lowered one knee into the sand.

"It's time for lunch, Gabi," Kelly said. A thin wisp of her wavy brown hair drifted across her eyes in the gentle breeze. "Let's go find your mom, okay?"

"I don't want to," she protested.

"It's time, honey."

"But I don't want to! I want to play!"

Kelly took Gabi's tiny hand into her own and stood up. "You can do that later. Come on, let's go."

"No," Gabi whined.

The older girl tugged gently at her arm. Gabi pulled back and dug her heels into the sand, but could not break Kelly's grip. She forced a sob to see if Kelly would give up, but she didn't; the Vandemark girl kept pulling her firmly along the beach. Kelly turned her head left and right every few steps.

"You're mean," Gabi pouted.

"You can go back to the beach as soon as you're done eating, I promise."

But that will take forever!

They reached the spot where the river flowed into the sea. Kelly paused for a second and turned her gaze up over the bank. She squeezed Gabi's hand and knelt next to her, then pointed to the river bank a hundred feet away.

"There's your mom. Go on, sweetie."

"No, I don't want to!" Gabi stamped her foot in the sand.

"Come on," Kelly smiled. "It'll be real quick, then you can come back and play. Now, go to your mom."

Kelly gave Gabi a slight nudge in the back, which made her stumble forward. She looked back at the older girl, who kept smiling brightly as Gabi walked away.

I don't want to, she repeated to herself, though her legs carried her onward.

Each step felt as if her feet were made of stone. Her toes dragged and her shoes, now mud brown instead of a brilliant pink, cut erratic curves in the dirt and leaves on the jungle floor.

Her mother sat, hunched over, at the edge of the river, looking down into the lazy waters. As Gabi approached, she could tell that she was crying. Her sobs sounded like a pitiful song of sorrow. Gabi slowly approached and put her arms around her mother's shoulders and hugged.

Her mom's shoulders jumped and fell with each gasp and sob. She did not acknowledge Gabi or return her embrace.

"Mama, what's wrong?"

The heartbreaking sound of her mother's cries made Gabi's heart sink and her lip quiver. When Gabi spoke, her mother only wailed louder. Still she did not touch Gabi or speak.

"Mama, what's wrong?" she repeated.

Her mother rolled away, breaking Gabi's embrace, and scrambled to a tree a few feet away. There was no eye contact. Her mother spoke no words, and now had pulled away from Gabi. She felt a panic start to rise within her, and her vision began to blur as tears filled her eyes.

"Mama, you're scaring me."

"I can't do it, Mija," her mother choked. "Not alone, I can't. I'm sorry."

"Mama?" her tiny voice quaked.

"Your Papa and I could do it together. He always knew what to do."

Gabi's mother sank to her knees. Muddy tears rolled down her cheeks in torrents, and Gabi could see her mother's open mouth, twisted by the pain and anguish that poured out with every cry. Without warning, she grabbed a vine of a pepperine shrub, screamed at the top of her lungs, and tore it from the plant with her bare hands. She twisted and folded the vine time and time again until it was nothing more than a pile of green and blue fibers at her feet, tinted red with blood from fresh wounds on her hands.

"I can't do it, Gabi," she screamed.

Gabi took a step back. It took a moment for her body to react, but her mind raced as it processed the terrible outburst that she saw from her mother. It told her one thing.

Run.

As she began to cry, Gabi ran away toward the beach. She reached the bank and stumbled over. She thrust her hands out in front of her, and they broke her fall as she avoided landing face first. Gabi picked herself up and sprinted along the beach as quickly as her short legs could carry her. She tried to find Kelly or Kristin Vandemark, but the beach was empty except for a couple fishermen dragging their dugout canoe onto the shore.

Gabi fell to her knees, exhausted and alone. She cried as loudly as she could, trying to shake off the memory of her mother ripping apart the plant with such anger that she didn't seem to feel the cuts that the vine inflicted in her hands. Even as she tried to put aside this memory, other older ones haunted her; watching her father being beaten to death by the side of the river, and witnessing the death of her father's killer at the hands of her friend Haruka.

She felt a warm, sandy hand on her back. "Are you okay, dear?"

Her eyes opened, and through her tears she saw the two fishermen kneeling beside her. One man looked very squared and muscular, and the other was so lean that she could see his ribs whenever he shifted. Though both men sported coarse, stubbly beards, they regarded her with soft, kind eyes.

"Are you lost?" asked the muscular man.

Gabi shook her head and sniffed. She continued to sob, but only softly; the presence of the men and the feel of a comforting touch calmed her nerves.

"Did something happen?"

She nodded. The fishermen exchanged glances and nods.

"Are you hurt?" the lean one asked. Gabi shook her head. "Are you looking for your friends?"

She nodded slowly. She took two deep breaths, wiped the last tear from her cheek, and settled down.

"You want us to take you back to them?"

Again she nodded. The muscular man handed his bucket to his friend, and then hoisted Gabi up to his chest. She threw her arms around his neck and rested her head against his broad, solid shoulder. He rose to his feet in one smooth motion and started along the path that led to the village, followed closely by the leaner man, who carried a bucket and two long, pointed sticks.

"Wow, you're a big girl, aren't you?" he asked. She paused for a second then nodded. "What's your name?"

"G-Gabi."

The lean man's eyes got wide for a second. "The Serrano girl."

"Oh, Jesus," the other man muttered.

"Better take her to Dad."

"Yeah, good idea."

Gabi watched over the muscular fisherman's shoulder as they climbed the hill. The sun shimmered on the endless expanse of water. She easily picked the dull gray form of the broken sleeper pod out of the landscape; it contrasted starkly from the white sands and green shrubs that surrounded it.

At last they passed between the two nearly completed huts that marked the entrance of the village. Camp Eight was very much alive, buzzing with the sounds of conversation and construction.

The fishermen took her inside Dr. Petrovsky's house. She was set down on the floor, and the doctor appeared from behind a short wall an instant later.

"Gabi?" he asked, then cocked his head to the side and looked up at the two men. "Nick, what happened?"

"I don't know," replied the lean man. "We found her crying on the beach, with no one else around."

"Thank you for bringing her back," Petrovsky replied with a sigh. "I'll take care of her."

The fishermen took their leave, but did not secure the storm curtain. Bright patches of light illuminated the clinic floor, dancing and swaying as the winds dangled the curtain. Dr. Petrovsky led Gabi to a bed near the back wall and sat her down.

"Have you had lunch yet, dear?"

"No," she said, shaking her head.

"Alright. Stay here, I'll be back in a minute, okay?"

Gabi nodded curled up on the rough bed as the doctor went outside. The clinic was quiet; no one else was in the room. Only brief clips of conversations as colonists walked past the clinic broke the monotony of the rustling curtain. Gabi's stomach began to growl, and after a few minutes she became restless. She wandered the clinic, looking at every bed, pillow, and piece of stray bark in the room as she hummed a soft tune.

More time passed, and she began to wonder if Doctor Petrovsky was coming back with her food. She returned to the bed and threw herself down. Her stomach rumbled again, and with it she felt a faint twinge of pain.

Mama yelled at me, and Doctor went away.

She buried her face in the fibrous green cover of the bed. She felt the tears about to burst forth from her, but then sat bolt upright as she heard the storm curtain being pulled back. Her heart skipped a beat in anticipation of the doctor's return, but instead, Haruka emerged from the brilliant sunshine that shone through the open portals. She saw Gabi and smiled, taking long strides to reach her.

"Hi, Gabi! How are you, sweetie?"

"Hungry," she whined, and put her hands on her gurgling belly.

"I'm sorry. Where's Doctor Petrovsky?"

Gabi pointed her finger at the door.

"Alright. What about your mom? Hasn't she given you lunch?"

Gabi turned away and folded her arms across her chest. She folded her chin down so far that it almost touched her chest.

"Gabi? Where's your mom?"

"Mama doesn't love me anymore," she muttered under her breath.

Haruka paused, and then her gentle hand fell on Gabi's shoulder. "I'm sure she does, sweetie. She's just…"

"No, she doesn't love me," Gabi screamed. "I hugged her and she screamed and yelled and ripped things up and threw them and yelled at me some more."

"When you hugged her?" Haruka gasped.

"Yeah. She was crying and I wanted to make her feel better. But she didn't want a hug, and yelled at me."

"Oh, I'm so sorry, sweetie," Haruka said and slipped her arms around Gabi's slender body. Gabi returned the embrace, comforted by the warmth of her friend.

"I don't know why she doesn't love me," she said, her voice trembling.

"She loves you. I bet there was some other reason she's upset. I don't think she's upset at you."

Gabi wiped her eyes and looked at her friend. "Are you sure?"

"I'm sure. I promise."

Gabi nodded. Haruka let her go and stood up. The storm curtain opened again, and Dr. Petrovsky stepped through the threshold with a coarse wooden platter laden with fruits and baked roots.

"Good day, Captain," he said cheerfully. "Gabi, I have something for you."

He walked to the short stump near the rear of the clinic and set down the platter. She could smell the roots and caught a glimpse of a pepperine. She bolted from the bed and had her hands in the food in a matter of seconds. The pepperine was juicy, squirting its sweet nectar all over her hands as she sunk her teeth into it. Gabi closed her eyes and savored every bite of the fruit. She then tore into the tubers, which had a hint of sweetness to them.

In the background, Dr. Petrovsky and Haruka were engaged in a conversation. Gabi only caught a few of the words that were spoken, but forgot about them as she gorged herself on the planet's newfound foods.

Darius Owens
13 April, Year of Landing, 06:43
Gabriel landing site
>|

Something Rory had mentioned as he spooned a glop of reconstituted eggs on Darius's plate had stuck with him longer than the breakfast itself had.

You've said that this doctor guy was being charged, and that one of your shipmates was charged as well. So why hasn't there been a court martial?

It was a question that couldn't be ignored. No matter how Darius attacked the problem, he couldn't figure out an answer.

Why? Why hasn't Eriksen started proceedings against Lieutenant Reid?

It didn't make any sense. Colonel Eriksen was very insistent on the process of Doctor Kimura's trial being quite public, with the exception of Darius's possible testimony.

Something doesn't add up.

The camp that surrounded the rear flank of *Gabriel* had become disorganized. Several of its occupants had moved on to other tasks, some far away from camp. Others had moved from tent to tent, searching for a prime location for their families to operate from. Some valued shelter close to the hull of the ship, while others were inclined to seek out plots that were close to camp amenities such as the wash station or the kitchen. Darius knew that Don Abernathy had relocated his family, although he was not entirely sure where. Darius searched the row along *Gabriel's* wall, but did not find any sign of the attorney or his family.

Come on. Where are you?

He continued along the far row, extending out from the wall toward the river. He found the Abernathy family in the corner, far from the wall, with no neighbors occupying the adjacent tents.

"Mr. Abernathy," he said as he approached, hand extended.

Don took his hand and shook vigorously. "Darius. What brings you to see me today? I thought you were working."

"That can wait," he replied. "I've got a bit of a problem, and I think you can give me the best advice."

"Am I going to have to charge you for this?" Don replied with a smirk.

"If you have to. Put it on my tab."

"Very well. What's on your mind?"

Darius sighed and rubbed the bridge of his nose. "What do you know about Lieutenant Brandon Reid?"

"Reid. Reid. Isn't his court martial scheduled for the twenty-third?"

"Of this month? Wait a minute, isn't that just after Doctor K's trial starts?"

"Just a second, please." Don turned and pulled aside the flap of the green canvas tent. He rooted around inside for a moment and then returned with a small notepad. He flipped through the first few pages, and then read something off of one of them. "Yeah, the twenty-third. Hmm. It seems like that's a bit close to the other trial."

"Why the hell would Eriksen schedule the court martial that close to Kimura's trial?"

"I couldn't tell you. I didn't even hear of this first-hand. Fred told me about it when our families got together the other night. The weird thing is that he doesn't know who will be representing Lieutenant Reid. And when I asked the colonel, he just told me that it was taken care of."

Taken care of? Darius shook his head. *I doubt it, Colonel.*

"Do you know where they plan to hold it? Or why I wasn't interviewed as a witness?"

Don raised his eyebrow. He pulled a pen from his pocket and scribbled something on the notepad. "You weren't interviewed. That's very interesting."

"I suppose this means something to you?"

"Yes, Mr. Owens."

"And just what is that?"

"That Reid is not going to get a fair trial."

God damn it, Colonel. He's your own man. What could you possibly gain from doing this?

"That's a mighty big accusation, Mr. Abernathy. Are you sure?"

He closed the notepad with a very deliberate motion and tossed it aside. "No offense, Mr. Owens, but when you've seen as many courtroom antics as I've seen, you know a shady deal when you see one. This reeks of it."

"I see." Darius offered a handshake which was returned. "Thank you for your time, sir."

"It's my pleasure, Darius."

Darius turned from the meager accommodations that held the Abernathy family. He headed into the depths of the camp, but had no destination in mind. He tried to wrap his mind tried to wrap around the commanding officer's secrecy.

He doesn't want a fair trial. But he will still have to punish the lieutenant. Why hide the trial if it's going to be public in the end? Very public. The punishment for treason is...

Darius stopped in his tracks. He felt his heart sink as his head swiveled to the right, capturing the gray silhouette of *Gabriel*.

To show that crimes will be punished. Severely. As Darius swallowed, his throat tightened and threatened to constrict the air that his lungs drew in. He took several shallow breaths, and he felt a bit faint. *Maybe he values Kimura more than Reid, but one of them has to suffer.*

His legs pumped with almost no thought. They carried him closer to the towering walls from which he was forbidden to go inside.

Eriksen doesn't trust that Kimura will be convicted, so he'll make sure someone is. Even if his motives were for his family.

He drew nearer to the walls of the ship. Somewhere inside, Darius knew, Eriksen was directing not only the affairs of the colony, but whatever scheme he had concocted. Darius was forbidden from stepping foot on the ship without permission and an escort, and he was not a devious man by nature. The fleeting idea that he could somehow sneak aboard the ship and find out what Colonel Eriksen was planning passed with little more than a shamed shake of his head.

Maybe Mr. Abernathy could challenge Eriksen and force his hand. This, too, felt pointless. *No, not with a military court he couldn't. The colonel would have him booted off the ship in two seconds.*

Frustration began to mount within him. Unconsciously, he flexed his fingers. He turned from the ship and walked toward the river, picking his way through the endless sea of green canvas that made up the camp. Darius found the muddy path that ran parallel to the line of utility poles he had helped erect. His boots made a soft squishing noise as the mud flowed from the tread on the soles with each step. The rhythm of his march stirred a fire within him, and before he realized it, he was running along the path.

In only a few minutes, he reached the now bare banks of the river. Stumps marked where once mighty trees stood, felled both for their precious timber as well as to clear space along the bank for the inevitable construction of industrial facilities. He stopped just feet from the edge of the wide, slowly churning river. He reached to the ground at his feet, unearthed a stone just smaller than his fist, and heaved it into the water with a furious scream. It arced high before it breached the surface of the river just over a hundred feet from shore. The plume of water from its impact was short lived, barely longer than the deep thud created by the impact.

Though it did nothing to solve his problems, hurtling the rock did feel good. He repeated the process with another rock of the same size, and then a rock large enough that he had to pitch it with both hands. The latter only went a few feet into the river, but the splash it created chipped away at the stress of the situation.

Darius continued throwing rocks into the river as he rolled over the information in his head time and time again. He then changed to skipping rocks until his arm ached. Still no solution presented itself, so he sat on a stump and looked across the river at the *Michael* side. As with the *Gabriel* side, their counterparts on the far bank had also cleared trees for river access, although they had done so farther downstream. He could see little through the wooded area directly across from him, save for the ship itself. Faint echoes of heavy machinery surrounded him, though from where he sat he couldn't tell which side of the river they came from. Both ships were equipped with exactly the same heavy equipment, and worked from the same operational guidelines.

That's why I still don't get why Eriksen had us land on the opposite side of the river. He knew both crews would be performing the exact same tasks. There was no conflict of interest. This was all supposed to be a big collaboration between all three ships.

Darius grimaced as he thought of *Raphael's* reactor going critical. Neither ship's crew had picked up any further broadcast from the doomed sleeper ship or its pods. Other than the radio beacon that *Raphael* sent before landing to mark the spot where they intended to start the colony, no other pieces of the ship had been detected or recovered.

Over two thousand dead on a ship that never made it to the surface. Two CO's who can't see eye to eye. Who can't put aside their differences for the sake of another four thousand colonists. What the hell has come between these two men that it's come to this? It's almost like the loss of the other ship has thrown everything to hell.

Darius rose from the stump and plodded back along the trail toward *Gabriel*. His thoughts shifted to *Raphael*. He tried to remember every detail that he could that might matter to Eriksen.

She was the largest ship. She carried full medical facilities so that we wouldn't have to build a hospital right away. She carried far more cargo than either of the other ships. Maybe there was something in the cargo manifest that he needed?

Darius shook his head at that thought.

No, each ship still carried what it would need to survive and build. Having the manpower and equipment of Raphael would have made things easier, but not really that different. Lieutenant Kimura was on that ship by accident, but I don't see how that would affect the colonel.

He began to go through the personnel records in his head, as he had seen much of the manifest when Captain Quinn had tried to work out who the assassin on board may have been. The work had ultimately proven futile when the ship was destroyed.

Colonel Fox. Hmm... no, from what I remember, he didn't care for her much at all. Major Emberley. Don't know much about him. I guess Eriksen would have met him during the command briefings. Who else was there? Bartrand. Singh. Ford. Mancini. Maynard. Morado. Cormack. No one else really stands out. What the hell was it? It's not cargo, and it's not an officer. It couldn't be a passenger, that's just too weird.

His head snapped upward and looked at the gray mass of the ship.

A passenger. When I talked to Drisko over on Michael, he said that one of the passengers was assassinated. God, who was it? Think, Darius!

He began to pace back and forth along the width of the track, trying to recall the name of the murdered passenger from the other ship. In his zeal, he failed to notice his old ops partner, Lieutenant Roger Miller, walking down the track.

"Darius?" he asked, causing Darius to jump back and his heart to race. "What are you doing out here?"

"Damn, Roger, you scared the crap out of me. What are you doing?"

"Inspecting the poles that you and your crew put up. Seriously, man. You look like you're about to rip your scalp off the way you're rubbing your head like that. Is something wrong?"

"You have no idea. Can I ask you a random question?"

"Always," Miller nodded.

"Do you remember the name of that passenger on *Michael* that was killed by the code bug in the sleeper routine?"

"Of course. It was Doctor Fairweather. How can you forget a thing like that? I mean hell; he, Benedict, and Kimura practically designed the ships themselves."

Darius pinched the bridge of his nose. "Of course," he echoed sheepishly.

How could I have forgotten? It makes so much more sense now.

"Time for another odd one. Doctor Benedict was supposed to be on *Raphael*, before he decided to stay behind, right?"

"I think so. Why?"

"Just been trying to figure this whole damn thing out, that's all."

"You still on the whole landing on the wrong side of the river thing?" Miller asked. His wording choice gave away to Darius that he was trying to hide his irritation.

"Don't tell me it doesn't bug you at all?"

"Of course it does. But what's done is done. Give it up, man. We've got bigger things to worry about now."

"I can't."

"Why not?"

"Because I think this is a bigger problem than anyone realizes. I think it has something to do with the whole Project itself."

Miller rolled his eyes. "Am I going to have to get your tinfoil hat for this one?"

"Can you just promise to hear me out?"

"Fine," he sighed, and gestured with his hand that Darius was free to continue.

"Doctor Benedict died on Earth dying to protect the secrets of Project Columbus. This is according to Doctor Kimura, and I have no reason to doubt him."

"Other than the fact that he's admitted to treason."

"Good, we're on the same page. We have an honest traitor. Let's give him the benefit of the doubt and continue to assume that everything is true, as it has been up until this point."

"Fine."

"So all three ships are cruising in deep space, when someone figures out how to use a code exploit between the com and stasis systems to assassinate Doctor Fairweather. This same exploit is used to attempt assassination on both Doctor Kimura and Lieutenant Reid."

"That's a bit of a stretch to think someone did that on purpose."

"No, it's pretty clear that's what was intended. I have the proof, too. It's in the version of the com software. It was rolled back on all ships prior to launch. I just didn't notice it until we were about to go to sleep for the first time, and didn't think much of it until I saw the code fragments that my null mailbox captured."

Miller's eyes widened and the color drained from his face. "W-what?" he stammered. "Why didn't you tell me about this?"

"Colonel's orders. Only he, Quinn, and I knew about it. Doctor Kimura figured it out too, but knew better than to talk about it. There were a few guys on *Michael* that figured it out after they were hit, but I can only assume they were ordered to stay quiet as well."

"S-so someone murdered Fairweather?"

"And tried to do the same to other accused conspirators. Someone out there didn't want these men to live. Maybe they knew something else. Something more dangerous. Then, all of a sudden, Colonel Eriksen orders a new landing site, and goes out of his way to exclude me from Doctor Kimura's trial. I just can't figure out why."

"Maybe he's the assassin?"

Darius pursed his lips and thought about it, then shook his head. "I was able to tell from the code fragment that it came from *Raphael*, so the killer was on that ship. Besides, if he was, he wouldn't have had Doctor Kimura continue his duties after his confession. He would have had him killed."

"Unless he wanted to throw suspicion off."

"Or have the assassination legitimized. Through a court," Darius added.

"So with an accusation of treason, and treason being punishable by death, Colonel Eriksen can wash his hands if Doctor Kimura is convicted."

"Exactly. Lieutenant Reid, too."

"Oh shit," Miller exclaimed. "That explains why I was ordered to defend Reid."

"What?" Darius gasped. "You?"

"Exactly what I said. I told him I'm not a lawyer, but he told me that no one on the crew was, and all that mattered is that an officer represented him."

"That's complete bullshit. He has civilian attorneys he could choose from that would do a better job. But still, why would he pick you, when we were partners for so long?"

"Ah, that's where my keen awareness of keeping my ass out of the fire came into play, and then promptly backfired."

"What do you mean?"

"Well," Miller replied. "Colonel asked me if I had seen you since we landed, which I told him that I had not, which seemed to please him. So when he asked me if I had any issues keeping you in the dark for a while, I lied and told him no. I figured if it was that big of a deal to him if I chatted with you, he might drum me out just like he did with you."

Oh, so that's the story he's telling? I remember it a little differently.

"And about that, we probably shouldn't be seen together. He might shit a brick if word got out that I even spoke with you."

"Can you at least keep me in the loop as to what's happening?" Darius pled. "I didn't even know the court was being set up, and even Don said something is wrong with the whole situation."

"I'll see what I can do, but we both need to lay low a bit. Something stinks here big time, Darius. I'll sniff it out for you. If I hear anything, I'll send word through one of your boys to meet me. That is, if they can be trusted."

"They can be trusted, Roger. I have no doubt about that."

"Take care. And for God's sake, keep your head down for a couple days."

"I will. Thank you."

Darius turned from his friend and jogged back toward the ship, mind still racing about what Eriksen's grand scheme might be.

Calvin McLaughlin
14 April, Year of Landing, 09:01
Michael landing site
>|

Cal's foot pushed down on the throttle a little harder. The turbocharger began to scream like a boiling tea kettle, and the crawler's nose lifted toward the sky as it ascended the hill. Cracking and scratching from under his feet told Cal of the presence of a bush he hadn't seen, now mowed down by the heavy skid plate. The body of the crawler rocked for a second as the offending vegetation disappeared under the left track. Glass rattled in the back seat as sample jars teetered in their precarious perches.

Easy, Cal. Easy. Just get it all there in one piece. That's all that matters now.

Cal glanced over his right shoulder. Neil was in the rear passenger seat. His glasses were off and his eyes closed. He was not asleep, though, as his hand shot out to steady an awkward load of glass jars nestled between his legs. In front of him sat Traci Josephson. Her scratched and bruised face bore a blank expression as she stared at a point somewhere beyond the windshield. There was nothing there; Cal knew she was lost somewhere back in the wilderness.

It was better that way, he thought. When her mind was distant, it couldn't focus on the physical pain she bore. Her left arm was bandaged and placed in a makeshift sling. He knew that she was bruised on her chest as well. The amount of pain she had been in for the past two days made him suspect that she had at least one broken rib. Neil had almost completely forgone sleep in order to attend to her in case she received a concussion when the beast tossed her like a ragdoll.

Cal turned his attention back to driving. He dared not look behind him at the seat occupied by sample jars and camp supplies. He tried to push from his mind the fact that Elaine Montoya had been replaced by cargo, and her body rested instead in the bed of the crawler. As the machine crested the hill and its hood pointed downward again, *Michael* came into view, dominating the entire windscreen. Their journey home had been almost without conversation; only the song of the diesel motor kept them with constant company.

Josephson's right hand stretched out for the radio microphone clipped to the dash. Cal watched her wince as she tried to lift her twisted body to reach it. Cal unclipped the microphone and stretched across the cab to hand it to her.

"Here," he said.

"Thanks." Her tone was as dead as her expression. She lifted the mic to her face and clicked the transmitter. "*Michael*, Echo Foxtrot Four. We're coming home. Be ready at the rear hatch."

After a moment of static, a familiar, cheerful voice welcomed them home. "Understood, Echo Foxtrot Four," Cameron's voice filled the cab. "We're looking forward to seeing you. Lieutenant Ceretti will be waiting for you."

The microphone clattered to the floor as Josephson let it go. She curled her fingers up and put them to her mouth, returning to her world of thought.

She didn't tell them.

There had been no earlier communication with the ship to warn them that the expedition party was returning to base. There had been nothing to warn them of the fatality that had occurred on the excursion. Sergeant Cameron Drisko had joyfully welcomed them back, without knowing the sorrow that the single crawler's return would bring.

Cal steered the crawler a little to the right, aiming it just beyond the rear of the ship. He released the accelerator, allowing gravity and momentum to carry the heavy machine forward.

"You were right, Calvin," Josephson spoke so softly she could hardly be heard over the engine.

Cal furrowed his brow in confusion. "About what?"

"Me. That night around the campfire."

He sighed and closed his eyes for a moment before fixing his gaze on the looming tail of the sleeper ship. "Look, I'm sorry. I was just really upset and said some things I shouldn't have."

"Maybe, but it was the truth. As much as I wanted to deny it, you were right. I'm too hard on people around me. I sabotage myself and then I blame others for what happens to me. There's no one else to blame for this. I failed."

"At what?"

"She's dead, Calvin. It was my duty to protect her."

Cal caught a flash of metal out of the corner of his eye and the unmistakable click of a safety being released. He slammed on the crawler's brakes, and jammed up against the seatbelt as it skidded to a halt.

Glass clattered and Neil cursed from the back seat. Cal unlatched his belt and lunged at Josephson just before the pistol reached her temple. He grabbed the barrel and twisted backwards, causing her to shout in pain as he wrested it from her left hand.

"What the fuck, Josephson?" he shouted.

"God damn it, at least let me go back as a corpse," she screamed. "She died. Under my watch. Doesn't that mean anything to you?"

Neil interrupted. "Traci, you did everything you could to get that monster away from her."

"It wasn't enough." Josephson broke down and began to sob.

Even as he ejected the magazine and cleared the chamber of her weapon, Cal couldn't help but feel sorrow for Josephson. The deep emotional toll of Elaine Montoya's death was too great even for the hard façade of the lieutenant. For the first time since he met her, Cal saw the human side of Lieutenant Josephson. The image in his mind of the aggressive, dictatorial officer played in stark contrast to the wounded, vulnerable woman in the seat next to him who wanted to take her own life.

It was always about duty, he realized. *The fact that I came out of sleep early and became part of the crew, even though I wasn't a member... That's why she couldn't stand me.*

Cal dropped the pistol over the back of the seat, where it clanked on a sample jar as it dropped to the floor.

"You gave all you could," Cal added. "You let that thing beat the tar out of you and you kept going. You kept trying to pull it away."

"I couldn't. No matter what I did, I couldn't keep it from finishing her off."

"Because it's an animal, not a soldier. Hell, it's probably never seen a gun before. If it was hungry, how was it supposed to react? Catch the prey."

"Fuck you! It should have attacked me instead," she screamed through her tears.

"If it did, we wouldn't have gotten there in time. Elaine would still be dead, and so would you. I mean, did you see that thing? It was twelve feet long, jumped like a cat on steroids, and the claws on that thing... shit, it might as well have been the grim reaper."

"Huh," Neil added. "A reaper bear. Now isn't that something scary?"

"It would have been better if it killed me," she continued, ignoring them.

"Why?" Cal asked callously. "So you wouldn't have guilt over this dumbass idea that your death would have meant something?"

"It would have," Josephson insisted.

"Not if both of you died," Cal retorted. "I'm sure if death was inevitable, Colonel Dayton would rather it be only one instead of two. And since it would have been two if that thing killed you first, I don't see much more to the argument. Yes, it sucks that Elaine died. Yes, I'm upset that she died, and am sure as shit her husband and kids are going to be devastated, but it's done. You're alive, and we still need you."

"For what? I can't go back out there. I can't put anyone else's life on the line when I've already lost someone."

"Take a break," Neil soothed. "You need to rest up first. I'm sure we can find you something around camp to do."

"Neil's right," Cal said. "I'm sure Hunter or Dayton will find something you can do."

"The only thing that Colonel Dayton is getting from me is my resignation."

"If that's what it takes to clear your head, then I'll back you up on it," Cal retorted.

"Right. Like you'd ever do me the favor."

"I would." Cal crossed his hand over his heart. "Swear to God. I know you don't believe me given our history, but I swear that I will help you get back on your feet when we get back to camp. And if that means going to bat for you with the colonel, then that is exactly what I'll do."

She eyed him with suspicion. "Why would you do that for me?"

"Because everyone deserves a second chance when they've been knocked down."

Seconds ticked by, but Josephson neither spoke nor moved.

"Come on, Traci. Let me help you."

"I don't deserve help."

"Neither did I, but Dad believed I did. Trust me, if you knew anything about me before we left Earth, you probably would have agreed with me." He laughed nervously and shook his head. "It turns out Dad was right. You can make up your mind later whether or not you agree with him, but you have to take the chance first. Please."

She looked through the windscreen at the lively camp extending between the river and the ship. After a long pause, she sighed.

"Alright."

"Thank you," he said as he exhaled loudly. The air of relief in the cabin was palpable. Even Neil let out a rush of air as he settled back into his position in the rear seat.

Cal released the brakes and coaxed the crawler back onto course. The rest of the short trip back to *Michael* was spent in near silence, and he couldn't wait to open the door and leave the expedition behind for good. The crawler reached its destination, and Cal turned off the turbo-diesel engine, which let out a cough before it settled in to rest. Cal's fingertips rested on the door latch for a moment. His head touched the window sill and he took two deep breaths before opening the door and sliding onto the running board. Hunter awaited them with a broad grin and tussled sandy hair.

"You're home early," he grinned. "Couldn't stay away from Alexis, could you? She'll be here in a minute, along with Elaine's family."

Cal dropped to the ground and trudged slowly to the base of the ramp where his friend waited. He could not bear to look at him except for a couple short glances. As he approached, he looked up one more time, and saw that Hunter's grin had disappeared.

"What's wrong?"

"Get Doctor Taylor. Traci's hurt."

"Oh my God, is she alright?"

"She's messed up." Cal took another step up the ramp, starting to walk by his friend. He paused and turned to him again. "Oh, and keep her away from any guns or knives for a bit."

"Why? What the hell happened out there?"

Cal swallowed hard as a shiver ran down his spine. "Elaine's dead."

Hunter was caught speechless and slack jawed. His eyes moved to the giant truck, where Neil was helping Lieutenant Josephson down to the ground. Moments later, Alexis bounded up to the bottom of the ramp, with a broad shouldered man and two children, a boy and a girl. Calvin took one look at the girl's face and saw the reflection of Elaine Montoya looking back at him. Alexis came up to throw her arms around him, but he brushed her off and walked straight up to Trevor Montoya.

"Mr. Montoya, sir," he cleared his throat. "I have something to tell you."

Cal used every ounce of courage he had left to tell Trevor of his wife's death, and to console him for his loss. The man crumpled to a heap at his feet, weeping. His children gathered around him and hugged him, bursting into tears themselves.

Cal turned on his heels, his lip quivering, deep emotions rising up within him. He marched past Alexis, who he again brushed off, as he darted down the stern of the ship and turned the corner around the port side. The instant he was out of sight, he fell to his knees and wept for another family crushed by the dreams of Columbus.

Capt Haruka Kimura
14 April, Year of Landing, midday
Camp Eight
>|

Come on, Maria. Where are you?

Haruka tried to keep still as she waited in the makeshift foyer of the Palm Palace. Her legs wanted to pace as she kept watch for the elder Serrano, but she forced herself to stay put, so as not to miss Maria passing by the building. Haruka's palms began to sweat. She was nervous about confronting Maria, but time was up; Haruka needed her to start contributing to the village workload. Even more disturbing was the fact that Maria seemed to be failing in her responsibilities as a mother. Gabi had, twice in the past week, been found alone by other villagers, and would refuse to go back to her mother when she was brought back. This led Haruka to ask Kelly Vandemark to split her time and watch Gabi when she could.

She pulled the curtain aside a few inches and scanned the village common, but there was still no sign of her. This was discouraging, but not surprising. Maria had no set habits, either. Haruka knew that sometime in the late mornings, she would leave the village to go to the river. She knew that Maria was in her hut when she decided to lay the trap. Only one path ran between the village and the waterways, and Haruka had not seen Maria in the roughly two hours that she had been watching.

Haruka's stomach growled, but she ignored it. Leaving the Palace for food might mean having to wait another day to confront Maria, and Haruka could not accept wasting a large portion of her own day to come out empty handed.

Come on, she chanted to herself. Though she did not speak, her lips moved ever so slightly in rhythm with the words in her mind.

As if Haruka had willed it, Maria walked past the Palm Palace and headed for the path to the water. She went to launch from her hiding place, but paused as the idea of her ambush devolving into a screaming match crossed her mind.

No. Follow her down. Get her alone.

Haruka waited until Maria disappeared below the hill's horizon and then slipped from inside the Palace. She moved to the edge of the village, confirming that her target was still oblivious, then began to follow her down the path at a distance. Whenever a colonist would come up the path, Haruka bowed her head and danced to the side of the path, obscuring herself behind a tree whenever she had the opportunity; her nerves tingled at the prospect of blowing her cover.

Gradually the path flattened out and then split; a smaller game trail wandered to the right through thick, often thorny undergrowth on its way to the river. She knew Maria would have taken this offshoot, as it was more secluded, and led to nearly the exact spot along the banks where her husband was bludgeoned to death. Maria had been spending more time at the site over the past week. Dr. Petrovsky had told her that Maria would need space to heal in her own way, but Haruka could not fathom why Maria would choose to walk the site of her nightmare day after day.

Haruka took a breath to steel her nerves before plunging down the path after Maria. Branches brushed against her legs as they carried her. She gained a singular focus on a rock formation just barely visible through the tall trees and dense shrubs. She came around a particularly large flower vine, and caught Maria off guard at the base of the boulder.

"What the hell are you doing here?" Maria screamed as she backed against the rock.

"We need to talk."

"No we don't."

"You can't just ignore me like you do the doctor," Haruka retorted sternly. "You can grieve if you have to, but you also need to become a functioning member of the village. I can't have you moping around forever when we're in desperate need of hands."

"I can't do it," she said, biting her lip.

"You can do *something*."

"I can't. You don't understand."

Haruka's eyes narrowed. "You're not getting out of this. Other than the doctor and his clinic, you were the first person in the village to get a home. We've let you grieve for months. Your wounds have healed. Well, your physical ones. I don't care at this point what's going on in your head, because I can't carry your workload for you anymore. Kelly can't carry your workload for you anymore. Kristin, Gina, Charlotte, Nick. None of them can carry you any longer."

"I can't do it. I'm not strong enough." Maria's voice wavered as she turned her head away.

"Bull. This is coming from the mouth of the woman who braved the uncertainty of unproven space travel. The woman who took two orphans under her care after the crash of the pod. The woman who cared for and protected three children as the survivors blazed through an unknown jungle to reach this site." Haruka paused and pursed her lips. "I hear the voice, but I'm not looking at the woman. No, the real Maria Serrano would have taken tragedy and built a stronger self. She's not this crying wreck that I see every day."

Maria squeaked a reply. "You don't know me then. You don't know why I can't do this alone."

"God damn it, you're not alone. You have the whole village pulling for you, ready to give you what you need when you need it. And they give it, too. All you do is take." She shook her head. "No, I take that back. You gave us Gabi, when you decided to stop caring for her. She's terrified of you, Maria."

"I'm so sorry," Maria whispered in reply.

"Stop being sorry and *do* something! Anything. Weave some roof panels. Cook a meal. Chop some firewood. I don't care what."

"I can't do it without him." Maria's hands fell to her belly. Haruka's heart sunk into her feet.

Oh God.

"You're… you're… Oh, Maria." Haruka reached her hand out to comfort Maria, who shrunk back slightly. Haruka slowly withdrew her hand and shook her head. She knew that her bridge with Maria had forever been burned, and that consolation from her would be unwelcome. "How… how long have you known?"

"What does it matter to you?"

"Because I'm your friend."

"You *were* my friend," Maria corrected. "I have no friends."

"That's not true. Emilia and Ken. Troy and Gina. The Vandemarks." Haruka waited for a response, but got only a shoulder roll and a turned cheek. "They all care about you. They all love you. They want to see you happy again, and would do anything for you."

"Yeah, right."

"Who have you been confiding in?"

"I can't. No one understands."

"Then who told you you're pregnant?" she asked bluntly.

"Ken," Maria sniffed.

"Good. That's a good start. Can you talk to him more about what's going on?"

"No."

"What about Emilia? She'll understand."

"No. No one understands." Maria stepped from the side of the rock and brushed past Haruka. "You're the last one that would understand. You didn't have to lose the love of your life."

"No," Haruka admitted. "I didn't have to lose my love. Just everyone and everything else."

Maria stopped at the edge of the path. Her fingers traced a brilliant orange flower vine dancing in the breeze at the level of her shoulders. "You still have everyone."

"No, I don't. I don't have my mother, or my sister. Or my father."

"They're all alive."

"I have no way of knowing that." Haruka gestured sharply into the air. "The other ships could have blown up like *Raphael* did, and we would never have known it." She then let out a solemn sigh. "Besides, even if the ships landed, they have to know that ours blew up, which means I'm as good as dead in their eyes. Plus, I'm not sure if my father made it very long. I found out before we got here that he was accused of a serious crime. One punishable by death. "

"Isn't that ironic," Maria shot back callously. "The executioner's father is a criminal."

"I only pulled the trigger because it needed to be done. Would you rather he killed someone or dragged them off into the jungle that day instead? Would you rather see his arrogant face in your dreams, knowing he's still out there?" Only the rush of the river answered her. "That's what I thought."

"You still didn't have to watch your world die. You will never understand that."

Haruka gritted her teeth and closed her eyes. For a moment, she saw the impish grin of Marco Mancini. His face faded quickly, and she relived the moment that Agent Evans thrust her blade into his back and discarded him.

"You don't know the whole story. I had to watch my best friend die on this planet, with nothing I could do to save him. He, too, was murdered. By a traitor on the crew. I've never told anyone else about it."

"You're just saying that. Quit trying to make Luis's death into nothing," she screamed.

"I'm not lying," Haruka cut her off. Her voice was stern, but controlled. "I'm trying to get you to understand that you're not alone. You're not the only person who has had shit go wrong." She took a deep breath, and lowered her voice. "I won't pretend that I understand the trauma of being raped. I truly can't express how sorry I am for what you've gone through. But it's time to move on. Make the choice to be strong again. And if you need to, find someone to lean on, before your support system falls apart."

Haruka did not give Maria time to respond. She marched quickly downstream along the banks of the river, towards her own sanctuary near its mouth. She knew her own wounds needed tending, her own demons would rise again, and she would need the serenity to deal with them.

The thick, black power line tugged taut and then slacked. Darius looked up, squinting as the bright late morning sun shone in his eyes. Miguel, high above the ground in the white lift bucket, had his gaze was fixed on his work at the top of the utility pole. Instead of acknowledging Darius with eye contact, he jerked his thumb skyward twice. Darius grabbed the line and unwound two turns from the spool. Miguel took up some of the slack, and the aerial span running to the next pole sloughed to a normal hang.

"That's good," Miguel called down and his hands went to work fastening the line to the pole.

Good. At this rate, we'll be able to plug the grid into the reactor tomorrow.

Darius uncoiled several more loops from the spool. He heard the whirl of a motor as the boom lowered back to its parked position. Miguel dropped to the ground and gripped the line in his thick gloves. He helped Darius twist the line to straighten it as Ivan slowly reversed the crane truck in the direction of the sleeper ship.

"You know, there's something about you I don't get, Miguel," Darius said.

"Yeah? What's that?"

"This line's completely dead. We started at the river and are working back to the ship. There's no way power can go through the line until we stretch it all the way back to *Gabriel*. So why do you wear those gloves?"

Miguel shrugged his square shoulders. "Habit. Never touch a line without 'em. After you work a crew for a while, it gets in your head that if you touch it you die."

"I never thought of it that way. I guess it makes sense."

"There's probably stuff you used to do out of habit when you worked with those computers of yours."

Darius considered the point. "I suppose you're right. I always organized my programs in a specific order. At first I did it for efficiency, but then I found later that if I screwed up the order, I'd get lost altogether. I guess it became a crutch for me."

Miguel leaned left, peering around the slowly lumbering machine.

"Oh, what's this?"

Darius ducked under the line and craned to catch a glimpse of what Miguel was looking at. A small trail of dust rose from the top of the hill, and a rider could be seen galloping his steed along the telegraph road, straight toward them.

"Messenger?" Darius asked.

"Yup."

As the rider approached, Darius recognized the familiar paint that was becoming a fixture of communication for the work crews not equipped with radios. He realized that the rider was not one of the two men who were becoming as recognizable as the horse, but rather a blonde, petite teenage girl. She wore a grin on her face that looked more like elation of freedom than desire to see any of the crew members.

Must be a busy day if they can't even spare Smith, he thought.

The blonde girl pulled her mount to an abrupt halt when she reached Darius. Her eyes darted between him and Miguel, and her smile waned slightly.

"I'm… not sure I'm in the right place. Are either of you Ivan Novak?"

In unison, the two men pointed to the cab of the truck. The rider turned the horse around, and Ivan emerged from behind the controls. He took his hard hat off and wiped his brow as he walked to the messenger.

"Ivan Novak?" she repeated.

"Yeah, that's me."

She reached into a leather satchel strapped to the right side of the saddle and fished out a few letters. She read the names on them, plucked the correct one, and offered it to him. "You have a message from Rory Baines."

Darius gulped hard and he froze in place.

"Thank you," Ivan nodded as he took the folded paper from her.

The rider scanned the horizon, looked at the remaining letters, and back at the scenery. She lingered for a moment, patting the paint on its shoulder.

"Anything else I can do for you?" Ivan asked impatiently.

"Sorry, just a little lost. I know where I'm going now." She squeezed her legs and the horse took off at a trot, back along the dusty trail.

The work crew waited until she was out of sight. Darius walked up to Ivan and took the letter from his hands.

MR. IVAN NOVAK

OUR MUTUAL FRIEND HAS SOME INTERESTING NEWS
ABOUT DEVELOPMENT OF THE POWER GRID. HE THINKS
THERE MIGHT BE AN OVERLOAD IF ADJUSTMENTS ARE NOT
MADE, BUT IS NOT SURE ABOUT HOW TO GO ABOUT THEM.
HE WILL BE COMING TO DISCUSS THEM WITH YOU AT THE
END OF THE LINE AT HALF PAST NINE. HE WILL BE BRINGING
YOUR CONSULTANT WITH HIM AS WELL. YOUR CREW CAN
CONTINUE THEIR WORK WHILE YOU HAVE YOUR MEETING
ABOUT THIS ISSUE.

RORY M. BAINES

"Is it your friend?" Novak asked quietly.

"Yes."

"What's going on?"

"He needs to meet me in a few minutes. Can you guys handle this
on your own?"

"No problem," Miguel replied. "Go do what you need to do. Me
and Novak will take care of business here."

"Thank you," Darius nodded, and jogged away toward the river.

Darius knew that the letter was a ruse. The message was in code,
and sent by Lieutenant Roger Miller. He had devised the method of
communication with Rory, and Ivan and Miguel knew that any letter
to them from Rory was actually a message for Darius, and he trusted
them to keep any communication quiet. Rory was also trusted, as the
former staff sergeant quickly sided with Darius after learning of Colonel Eriksen's threats.

Power grid, Darius mused. *Overload. Nice way of putting it, Roger.*

The letter was about Colonel Eriksen. Darius knew that something
important had come to light; otherwise Roger would not risk a meeting, even away from the crew of *Gabriel*. There was still something odd
about the letter: a phrase that Darius could not interpret.

He will be bringing your consultant with him as well, he recalled.
Consultant? Who? Is Roger bringing someone with him?

Darius came to a stop to catch his breath. A disturbing thought crossed his mind.

What if it's a trap? Has Eriksen figured out our code? Or has Roger turned on me?

He shook his head and continued on. There was a chance that the colonel had broken or turned Roger, but he had to take the chance. If Eriksen wasn't involved, Darius needed to know what was going on. Dr. Kimura and Lieutenant Reid could be endangered by any scheme of *Gabriel's* commander, and Darius could not stand idly by and watch while one or both were put to death. At least not if they didn't have a fair trial to begin with.

Darius reached the last pole in the line, about two hundred feet from the river bank. A single bulldozer sat in the middle of a wide clear cut. Stumps had been blasted or pulled out from half of the cut, and the machine rested by a tall mound of dirt, waiting for its absent operator to finish the project of flattening the land for building. He looked around the construction site for any workers, but found none.

They might be on a lunch break, he thought.

Darius glanced at the pitted metal watch on his wrist. Though the hour hand on the Earth-made timepiece was useless, the minute hand told him it was twenty-six minutes past the hour. He paced back and forth, then made a trip to the river bank to make sure no one was there. He then inspected every inch of the lonely machine, making sure no one was hiding in or under it. Satisfied that there were no agents of Colonel Eriksen to be found, he selected a stump with a good view of the shallow, wide river, and sat.

It did not take long for Lieutenant Roger Miller to arrive. He greeted Darius as he approached. Darius felt a moment of shock when he saw Don Abernathy arrive at Roger's side.

My consultant, he thought. *Clever.*

"It's good to see you, Roger," Darius said.

"Likewise. I wish it was under better circumstances."

"You have news, then?"

"I do." Roger sighed and sat on another stump a few feet from Darius. He cast his eyes at the dirt and his shoulders slumped as if weighed down by the tree that once stood in his spot. "I thought you were crazy at first, I'll admit it. I thought I was just playing along to keep you from snapping. Back on Earth I accidentally stumbled across Doctor Kimura's files on hibernation psychosis, so I thought you might have been suffering from it. But after what I heard this morning, I know you've been right all along."

"Go on," Darius replied, shrugging off the suggestion of insanity.

"I accidentally left the bridge recorders on this morning during a routine com check. I guess when Colonel Eriksen barged in and ordered me out immediately, I just… forgot."

Darius nodded and leaned back slightly. *So he accidentally recorded Eriksen.*

"The weirdest thing about it was the fact that as I left the bridge, Major Kintney was going to the bridge, along with Captain Quinn."

"Sorry, Roger, why is that weird?" Darius asked, slightly confused.

His former partner lifted his head and looked Darius dead in the eye. "Major Kintney was supposedly assigned to an expedition group five days ago. I saw him get in the crawler myself. Every log I've seen confirms that assignment. No one I know has seen him for days. So I did something… impulsive. I checked his rack in the crew pod. He's definitely been living there. His bed was still warm, and there are too many food pouches and dirty suits stashed away in that section of the ship."

"So he's been hiding on *Gabriel*? What for?"

"I don't know. But when I got back to the bridge and found the recorders on, I stashed the conversation on a thumb drive before purging the computer."

"Good thinking," Darius added.

"In any case, I had to do a redundancy check on the mainframe this morning, so while I was locked in the computer core I took a few minutes to listen to what happened on the bridge." Roger paused for a second as he scratched the stubble on his chin. "It's pretty shocking. They were going over a list of points to bring up at the court martial. Lists of witnesses. They mentioned you."

"I thought they made it clear they didn't want me at Doctor Kimura's trial," Darius sneered. "Why would they want me at Reid's?"

"They don't. Colonel Eriksen said that you were to be 'excluded.' The colonel almost went off the deep end when Quinn asked him why, and kicked him off the bridge. Anyway, Eriksen knows that his efforts to push you away from the Kimura trial failed, so he told Major Kintney to make sure you don't testify at Reid's trial, and to keep your legal 'watchdogs' at bay."

"It's clear this man has no regard for legal procedure or consistency," Don noted. "Unfortunately, when it comes to a military court, I don't have any real power. Fred Hausner and I are doing all we can to keep him from interfering with Doctor Kimura's trial, but I'm afraid I can't help you get your foot in the door with respect to Lieutenant Reid."

Darius thought hard about the information and what it all meant. The fact that Eriksen's second-in-command was hiding on the ship while assigned elsewhere was very strange. Kintney had been in stasis for the entire journey, so he did not get a chance to see how Dr. Kimura kept his end of the colonel's bargain. His head began to swim, and he knew he needed to be alone to sort out his thoughts.

"Thanks, Roger," he said as he rose. "At least we know the colonel's in this to lay down the law. We should probably leave before the work crew comes back and sees us together. I wouldn't want that to get back to the colonel. You don't need that kind of trouble."

"There's more, Darius," Roger said as he grabbed Darius's elbow. "None of the men assigned to Kintney's expedition group were civilians. They were all Air Force. And I think all of them are camped out on *Gabriel*, just like Kintney. I think the crawler's there, too. I didn't want to open the cargo pods because it would leave a trace in the system, but I ran a calculation through the mainframe when I was working on it earlier. *Gabriel's* load sensors show that it's between six and twelve tons too heavy on the starboard front quarter right now."

"A crawler weighs eight tons," Darius remarked. "That's a lot of metal to be hiding in plain sight. Who else was assigned to that expedition?"

"Camp, Garza, and Marks."

"Can you keep an eye out for them? Send a message through Rory if you see them."

"I will."

Darius shook hands with the two men. He then walked to the steep bank of the river and looked across at the other sleeper ship. He wondered if their crew was struggling with how to handle any conspirators that might have been on board. He wondered if they had the luxury of being able to concentrate solely on colonial life. For a moment, he yearned to be on the other side of the river, to be able to walk freely among the other crew.

He walked downstream along the river, searching within for many answers.

Cal's hand shot out and grabbed Alexis's arm as she nearly stumbled face first into the swift, sparkling water. Her weight pulling on him made his foot slip, and he was forced to take an awkward step to avoid dunking his backpack in the river. His left hand dropped, and with it, their shoes plunged into the cold water.

"Damn it," Cal muttered.

She regained her footing and straightened up. The knee deep water lapped at her soaked jeans. They had rolled up the cuffs as far as they could, but even at the shallow crossing to the islands, the river was just a few inches too deep to keep their clothing dry.

"Sorry, I slipped," she said sheepishly, almost drowned out by the river.

"It's okay." He held up two drenched pairs of sneakers and grinned. "We'll just bring the river with us when we walk."

Alexis wrinkled her nose. "I'd rather go barefoot, thank you."

They crossed the last fifty feet of river with great care; their feet would alternate between finding solid, smooth stones and sinking a couple inches into muck in the river bed. When they reached the shore of the near island, disappointment set in. Cal gingerly picked his way around the downstream shore, only to find that the entire island was nothing more than a heap of mud, accentuated with numerous felled trees and only a half dozen or so that were still standing. He could not find a patch of dry ground anywhere he looked, so he returned to Alexis.

"A bust?" she asked, pouting slightly.

"Yeah. Shall we try the other one?"

Alexis turned to the narrow channel of churning water that lay between the two islands. It was nowhere near as wide as the fork of the river that they had just crossed, but the white rapids that dotted the span as far down as the downstream tip of the island made Cal question the safety of the idea. He was a strong swimmer, but was more used to lakes and pools than anything else. He knew that one false step in such a current could be disastrous.

"I think so," she replied. "It's fast, but I think it's pretty shallow, too."

"You sure?"

"You bet. I'm not wasting a day off just so we can mope around back at the ship. I'll go first," she said as she grabbed a long, soaked branch from the ground.

She waded into the river, prodding the river bottom as she went. Cal followed just behind. He kept one hand just behind her, ready to reach out in case they fell. The water pulled at them, threatening to sweep them from their feet if they made a false move. But the river bed was lined with rocks, and had only gradual shifts in depth. The water barely rose to their knees before they closed in on the far shore, and the channel once again became shallow.

The second island rose farther from the river, and was topped in lush vegetation. Birds called from the trees above, and the midday sun helped to ease the chill of their waterlogged jeans.

"This looks more promising," Cal chirped as he took a few steps downstream and scrambled up the tall bank. As he emerged on top, he caught a glimpse of something metal from the corner of his eye, buried in the vegetation. He walked over to a tall, half flattened bush and found an eight foot tall cylinder with four legs splayed out on the underside. It sat at a sharp angle on only two of the legs, with a fallen trunk wedged underneath it. Alexis bounded up to his side.

"What is that?" she asked as she brushed a clump of dirt from the side.

"I think…" his voice trailed off. He skirted around the other side and pulled back a branch full of tiny blue leaves. Underneath were thick block letters, scratched from its hard landing.

USAF. XCS-03-R.

"Yeah, that's *Raphael's* landing beacon, alright," he confirmed.

Alexis had her eyes glued on the beacon as she walked around it, one hand firmly planted on its skin. "I thought that there was nothing left of that ship?"

"No other part," Cal corrected. "Hunter said this was launched as part of their approach, well before they had a problem. We knew this piece was here, I'd just never seen it in person before."

An uneasy silence fell between them as they inspected the only artifact from the doomed sleeper ship. Cal's nightmare of the burning wreck began to play in his head, but he shook it off before it could consume him.

"Come on," he beckoned toward the high point near the center of the island and laced his fingers with hers. "I've done enough swimming and sightseeing. It's time to eat."

They walked slowly along the low ridge, avoiding shrubs and sticks that might poke into their unprotected feet. Just below the top they came across a grassy patch with a lone felled tree below a shaded canopy from three others that were standing. Cal cast aside their shoes and slipped out of the shoulder straps of the pack. He set it down and carefully removed the belt and holstered pistol, which he then set down next to the pack.

Please be intact. Please be intact.

Cal dug further into the container, removing meal pouches that had been rolled and clamped to seal their slit tops, and the skin of scotch that Dr. Taylor had gifted to him. Though the alcohol had been consumed the first night on Demeter, Cal had refilled it many times before, even taking it with him on the scouting excursion. On this occasion it was filled with coffee that Gail helped him sneak from the kitchen just before he and Alexis had left the camp. Cal hoped that it had retained enough of its heat to remain palatable; the bladder of the bag was not well insulated. He laid the items out on the ground next to the log.

"Oh, so this is your idea of a romantic first date?" Alexis teased. "I see how it goes. Woo a girl, take her out to a stunningly beautiful and secluded place, and then feed her a bag of military chow."

"Really?" he feigned indignation. "What kind of guy do you take me for?"

He handed her a plastic fork, unrolled the pouch, and then pulled the top open so she could see. Spicy and sweet smells wafted from inside, and the bag felt warm against the palm of his hand. He smiled, trying to hide his relief that the food had not gone completely cold.

"What… what is this?" she gasped.

"Some of the testing came back on the plants right around the ship. Most of it was inedible, but there were a few things that are. There's turnips in there… well, Demeter turnips, anyway. Wild onions. Shredded greens. Gail said she might toss some bacon in there. A little pepper in there, too; I convinced Dayton to loosen up a little on the spices, just for a few days."

Alexis poked her fork into the pouch and withdrew a small, oblong onion. She popped it in her mouth, and her eyes rolled back and her lids closed slowly as she chewed. She let out a moan of approval, and opened her eyes again.

"Wow," she said.

"Good enough for you?" he grinned.

"It's been so long since I've had fresh food. I was almost afraid I'd never taste it again."

"That's not the only surprise I have for you." He unrolled the other bag, which let out a smoky smell. He reached in and flaked off a chunk of smoked fish, then offered it to her. "I owe a couple favors for this, but it's worth it."

"You're kidding, right?" she said as both her eyes and her smile widened. "Oh, Cal! You... you really went out of your way for this, didn't you?"

"I made you a promise, didn't I? An unforgettable first date."

"You did. And it is." She leaned in and kissed him on the lips. "Thank you."

"It's nothing," he replied shyly.

They shared the meal in the shade as they talked about the local birds, the landscape, and friends back at camp. The conversation turned to Alexis and her duties with the camp kitchen. He began to fidget, and his smile disappeared. He knew his prospects for work back at the ship were still very slim, and it hurt him that he might have to leave her side again. The death of Elaine on the exploration mission brought his own mortality to the front of his consciousness.

Alexis must have sensed his concern. She placed her hand on the back of his and her green eyes pierced him, as if she could look into his soul. "What's wrong?"

Cal shook his head and sighed. "I don't know how to bring this up. I still haven't been able to find work around *Michael*. They're sending Neil back up to the hills. He wants me to go with him, to give a hand to him and the crew going up there. I asked Hunter for more details, and he said that about twenty people are going up there to start an outpost. Mining and logging, I guess."

"What?" she gasped. "They want you to leave again? When?"

"In three days."

"But you just came back! They expect you to go back out there with those... things? No. Whatever it is, it can wait. You can find something around camp. There has to be *something*."

"I haven't told them anything yet, Lexi. I needed to know something." Cal cupped her hands in his. "They need a cook. We could..."

"No," she shook her head.

"I need to get back to work. We could go together and..."

"No," she shouted and pulled her hands back. "Are you nuts? I barely feel safe at home as it is. I'm not going out there with those monsters in the woods."

"Then I have to go back alone."

"No, you don't." Alexis crept forward on her knees and put her arms around him. "You can't. I don't want to be without you any longer."

"I want to stay, believe me. If there was any way that I could stay, I would."

"I'll twist Dayton's arm until he gives you a job, if I have to."

Cal chuckled. "I bet you would."

Alexis scrambled to her feet and pulled him up. "Let's go find him now," she grinned. "I'll convince him for you."

"Our date's over already? Damn, that went by too quickly."

"You have something better to do?"

"Of course. A walk on the beach, maybe?"

"Alright, if I can't beat up the colonel, I suppose I can settle for that."

Cal packed up the waste and the mostly empty skin of coffee. He shoved their wet shoes in the top of the bag and slung it over one shoulder, then wrapped the gun belt around his waist. He helped her down to the beach on the far side of the island so they could make one loop before heading back.

The far beach was covered in fine, black silt, which squished between their toes as they walked along slowly. Cal grabbed her hand and pulled her in close as a flight of birds skimmed along the surface of the water.

"You know I'll find a way to stay with you," he whispered. He felt her nod against his chest before letting go of their embrace.

"I just can't lose you. You're all I have left."

"I know. Trust me, I know."

Alexis smiled and nodded. Her smile quickly faded, however, and she stepped to the side. Cal turned around to see what she was looking at. On the far river bank was a man, shouting and waving his arms at them. Cal could barely pick him out from the dark earth of the bank itself; the man's black skin and tan overalls almost made him blend in to his surroundings.

"What the hell?" Cal grumbled. "Is that Donnell?"

"What's he doing on that side of the river?" Alexis asked. "I thought Colonel Dayton ordered no contact with the other ship."

"He did," Cal shot back. "Dayton's going to be pissed."

Cal's heart sunk as the man plunged headlong into the river and headed straight for them. Shock sank in as he waded out halfway into the channel.

"What the hell, Donnell," he cursed. "Be careful."

In a flash, the man slipped and pitched forward into the water. Cal shouted a curse and fumbled at the clasp on his belt. He tore it loose and dropped it into the muck without a second thought. A second later, the backpack dropped to the ground next to it with a thump.

"Hang on, Donnell!" Cal shouted. "I'm coming!"

The larger man struggled and flailed against the current, and was swept downstream. Cal burst into a full sprint down the length of the beach, trying to stay ahead of his friend. His feet pounded into rocks every few steps, challenging him to keep his pace as wave after wave of pain ran through his legs.

Don't stop. Don't stop!

He came to a point where the beach turned rocky and decided to lunge into the river just before reaching it. He took three powerful strides before leaping hands- first into the river. He was caught in the current just downstream of the thrashing victim. Cal kicked and thrust his way deeper into the channel, struggling to go against the current even as he carried himself farther out. A flash of brown streaked his way, and he lunged once more. Both hands clawed into the chest of Donnell's coveralls.

"I've got you," he shouted as he tried to find bottom with his feet. "Put your feet down!"

Cal's feet ached as they bumped off of rocks just too far for him to push against. Roiling white rapids filled his vision as they rushed down the river.

Oh shit, he thought.

He thrust his feet down again, and this time they hit shallow rock. He bellowed in pain from the impact, but rose up in the water and slowed. Again he stretched his legs to the bottom and found another rock. The pain was nearly unbearable, but this time he slowed enough to where he was able to stop their momentum. In searing pain and half drowned, Cal put his arm around the hunched shoulder of his friend and, limping, escorted him back to shore. Cal helped him sit down, and then his heart leaped and his hands tingled.

You're not Donnell.

Darius Owens
15 April, Year of Landing, 11:01
River Islands, 1 mile east of Gabriel landing site
>|

"Who the hell are you?" asked the gangly, blond-haired boy who stood over him, favoring one leg.

Darius coughed violently and spat up a mouthful of water.

"Are you from the other ship?" his rescuer asked. He could clearly hear apprehension in the kid's voice.

"Yes," he managed in a hoarse whisper.

"Why are you here?"

"I need to talk to Colonel Dayton."

"Dayton?" the kid looked confused. "Why the hell would you need to... hey wait, are you from *Gabriel's* crew?"

Darius nodded as he rolled onto his hands knees and retched up another round of river water. He took a moment to regain his breath and then leaned back onto his ankles. When he opened his eyes, a brown-haired girl in soaked jeans and a green form-fitting top had joined the fray. She held a weapons belt in one hand and with the other pointed a Beretta at Darius, though her hand was trembling. Her emerald green eyes almost burned as she tracked his every move. Darius slowly raised his hands and bowed his head.

"Why are you..." the boy started. "Lexi, put it away."

"That's not Donnell," she shot back. "He's from the other ship."

"That's right," Darius interrupted. "I'm not Captain Gibbins. I'm from *Gabriel*, but it's not what you think."

"Lexi, stop. Let him speak," the boy said. He had a definite twang to his voice, which Darius instantly recognized as being Texan. He turned to Darius and repeated, "Your CO broke his word and landed on the wrong side of the river. You know we're not supposed to have contact with you. Who are you? Why are you here?"

"My name is Darius Owens, and I'm here because something has gone terribly wrong," Darius replied. He slowly rose to his feet and lowered his arms.

The girl reaffirmed her aim. "Don't move. I don't want to hurt you," she shouted.

"I don't want you to either. But with all due respect, Miss, you can't. Not with the safety on, anyway."

She lowered the pistol and turned it to the side to inspect it.

"Besides," he continued, "I owe your friend here my life for fishing me out of the river. I'm here seeking help."

"Help?" The boy folded his arms across his chest. "I'm pretty sure Colonel Eriksen made it clear how he felt about our crews helping each other when he landed on that side of the river. You can't tell me that was a mistake."

"It wasn't. The colonel did that on purpose, but I don't know why." He looked down at his drenched flight suit that clung to his skin like a cold curtain of shame. "He'd probably tell you that he threw me out of the crew for asking why."

"Did he?" the girl asked.

"Threw me out of the crew, yes, but that's only scratching the surface of why. That's why I need help. Now, I know you're not part of his crew, but I need… no, we need you to give him a really important message."

"Who is we?"

"Two men who stand to die for the sin of saving lives. Doctor Kimura and Lieutenant Reid. Colonel Dayton should know who they are."

"I know who the doctor is," the boy replied. "He was one of the Project Columbus lead researchers, and is accused of treason. The same treason that Major Forrest is accused of. The same one that my father…" his voice trailed off and he paused for a moment, lost in thought. He then cleared his voice and spoke again in an eerily calm voice. "Lexi, put it away."

With only the slightest hesitation, she lowered the pistol and stuffed it into the belt's holster.

"Pardon me," Darius said, "but you seem to know an awful lot about what's going on."

"It hits close to home." The boy avoided making eye contact with Darius, casting his gaze into an eddy at the edge of the shore.

"Your father. Was he part of the Project?"

"Not directly, but he did help Doctor Kimura."

"Was he Air Force?"

"Yes," the boy sniffed and looked Darius in the eyes. He extended his hand. "I'm Calvin McLaughlin. This is my girlfriend Alexis."

"McLaughlin," Darius repeated, as stunned as he was shaken. "Son of General Andrew McLaughlin, and grandson of Colonel Christopher McLaughlin."

"That's right."

Darius's hand trembled as he reached for Calvin's. He shook it, though timidly. "I'm very sorry for your loss, Mr. McLaughlin."

"It's just Cal, and thank you."

Darius nodded. "I've never known Doctor Kimura to be a boastful or dishonest man. He told me… no, he told us all about the role that your father and his men played in protecting and transporting the civilians bound for Laramie. I can't say that I would have had the courage to do the same, if I were in his shoes."

"Thank you, again." An awkward moment of silence swept through. "So what was this message that you needed me to take to Colonel Dayton?"

"That Colonel Eriksen has been overstepping every boundary he possibly can in order to make sure one, if not both, of the accused men is convicted. I can't say why for sure, but I think he wants to make it clear to the other colonists that crime won't be tolerated. He's rigging the deck as much as he can in the trials."

"And you want to save these men?" Calvin asked.

"I just want them to have fair trials," he replied. "If either of them are convicted in a fair trial, then so be it. I think it would be a terrible blow to the colony to lose either of them, but justice would be upheld. What Eriksen is doing is playing with lives to make a political statement."

"He seems to be full of those."

"That's part of what concerns me. Letting him get away with what he's doing is a slippery slope. He could just stop and life will go on, but I get the feeling that it's going to corrupt him even more, once he gets a taste for it. Please, Colonel Dayton has to help us."

"I hear you," Calvin replied, "but Dayton is still spitting fire about what happened during the landing. Pardon me for asking, but what exactly does he get in return?"

"I can speak for at least twenty officers and colonists whose loyalty he would earn right away. I have no doubt that many other colonists would put their weight behind Dayton if they knew what Eriksen was up to. It could topple like dominos, and maybe, just maybe, we could all finally live as one colony, like we're supposed to."

Calvin thought for a moment and then nodded. "I'll bring your message to him. I'm not sure how we'll get in touch with you if he responds, but at least I can do this for you."

"Send smoke signals if you have to," Darius replied. "But I might be able to get someone to turn on part of the extracom on *Gabriel.* It's only a data stream, so no voice, but I know a little bug that can be used to capture a message."

"I'll let Dayton know that as well. You should probably get back before it gets any later."

"Right." Darius looked at the roiling, inky waters of the river. "Any idea how I can do that without drowning?"

Calvin walked to the edge of the river and pointed to a spot in the channel. "Right there. You went into the water where it was too deep. Your body lifted up and that's why you got swept away. I know it looks more dangerous, but it's a lot shallower there, probably just up to your knees at the deepest. Just go slow and you should keep your feet under you."

"Thank you." He shook Calvin's hand again, and then nodded to Alexis. "Miss Alexis, a pleasure."

The pair from *Michael* started along the beach as Darius drew in a breath, as well as the courage to ford the perilous channel.

"Gabi, honey," Emilia smiled at her as she stooped over Gabi to pat her shoulder. "Can you play for a little bit? I'm going to check on your mom here for a minute."

"Is she sick again?" Gabi asked.

"No, I just want to see how she's doing. Where's Pelusina?"

Gabi turned and walked a few paces to retrieve her prized stuffed cat. She held it up for Emilia, who nodded and mussed up Gabi's hair. "There you go. This will take just a few minutes, okay?"

"Okay," she replied.

Gabi skipped from the rear of the clinic to the front, tossing the animal in the air and trying to catch her on the way down. She dropped Pelusina several times, which added to the fine coating of dirt that the cat's hair had accumulated over the months in camp.

She then spent a few minutes trying to jump from bed to bed, tossing the animal onto the next bed before making each leap. Once she made a complete circuit of the clinic, she sat down on one of the beds and restarted the game of tossing the animal in the air and trying to catch it. Each time she threw a little harder. Then she lay on her back and threw her arm out as hard as she could. Pelusina arced high into the air, almost brushing the ceiling with her belly as she did a mid-air spiral. She then did a face-first swan dive into the dirt, right in the middle of the adults.

"Gabi!" her mother shouted as she scowled.

"Sorry, Mama," she squeaked.

"Pick it up and go back to playing."

Gabi skittered over to the thick stump where her mother sat. She was flanked on either side by Dr. Petrovsky and Emilia Reiber. The doctor glanced up at Gabi for a moment, then went back to looking at her mother's wrist, which he held in his fingers. His lips twitched.

"What are you doing?" Gabi asked.

"Shh, go away," her mother hissed.

Dr. Petrovsky's lips moved more, and she could hear him counting under his breath. With her free hand, Gabi's mother shooed her away. She squeezed Pelusina and walked around the partition wall, then rolled onto Dr. Petrovsky's bed. Gabi set the cat down on top of the doctor's blankets and began to bounce her up and down, as if she was pouncing on some unseen insect. The voices of the adults carried over the wall as she played with her dingy stuffed toy.

"Everything looks good," the doctor remarked. "How are you feeling?"

"No nausea," her mother replied, "but Haruka sure made me feel like crap."

Gabi turned her head when she heard the name. She sat still for a moment to listen to what her mother and the doctor were talking about, but they went back into a boring conversation about her mom not being able to work. Gabi picked up Peluisina again and rolled onto her back. She held the cat high above her head with one hand and made a sweeping motion, combined with a whooshing noise. She imagined the fat, stuffed cat was flying, trying to catch an evil mouse with a rocket pack that had stolen her food.

After a couple minutes, Pelusina caught the imaginary rodent. Gabi kissed the cat and gave it a squeeze. She sat up, and could hear the voices from beyond the wall again, this time a little louder.

"Haruka doesn't care about me," her mother's shrill voice rang out. "She already said she doesn't care what you have to say about it either, Ken."

Dr. Petrovsky spoke in his soothing tenor. "She's got a lot of weight on her shoulders, Maria."

"Then someone needs to do something about it."

"Like what?" Emilia asked. "If she's not listening to us, there's nothing we can do."

"Then get someone to remove her!" Her mother's voice jumped almost another octave. The piercing sound made Gabi curl her knees to her chest, and squeeze Pelusina tight.

"Shh," the doctor soothed. "Calm down. There's no reason to be so harsh."

"Isn't there? She doesn't care about me, she's ignoring you two altogether. She's running Troy and his crews ragged. Is she trying to work everyone to death?"

Stop yelling, Mama!

"She has a point," Emilia added. "When's the last time she didn't put us on the back burner? How long was poor Will back before she sent him back out scouting again? Did he even get to say goodbye to his mom before he left? And she's pushed Nick back to work before he was really ready."

"You're damn right, she did."

"Mama, bad word!" Gabi called out.

"Be quiet, Gabi!" she shouted back.

She shrank back into a ball and buried her nose in Pelusina. Gabi's lip began to quiver as she wondered what she had done to make her mother angry again.

"Take it easy on her," Dr. Petrovsky said in a stern tone.

"Stop telling me what to do. She's *my* daughter."

Gabi heard footsteps approach her and heard the soft rustle of fabric on the sleeping bag that was draped over the bed. She peeked out from her soft, albeit dirty, protection. Emilia offered her hand to Gabi.

"Come on, Gabi. Let's go somewhere else and play for a while, okay?"

She nodded and took the nurse's hand and was led out of the clinic. The sun was slowly sinking toward the sea, streaking the scattered clouds above with brilliant shades of pink and orange.

"Let's go to the Palace," Emilia said as she pointed to the long building across the street.

"Why?"

"To see if Caleb or Karina can play."

Gabi glanced back at the clinic, then down the street at the small hut that she shared with her mother. It stood silently at the end of the street, with its storm curtain rippling in the cool breeze. For a second she thought about asking Emilia if she could go home instead, but without her mother or friends there, the hut could feel very lonely and frightening. Though she didn't really want to play with Caleb, she agreed to go in the Palace anyway.

As they rounded the corner to find the entrance, Caleb and Karina skipped through the village square with the Vandemark sisters. Kristin spotted Gabi as she sped by, giggling and joking with Karina.

"Hey Gabi," she called. "We're going to the beach to have a fire and sing songs. Want to come with us?"

Emilia leaned over and whispered to Gabi, "That sounds like fun. You should go."

"But what about Mama? She won't know where I am! And Pelusina is afraid of fires!"

The nurse plucked the stuffed cat from her hands. "It's fine if you go with them. I'll tell your mom where you are, and make sure Pelusina is waiting for you at home when you're done."

"Yippee!" she exclaimed and hopped up to the younger Vandemark girl. Her heart raced with excitement; it had been far too long since she had sung.

Calvin McLaughlin
15 April, Year of Landing, 17:09
Michael
>|

Cal looked aft down the brightly lit upper gallery. The utilitarian panels and braces that were so dark and eerie during their journey were now just an endless repeating pattern of steel; creases and bolts flowed into a linear sea as the vastness of the gallery stretched before him.

Why does this feel so much like home? Cal asked himself as he ran his hand along the cold metal bulkhead that contained the airlock. The flight suit he had changed into after his earlier swim tightened a little around the cuff as his arm extended. *There's something about being here. About participating again.*

Dr. Taylor leaned against the wall just on the far side of the airlock. She had a worn paperback copy of *A Tale of Two Cities* splayed open in one hand, and she was thoroughly engrossed in the story. Captain Donnell Gibbins and Sergeant Cameron Drisko stood a few feet away, poring over a clipboard full of reports of colonial activity for the last few days. The sight of what he expected from the crew helped calm his frayed nerves. He still knew that the meeting they were about to have would be anything but relaxing.

Hunter emerged from the airlock and greeted him. "Colonel Dayton is ready for you." His eyes darted around the group. "All of you. Please, come to the bridge."

Cal stepped through the portal that joined the command section to the upper gallery. The familiar split staircase sat ahead, and Cal marched up the stairs, every motion of his legs and feet deliberate. Each rising step made more goose bumps rise on his skin, and when he reached the top and saw the massive glass canopy, he shivered.

The glass was streaked with tiny rivers of water. A light rain had started to fall right at sunset. Though the skies were now dark, the light from inside the bridge clearly reflected in the water that pooled up at the very top of the ship. Under the panorama, the command chair sat on its raised platform. Colonel Dayton stood at the chair's side, resting his arm on the back. His back was turned to the group as he stared into oblivion somewhere off the starboard bow.

The others took positions in a semicircle around the command chair. Cal stopped about six feet from it and leaned against the metal railing just above the engineering terminals. His hands gripped the smooth, slightly tarnished steel out of habit. Hunter stopped on the other side of the chair back from Colonel Dayton and softly cleared his throat.

"Colonel, sir," he said, bobbing his head in Cal's direction.

The ship's commander turned around and scanned the gathered crowd. His crow's feet looked like they had doubled in size, and formidable, dark circles under his eyes told the story of a man who desperately needed sleep. His beard had grown as well, and was not as well groomed as Cal had remembered.

"Mr. McLaughlin," he said in his thick New England accent. "Lieutenant Ceretti tells me that you have some interesting news. Something about our friends on the other side of the river. I understand that you have had contact with one of them, against my orders."

"Yes, sir," Cal replied, making an effort not to stutter. "I didn't realize who he was at first. To be honest, at a distance I mistook him for Captain Gibbins. But I guess I would have talked to this guy no matter what, since I saved him from drowning in the river."

Dayton nodded. "I don't blame you for doing that at all. But from what I understand, the contact wasn't accidental. Ceretti mentioned that he ran into the river to… speak with you?"

"That's what I figured. He was definitely trying to get the attention of Lexi and me. He did a good job at that when he fell in. We were both a little freaked when I fished him out and found he was from *Gabriel*. But he wasn't armed, and he wanted me to give you a message, and ask for help."

"Help," Dayton spat. "They had their chance at that. And then they landed over there."

"Please hear him out, sir," Captain Gibbins interrupted.

"Fine. Go ahead."

"He said that he was part of the crew, but that Colonel Eriksen booted him when he questioned why they landed on the far side of the river," Cal continued. "He told me that Eriksen has gone out of his way to twist the trials of Doctor Kimura and Lieutenant Reid to force at least one to be convicted. He fears that if Eriksen succeeds that he might become even more corrupt, and he's afraid of what that means."

"*Was* part of the crew?" Dayton scratched at his thick brown beard. "So we're taking the word of a disgruntled former crewmember."

Captain Gibbins took a single step forward. "Sir, I know this man. He's one of the most devoted officers I've ever seen. Back at Laramie he would pull extra shifts when things needed to get done, never once complained about it. Hell, I even saw him showing some of the refugee kids how to tuck down a bed properly before we left Earth."

"Who is he, Captain?"

"Lieutenant Darius Owens."

"Owens… Owens. I know that name. He was the officer that relayed messages to Eriksen for me."

"Sir, I know a little about Lieutenant Owens myself," Hunter added. "He's my counterpart on *Gabriel*. He's the one who found the bug in the extracom software that the assassin was using against his prey. I can hardly believe that a man like that would be going behind Colonel Eriksen's back because of a simple grudge."

"It's not just him either, Colonel. He told me that there are at least twenty others that he could vouch for who were concerned by Eriksen's actions. He believes that the majority of the colonists would too, if they knew what was going on."

Colonel Dayton took two slow, measured steps around the command chair, not making eye contact with anyone. He lowered his body into the chair, lost in thought.

Come on, sir. You know that I'm telling you the truth.

Cal wasn't convinced by his own words. Some bitter rift between the colonels of all three ships had flared up at some point. One was now dead; Cal considered her the lucky one, as she didn't have to play games with her colleagues – or the lives of the colonists – any more.

"I'm not sure what to say to all of this," Dayton finally replied. "If this is true, then Colonel Eriksen and myself are in two completely different frames of mind as to how to run things. He's rushing through two trials, while I haven't even thought about conducting Major Forrest's court martial. He's putting pressure on his people, while I am trying to keep morale as high as possible. He's agitated someone enough that they risked drowning and God knows what else just to send us a message, with no guarantee that we're even listening."

His chin rose up and he looked to Captain Gibbins. "Is Lieutenant Owens a bold man?"

"Not really, sir. He's friendly, but can also be quiet and reserved. He never signed up for combat, and he was also real nervous about the idea of space travel."

"To me, that alone speaks volumes. I'd like everyone's opinion on the situation. Ceretti?"

"If Colonel Eriksen is losing grip on his colony, or even if he thinks he is, it could be a dangerous situation. I don't know if it's more dangerous for us or the civilians under his watch, but I don't think I could stand by and watch innocent people get caught up in this."

"Drisko?"

"What are we even going to be able to do about it, sir?" Cameron replied. The passion in his voice emphasized his grave concern. "We don't have any boats, and if we march up there and try to take over, he'll see us coming a couple miles away. We can't send any civilians over there, either. It's too risky."

"Thank you. Mr. McLaughlin?"

"I don't know. This guy seemed truly upset and desperate. If it's that bad, shouldn't we help? *Can* we even help?"

"Doctor?"

"It's not my place to say anything, Colonel. But please, let me know if whatever you decide may end up in bloodshed. I'm not a trauma doctor, so any surprises might end up proving deadly."

Dayton nodded. "Captain Gibbins?"

"If they are in a sticky situation over there, what better way to prove that we're serious about working together than to help them without asking for reciprocation? If we show them that we've got their backs, then don't you think they'll have ours when it comes down to it?"

The colonel slumped into his chair. He craned his neck upward and stared at the torrents rolling down the canopy above. No one in the circle moved; Cal supposed that, except for Dr. Taylor, the rest were trained to wait for Dayton. But the wait was not sitting well with Cal, and he wrung his hands nervously on the metal railing.

"I need to sleep on it," Colonel Dayton grumbled. "Thank you, gentlemen, Doctor. You are dismissed."

Cameron, Hunter, and Gibbins gave quick salutes before they turned away. The five companions silently filed down the stairs.

"I'm going to get some rack time," Hunter said as he took the turn down the lower stairway to the crew pod.

"Me too," yawned Cameron, who followed suit.

Donnell Gibbins clapped Cal on the back. "Thank you for fishing Owens out of the drink. Not many people I know would stick their neck out for someone like that."

Cal nodded, though his fatigue and shyness kept him tongue tied. He watched as the captain followed the others down into the crew pod.

He was left alone with Dr. Taylor, who stepped in front of him. She held her book to her chest with one hand and tucked her reading glasses into the other.

"Do you know why I didn't offer an opinion in there?" she asked. Cal shook his head. "It's that I'm not certain about what's going on. I only have parts of the picture, and they're not pretty. Throughout history there have been wars fought for religion, land, and slaves. Others were the sole product of political ideals. Those are the ones that can be the most inspiring, but also the most treacherous and devastating."

"I don't know where you're going with this, Doctor."

"I didn't think you would," she retorted. "You're still young and idealistic. You've got the grand and beautiful notion that we can reach out and save friends, loved ones, and strangers alike with a gesture. But there's an opposing force that might take issue with that gesture, and we have no idea how strong it is or how it will react if pushed. With Dayton and Eriksen already feuding, how much do you think it will take to start a full blown war between the two crews? And in a very literal sense, all of the civilians are caught in the middle. Remember that when you return to your tent with Alexis tonight."

Calvin swallowed hard as a sketch on the foggy windshield of the crawler returned to his memory.

The Battle of Concordia. Great. Just great.

Darius Owens
20 April, Year of Landing, 11:00
Gabriel
>|

"The court's recess is over," Captain Quinn boomed over the din of the crowd that gathered at the base of *Gabriel's* loading ramp. "As the prosecution has rested, it is time for the defense to call its first witness."

Eriksen had to put a pawn somewhere, didn't he? Quinn acting as judge. How thin is your veil, Colonel?

Darius rocked from one foot to the other as he anticipated his turn on the stand. Don Abernathy appeared at the top of the ramp from within the long hallway beyond. He was dressed in a flannel button down shirt and jeans. The Hollywood image of a lawyer in a fine suit, strutting in front of an enraptured, seated jury was shattered by the day's events. Don and Fred were both dressed in their finest attire, which did not include a shirt or even slacks for either man. The jury was composed of six men and six women randomly selected by lottery; this was the lone guarantee against Eriksen's scheming that both counselors came up with. They stood in a row at the base of the ramp, three paces in front of the throng of colonists that had come to watch the trial.

Along with Quinn and Don, the top of the ramp was host to Colonel Eriksen, Fred Hausner, Doctor Kimura, and Lieutenant Reid. Reid was bound at the hands with rope, though the doctor was allowed to stand without bondage.

The lieutenant had been called as a prosecution witness early in the morning, and was questioned about his contact with the doctor, as well as the role that the research staff had him play. It was damning testimony, but freely given. Like Dr. Kimura, Reid seemed to cooperate completely, never once hesitating to answer any question that was thrown at him.

Admirable, even if they are convicted.

In an unusual move, the prosecutor called the defense attorney, Don, to the stand after Lieutenant Reid. He answered only a few questions, all of which were legal definitions of the crimes that had been leveled against Dr. Kimura: conspiracy, theft, and treason. Colonel Eriksen had turned beet red and ground his teeth at this display, which was the only amusement that Darius had all week.

"The defense would like to call Doctor Tadashi Kimura," Don belted out loud enough for all to hear.

Darius felt a hand clasp his left arm and squeeze lightly. He looked to his left at the doctor's wife, Sarah, as she clutched to him. Her eyes were fixated on the spectacle above them, and her face was almost ghost white. Just beyond her stood her daughter, Saika Reid, and Lieutenant Reid's sister, Kayla. Kayla held her arm around Saika, whose head rested on her shoulder. She wiped her cheek with a handkerchief.

Doctor Kimura walked to the center of the deck, just in front of Captain Quinn. Quinn held out a Bible and raised his hand. "Place your hand on the Bible, and repeat after me." Kimura obeyed. "Do you swear to tell the truth, the whole truth, and nothing but the truth, so help you God?"

Dr. Kimura responded, though the words were inaudible, even from where Darius stood. Don then moved to a position at the edge of the ramp and looked out over the captive audience.

"Doctor Kimura, one of the charges against you is sabotage of government property. Do you know what property this charge refers to?"

Dr. Kimura nodded and Darius could see his lips move, but could not understand the words.

"I'm sorry, Doctor. I need you to speak up. I can barely hear you, so I know our jury cannot."

"They refer to the selection algorithm for Project Columbus," Kimura replied, this time with near perfect clarity. Darius could tell by the strain in his voice that it had been a long time since he had to speak so loudly.

"And can you please describe what it does?"

"It was designed to select passengers for the sleeper ships. It had parameters for many aspects that would need control for initial colonization, including profession, age, marital or familial status, et cetera."

"And who designed the algorithm?"

"It was a collaborative effort between myself, Doctor David Benedict, and two of the initial Project Columbus researchers, Doctors Johann Weiss and Robert Fairweather. Most of the early programming was done by Doctor Benedict, with Doctor Jonathan Fairweather taking over the final work after his father's death."

"And yet you are accused of sabotaging this work?"

"Objection," Fred interrupted. "Asked and answered."

"Sustained," Quinn remarked.

"Very well," Don continued. "After the algorithm was completed, what was the next step, under the Project guidelines?"

"We were required to submit the algorithm to Congress, along with detailed information as to its operation. We were not allowed to populate a manifest without their approval."

"Did you comply with their requirements?"

"Yes," Kimura nodded. "We submitted everything as instructed. It was placed in committee, as expected, but it was debated for five years before it was sent back with an approval, but it had been changed before it came back to us."

"How so?"

"When we began testing the algorithm a few years later, we noticed something very unusual about the citizens it selected. No matter how many times we ran the simulation, an unusual number of Congressmen and their families ended up on the passenger manifest. When we took them out of the equation, we had only around four thousand five hundred colonists, instead of six thousand. And several professions were severely short changed, as well. There were nearly no civil engineers or biological scientists, no culinary workers, and the number of Congressmen exceeded the number of teachers."

"And can you explain why this mattered so much?"

"Enough critical early professions were eliminated or so drastically reduced that we did not believe the colony could survive past the exhaustion of the food supply carried on the ships themselves. The replacement passengers had few or no skills useful for creating infrastructure or cultivating forms of food or resources. Also, many of them were older than our age guidelines, which were put in place to ensure the colony could grow from within by having children on the planet."

"You mentioned that these replacement passengers were Congressmen and their families. Were there any patterns as to which ones were selected?"

"Objection!" Fred growled. "Speculation."

"O-overruled," Quinn stammered after a brief hesitation.

"Yes," Kimura replied. His voice sounded as if it was getting hoarse. "The same four appeared every time. Most notable was Senator Ryan Evans, who sat on a key Senate financial committee during the time the algorithm was under submission."

The crowd began to mutter. Darius could hear bits and pieces from other colonists, registering disapproval of what they were hearing, though he couldn't tell if it was about the accusation or the implications it carried.

"So the program that you *actually* altered was not your original one, but the one that Congress approved after they modified it, correct?"

"That is correct. We restored it to nearly the same parameters as the original. Once our tests showed that the manifest would reliably populate what we projected would be a successful skill set, we returned our focus to other aspects of the Project."

"Thank you Doctor. With respect to the theft of government property, do you know what property you are accused of stealing?"

"Yes. The sleeper ships *Michael, Gabriel, and Raphael.*"

"Why are you accused of stealing them, if their creation was your life's work?"

"Because we never resubmitted the algorithm to Congress for approval. We were in breach of our operational guidelines," Kimura admitted.

"Thank you. And the treason?"

"Is for the same reason."

"That will be all." Don motioned to Fred Hausner. "Your witness, counselor."

Good. Paint the picture for them, Doc.

Fred took the place at the top of the ramp vacated by Don as he turned away. He rolled up the cuffs on his sweater and paused for a moment.

"You and your colleagues launched the sleeper ships in a time of war, correct?"

Once again Dr. Kimura's response was too faint to hear.

"Please speak up, Doctor. For the sake of the jury."

"Yes, that is correct."

"Did you receive authorization from Air Force Space Command to proceed with the launch?"

"No, we did not."

"Did you receive authorization from any governmental agency to proceed with the launch?"

"No, we did not."

"How were you able to get the Air Force crews to comply with your unauthorized launch?"

Dr. Kimura bowed his head slightly. "We had assistance from other officers inside the Air Force. General Andrew McLaughlin issued an order to the command staff of the Project Columbus crews to proceed with launch."

"Did General McLaughlin have this authority?"

"No, he did not. He falsified information to assume command of the crews in violation of the chain of command."

"When you and your colleagues modified the selection program, how many people were removed from the list?"

"Objection," Don interjected.

"Overruled," Quinn replied.

Kimura mumbled an answer.

"I have to remind you to speak up, Doctor."

"Approximately fifteen hundred."

"And these fifteen hundred people, who had been authorized by Congress to join the colony, were instead left behind on Earth, during a time of war?"

"They were replaced by…"

"It's a yes or no question, Doctor," Fred shot back testily.

"Yes."

"Thank you. Nothing further."

Damn it, Darius cursed under his breath.

Sarah Kimura again clutched at his arm. "Oh, Darius," she whispered. "That made him look so cruel."

"Don't worry about it," he soothed. "Doc's a good man, and he did what he did for the right reasons."

Do they see that, though? Doubt seeped in as to whether or not the jury would agree with him.

Don retook his place on the platform. "The defense would like to call Colonel Charles Eriksen."

"What?" Darius gasped. He looked around at the dagger-like looks he received from those near by.

I thought I was supposed to be next? What the hell are you doing calling Eriksen up there?

Gabriel's commander seemed equally perplexed. Even from where he stood, Darius could see the man's eyebrows knitted tightly together as he approached Captain Quinn and was sworn in.

"Colonel, are you in agreement that we are currently on this planet illegally?"

"Yeah." Eriksen crossed his arms and a smug look crept onto his face.

"And you believe this because the ships were launched because of an illegal order stemming from someone involved in the conspiracy to send the ships?"

"Correct."

"Was one of the original objectives of Project Columbus to create and annex an extrasolar colony for the United States of America?"

"Yes it was."

"If we are here illegally, is our mission still valid?"

"Objection," Fred cried. "Leading the witness."

"Overruled."

Eriksen's eyes narrowed and Darius could see him snarl. "We would have to receive confirmation of our mission AFSC."

"Do you or anyone in this colony have the ability to contact them?"

"No."

"Thank you, Colonel, that will be all," Don said, looking over his shoulder as he walked away. "Your witness, counselor."

"That's it, you little shit?" Eriksen blurted out.

"Colonel," Quinn said as he took a step forward.

"Shut up, Captain." He turned back to the attorney. "No more questions? You're just going to leave it there?"

"With all due respect, sir," Don replied with a grin, "I have asked you every question I needed answered. Now if you will excuse me, it's the prosecution's turn."

Colonel Eriksen stood still, glaring at the defense attorney. From his opposite side approached Fred Hausner, though he did not take notice until the prosecutor cleared his throat loudly.

"Colonel Eriksen, without confirmation from Air Force Space Command as to the validity of the Project Columbus mission, do you and the crew operate under the assumption that the mission is valid, or invalid?"

"Valid, until we receive clarification that says otherwise."

Hausner nodded. "That will be all."

Eriksen lingered at the top of the ramp for a moment, then turned away and took a position behind and to the right of Captain Quinn. His brow was furrowed and he shook his head once he settled in. The corners of Darius's mouth twitched as he held back a grin.

That must have burned him up. Let's see what we can do when I'm up there.

Don paced back to the edge of the ramp. "The defense rests."

Darius felt his heart drop and his stomach knot. *What? I'm not being called? But...*

"Very well," Quinn boomed. "Make your closing argument if you will, Mr. Abernathy."

"Thank you." Though dressed in an unexpected manner, Don took an expected pause and paced across the width of the loading ramp. "Ladies and gentlemen of the jury, there is no dispute here about what actions Doctor Kimura took on Earth prior to the launch of the ships. He freely admits to the course of action he and his companions took. This is corroborated by the testimony of Lieutenant Reid, who also spoke freely. Bear in mind that it was the prosecution who called Lieutenant Reid as a witness. Two men giving the same testimony. One for the defense, one for the prosecution." Don wagged his finger in the air at nothing in particular. "Two men, apparently, with nothing to hide. Why is that, I ask myself? The answer comes from the testimony of Colonel Eriksen and the prosecution counsel.

"Colonel Eriksen himself believes that we are here illegally, and thus we have not established a legitimate colony of the United States. On the other hand, Mr. Hausner defined treason earlier today. In his own words, it is to help a foreign government overthrow a government, or to seriously damage one's own government. But how can Doctor Kimura's actions have further damaged a government that is four light years away, that was already in the process of collapse from an extended war that spilled onto its own soil? The government of the United States doesn't exist here. If you have any questions about that, just look at the judicial process that has been laid out before you today. When's the last time you saw a military officer preside as judge over a civilian's trial?"

Don walked away and took his place at Doctor Kimura's side.

I'll be damned.

"What... what does it mean, Darius?" Sarah whispered.

"If the jury agrees, the trial never should have happened," he replied.

"So he's going to be free?"

"He might be, but we're not done yet."

Fred Hausner approached the impromptu stage. One finger was up to his pursed lips, and his head was cast slightly down. His eyes scanned the audience with the scrutiny of a hawk.

"Don't let the smooth words of the defense counsel trick you into casting aside the laws that have governed us since the days of George Washington and Thomas Jefferson. We are a free nation, full of patriots and heroes. Their sacrifice was not made, and their blood not shed, so that we could decide on a whim whether or not threats to our country would be ignored or not. Imagine, if you will, what the US would have been like if Lincoln had let the Confederacy secede after they fired on Fort Sumter. The world certainly would have been different, and almost certainly not for the better.

"We have laws for a reason," he emphasized. "Doctor Kimura admits to breaking these laws. There should be no further thought about it."

Fred paced back from the ramp, ending up against the opposite wall from Don Abernathy. He looked over at his colleague and nodded once.

"The jury is hereby ordered to deliberate on the matter," Quinn announced. "Please report to pod seven. An appointed officer of the court will be waiting outside for your verdict."

Slowly, the men and women at the front of the throng walked up the ramp. Captain Quinn escorted them inside the ship, followed by the two attorneys, and finally Doctor Kimura, Lieutenant Reid, and Colonel Eriksen, whose glare found Darius in the crowd.

"What now?" Sarah asked.

"We wait."

The trek up the short, round hill to the south of the village made Haruka's legs ache. Though the rise was not as high as the one that gave Camp Eight its commanding view of the sea, the incline was a little more sharp. Recent work on the hillside had stripped many of the trees that once shaded its slope, and patches of tilled ground dotted the flanks of the path they walked. Occasionally the path itself was churned up, and the loose dirt would slip from beneath her feet.

"Watch your step," Troy said, grabbing her arm as she was about to tumble forward.

"Thank you."

Haruka scrambled to her feet, rubbed the dirt from her hands onto her dusty flight suit, and resumed the ascent. There was a lingering taste of dirt in her mouth, and after a few minutes, she turned her head aside and spat in an attempt to vacate the offending particles. To her satisfaction, the taste subsided.

They reached the skeleton of a small structure just below the crown of the hill. A small pile of timbers lay in a precarious stack a few feet away from the incomplete, four-foot tall log walls. Posts inside marked the points from which the roof structure would eventually sprout. Haruka walked to the open maw of the front door. Piles of thick green and blue fronds waiting to be turned into roof panels lay within.

Haruka produced a torn scrap of another flight suit from her pocket and dabbed the sweat from her brow. "So what are we looking at for timeframe here?"

"Well, the slope is playing hell with our ability to get the wood up here. It would be easier if we could find one of those pods with the tools in it."

"I know. I have Will climbing every hill from here to the mountains and back. It's going to take time, though. We've only found two pods so far."

"And the workshop one you found was all power tools," Troy sighed. "Two weeks, maybe. That's just to finish the work on the structure. Clearing and tilling the whole hill? That's a lot, and we only have a few shovels."

"I get that," Haruka snapped. "But if we don't get something in the ground and growing, we're going to blow through all the edible plants around the village in just a few months."

"We still haven't tested all the plants around here to know if there are others we can eat."

"We're working on it. In the mean time, we still need to find a way to grow our own crops."

Troy nodded and knocked on the short wall. "We'll do our part. What have you come up with for us?"

"A lot of samples, but I don't know how much of it will take here. I'm sure most of what we've got seeds for will die out here if we even try to grow it. I just hope some of the grains take."

Troy's mouth tightened and he stroked his chin. "That's not very comforting. What if we dig up this whole hill and nothing grows?"

"Then it might boil down to trial and error with the native plants." Haruka shuddered.

Troy cast his eyes down at the dirt and shuffled his foot. The thought that colonists might voluntarily need to eat unknown plants was something that not even Haruka wanted to consider. It was a worst case scenario, but their settlement was months away from the point where desperation might force her hand.

This had better work.

"You know they're never going to buy that, right?"

"It won't come to that," she replied. "I promise."

"Alright." A slow nod accompanied Troy's response. "Are we done here?"

"Yes, thank you."

They turned back down the hill toward the settlement. The sun, though not far above the horizon, still beat on them mercilessly. Haruka paused halfway down to take a drink from her canteen and wipe the sweat from her brow again before continuing on. They reached the path and turned left, where the dead hulk of the sleeper pod rested in the sands. Without a word they entered by way of the frozen ramp and entered the cockpit at the front of the pod. A rancid smell assaulted her nostrils as they pushed open the door. The windows were fogged up from the inside, and black blotches of mold dotted the fabric of the seats. Red flakes of rust could be seen on the edges of most of the metal panels on the control console.

"Wow, this is a real mess," she grumbled as she covered her nose with her mouth. "James really thinks he can make something of this junk?"

"He does. He's not sure how long he can keep it running, though. Maybe an hour. Maybe just a few minutes."

"That's all we'll need, if it works."

That's all we'll need to let the others know we're here.

She stretched her arm out and her fingers brushed the knobs and switches on the radio control panel. James Vandemark was off scavenging equipment from the crashed workshop pod that he believed would bring the dead radio on the craft back to life. His plan relied on generating enough wind power to power the circuitry, but after his first mission to the wreckage of the workshop, he was bursting with enthusiasm.

Dad, she thought. *He'll want to know that I'm alright.*

"What do you think?" Haruka asked.

Troy shrugged. "Leight says this thing isn't worth its weight in scrap anymore. Hell, how many times have the lower levels of the pod been flooded?"

Four.

Haruka shook her head and walked away. "It's better to try, at least."

"Is it?" he retorted. "You've been so stuck on getting Maria to join the work force, but you've taken away James. Call me crazy, but that's not an even trade."

She stopped at the edge of the ramp. She leaned on the wall just inside, and looked back over her shoulder. "It's not a trade. You know as well as anyone that I have to prioritize where resources go. That includes people."

Troy crossed his arms and scoffed. "Fine. You want it blunt? I'll give it blunt. Fixing the damned radio is a waste of time. I'm with you on needing to grow crops, but it would sure as hell make me feel better if someone here knew what would grow, instead of just throwing a bunch of seeds in the ground and praying."

She whirled around and snarled at him, "And what am I supposed to do? Magically pull a farmer out of the air?"

"There had to be some on the ship," he snapped back. "You said the people on board were balanced out. A little bit of everything. So there's got to be someone out there that's got the knowledge we need."

"Even if I knew who all survived, I couldn't tell you who did what back on Earth." She pointed her finger at the open cockpit door. "The computer on this rust heap wouldn't tell me either. I'd need *Raphael's* mainframe to tell you that. Even if we found more survivors, we might not get what we're looking for. And then we're just stretching ourselves even thinner for food."

"What about that other camp that you told me about?"

Haruka lost what little control she had left over her patience. "What about them? They're dozens of miles away, and we have no radio. Unless you're planning on walking all the way there, we have no way to talk to them and find out. And let's not mention how ridiculous that idea is, since we have no clue where exactly they are."

"They know where *we* are."

"Yeah. In case *their* camp fails. I thought we'd be in a better position by now, but I guess I underestimated how deep of a hole we're dug into right now."

"Well, I'd ask you to send out a scout to find out where they are and talk to them, but I guess I know what the answer is going to be."

"That I'd rather have my precious few scouts looking for saws and shovels for you?"

Troy gave her a hard glare for a minute, but then he relaxed his shoulders and nodded. "You're right. I suppose we have to pay for everything we do somehow."

"We do," she said, taking a deep breath to calm her nerves. "So let's make the most of what we have. Come on, it's chow time."

She led him out of the pod and back to the winding path up the hill to the village. They were about to begin the ascent when Haruka heard a rustling in the bushes a few feet off the path, and caught a flash of brown out of the corner of her eye. In an instant she drew her pistol and flipped off the safety.

"What is it?" Troy asked, frozen in place.

"Shh."

Haruka inched forward and trained the weapon on the pepperine shrub. Another flash of brown was visible through a gap in the leaves. She craned her neck and put her foot another step forward. The animal burst through the back of the brush with a squawk, sending Haruka leaping back, her heart pounding.

"What the hell?" she gasped as the animal scurried away in a feathered blur.

"Was that…"

"I think it was." She holstered her weapon.

"I am so going to make the most of *that*," Troy grinned.

"Capture them. As many as you can."

"You don't have to tell me twice."

The animal stasis pod must have crashed near here. How else could that chicken have gotten here?

Calvin McLaughlin
21 April, Year of Landing, 07:45
Two miles west of Michael landing site
>|

"This is nuts," Cameron muttered under his breath as he plunged the shovel into the water and stroked. He had traded his usual flight suit in for a pair of jeans and a white t-shirt borrowed from the wardrobe of another colonist. Without his sidearm or uniform, Sergeant Drisko looked like any one of a dozen young men that you could find in a crowd anywhere on Earth.

The bow of the raft slowly rotated downstream. Cal edged farther forward and dug his shovel into the water over and over, digging hard into the river with his makeshift paddle.

"What part of it? Dayton's plan or trying to cross the river on these toothpicks?"

He checked his balance with one hand as the tethered logs creaked and rocked unexpectedly. Their forward momentum slowed, so they paddled in rhythm. The cumbersome raft moved faster, but was also being carried downstream by the current. They were still two hundred feet from shore, and the flow was clearly too strong for them to make their original landing spot on the far bank.

"Never mind," he grunted as he dug in over and over. "I answered my own question."

There was a ripple ahead in the water, which Cal recognized as something just under the surface. Whether it was a rock or a tree limb did not matter, they needed to navigate around it. Doing so forced them to point their craft even farther downstream. He looked up at the looming gray hull of *Gabriel*.

"We need to hurry up," Cameron said. "We can't let them see us cross."

Cal gritted his teeth. "I know, I know."

The raft neared the bank. Cal scanned the edge of the water for a safe place to set the raft ashore, but they had drifted several hundred feet downstream of the sand bar they had picked out. The shore was dotted with large boulders and snags from felled trees, and the bank rose like a cliff, darkening the churning waters that lay below.

"We have to go farther down, Cam."

"Are you nuts?" he shouted. "They'll see us!"

"Take your pick then," Cal snarled. "They see us or we bash against the rocks and take a swim. Either way you're going to have a bad day. I'd rather be dry than drowned."

Cal didn't let the sergeant make a choice. He thrust his shovel into the water and backpedaled, sending the front of the raft careening downstream. The momentum of the craft and the swift water hurtled them along the river, jostling them and pitching them around. Cal sunk lower onto his ankles and steadied himself as he sought a safer landing zone. His efforts were rewarded with a broad shore of rolled gravel and small stones.

"There," he pointed.

They steered the soaked raft toward the shore and let the river carry them near their new target. They then slowed down with careful maneuvering, and slid onto the shore with a soft crunch. They jumped from the raft and pulled it onto the bank far enough that they were satisfied the river would not carry it away, and then hid the shovels under the slightly elevated front edge.

The bank rose less sharply here, and it was almost devoid of trees. A few feet farther down, the trees disappeared completely, only to pick up again three hundred feet downstream. They were in the open, and an easy target to pick out for anyone who might be watching. Cal reached to his waist, but the familiar bulk of his pistol was not present; Colonel Dayton had ordered them to go to the *Gabriel* settlement unarmed, so as to minimize suspicions as they attempted to contact Darius Owens. The absence of his protection left him with a distinct feeling. Naked.

"Great, we're here," Cameron whispered sarcastically. "Now what?"

"We find Owens."

"Good plan. Know where he is?"

"Not a clue, but I've got a good idea how to find out."

"Oh, that just makes it all better."

Cal crept up the bank and peered over the edge. Stumps marred the ground between the scattered trees, and felled logs were piled up in a wide clear cut, guarded by a pair of bright yellow construction machines. No sign of their operators could be found, so the infiltrators quickly made their way west into the woods and then south toward the encampment. Cal's pulse raced as they covered the ground. He was not sure of how the camp was laid out, or what would happen when they ran into one of the colonists.

Their mission, as laid out by Colonel Dayton, was to infiltrate the

Gabriel camp by any reasonable means and attempt to contact Darius Owens. If such contact could not be made, they were to try to find any possible sympathizers or allies that might be able to relay a message to him. There was a concern that Cal and Sergeant Drisko would be discovered by Colonel Eriksen or someone loyal, in which case they were not to resist.

Not to resist. Just give up.

The uncertainty behind what might happen was deeply unsettling. Colonel Eriksen might simply give them a slap on the wrist and a message for Dayton, or he could imprison them. Even darker ideas dwelt within his mind, but Cal did his best to avoid them.

"Remind me again why I'm here?" Cameron complained as they came around the shoulder of a hill and saw the massive encampment spread out in front of them.

"Because Josephson is still beat to hell, and Dayton thinks the rest of his senior officers would be recognized," Cal replied. "Come on, this way."

Cal turned them toward a low rise just north of the ship where a large tent sat, a long line of people trailing from it like a giant serpent on an equally impressive rock.

"Are you kidding? There's too many people there," Cameron complained.

"Exactly. Best way to blend in. Now act natural when we get there. And shut up if you can't."

"Fine, let's get this over with and get home."

Cal led them into the thick of the camp. He looked over his shoulder after passing each of the first few rows, looking for anyone who might be pursuing them. Though it gave him a momentary sense of being James Bond, he soon realized how ridiculous he must have looked when Cameron smacked him on the back of the head.

"Cut it out, stupid."

"I was just…" Cal sighed. "Never mind."

They then took a meandering route through the sea of green canvas and up the hill, where they formed up at the back of the line. Cal's skin began to crawl and his hands grew clammy. Still, no one ahead of them in line gave them so much as a second glance. A few more colonists formed up behind them, but again Cal and Cameron were given no more attention than they would have expected in the same line back home. The crowd slowly moved forward as breakfast was served to all who waddled through the double file line. The unmistakable odor of reconstituted eggs soon was upon them. Cal put his fingers to his nose for a second to block the stench as his already upset stomach turned sour.

Don't puke. Don't puke.

He was able to hold back, and finally came to the head of the line. A stout man with a weathered face and overly perky expression greeted them with a coffee stained smile.

"Ready for another day in paradise, my friends?" he asked.

Cal took a plate from the neat stack on the end of the table next to the cook station. He smiled and replied, "Every day I live and breathe."

The cook jabbed his long metal spoon into a tray of eggs and drew out a heap, which he slopped onto Cal's plate. "So, are you on detail today, or are you going to watch the trial?"

They're holding the trial? Crap, did Dayton wait too long?

"Don't know yet. We haven't seen our boss today, and I can't find him. Maybe you know where he is?"

"I know everyone, son. Who's your boss?"

Cal took a deep breath as the cook was speaking, trying to settle his nerves.

"Darius Owens."

The cook paused and rolled his tongue around inside his cheek. He nodded. "Yeah, I know where. Come on with me." He turned and shouted to someone behind him who was cleaning dishes. "Karl, I need to step out for a sec. Can you finish up here?"

The lumbering dishwasher took his place at the serving station, and the cook motioned for Cal to follow. He did, with Cameron at his heels. They walked about twenty feet from the tent, and then he stopped and turned around, leaving the two with their backs to the kitchen. The cook leaned around them to take one more look, then his smile disappeared in favor of a snarl.

"Don't fuck around with me, kid," he said in a low, grave tone. "You're not from around here, and you're poking around somewhere you don't belong."

"Back off, old man," Cameron said as he took a step forward. "If it wasn't for the lieutenant coming to us, we'd have stayed on our side of the river. I don't see why it's any of our business to poke around here when your colonel broke his word and left us alone. You guys should have been left to rot."

"Watch your tongue, soldier," he retorted. "He's not my colonel. And Owens isn't an officer anymore. If you'd actually talked to him you'd know how he wanted you to contact him. Give me one good reason not to snap both of your necks right here."

"A bug in the computer," Cal interrupted. The cook looked at him, a twitch of shock cracking the hard façade he wore. "He said he knew of a bug in the computer that would let us leave him messages."

The cook took a step back and nodded. "It's too bad he couldn't tell you why that hasn't worked. Now that I know you're from *Michael*, and not Eriksen's skulks, I can tell you the obvious. Mr. Owens was a witness for the trial, so he's going to be there. I wouldn't go there if I were you, though. Too dangerous."

"Why?" Cal asked.

"Are you hard of hearing or something, son?" the cook growled. "Besides the fact that you two probably stand out like a pair of weasels in a henhouse, Mr. Owens has found out that Colonel Eriksen has stashed away a squad of goons somewhere near the camp. No one has seen them, and no one knows what they're up to. The fact that Darius's contact inside the ship can't account for them scares the living bejesus out of me, and it should scare you too."

"He's right, Cal," Cameron interjected. "We shouldn't be here any longer than we have to be. We know we can't contact Owens directly right now, so it's time to go."

"Just a minute, Cam," Cal said as he laid a hand on his friend's shoulder. "What do you know about the trial? What's happened?"

The cook picked at the food particles that clung to his apron. "Well, I heard that the defense attorney did a complete end run around the law, and is trying to get the jury to basically declare us as an independent nation."

"What good does that do?" Cameron asked.

"If we're not Americans anymore, then we can't try Kimura."

"Smart," Cal commented. "Will it work?"

"If what I've heard around the grill is accurate, he might have pulled it off. Not everyone is happy, though," he sighed. "I've heard a few folks grumbling about how it doesn't matter what the end result of Doctor Kimura's actions were, they're with the colonel; send a clear message."

Cameron shrugged. "I don't care what he did either. I just want to get this over with."

"Then join the other sheep, kid," the cook sneered. "Just because you're Dayton's men doesn't mean you should be any less thankful for what he did."

"I'm not one of Dayton's men," Cal corrected. "And I *do* care. I owe it to my father to do this. Is the trial almost over?"

"Will be today. They should be giving the verdict in an hour or so. See the crowd at the back of the ship?"

Cal looked at the massive sleeper ship that dominated the low terrain. At its rear the ramp was down, and a crowd had already gathered. He estimated around three hundred were already gathered, and more were streaming in by the second.

"That's where it's all been going on. That's where our friend is." The cook crossed his thick arms across his stained apron. "Will that satisfy your commander's curiosity?"

"It will, thank you," Cameron replied.

The cook nodded. "Get out of here, then. Now is not the time for you to be here."

Cal and Cameron nodded and headed down the flank of the hill. Cal looked to his left and watched as the crowd swelled at the rear of the ship. He paused for a moment as he thought about the gravity of what was to happen in just a short time.

The verdict is being delivered today, he thought. *Colonel Dayton will want to know what happened.*

"Come on, let's get back to the raft." Cameron tugged at Cal's sleeve.

"No, we need to listen to the verdict."

Cameron's eyes opened wide and his jaw slacked. "No. No, that's insane. Do you have any idea what kind of trouble you're asking for there? Didn't you hear what that guy had to say?"

"I did." Calvin started walking directly toward the rear of the ship. His heart beat furiously within his chest, threatening to tear him apart from inside. "But we need to know."

Cameron hurried ahead and turned around, walking backward in front of him. "No. We're going back to the raft, now. That's an order."

"You can't order me, Cam."

"I outrank you."

"Only because I have no rank. Who did Dayton put in charge?"

"Are you serious?" his friend whispered hoarsely.

"Yup. Go back to the raft if you want, or stay with me and watch my back. I'm going either way."

"Thanks for giving me a choice in the matter," Cameron grumbled as he followed Cal down the grassy hill.

Darius Owens
21 April, Year of Landing, 08:58
Gabriel
>|

The droning of the crowd around him drowned out the sounds of the planet. In turn, Darius tuned them out to listen to his own thoughts.

So this is what it all comes down to. The plot of the conspirators. The years of hiding. The schemes of Colonel Eriksen. The trial itself. It all comes to an end.

There was no doubt that the trial would be at an end today. The jury had delivered a message to Captain Quinn stating they had a verdict. The revelation spread like wildfire as it jumped from lips to ears in the camp. Each new bearer of the news took it to their friend or neighbor, and in under an hour, there was not a single person left within the camp that did not know that Dr. Kimura's fate was to be announced at nine in the morning.

Some had taken breakfast early in hopes that they could find a spot in the front of the crowd with a premium view of the court stage above. A steady stream had followed, and the base of the ramp had soon been obscured behind a wall of bodies. As he looked around, he estimated that only a couple hundred colonists were not present, mostly children. The crowd still numbered over a thousand, and it fanned out for hundreds of feet in all directions from the ship's stern. Darius had not arrived early, and was near the rear of the crowd, and well off to the side.

Will I even be able to see Doctor K? Or hear what's going on?

Even when he had been at the front of the crowd during testimony, occasionally it was difficult for him to hear. He now had to rely on the lungs of the jury foreperson, as well as hope that his neighbors remained quiet through the process.

The intensity of the whispered gossip increased. Arms in the crowd shot up and pointed to the stage at something just beyond an overhanging bulkhead. Darius craned his neck to see, but could not get a view of anything but the rear of the ship, and an occasional glimpse of Fred Hausner against the far wall.

They're starting.

Darius straightened up and came to a parade rest out of habit. He waited for the crowd to cease its commotion as the seconds ticked by. The noise abated somewhat, but his hopes of being able to hear dimmed.

"Madam foreperson," Quinn belted out, though Darius could barely hear him. "Have you reached a verdict?"

"We have," Darius could just make out the voice of the speaker, though she remained hidden from sight.

"On the first count, treason, how do you find?"

"Not guilty."

The crowd seemed to let out a breath as one. Tension still hung thick in the air, and every eye was fixed on what part of the spectacle they could find. Fred Hausner, the prosecutor, was what Darius fixated on; the dignified lawyer gave no reaction except pursing his lips and bringing a single finger up to them.

That's gotta be eating the colonel up inside. Darius wanted to laugh at the thought, but dared not move.

"On the second count, sabotage of government property, how do you find?"

"Not guilty."

Another sigh of relief came from the crowd, though as he looked around, Darius saw a few colonists shaking their heads.

One more, Doc…

"On the final count, theft of government property, how do you find?"

"Guilty."

Darius felt his stomach tighten like someone had punched him. He opened his mouth and gasped. He was not the only one; others around him let loose similar displays of disbelief. At once gossiping began under the breaths of those around him, and the air was abuzz with chatter. He strained to hear more from the ship. Though he could make out that someone was speaking, he could not hear.

Less than a minute later, the throng erupted into curses and shouting, directed at the rear of the ship. Insults and boos hurtled at the passive, unyielding hull of the ship.

Darius edged forward with his shoulder, tapping the person in front of him. "What happened?"

"I don't know," the man shook his head. He caught the attention of someone in front of him, and repeated Darius's question. Darius waited a minute for the information to come back through whispers in the crowd. An incredulous gasp escaped the man's lips. "The colonel sentenced him to life in a sleeper berth. Both of the lawyers are arguing with him right now."

"Life in a sleeper berth?" Darius gasped. "For theft?"

"That's what I heard." He looked around. "I'd say that it's true, just by the way everyone's looking like they're about to riot. I don't know, man. I don't really think he was guilty of any of it. Not after what the government tried to pull."

A single shot rang out over the screaming crowd. Darius flinched, along with many others. Some shrieked and ducked.

What the hell?

Darius wove his way forward in the crowd to get a better view. He stopped after a few feet as he saw Colonel Eriksen's square form standing a third of the way down the ramp, holstering his pistol.

"It has been brought to my attention," he shouted, "that the sentence for Doctor Kimura's crime is excessive and cruel." He paused for just over two seconds. "It is a serious offense, make no mistake. As such, it should carry severe punishment. I stand by my sentence. Doctor Kimura is to be placed in biostasis and serve a life term. Because he will age only a little in stasis, I am defining life as fifty two years, which was Doctor Kimura's age at the time of launch. No parole will be considered."

Eriksen walked back up the ramp and out of sight. No one moved for a minute after he left, and even then only slowly. They talked amongst themselves and the crowd began to break up. Darius did not move with them; his feet were rooted, and he cast his gaze at the ship as he stood with a slacked jaw.

That might just be worse for Doc than killing him.

He was about to turn away back to camp when his eyes caught a familiar face in the crowd, meandering slowly in his general direction.

No.

Darius checked around him for onlookers and then sidled up to the slender, blond-haired boy and his shorter companion. "What the hell are you doing here?"

The boy startled, and his friend quickly stepped between them.

"We're just on our way out. We needed to see what was going on for ourselves," Calvin replied.

"Was satisfying your curiosity worth it?" Darius retorted in a low whisper. "Now do you understand why you should get your ass across that river as fast as possible?"

"It would be easier if you'd quit drawing attention to us," replied the dark-haired companion, Sergeant Drisko. "We know you're on Eriksen's radar as a threat, so give us some space."

"We couldn't contact you. Why didn't the computer bug work?" Calvin added quickly.

"Because my contact has been working too closely with the colonel to be able to get to the computer."

"Has he turned?"

"No, but he's being watched too closely to do anything."

Calvin nodded. "We'll find another way. Good luck, Darius."

The pair quickly distanced themselves from Darius and disappeared into the stream of colonists leaving the trial. His thoughts quickly returned to the trial, and the consequences of Doctor Kimura's conviction.

Fifty two years in a sleeper berth, he thought. *Sarah might as well be a widow now, since she'll never see her husband again. And Saika…* Darius shook his head and sighed. *That poor girl has got to be going insane. She may never see her father again either, her husband's still facing a court martial, and she's pregnant.*

He turned the corner around the rear of the ship and walked between its hull and the first row of tents in the encampment. The sun was starting to rise over the steel of *Gabriel.* As he walked, his face went from the blinding morning sun into the shadows and back again, and his vision became filled with dancing, phantom dots. Darius rubbed his eyes in a vain effort to shake them off.

At least Doc wasn't convicted of treason. Maybe Mr. Abernathy can find a way to get his sentence reduced, or convince the colonel to let him work it off. Maybe if we approach it as being a death sentence, because the ship's reactor only has another forty years of fuel…

He heard a rustling and footsteps behind him, and knew at once that he was being followed. The crowd had already dissipated. His skin began to crawl as he stopped and turned around. Darius saw the fist swing toward him, but had no time to react as it crashed into his right cheek. He spun around and fell to his hands and knees. A sharp pain burned in the side of his face. He wheeled around onto his butt and looked up.

Major Holden Kintney towered above him, dressed not in a flight suit, but in jeans and a light gray t-shirt. He bared his slightly crooked teeth through a snarl. Dark brown stubble adorned his chin, broken by bare patches just below his cheekbones where the hair didn't grow. His brown eyes flared menacingly as he shook his hand loosely into the air, then rubbed it with his other hand.

"Damn," Kintney growled. "Your head is just as thick as Colonel Eriksen said, Owens. That actually hurt."

Darius turned again onto his knees, intent on running away from the major. He did not make it to his feet, as he saw two more sets of denim-clad legs. He craned his neck upward to find Sergeant Marks and Airman Garza looming over him. Darius slowly rose to his feet and turned to face the major.

"So this is how the colonel is sending messages now?" Darius asked defiantly.

Kintney's snarl turned to a wicked grin, and he nodded once at the men behind Darius. They grabbed his arms and restrained him while Kintney delivered two punishing blows to his abdomen. Darius coughed and gasped for breath.

"I don't need any attitude from you, sympathizer. I'm just giving you a little something to think about."

Sympathizer?

"Yeah, I know, you want me to butt out while Eriksen makes an example of someone. I get it."

Kintney hammered home another hard blow, this time to the left side of his jaw. A stabbing pain shot through his tongue, and the acrid taste of blood filled his mouth.

"Reid isn't an example. He's a traitor. You're pretty close to that territory yourself, Owens. If I had my way, I'd throw you in the damned river and make you swim home where you belong."

"Do it," Darius taunted. "Watch how long it takes him to send someone else after you. Oh, and ask him why after you piss him off. He loves that."

Another hit slammed into Darius's face. His legs buckled, and for a moment he couldn't figure out how he stayed upright. He then remembered the arms holding him back. He shook his head and looked at the major, but his vision was blurred, and he could only make out the outline of his assailant.

"I've got your attention now, right? Good. Now what did you tell your sympathizer friends? The ones that came over from *Michael*?"

J.C. Rainier

"They're not my friends," Darius replied. "And I told them to go home."

"And what about before that?"

"Nothing. This isn't their business. I told them to go home and leave me alone."

"Looks like he's too dumb to understand, boys," Kintney said in a sarcastic tone. "Maybe I should make this simple." Darius saw the blur get larger, and his head was lifted by the chin. He was aware that the major was now in his face, and his rank breath nearly made Darius gag. "Stay away from Reid. Don't try to stop or sabotage his court martial. If you do, I'll take you swimming myself."

Darius was shoved roughly to the ground, where he rolled over onto his back and regained his breath. "I'll get my swim trunks ready," he muttered.

He lay on his back for some time. His body ached and his head felt like a shoe in a dryer. He spat out a glob of red-tinted saliva, and tapped his tongue on his cheek to see how badly cut it was. The taste of iron subsided, and his tongue didn't throb, so he figured that it was not severely damaged. He sat up and looked around at the nearby tents, which came into focus after a minute. No other colonists were around.

Damn it. No one saw that, did they?

He climbed to his feet and made his way for the mess tent, hoping to seek the counsel of either Rory or Don. He stumbled many times along the way. The fourth time he fell, about halfway between the ship's hull and the mess, he was stopped by a familiar voice.

"Didn't I tell you to stay out of this whole Kimura business?" Quinn asked, seething with animosity.

Darius sighed and squared himself to the redheaded brick. "You did. I didn't think you'd resort to this, though."

"I wish I could take credit. This is all Eriksen. Though he does have an interesting way of persuading people, I have to admit."

Darius coughed once as he continued past the captain. "I'm not convinced. Tell Eriksen he'll need to send the major to talk to me again. I didn't quite hear what he was saying."

Calvin McLaughlin
21 April, Year of Landing, 10:01
Michael
>|

"It'll be just another minute, guys," Hunter said. His feet clanked on each step as he hustled down the stairs from the bridge. "Colonel Dayton has been in briefings all morning with field teams and the civil engineering staff. He's just wrapping up his last meeting now and will be ready for you then."

"Busy day?" Cameron sneered mockingly as he leaned up against the bulkhead next to the airlock.

"Sorry, Cam," he replied. "He wanted to see you the minute you got back, but the civil engineers have been arguing with each other and talking his ear off. They wouldn't go until he finished mediating a dispute with the parceling of the planned city."

Only a few moments later, the clank of footsteps rang out from the bridge above. A tall, gray-haired man in a fleece jacket came down the stairs with a stack of papers in his hands, followed by a short, slender, middle-aged woman and a rotund, flannel-clad man with a shaggy beard and receding hair line. Cal watched as they passed, and caught Cameron giving them a dirty look as they exited the crew section of *Michael*.

"Come on up," Hunter said as he beckoned to the bridge.

Cal stretched his weary legs before he walked side by side with Cameron up the familiar stairs. The command chair was facing them, flanked on all sides by abandoned workstations, their screens glistening with the reflection of the mid day sun. Colonel Dayton sat in his familiar seat, rubbing his eyes. As the two approached, he leaned forward and folded his hands in his lap. Cameron snapped to attention as soon as he stopped.

"Sorry for the delay, gentlemen. I'm starting to remember why I decided to go career in the military. Too much bickering and not enough compliance today," he said with a weak smile, waiting for a response that never came. "What do you have to report, Sergeant?"

"Sir, we went over to *Gabriel's* camp as requested. There was something going on over there, and we had a difficult time finding our contact at first. One of the colonists confronted us when we asked about Lieutenant Owens. It seemed that he was protecting Mr. Owens, but once we relayed that we were also working with Owens, he gave us some useful information."

Cameron paused for a moment. Dayton raised his eyebrows and asked, "And that was?"

"That Doctor Kimura's trial had completed, and the jury was delivering their verdict. He also let us know that the situation was too dangerous for us to stay around and risk getting caught." He cleared his throat and gave Cal a cold glance. "But Cal ignored that and went to attend the trial anyway, forcing me to stay with him for his own protection."

"I see," Dayton replied as he scratched at his freshly trimmed beard. "Were you able to get anything from your risky little venture there, Mr. McLaughlin?"

Cal nodded. "It was worth it. Doctor Kimura was found guilty of only one of the three charges."

"Which one?"

"Theft of government property. Colonel Eriksen gave him a life sentence in stasis."

"Life in stasis?" Dayton asked, a confused look creeping onto his face. "How the hell do you define life in a box that basically suspends your life?"

"He clarified it right after, sir," Cameron interrupted. "As being Doctor Kimura's age when they left Earth. I think it was fifty some odd years."

"Fifty two," Dayton corrected. "The command staff attended his last birthday party." He let out a heavy sigh and cast his gaze at the deck plate for a moment. When he raised his head, he had paled, and his eyes were full of sorrow. "Either he's a colossal idiot, or he's found a clever loophole. He just passed a death sentence on Doctor Kimura."

"What?" Cal gasped.

"Colonel's right, Cal," Cam added in a hushed voice. "The ships were loaded with enough fuel to run their reactors for eighty years. Forty or so in space to get here, the rest on the ground to power the colony. The sleeper units will run out of power when the fuel's expended, and they will shut down. He'll choke to death before he can wake up and escape."

"What the hell is he hoping to prove over there?" Dayton mused. He stood up and straightened his flight suit, then walked to the railing between the nav and ops consoles. He looked out of the massive, open canopy at the trees on the far bank of the river. "He's doing everything he can to prosecute and punish the conspirators in his custody. I'm trying to stall the legal hounds on this side of the river and keep Major Forrest from having to face a trial. If they get wind of what Eriksen has been up to, I'll be forced to hold a court martial over here."

"Excuse me for asking, Colonel, but why *are* you delaying a court martial?" Cal asked.

"Because what's done is done. I can't go into the past and reverse what the major is accused of doing. A part of me wouldn't want to, even if I could. After interviewing him, I'm not convinced that he was wrong to do it. But he's accused of a capital crime, and that would mean death if he is convicted. And for what? To exact revenge on him for something done decades ago to a government we're not even sure exists anymore? No, I'd rather have him working to better the colony. Everything that he has done so far has been to that end."

"So has everything that Doctor Kimura has done," Cal retorted. "Look where it got him."

"I know, Mr. McLaughlin. I know."

Silence blanketed the bridge as Colonel Dayton walked slowly back to the command chair and sunk into it. His stare seemed a thousand miles off, somewhere in the distance beyond the ships.

"Is there anything else, sir?" Cameron's voice shattered the tension.

Dayton chewed on his thumbnail for a second before responding. "Did you ever find our contact?"

"Actually, he found us, sir. Sent us packing after the verdict."

"Did he have any insight as to what's going on over there?"

"Not much. Just that his contact hasn't been able to get to the computer to get any of the messages we sent, or send any of his own. He's being watched."

"By that damned clown Eriksen I bet," Dayton growled.

"Yes sir."

"So other than knowing Kimura's fate, we're still in the dark. Just like before."

"Maybe not," Cal interjected. "I heard people talking as the sentence was being given, as well as on our way out through the crowd. I don't think a lot of people were thrilled with Eriksen's handling of the whole thing."

The creak of the command chair swinging around could barely be heard over Dayton's feet shuffling on the deck. "How many people did you overhear, Mr. McLaughlin?"

154   J.C. Rainier

"I don't know, maybe thirty or forty."

"Out of almost two thousand, that's not a whole lot," Dayton sighed.

"Maybe not, but I didn't hear a single one of them agree with Eriksen. And if I could hear that many upset with the decision, there's got to be more, right?"

"Hmm. You've got a point. It certainly complicates things, however."

"How?"

Dayton waved his hand and shook his head. "I'm sorry, I'm getting ahead of myself. Thank you for what you have done today. Dismissed."

Cameron turned and marched down the stairs. Cal followed closely behind, casting one last glance back at the troubled commander as he took his leave from the bridge.

"I don't like it," Cameron remarked as they passed through the airlock into the upper gallery. "This makes me nervous. We should just leave them alone to do whatever they're going to do. It was a mistake for us to go over there."

"Calm down, Cam. It's over now. We're home," Cal soothed.

"Yeah, home," he replied tersely.

Cal put his hand on Cameron's shoulder. They stopped, and Cameron turned around. Cal smiled. "Hey, don't live in the past when there's so much future for us to build. We're home. We have nothing left to do today because we weren't assigned anything else. Go take a walk, skip some rocks across the river or something. Clear your head of what happened this morning."

"I don't know, Cal."

"I do. There's one thing I know for sure tonight, too."

"Huh? What's that?"

"You better bring your guitar with you, or Lexi and Doc are going to be disappointed. Did you forget that it's bonfire night?"

"Ah crap," Cameron cursed. "I forgot. I've been looking forward to it for a week."

"Well then, it's a good thing I reminded you," Cal said as he slapped his friend on the back. "Lexi can be pretty vicious when she doesn't get what she wants. I've probably just saved your hide. Literally."

"No joke." Cameron managed a wry grin.

As they climbed down the ladder to the lower gallery and made their way down the length of the ship, they exchanged memories of the first few days and nights on Demeter. They got onto the topic of Hunter and his management of the colonists, recalling a story about a particularly difficult architect who refused to get his hands dirty around camp, and how Hunter tricked the man into setting up tents by giving him a band of clueless teenagers to oversee in the task. Cameron burst out laughing as he recalled the shade of red that the architect had turned as he futilely showed the youths how to erect the tents, then gave up and set them all up himself.

Cal squinted for a brief second as he emerged from the dark belly of the ship with his friend at his side. The midday sun burned overhead, wrapping his bare arms in its warmth. The slightest breeze blew from the river, bringing with it the smell of the cramped camp mixed with coffee and fish from the kitchen. He took a deep breath and drew in the scent, exhaling from his mouth.

Cameron walked a few steps and then stopped. He raised his hand to shield his eyes from the sun and turned to Cal.

"I'm going to go up to the farm and do a little pest control. Maybe come up with something else special for tonight. You coming, man?" he asked.

"No, I'm going to grab something to eat and say hi to Lexi."

"Alright. See you later then."

They exchanged a quick fist bump before departing ways. Cameron headed away from the river toward the skeleton of a building on top of a low rise, about a kilometer from the aft loading ramp of the ship. Cal trod the familiar path up to the three tall canopies that marked the kitchen. The grass along the shoulder of the hill had been trampled by countless feet grinding into the dirt. A narrow path of bare, packed dirt now marked the way he followed.

Cal formed up at the rear of a modest line of pioneers seeking their lunch, and in moments others joined in behind him. He slowly shuffled his feet as the line inched forward, and was rewarded a few minutes later as he reached the first tent. Cal picked up an enameled metal plate and a fork as he stepped inside.

Gail, the cheerful middle-aged woman charged with running the entire kitchen, threw a raw fillet of river trout onto the grill in front of her. It hissed and sizzled as the heat began to sear its thick skin. Gail carefully laid a few sprigs of a native plant across the top of the fish, then looked up and smiled at Cal. With a nod, she used a long metal spatula to cut a portion from a cooked fillet resting on the other side of the grill, and slid it onto Cal's plate. As he passed through the second station, a similar flourish of culinary skill was displayed by Roy as he worked on a hash of native potatoes and spices. Cal collected his portion and carefully hoisted and settled an enameled cup full of steaming coffee onto his unsteady plate, then walked around to the back side of the kitchen.

Alexis sat at a folding camp table in a matching folding chair. Her eyes were firmly fixed on her work scaling and filleting a pile of trout that the camp's fishermen had provided. She did not notice Cal approach, nor did she notice when he pulled up another chair and sat down, careful not to drop the scalding drink into his lap. He took a bite of fish from his plate; the flaky white flesh melted in his mouth, and the native herb used in its cooking gave it the slightest hint of mint.

"You can tell by the quality of the fish, and the simplicity of its preparation, that this restaurant is so…" he paused and twirled his fork in the air grandly. "Unique."

She startled for a moment and looked over her shoulder at him. A grin spread across her face before she turned back to her work. "You're such a nerd."

Cal chortled under his breath as he began to work on his meal. Alexis beheaded, de-boned, and filleted three fish as he took several bites and downed most of his coffee.

"So I didn't see you this morning," she said, slicing into another trout.

"Yeah, sorry. I had a job to do this morning that took me out of camp."

"Well, at least it didn't take you far. Did Hunter find you something good to do today?"

"Not Hunter. Colonel Dayton."

Alexis set her knife down and quickly wiped her hands on a dingy towel. She cast her legs to the side of the seat and her green eyes fixated on him. "Dayton? Why would he be giving you work?"

"It's a long story," he replied as he shoveled a forkful of potatoes in his mouth.

"Well, I want to know," she insisted.

"Don't worry about it. It's over with."

Alexis stood up and swung the chair in front of Cal and sat down to face him. The smile had disappeared from her face, and her eyebrows arched slightly. "I'm not going to stop worrying until you tell me what it was."

Cal paused and set his fork on the plate. He realized that telling her as much about the job as he had already let on was a mistake, but he had already broached the subject. Alexis was privy to much of the gossip of the settlement, and she was not clueless about its operations, either; she knew that Colonel Dayton only gave tasks either to his crew or to colonial department heads. Cal was neither, and to deceive her would be futile.

"Fine. The guy we fished out of the river the other day was supposed to exchange contact with us through a coded method. We hadn't heard from him, so Colonel Dayton sent Cam and me across the river to find out what was going on. We found him, but we also found out all kinds of messed up stuff that's been happening over there, too. We just finished briefing Dayton on it."

"My God, Cal," she gasped. "Are you nuts? Everyone on both sides of the river is paranoid. Do you know what they'd do to you if they caught you?"

"But they didn't," he cut her off. "And it's over. I did what he wanted, and now I'm done."

Alexis rose to her feet slowly. "You're not done, are you?" she asked, just barely audible over the rustle of the canvas canopy.

"I did what he wanted. I'm done."

"And if he asks you to go back?"

"I don't need to. Darius should be able to communicate with us again soon."

"And if he can't?" she shot back.

Cal chewed the last bite of fish pensively and washed it down with the last of his coffee. "I've come face to face with all kinds of nasty shit on this planet, from reaper bears to some old dude in the other camp that wanted to break my neck. I'm done with that. Colonel Dayton's just going to have to send Cam alone if he needs someone to go back."

"Promise me you'll stick to that."

He gained his feet quickly and took her fishy, greasy hands and looked into her eyes. "I promise. I'll go on pest patrol at the farm if that's what I need to do, but I stay here with you."

"Thank you," she said with a slight grin. She leaned in and gave him a gentle kiss on his cheek.

"I'm going to take a nap and then come back to help you in a bit, okay?"

"Help?" she asked, cocking her head to the side.

"Yep. We've got to get you out of here early tonight so we can go to the bonfire. I figure I can scrub dishes to help."

"That would help a ton." They kissed before she returned her seat to its position and resumed her duties. "Remember, dishes on *this* side of the river, mister!"

"Damn," he chuckled. "I guess I won't be seeing my other girlfriend tonight then."

Haruka sipped on the spicy tea steeped from pepperine leaves as she rubbed her throbbing, fatigued right leg. Her back ached from a restless night sleeping under a thin, gnarled, spider-like tree near the empty husk of the sleeper pod. The particular species of tree had earned the name "vinewood" because of the way its trunk resembled a woven tangle of pepperine plants. Unlike the towering palm trees, they provided good shade without the threat of seed pod bombardment from high above.

Troy stood aside her on the glittering white sand of the beach, just outside of the long shadow cast by the palms as the sun crept over the eastern horizon. With one hand shielding his eyes from the glare, he surveyed the activity of three new wooden fishing canoes on the water. A gull with a full beak cackled and swooped low, gliding onto the top of the sleeper pod and landing with a clatter. Two more joined in short order, and an argument of squawks ensued over the first gull's meal.

"Looks like those canoes are paying off," Troy remarked. "They can go farther out. They look stable, too; not going to roll over in the surf."

"One problem down, a thousand more to go," Haruka muttered into her tea as she took another sip, then emptied the enameled steel cup onto the sand with a flick of her wrist.

She raised her head as she heard the clank of footsteps on the deck plating within the pod. James emerged from the dark maw, wringing a tattered blue rag with his dirt-caked hands. He took long strides as he walked down the sand covered ramp, and he bore a wide, toothy grin.

"If I you could lend me a hand, Troy, I think I've got it worked out."

Troy grunted and shook his head, but walked to the rear of the pod and followed James. Haruka kept her distance a few feet behind. She sidestepped a long, rough wooden pole about four inches in diameter, and leaned against the bulkhead just outside of the cockpit as the two men entered.

"So I knocked out the top glass on the far side here so we can tilt it up and out," she heard James say from the other side of the wall. "Then we should be able to seat it, and I can get up top and rig some sort of sail. It should turn the generator and slowly charge the batteries I wired up in the upper hallway."

"What about keeping the water out?" Troy asked.

"Already ahead of you. I've got a couple leftover roof panels from the village to cut down on that. It won't be perfect, but we should be able to keep the electronics dry. The batteries are upstairs, the roof is still sealed, and even those damned mega tides can't get up that high."

"Alright."

Troy emerged from the cockpit and stopped at the end of the pole. He gripped the end and lifted it slightly off the floor. The pole lifted high on the front side as James lifted and guided it from inside the cockpit. After a moment, Troy walked back into the cockpit with the bottom portion, and Haruka peeked around the corner to watch them affix it to the generator with salvaged cargo straps. Another two sets of crisscrossing straps were run just under the roof of the cockpit to stabilize the pole and limit horizontal movement to either side. Haruka stepped into the doorway and admired the work.

"So this will really generate the power we need to run the radio?" she asked.

"Not directly, no," James replied as he checked the fit of the pole's base. "It doesn't make enough to run it real time. The radio will still run on batteries. This just charges the batteries."

"How long will it take to charge?"

"I think about three days for every hour you want to run the radio."

"If it even works," Troy interjected dourly.

James looked up through the missing glass and tapped the pole with his hand. "It'll work. We'll be able to talk to the other camp again. Maybe, if I can boost the signal a bit, we'll catch a break and get one of the other ships on the line."

The other ships, Haruka thought. *Dad.* She pursed her lips and took a deep breath to check the excitement that was building within her. It had been too long since she had spoken with her father, and the idea that in a few days' time she might be able to hear his voice again did more to lift her spirits than anything else since the refugees crashed on Demeter.

"Well, I've done my bit to help with this nonsense," said Troy. "Back to work on something that's actually useful."

Haruka's brief moment of elation came crashing to the ground with these words. Troy brushed past Haruka as he marched purposefully down the pod's main hallway. He disappeared down the ramp into the bright blur of the beach sands. James took a few short steps into the hallway and shook his head as Troy left.

"Ignore him," he said. "This will be worth it in the end."

"I hope so. I hope this hasn't been for nothing."

"I wouldn't have done it if I didn't believe that we could get the radio back. I know how much time I've invested in this, and how much that has taken away from my duties in the village. Thank you."

"For what?"

"For letting me see it through. And for picking up the slack in my absence."

Haruka paused for a moment to collect her response. "I didn't really pick up any slack. There wasn't any to pick up. You've done such a good job making everyone understand exactly what they're supposed to do that they just do it. All that's been left is to collect reports."

"You don't have to butter me up, Captain."

She sighed and began to walk toward the rear of the craft. "I don't pander. It wouldn't do either of us any good. Not out here."

Haruka squinted as she emerged from the hulk into the bright morning air. She glanced over her shoulder briefly to make sure that James did not follow, and then made her way to the village. Other colonists, old and young alike, greeted her as she ascended the hill. She returned smiles, but was lost in thought.

Letting James work on the radio was a huge gamble. Troy still disagrees with my decision. I'm starting to think he's right. Troy's disagreed with me before, but never like this. Not to the point of getting snarky about it. Now I have to just hope that I was right.

She reached the curtain that sealed the entry of the clinic and reached for it. She paused for a moment with one lingering thought.

Or find a way to make a huge improvement in the village.

She swept aside the curtain and stepped inside. The familiar straw beds along each wall greeted her, along with Dr. Petrovsky's makeshift table at the rear of the room. The front of the clinic was quiet. Haruka had to strain to hear any sign of habitation over the rustle of the curtain.

"Hello?" she asked softly. "Doctor Petrovsky?"

Gabi walked around the partition wall in the rear. She rubbed her eyes and clutched her worn stuffed cat to her chest. Gabi blinked as she regarded Haruka, and then smiled and skipped up to her, throwing her arms around Haruka's legs and hugging her.

"Good morning, Gabi."

"Good morning!"

"Is the doctor around?"

Gabi shook her head.

"What about Emilia?"

"No, she's with Mama."

Checking on her, no doubt. It would be nice if she took Gabi with her instead of just leaving her alone.

"Do you know when they're going to be back?"

Gabi shook her head again.

"Have they been gone long?"

The corner of Gabi's mouth twisted upward, and her eyes darted upward as she thought. "Yeah. Mama told me to stay here and that she'd be back in a few minutes, but I really don't know when she's going to be back. Do you?"

"No, sweetie, sorry. I haven't seen her. Is it okay if I wait here with you until she gets back?"

Gabi smiled and nodded. Haruka took a seat on one of the beds, and the young girl bounced down next to her on the mattress. She rolled over and pretended to fly her cat through the air. Gabi paused for a moment, flat on her back with her arms sticking straight up in the air holding the animal, and gazed quizzically at Haruka.

"Why do Mama and Emilia want to get rid of you?" she asked.

Haruka's jaw dropped, and she stopped to run the question through her head again, unsure that she had heard it correctly.

"What do you mean?"

Gabi rolled her shoulders in a shrug and sat up. "I keep hearing Mama and Emilia talk about how they want to get rid of you. I don't know why they want that, but they won't tell me when I ask. Mama just gets really angry and yells at me to go away."

Haruka grabbed Gabi around her midsection and gave her a hug. "I'm sorry, honey." She paused for a moment and asked, "Do they talk about this around you?"

"Sometimes. Sometimes they talk about other stuff."

"What do they say when they talk about it?" she pried.

"I don't know. Mama doesn't like you anymore, I guess. Emilia says you need to stop bossing people around."

So this is about me pressing Maria into the workforce, then.

"Does this mean Emilia doesn't like you either?"

"No, sweetie. I think she just doesn't like some of the things I say. It's normal for adults to disagree," Haruka smiled weakly.

And stab each other in the back, apparently.

"I guess Doctor Petrovsky doesn't like what you say either," Gabi added.

Haruka blinked twice and her smile began to crack. *The doctor too, huh? Well, that's an easy way to get rid of me, isn't it?*

"I guess. I need to go talk to James, but I don't want you to stay here alone, okay?"

"Can I come with you?" the girl's brown eyes widened and lit up.

"Sorry, sweetie. He's working on the pod, and it's too dangerous for you to go there. I'll find someone who can play with you, alright?"

Gabi's shoulders slumped and she let out a loud, dramatic sigh. "Okay."

Haruka took Gabi by the hand and led her down the path to the beach. Gabi filled the time by singing several of her favorite nursery rhymes and skipping down the path, then running back to Haruka when she got too far ahead. When they reached the shore, Haruka found Gina Bryant watching over a small herd of children, and left Gabi in her care. She then quickly made her way to the cockpit of the sleeper pod, where James was making adjustments to his palm frond water barrier, where the broken canopy window once was.

"Look, Captain," he began when he saw her, but she cut him off.

"We need to talk. And we need Troy, too."

Darius dipped his arm low to the side and whipped it forward. The smooth stone shot from his hand, arcing slightly upward before it slammed into the surface of the river with a loud slap. It bounced upward and began to tumble end over end, and when it landed on the water again ten feet away, it broke through the surface and sank at once. He muttered under his breath about angles, and then stooped down to pick up another rock. Darius winged it over the river, and was rewarded by four skips before it plunged beneath the river.

Much better.

He brushed the dirt from his hands onto the leg of his jeans and began to walk slowly along the river's edge. A movement on the opposite bank caught his eye, and he looked up to watch. Over the course of the previous month, a five-hundred foot section of the bank had been cleared of trees. Darius could see two large stacks of rough-hewn timbers, likely harvested from elsewhere as the native trees that lined the river were far too short and thin to have produced such stout logs. One of *Michael's* bucket lifts hefted a timber into the air and drove to the end of a line of support poles. Three men followed the machine on foot and guided the pole into the ground, where they then buried the base. He scanned the tops of the poles and found where the power wiring ended near the construction site, but none of the supports appeared to be at the right height or position to extend the line.

I wonder what they're building.

As Darius continued along the river's edge he glanced up the steep bank beside him at a matching clear patch of ground created by the colonists of *Gabriel*. While Darius was part of the team that brought power to the river's edge, the other work crews had stopped almost a week earlier, and the plans for industrial buildings along the river's edge had stalled.

Another casualty of Eriksen's crusade.

He tried to push aside the lingering animosity he felt toward his former commander. Darius focused again on the far side of the river. This time, he picked out a short hill beyond the sleeper ship. Its round top was barely visible over the bank from where he stood, but he could clearly make out a building taking shape near the top. The hill was the deep-brown color of plowed earth, and tiny specks moving about on its face told Darius that the fledgling farm was active. He paused to think of what crops the colonists had planted, and if other fields had been tilled in the gently rolling hills beyond.

Yet every thought Darius had of the other colony led him back to *Gabriel*. The other colony was building along the river, but *Gabriel's* leadership had stalled development of the equivalent structures in the planning phase. While both sides of the river had fields tilled and planted, it concerned Darius that there were only three distinct crops that had been planted: corn, wheat, and onions. He wasn't about to question this decision, however, as Colonel Eriksen had appointed two of *Gabriel's* crewmembers to oversee farm operations. His last run-in with Eriksen's subordinates had not gone well for Darius; though difficult to distinguish from the surrounding flesh, he could see the outline of his black eye when he examined his reflection in the river.

I doubt that Colonel Dayton has ordered his men to beat the shit out of someone for disagreeing with him. Darius shook his head and flung another stone into the river. It sank without skipping, but he barely took note. *I also doubt that he's devoting so much time to crucifying the conspirators. That McLaughlin kid is proof enough of that.*

Darius had played Major Kintney's words over and over. They haunted him in his sleep, and lingered through the day like a whisper deep within his ears. Even as he scaled the bank and made for the camp at a brisk pace they came back to him. It didn't take Darius more than a couple hours to figure out why he had been labeled as a "sympathizer," or what that meant. Calvin McLaughlin seemed to be the key to that.

He thinks that Colonel Dayton is part of the Project Columbus conspiracy. He believes that Calvin McLaughlin serving on his crew before the landing instead of being in custody is proof of that, as Doctor Kimura said that the boy's father was a key figure in covering up their tracks. He sighed heavily. *And now I'm lumped in with them because I voiced my opinion that we should band together with them. Not because I'm in league with them, but because I thought we should follow the mission guidelines.*

From what he knew of the crew of *Michael*, Darius did not believe that they were part of the conspiracy. Major Forrest had been placed under arrest as ordered. Doctor Fairweather died in transit to the planet, a victim of the assassin's stasis disruption algorithm. The idea that, assuming he *was* part of the conspiracy, Dayton would kill one of his own was ridiculous as it was, but Darius knew that the assassin had been on board *Raphael*.

But the dead can't talk, and the secrets of the killer burned up with the ship.

"Darius!" he heard a shout from his left as he neared the camp. He looked up the hill toward the kitchen tents, where he spotted Rory Baines. He was in a near sprint coming down the hill. Rory's apron flapped loosely at his side as he ran forth waving his arms in the air and calling out to Darius repeatedly.

Darius paused and waited for the old cook to catch up. Rory doubled over and wheezed for a moment. "Rory? What's going on?" Darius asked.

"Where… where the hell have you been?" he gasped.

"By the river. Why?"

"Eriksen… Miller said…" Rory had to stop as he panted.

"Miller said what?" Darius began to feel his stomach knot.

If Roger talked directly to Rory… in broad daylight…

"Court martial. Eriksen is holding Reid's court martial today."

Darius muttered a curse under his breath. "Did he say where?"

"On the ship. Forward part of the lower deck."

"Damn it. Why didn't Don tell me about it?"

"He probably doesn't know," Rory replied. "Hell, I just found out from Miller. He only figured it out because Fred Hausner passed him a note as he boarded *Gabriel*."

Darius arched his brows. A note was a bold, desperate move on the part of the attorney. "A note? What did it say?"

Rory outstretched his hand with a folded scrap of paper tucked neatly between his middle and index fingers. Darius took it as he watched the expression of his companion. Rory normally had a cheerful demeanor, but the only hint of emotion was a twitch at the corner of his mouth. This reaction made his blood run cold. Darius could not shake the feeling that Rory was close to doing something extreme. He cringed as he imagined how that might manifest. Darius pushed aside the thought and unfolded the rough edged scrap, torn from the pages of a sketchbook.

HAVE BEEN ORDERED TO DEFEND LIEUTENANT REID TODAY. WASN'T GIVEN TIME TO PREPARE OR REVIEW CASE. HELP. UNDER DURESS.

Duress. No preparation. He couldn't win a fair trial, so he's rigging the court martial.

Darius crumpled the paper into a tight ball. His fist squeezed so hard that the tiny mass pressed into his skin, leaving marks after he shoved the paper into his pocket. For a minute he stood frozen with his eyes locked onto the hull of the ship, as if he could tear a hole in it with his gaze and expose the fraud within. Then he began to run.

"Wait, Darius! Where are you going?" Rory called after him.

"Keeping a promise," he shouted back as he picked up speed.

"To who?"

My mother, he answered in his mind.

His long strides took him around the outskirts of the sprawling tent city. His first stop was well known, and he picked through the last row of tents to the canvas abode of the Abernathy family. The back side of the tent, which normally was flanked by a field of grass and short shrubs, was instead surrounded by dozens of young children, sitting in the field and hanging on every word that Don Abernathy spoke as he read from a book. Darius slowed only enough to keep from tripping over a young boy as he approached the attorney.

Don removed his glasses and looked directly into Darius's eyes. "Can I help you, Mr. Owens?"

"You need to come with me, please."

"I'm in the middle of a class here," he said as he swept his glasses in the direction of the children.

"Sorry," he said, pushing through his short breath. "It's an emergency."

Don paused for a second, nodded, and closed the book. He turned to the class and spoke. "One moment, children. I need to go, but your story will be read to you in a few minutes. Just wait here."

He walked with Darius to the front side of the tent. "What's this about?" he whispered abruptly.

"Eriksen is court martialing Reid today. No warning. Fred Hausner might be in danger, too."

"Damn it. Where?"

"On the ship. Let's go."

Don's arm shot out and caught Darius's elbow as he turned toward the rear of the ship. "Wait, how do you expect to get on the ship? Surely Eriksen will have guards ready to arrest you if you show up."

Darius nodded. "He will. That's how we get in." Don gave him a puzzled look. "C'mon, one more quick stop to make."

Darius did not let the attorney deliberate on the matter. He jogged along the side of the hull toward the rear of the ship. Just behind the rearmost cargo pod he found his entry plan, right where he expected to find them. Novak and Barajas were at work assembling the reactor-grid interface module that would serve to transfer power from *Gabriel's* reactor to the colony. Barajas leaned over the edge of the lift bucket, high above the ground, as he adjusted a line connection on the transfer port. Novak sat in the cab of the lift with his hands on the controls, ready to move his partner at a moment's notice.

Darius came to a stop at the cab's door and gently rapped on it. Novak startled, and his hand hit the controls, which dropped Barajas about three feet. Barajas let out a high pitch scream and ducked into the bucket.

"Bloody hell, Owens," Novak grumbled. "I should knock you upside the head. Though hearing Barajas scream like a girl was almost worth…"

"Shut up and come with me, both of you," he interrupted.

"This is getting out of hand, Mr. Owens," Don said, his voice raised slightly. "Leave them out of this."

"Out of what?" Barajas asked as his hard hat and eyes became visible over the edge of the lift.

"Reid's in trouble. Eriksen's rigged the court martial so he doesn't stand a fair chance," Darius replied.

"Your friend? The kid with the pregnant wife?" Novak asked as he lowered the boom lift and jumped down from the cab.

"Yeah, that's him."

"That's some real shit that the colonel's pulling," Barajas barked. "What do you want us to do?"

"Now, guys," Don tried to stop the infuriated construction workers by stepping in front of them. "I don't want to see you get involved in anything…"

"No offense, Mr. Abernathy," Novak cut him off. "Hats off to you for what you did for that doctor during his trial, but this Eriksen guy is really pissing me off. I'm with Barajas. What can we do for you, Owens?"

Darius patted Don on the back and nodded, and the attorney stepped aside. "They're expecting me to show up. You guys hide at the side of the ramp and rush them when they come to take me."

"You got it, boss," Barajas grinned.

"Let's do this," echoed Novak as he jogged ahead of Darius. Barajas joined right on his heels, and Don hurried behind, uttering a protest that did not slow the strides of the group.

When they approached the rear of the ship, Darius pulled up and let his two muscled cohorts slip under the massive bells of the main plasma drive. Don stopped next to him and opened his mouth to speak, but Darius silenced him. They waited for a few minutes, with Darius reminding the attorney every thirty seconds or so to be quiet, as the man protested several times.

"Now!" Darius whispered hoarsely and stepped from his obscured position at the side of the ship. He moved at a casual pace to the end of the ramp, where he glanced up to confirm the presence of guards. His skin began to crawl and his lip curled when he caught sight of Major Kintney at the top of the ramp, crossing his arms across his broad chest, a wicked smiling snarl contorting his lips. He was flanked on either side by the cronies that helped deliver his recent beating, Marks and Garza.

"Owens!" Kintney bellowed as he started to walk down the steel incline. "We knew you'd try something. Just didn't think you'd be so stupid as to stroll right up here like this."

Darius squared himself toward the major as Don bowed his head slightly and shuffled three steps back.

"If you knew I was coming, why'd you wait for me?" Darius replied, forcing his voice to carry the distance. "Why not just come and beat me again when no one's looking, like last time?"

Kintney raised one arm in the air and motioned forward with his fingers. His companions took a few steps into the hold of *Gabriel* and knelt down to lift something.

"Sending a stronger message this time. Couldn't do that with what I had in mind."

Sergeant Marks marched forward in lock step with Garza, dragging a bloodied and nearly limp body dressed in a stained flight suit. The victim raised his head slightly as he was being dragged down the ramp, regarding Darius with the one eye that was not swollen shut. Darius clenched his fists as fury ripped from deep inside.

Roger! Damn them...

They threw him at Darius's feet. Marks delivered one last kick to the ribs of the defenseless Lieutenant Miller, then the pair calmly walked back to the ship. As they did so, Barajas and Novak came charging out from the side of the ramp. Darius quickly shook his head and motioned to his former partner. The construction workers slowed, then changed their course to tend to their beaten fellow, as Darius knelt in the grass to do the same.

"You just don't know when you're beaten, do you, Owens?" Kintney said with a mocking laugh.

"It's about doing what's right, Major."

"I expected as much from a sympathizer. You're a nuisance. You have no idea what kind of damage you're doing to the mission."

Darius glanced to either side and noticed a small crowd start to form near the flank of the ship. Colonists of all walks timidly shuffled into a circle, watching the spectacle with eyes wide and mouths agape.

"Damage?" Darius scoffed. "Don't talk to me about damage. Colonel Eriksen has done way more than I ever could. This insane crusade of his…"

Kintney cut him off with a snarl. "There's nothing insane about upholding the law."

"Not true," Don Abernathy belted out as he stepped in front of Darius. His voice, though well projected, was calm and smooth. "There is no justice done when the law is upheld through illegal means." He turned and addressed the gathered crowd. "Inside that ship, a man is fighting for his life in a trial without proper representation. He was denied that by Colonel Eriksen. Can any of you out there tell me that's just?"

"It's a court martial," Kintney snapped.

Abernathy turned again to face the imposing major and his small entourage. "Then tell me which member of *Gabriel's* crew is qualified to present a competent defense in a military court? There are still rules that your commander must follow in order to properly conduct the trial. He hasn't done so."

Grumblings began to rise from the gathered colonists as they began to quietly debate Don's presentation. Major Kintney's jaw shifted from side to side, and Darius could swear he heard grinding teeth over the din. The major then looked over his shoulder, and moved to the side of the ramp with his cohorts as Colonel Eriksen appeared from the lower gallery of the ship. He was flanked by Fred Hausner and Captain Quinn, whose heads were lowered and their shoulders stooped. Quinn caught Darius's gaze, and his lip curled upward, baring his teeth.

That can't be good.

Eriksen stopped at the top of the ramp, allowing the attorney and engineer to pass him as they shuffled their way to the grass below. He scanned the growing crowd with a look of shock.

"What's going on here?" he shouted.

"You tell me," Darius retorted as he pointed to Roger, who held a rag to his nose to staunch its bleeding. "You need to explain to us all why you sent Major Kintney to beat the tar out of Lieutenant Miller here. Or why you had them do the same to me just after Doctor Kimura's trial."

"Or why you denied Lieutenant Reid proper representation at the court martial you were just conducting inside the walls of *Gabriel*," Don added. "Restricted walls within which no civilian may step without *your* explicit permission."

The colonel shot a wilting glare at Kintney, who simply shrugged as he leaned casually against the inner hull. He straightened his flight suit and picked a point in the throng of colonists, avoiding contact with Darius.

"I've tried to keep this silent, for the good of the colony," boomed Eriksen. "I've given my former lieutenant more than enough chances to stop his destructive and subversive behavior. I've even allowed him to live and work in the colony, despite his insistence on trying to break it apart from the inside. But I can't ignore it any more. Not once I found out that he had been using Lieutenant Miller to record and report on confidential military conversations."

A few gasps rose from the crowd, and the hum of the rumor mill started to take on a chaotic pitch.

"I didn't have him record anything, Colonel," Darius shouted. "It was your own carelessness that caused that conversation to be recorded. He came to me because he was concerned about what you were doing. But he didn't want to stand up to you, because he saw what happens to people who do so."

Eriksen leveled his cold gaze at Darius. "You seem to be good at sowing dissent, Mr. Owens. I'm regretting not locking you up and putting you on trial as well. Not only did you turn Lieutenant Miller, you also got to Captain Quinn. He had quite the outburst a few minutes ago during the proceedings."

"Me? What the hell did I do? I've barely said twenty words to him since we landed."

"Unlikely. Listening to his insubordinate tirade reminded me of one I heard from you on the way down to the planet, Owens. Tell me again how you had nothing to do with that." Eriksen cleared his throat and addressed the crowd once more. "I'm trying to be reasonable with Owens and his sympathizers, whose allegiance clearly lies elsewhere. I have no more recourse at this point. For the sake of showing fairness, I'm going to give these men one final decision to make. Lieutenant Roger Miller and Captain Tyler Quinn are hereby stripped of rank, and shall take Darius Owens with them across the river to the other colony by sunset, never to return. If they choose not to take this option, I will have no choice but to have each of them arrested and tried for their crimes."

What? he said to himself as he gasped. His stomach knotted in an instant, and his head began to swim. The crowd's level of agitation grew again, but the tones were muffled by the sounds of his own shallow breaths.

"As for the matter of Lieutenant Reid," he continued, addressing Abernathy directly. "He was represented properly, by an officer with legal training."

"Who?" the attorney challenged.

"That information is a confidential military matter."

"And I suppose the verdict and his fate are confidential as well?"

"No. Because his crimes are against our government, all have the right to know. Lieutenant Brandon Reid has been found guilty of treason, and will be sentenced appropriately."

"You mean death," Don shouted, his voice beginning to lose its calm.

"That is correct," Eriksen replied coolly.

The crowd erupted in shouts, but Colonel Eriksen ignored them, as he retreated to the steel confines of *Gabriel* with Kintney, Garza, and Marks hot on his heels.

So pretense is everything, I guess. A tour of the farmhouse, she thought. *Believable. At least as long as we don't keep using the same excuse.*

Haruka relaxed and leaned her back against the inner wall of the skeletal farmhouse. She stretched her legs in front of her, then rubbed her throbbing calves. The fatigue of the hike began to fade as she waited for James to join their meeting.

"Maybe he just got hung up," Troy muttered as he peered through the open door frame. "Should I go find him?"

"No, we need to wait for him."

"What if something happened to him? What if they found out?" Troy's shoulders tensed up and he started to pace along a very short course on the packed dirt floor.

"What if?" she replied dismissively. "It's not like they can do anything to him. Maybe complain or start rumors."

"I'd be worried about rumors if I were you. If what I've heard is true, the villagers actually fear you."

"Fear me? Why?"

"Because of how you handled Carney," he replied. "Execution in full sight of everyone. No trial."

"Tell me how we would have handled one, and where we would have put him."

"I'm not the one you need to convince."

A loud crack of a snapping branch pierced the air, and both Haruka and Troy jumped. Her heart pounded in her chest and she scrambled to her feet, but her alarm was quickly relieved as James stepped into the hut from outside.

"Damn it, James," Troy berated. "You scared me half to death."

James rolled his eyes. "Sorry, next time I'll knock."

"Very funny."

Haruka rose and dusted off the legs of her flight suit. "Everything okay, James? You're late."

"Yeah, I was just testing the radio in the pod to see if it would work."

"Anything?" she asked. Though everything in the pod seemed to have been permeated by either salt water or condensation, deep within she still held onto a glimmer of hope that she might one day be able to talk to Saika again.

"No, sorry. I'll have to do some troubleshooting to find out where the problem is."

The glimmer became just a little less bright, now only the barest flickering flame in her mind. She sighed heavily. "Alright, let's get to this then. Have you guys found out anything about what Gabi said to me? About Maria and Emilia wanting to replace me?"

"Like I was telling you," Troy spoke before James had a chance to open his mouth. "There are some people down there that are scared. That whole Carney situation has them shaken up."

"I know that wasn't ideal, but I did what I had to do."

"I know that. He was dangerous, desperate, and in the middle of town square. But what happened has really made an impression. I heard a story about a guy who's worried about what you'd do if he took an extra meal ration."

"A story about a guy?" she asked. "You didn't talk to him yourself?"

"Well, no, but…"

"Then it's just someone's exaggerated opinion. The thought of someone having to worry about that scenario is just… I don't know how to describe it."

"I'd be interested to know if someone actually feels that way," James added. "We're talking about a group of a half dozen or so people here who want to see someone else in charge of the colony, but are afraid to challenge you directly, question you, or call for elections. Something like that could grow if it's being ignored, or if someone's fueling the fire from within."

"A half dozen? Do you know who else is with them? I mean, besides Doctor Petrovsky."

James nodded. "A couple of them, anyway. George Dormer and Mark Reiber. No surprises there. I've been very careful about how I've been doing this, to try to keep their suspicions down, so I haven't heard directly of any outside of that circle. Though I'm a little concerned when it comes to someone close to us."

"Close to us?" Haruka frowned. She did not want to consider that one of her trusted colleagues might be in on any plot against her. Yet curiosity spurred her on. "Who?"

"Seth."

She swallowed hard and took a step back to lean against the coarse wall. Sergeant Leight had, despite his early resistance, become trusted to her. He had a knack for pointing out viewpoints counter to her own, and helping her understand them.

No, not Seth. It can't be.

"Are you sure?"

James shook his head, a signal that gave her both relief and pause at the same time. "It's really hard to read him right now. He's keeping his distance pretty well, which makes me think that something's up. You know he's not a good liar, so I wouldn't be surprised if him avoiding us is his way of covering up. Or he could just be so buried in his work that he's oblivious to the whole thing."

"So why don't you ask him?" Troy asked.

"Are you kidding? If he's working with them, we'll have blown any cover that we have. He'll tell Maria and Emilia, and then our job of keeping an eye on this will be three times as hard."

"Seth's a really straightforward guy. If he's not part of it, he'll come clean. Maybe even help us."

"Yeah, *that* would be a good idea," James mocked. "I can just see him now standing outside the Palace, polling everyone who walks by as to whether or not they want to overthrow the Evil Queen Haruka. That'll help."

"You got a better idea there, Vandemark?"

"Yeah, keep doing what we're doing. Maybe start joining people for lunch and listening to conversations."

Troy groaned and folded his thick, tanned arms across his chest. "We really suck at this, don't we?"

His companion sighed, and a nervous laugh came out. "Yeah. Sorry, Haruka. You probably want to find guys better suited to the task."

"You're fine for the job," she shrugged.

And I can't trust anyone else, so you're stuck with it.

"Any ideas?" Troy asked.

"Maybe. Two parts. Don't talk to any of the kids about it. Gabi was the one who clued me in to begin with, so any of the others would probably gab about it if you two started poking around there. The other is Jenkins."

Troy and James exchanged glances. "What about him?" James

asked.

"I know that Will has worked a lot with him during scouting. Can you see if Will can get a read on Jenkins? Don't tell him to do anything else yet, but if we know what side he's on, we might have a way to get a clear picture of what Seth's thinking without tipping our hand."

"I haven't told Will about what's going on yet. Are you sure you want me to do so?"

A little gamble, but I need as many leads as I can right now.

"Yeah. Just make sure he doesn't talk to anyone else about it, okay?"

"Got it."

"Good. Now on to the life and death stuff. Have we found a survivor who knows anything about agriculture?"

Troy's stubbled cheeks stretched wide open as he smiled. "A whole family, if you'd believe the luck. Wheat farmers from Kansas. Good folk, too. I'd love to introduce you to them when we get back to town."

"No. I'm not going to meet them there."

His smile faded and his eyes widened. "Captain?"

"I'm going to meet them here, in their new home. Bring them here to take a look around."

Troy stood still for a moment, then exhaled loudly, shook his head, and laughed. "You had me going there for a minute. I can be back with them in an hour."

"Take James with you."

They nodded and turned to go.

"And bring some seeds with you, too."

Darius hunched low as he scurried from one row of tents to the next one closer to the river, careful to make sure his head did not rise above the peaks of the shelters. He held up for a moment and waited for Miguel Barajas to scan left and right down the next row of tents. Barajas then glanced back and signaled for Darius to advance again. He did so, nearly tripping over a rock jutting out of the ground. The dark of night shrouded the entire encampment. Few lights remained lit over the entire span of the temporary colony; most had gone to bed over an hour earlier.

"We're almost there," Barajas whispered. "Then we get you and Quinn to your hiding spots."

"We've got to stop this, Owens," Quinn complained as he caught up to Darius. The former captain was slowed by the laborious task of helping Roger Miller, who could not walk on his own.

Darius's eyes fell to the dirty white cast that immobilized the broken bones of his friend's leg. He imagined for a moment the satisfaction he might feel from returning the favor to Major Kintney. The injuries that he and his subordinates had inflicted on Miller made safe crossing of the river impossible.

"You got a better idea, Captain?" he replied, only remembering after he spoke that Quinn no longer bore the rank.

"Yeah, getting the hell out of here like we were supposed to. Not sneaking around the camp trying to hide from Eriksen and his cronies."

"Roger can't swim, and we can't just leave him here."

"That's your mess, not mine," Quinn shot back. "And you still managed to drag me into it. Why couldn't you have just listened? Everything would have worked out."

Darius turned to face his former superior. "Not for Doctor Kimura it wouldn't have. Now I don't know what kind of man you think I am, to expect that I wouldn't at least try to save a friend. Not to mention a man whose life's work allowed us to even be here. Alive. Far from the War."

"And so you had to make Brandon pay for it instead. But you screwed that up and now they're both fucked. We are, too, if any of the crew finds out we're still here."

"So leave, then," Darius snarled. "Go across the river. They'll take you in over there and you'll be free to live the rest of your life knowing that you left us to the wolves."

"I could care less about you at this point, Owens. You're poison."

"Fine. I can't argue with that. But you're still leaving Roger out to hang, and he's done nothing but try to help *both* Doctor Kimura and Lieutenant Reid. I hope the coffee over there is strong enough to wash that down every single morning."

"Stop arguing," Barajas hissed. "Do you want to wake up the whole damn camp?"

"Maybe that would be better," Quinn replied nonchalantly. "At least it would be over with."

"You're a selfish prick, dude," Barajas grumbled. "I'm out here risking my ass trying to save yours. Now shut up and move. We're almost to Clara's tent."

Clara, Darius thought. *Just an ordinary colonist, with nothing to do with me or Eriksen. Her husband is out with an exploration party, and she's willing to risk taking Roger in so he's safe for the night. Risking whatever wrath the colonel might bring down on her.*

Quinn opened his mouth to protest but Darius and Barajas moved down two rows without a glance back, forcing the disgraced officer to hurry along with them. They then turned to the right as a group, and moved to a cluster of tents about a hundred feet away. One tent glowed softly like a beacon in the cool night; the light of a single lantern within cast a diffuse glow through the fabric. Arion was slowly traversing its arc overhead, yet the full, dark moon did little more to illuminate the landscape than the beckoning lantern, and it would still be hours before Persephone was expected to rise.

Barajas led the group to the tent and pulled the flap aside. Inside the modest canvas abode, a small child rested in a sleeping bag, sound asleep. Her mother lay at her side, stroking her hair. She greeted the men as they arrived. Barajas motioned to an empty sleeping bag on the floor. It was square and pristine, as if its owner took the time to lay it out anew every day. Darius grabbed Miller's arm, and with Quinn's help, settled the injured man into the bed.

"Thank you, Clara," Barajas grinned. "We'll have him out of your hair before you know it."

The woman smiled back, and as Darius's companion closed the flap to the tent, she extinguished the lantern. Once more the men were enveloped in the mantle of the night. Far in the distance an eerie howl rose as a pack of native night predators heralded the start of their hunt. Darius had heard of the species, but not encountered it. From the description, he was thankful for that; they were essentially giant weasels that could glide between trees and swoop from above to attack.

Darius shook off the image of an aerial surprise and followed Barajas deeper into the camp. They twisted their way back toward the ship, and then again astern. This time the shelter that awaited them was not lit. Barajas opened the tent, and Darius and Quinn crawled inside, groping in the dark to find their respective bedding.

"Stay low, okay guys?" said Barajas. "Novak will try to wake you guys before dawn so you can get out. If you can't, keep a low profile and make sure no one is around."

"Where is he, anyway?" Darius asked.

A whisper from the dark next to him nearly made Darius scream in surprise. "I'm right here. Try not to wake the neighbors."

"Be safe," Barajas added as he closed and secured the tent flap.

Darius settled himself into the sleeping bag and tried to get comfortable on the cold, hard ground. Once he got a feel for the slope and irregularities of his patch of earth, he shifted again and finally found a balance that didn't threaten to have his back in knots come morning.

"Once I can see the other bank of the river, I'm gone," whispered Quinn.

"Good for you," Darius replied in kind. "Good to see you've given up just when you're needed most."

"Given up? God damn it, it's over. Kimura's in stasis. Brandon's going to be executed tomorrow. We're fugitives as long as we're hanging around, and you're saying I've given up? Just what the hell are you expecting to do for your grand finale there, Owens?"

Honestly? I don't know. It's not like I planned any of this, you know.

"I'm going to make a stand. Make a difference. Maybe even stop the execution."

"What?" Quinn choked. "After all that you've done, you're going to go back for more? Kintney's going to rip you to shreds."

"Seriously, man," Novak whispered from the darkness. "What do you think you could do at this point except get yourself killed? Colonel Eriksen was pretty clear about wanting you gone, and that major sounds like one psychotic fuck."

"Eriksen thinks I'm good at turning people against him. Really, it's just the way he's been carrying on that's the problem." Darius folded his hands behind his head and looked straight up. His eyes could not see the canvas just a couple feet from his face, but it seemed like he could see into the soul of the colony. Images of a colonial mob hurling insults and raising their fists in defiance coursed through his mind. "I know I'm not the only one that sees it. All they need is a little push."

"Who?"

"Everyone. The whole colony."

Quinn released an exasperated sigh. "Well, at least now I know you're nuts. That makes the decision to leave you here a lot easier."

"Then don't stay and help me out. Stay for Lieutenant Reid instead."

"By doing what?" The distress in Quinn's voice was apparent as he escalated beyond a whisper. "I don't know how many times it has to be explained to you. If we go back there, Eriksen will have us arrested. Or worse."

"Shhh," hissed Novak. "Keep it down."

"I don't care anymore," Darius replied. "I made a promise to help Doctor K, no matter what. I'm still standing, so I'll keep fighting."

"Yeah, you've really been doing a good job of talking Eriksen out of things. Keep it up."

"Maybe you could make a little more noise," Novak interjected.

Darius paused for a second, confused. "What do you mean?"

"Do you remember how Eriksen got control of the crowd after the doctor's verdict?"

Darius could not form an immediate response. The prospect of using fear tactics to counter the colonel made his stomach churn and his skin crawl. "You don't mean..." He paused. "No. No weapons. No way."

"You don't stand a chance without at least something."

"He'll have me shot on sight if I'm armed, Ivan. Besides, I'm not going to play at his level. If I have any chance at all of getting the colonists to demand his resignation..."

"His resignation?" Quinn snorted. "You think he's going to resign if the people get upset? He's still got all the weapons."

"Not all of them," Novak amended. "The scouts all have arms. So do the hunters, farmers, and some of the foresters."

"You're not serious," Darius uttered in unison with the former captain.

"Fine. Just don't say I never offered to help."

"Thanks, but I can't do that."

A couple minutes passed in suffocating silence. The tips of Darius's fingers flexed as he expected one of his companions to voice a further objection or idea, but only the feral sounds of distant alien wildlife filled his ears.

"If you change your mind," Novak's whisper cut the silence. "There might be a crawler at the edge of camp tomorrow that someone accidentally left unlocked. And there might possibly be a rifle or two carelessly left inside. Just saying."

"Give it up, Novak," Quinn replied. "He's too bull-headed to take you up, and I'm gone before sunrise. Thanks for finding us a place to bunk, but it's over."

Darius swallowed and clenched his teeth as quiet descended once more inside the confines of the canvas. After a few minutes he began to hear the snores of his companions on either side of him, and he knew that he was alone with his thoughts. He settled his nerves as best he could and tried to formulate speeches and arguments to anything that Colonel Eriksen might say. He knew that timing was key, and that Lieutenant Reid's life counted on Darius being able to incite the passion of the colonists before the execution could take place. After racking his brain for a half hour, he sighed and gave up.

Quinn is right.

The colonial camp was vacant. As they stole between tents to avoid detection, Cal realized that he and Sergeant Drisko were alone in the expansive sea of triangular canvas. Laundry on makeshift lines flapped in the gentle breeze, waiting for the rising orange sun to warm them up. Scraps of trash rolled lazily down the rows. But there was no human movement at all.

"Something's wrong here," Cameron muttered under his breath. "There should be *someone* here. I mean, where the hell did they all go?"

"Beats me. They didn't pack up and move, though. That's for sure."

"I don't like it. We need to get out of here."

"Not until we get what Colonel Dayton sent us here for."

"You mean Darius?" Cam laughed nervously. "Sure, point him out, let's get him, and go."

"Come on, they have to be around here somewhere. Let's get up on that hill over there and look," Cal replied as he pointed to a brown rise just on the far side of the sleeper ship's stern.

Drisko's lip curled and he marched away toward the target without a word. Cal followed a few steps behind. They reached the hill a few minutes later, and found that it had been tilled almost completely from top to bottom. A pair of horse drawn plows rested near the top, where the work had been abandoned. The parched earth revealed that the work had been done some time ago, but seed had only been planted in a few areas.

"What the hell have these guys been up to?" Cal asked. "Are they going to leave their fields open forever?"

"Why don't you ask Colonel Eriksen when we run into him?" Drisko sneered.

Cal shook his head and ignored the sergeant's demeanor. He bounded over empty rows of tilled soil. With each step, the question of why kept repeating itself, growing ever louder in his mental refrain.

Have they found more edible native plants? If not, they really need to get a move on.

As Cal trailed his friend up the broken, dirty hill, he noticed a bulge in the beltline of Cameron's jeans. A glimpse of dark steel caught his eye as a gust disturbed his shirt.

"What the hell?" Cal growled as he bounded up to Drisko's side. "Dayton said we were supposed to come unarmed. Just like last time."

"Then next time he can come out here himself. Last time was bad enough, but this shit's just too creepy."

"You know I'm going to tell him when we get back."

"Good. Maybe he'll stop sending me on these insane errands of yours."

"C'mon, this is important. I wouldn't have snuck out here without Alexis knowing if it wasn't. Do you have any idea what she'll do to me if she finds out that I broke my promise and started working for Dayton again?"

Cameron wheeled around as they reached the crest. His coal-black eyes were wild and full of fire. "You're not a kid anymore. Dayton expects you to man up, and part of being a man is accepting the consequences of your actions. Remember that when she kicks you in the nuts tonight."

Cal felt himself flush. He shook his head and turned away from his friend, biting back the scathing rebuttal that he wanted to deliver. Instead he took several deep breaths and began to survey the land beyond *Gabriel*. What he was searching for did not take long to find; hundreds of colonists were gathered in a mass near the edge of a solitary grove that loomed between two small rises, just over a kilometer away.

"There," he pointed and started down the far side of the hill.

"Wait, you're just going to charge right in?" Cameron complained as he hurried alongside.

"Going to take a look first. If they're gathered to watch something, we should be able to slip in like last time."

"Ugh. Here we go again."

They traversed the gap in the brush-pocked terrain in just over ten minutes. As they drew near, Cal confirmed that the colonists had indeed gathered to watch something, though a quick estimate told him there were only around a thousand present. Conspicuously absent were all of the children that he had seen the last time they had arrived in the colony.

Where are the kids? And the rest of the adults?

The crowd stood in a wide, deep arc, looking part of the way up one of the rises. At the point where the collective stare gathered, Cal could make out several men in flight suits. One knelt on the ground with a blindfold around his eyes and bindings on his wrists. Three more stood at attention, twenty feet downhill, facing the crowd. Each one had a rifle slung over their broad shoulders, and if not for the difference in their heights and hair styles, Cal might have thought his eyes were playing tricks. One final figure paced back and forth along the contour of the hill as he addressed the crowd in a grand speech. His frame was even more square and thick than his nearby cohorts, and his neatly trimmed red hair and beard were marred with streaks of white.

"Colonel Eriksen," Cameron whispered, standing stiff as if suddenly gripped with paralysis. "Shit."

Cal pulled his friend into the crowd and maneuvered forward to where he could hear what *Gabriel's* commander had to say.

"Don't think that I take this lightly," Eriksen's stern voice carried easily over the distance. "This is not a show of force or retaliation. Lieutenant Brandon Reid was convicted of treason. Treason against the government and people of the country he swore to protect. Treason against all of you. This execution is not because we cannot contain a criminal; as you have seen, Doctor Kimura has been placed in stasis for his crimes. Treason is a capital crime. There is only one punishment that we can give. For that, I'm sorry."

"And you're still full of lies," a deep voice belted out from near the front of the crowd. "You still stand in front of us and tell us your excuses for persecuting a man whose only crime was to save the lives of almost everyone here."

"Darius Owens," the colonel boomed as he folded his arms across his chest. "This, ladies and gentlemen, is exactly why coddling the traitors cannot be tolerated. Mr. Owens was once a trusted officer of mine, but he has become corrupted by the idea that grave crimes can be dismissed with a simple apology and swept under the rug. He threw away a promising career by constantly undermining what we're trying to build here on this world. And by staying, he's thrown away his freedom, too." Eriksen turned to the trio of officers and barked, "Major Kintney, please take Mr. Owens into custody."

"Yes, sir," the barrel-chested man in the middle replied with a smart salute. He handed his weapon to one of his companions and began the march down toward the crowd.

Darius clamored to a higher vantage point, and his head and shoulders became visible above the crowd. He turned his arms out in appeal and shouted, "Look at what's going on here. All I've ever done is talk. Words and reasoning that have fallen on his deaf ears. This man is so vindictive that he is willing to have me arrested in front of all of *you*, because I have the audacity to speak against him." He glanced in the direction of the major, then turned to face Eriksen. "I've never said anything bad about you before today. I have had nothing but the utmost respect for you as a commanding officer, sir. But this is all wrong."

"Take him," Eriksen snarled.

Major Kintney sprang and tackled from whatever high point he had gained, and both hit the ground with a thud. The crowd reacted with a collective gasp, and bodies began to mill about.

"He's not a threat," Darius called out. "His wife is pregnant. Please, think about what you're doing."

A high, shrill voice rang out from near the front of the crowd, cracking in panic. "God damn it, listen to him! Brandon never hurt anyone!"

"Shit, we need to get out of here," Cameron whispered as he tugged at Cal's arm.

"I need to see what's going on," he protested.

"Our mission's over. They've taken Darius. Come on."

Cam and Cal turned to make their way from the crowd, but the riveted audience paid no mind to their urgent need for flight; they stood fixated, and the pair from *Michael* had to press through to get anywhere. They did not get far before conflict flared up again.

"Let them go, Colonel," shouted yet another man from the edge of the crowd, just below where Eriksen's officers stood. Cal craned his neck to see over the mass of humanity, and caught a glimpse of a tall, young, and very muscular red-headed man in a filthy flight suit. "You have to stop, for the good of the colony."

Eriksen's scowl briefly changed to a look of surprise before his features hardened again and his lip curled. "Tyler Quinn. That's two renegades. You going to bring out Miller next?"

"Let them go," Quinn repeated firmly.

Eriksen paused for a moment, and for that short span of time, the tension in the air seemed to draw the collective breath out of the nearly thousand people present. Though he could make out what looked like the edge of the crowd, Cal found his movement hampered even further by the enraptured throng. He gasped for air as the blue sky and gray hull of the ship taunted him from far away, their safe haven beyond his reach.

"Marks, take Quinn."

"Yes, sir," one of the subordinates shouted. He rested one of the two rifles that he carried against a rock, and then started toward Quinn in a deliberate march, leveling the weapon at him. The red haired man stood firm, with his chin held high.

"Garza, carry out your duty."

"S-sir?" the last subordinate on the hill stammered.

"Execute the lieutenant," barked Eriksen.

"No!" shrieked the woman in the crowd, echoed a split second later by Darius.

Garza hesitated for a moment. He looked at the defenseless prisoner, and then back to his commanding officer. Colonel Eriksen's face turned a nearly infernal shade of red; even from where Cal stood, he could see the shade grow darker.

With powerful, long strides, Eriksen covered the gap to Garza in just three seconds. He snatched the rifle from Garza's grip and jabbed him in the gut with the butt, causing the young man to crumple into a writhing, coughing heap.

"No more," Eriksen bellowed at the top of his lungs. "No more questioning my authority. This traitor dies!"

From the corner of his eye, Cal caught a movement, and his head swiveled just in time to see Tyler Quinn take a side step and rip the weapon out of Marks's hands and deliver a punishing blow to the jaw with the stock. Marks staggered and dropped to his knees, reaching for his face. Shrieks rose from the crowd near Quinn. Cal felt the throng press against him, and Cameron slipped away as two women pushed into Cal, knocking him backward.

"Cam!" he gasped and shot his arm out, reaching for his friend as the shifting crowd enveloped him.

"Cal!" his friend called back, but Cal could not see him anymore.

A single shot pierced the air, and what little order was left in the crowd evaporated. In an instant, Cal was thrown to the ground. He crawled underneath a prickly blue-green bush to avoid the dozens of pairs of feet that trampled the ground where he had initially fallen. Shouts and commands were hurled between the combatants, and only seconds later the air was filled with the deafening reports of gunfire.

Though it was only a few seconds, it felt like an eternity to Cal. With each boom, he tried to curl farther under the bush. Throwing his hands over his ears and closing his eyes did nothing to quell the fear that rose as the battle ensued. He yelped as a hand clamped on to his wrist and yanked. His eyes opened to reveal Cam kneeling next to him, dragging Cal with one hand and wielding a Beretta in the other.

"Come on," he shouted. "Let's go. This way."

Cal stumbled to his feet and willed his legs to move with all their strength and speed as they crouched low, running across the nearly empty field that just moments earlier acted as Eriksen's makeshift amphitheater. A few dozen colonists lay scattered on the ground. Most who were unfortunate enough to be caught in the middle were on their hands and knees scrambling away. Others lay flat and pressed their hands to their heads.

"Get down!" Drisko yelled, and shoved Cal from behind as two eruptions of dirt darted up from bullets striking the ground a few inches in front of them.

He hit the ground hard, just behind a sizeable boulder. He winced from a sudden pain that shot through his left wrist. Loud reports ripped through the air as Cam discharged three rounds, and others echoed from farther away in response. Cam dropped to the ground next to Cal, though the thump was barely audible over the ringing in his ears. Cal inched his body to the left until his side touched the hulking rock, and did his best to draw his legs in so they were not exposed. Cam dragged himself slowly next to Cal.

"Shit," Cal muttered as he shook.

"Cal," his companion whispered. "They got me."

Cal rolled to his other side and his heart plummeted. Cameron's face was drained of color, and he drew his hand from his chest, completely soaked in blood. His shirt was awash with the red liquid, and a river began to pool on the ground in front of his stomach.

"Oh, fuck, Cam," Cal shouted. He rolled the sergeant onto his back, tore his own shirt off, and pressed it into the gushing wound.

"So... cold..."

"Fuck, stay with me, Cam!"

Drisko's eyes rolled back to attention, and he coughed. "Get out... get out of here. Leave me," he choked through a glob of blood that stained his teeth red. One hand rose to his chest, and he pressed the Beretta into Cal's grasp. "Go."

Cal shook his head vehemently. His vision blurred from tears, and a lump in his throat kept him from uttering a sound. He cast the weapon aside and doubled his efforts to stop the bleeding, even as he fought back both rage and anguish. The gunfire subsided, and shouts, screams, and warnings from across the battlefield could be heard. Cal drowned them out; his singular focus was on comforting his friend and tending to the wound. But the injury was too serious, and Cameron expired after a couple minutes of wheezing and gagging.

"No," he sobbed as he shook Cameron's limp shoulders in disbelief. Tears welled up in uncontrolled torrents and he began to sob softly.

No. No, no... fuck... no! Why?

He wiped his eyes as a moment of numbing calm washed over him. Cal looked over his shoulder as he slowly rose and wiped Cameron's blood off on his shirt as he surveyed the scene. Those who had been caught in the open or taken cover had gained their feet, and were carefully picking their way away from the carnage.

Lieutenant Reid lay in the arms of a slender, raven-haired woman, his bindings still fast around his wrists. The woman wailed as she held his lifeless body against her, and another woman clutched the first from behind, also in tears. Colonel Eriksen writhed in the green grass a few feet away, staining the verdant blades with his blood. Garza and Marks sat on their knees next to *Gabriel's* commander with fingers interlaced behind their heads in surrender. The red-headed hulk, Quinn, hobbled behind them, training his rifle alternately between the two men, while occasionally glancing at Eriksen.

Cal stumbled his way to the boulder and clamored to its top, still reeling from the shock of the sights that he took in. Darius Owens squatted in the grass, rubbing his massive hands – one of which clutched a pistol – over his shaven, ebony scalp. He made eye contact with no one. Major Kintney's body lay in repose within arm's reach of Owens, staring blankly out into nothingness through dead eyes. Three holes in his flight suit, ringed in drying blood, testified to his demise. A few brave souls moved from person to person, checking wounds and tearing clothing to serve as impromptu bandages.

Cal glanced back at his slain friend again, and in an instant the calm that held him together was washed away as his rage boiled over. He shouted an obscenity at the top of his lungs and kicked a foot over the top of the boulder. The outburst garnered the attention of several around him, and even Darius glanced up to find the source of the disturbance.

"What the fuck is wrong with all of you?" he screamed. He clutched his blond hair, marring it with the blood of his fallen friend. "He's dead. My friend... he's dead, because of all of you. Because you couldn't figure out how to handle your shit without it coming to this."

Cal watched as Darius rose slowly, looking down at the weapon in his trembling hands. His fingers splayed outward as he looked down at them, and the Beretta slipped from his grip, tumbling to the ground. Marks and Garza regarded him, captivated, and Quinn lowered his rifle, hesitating for only a moment.

"Whatever this stupid quarrel is, I don't get it. I don't get why that man," he continued, leveling his index finger squarely at Colonel Eriksen, "couldn't have just followed the plan and landed on the north side of the river with us. He had agreed to it, and then broke off at the last minute. Cameron. Oh, God, Cam." His voice began to waver, and a tear rolled down his cheek. Cal took a moment to regain composure. "He told me once that the three commanding officers had some sort of feud back on Earth. After *Raphael* blew up, Colonel Dayton tried to put all that aside and make amends, and look what happened.

"I'm just a kid from Texas. I don't really know what any of this shit is about. I don't care what any of it is about either, and neither should any of you. All I know is that none of us can survive on this planet alone, and that we're only going to pull through if we work together. That's why Cam and I came today; to try and help put aside whatever differences tore the two crews apart. And here we find that you can't even keep your own crew in one piece."

Cal looked down at Cameron. He began to feel hatred for the colonists on this side of the river, and how they could possibly be this indifferent as to who led them that such a situation could possibly arise. He choked back more tears as he turned once more to the slowly gathering crowd of survivors.

"Was it really worth my friend's life for you to figure out that you have a problem?" His eyes shot skyward and he laughed nervously. "God, none of you here are fit to lead anything. No one took action until it was too late." Then Cal leveled his gaze at Darius. "Except for him. He knew something was wrong. And when you all failed him, he did something about it. He came to us for help. You should listen to him. He gets it."

Cal regarded the anonymous crowd coldly before sliding down the far side of the rock. He returned to his friend's body and knelt beside him, drawing his eyelids closed with two fingers.

"I hate that I have to say this," he whispered, "but I can't thank you enough. You... you saved my life. I don't know what I did to deserve that, not after I dragged you out here." Cal picked up the Beretta from the ground and engaged the safety, then tucked it under Cameron's hands as he folded them over his chest. He sighed, and finally let the

J.C. Rainier

sorrow pour from within him.

I should have listened to you. I should have let these people rot. Then you'd still be here, and they'd have gotten what they deserved.

Cal felt a heavy hand fall gently across his shoulder. He wiped the tears from his eyes and glanced over to see Darius Owens kneel next to him. The man's deep brown eyes were full of sorrow, and he nodded once.

"I'm very sorry, Calvin," he spoke softly. Cal nodded and continued to grieve as the colonists slowly filtered their way back home.

Emilia ticked off the seconds in silence as she held her patient's wrist between her fingers. Gabi's mother ran her free hand through her tangled black hair, waiting for the nurse to finish the task. Gabi watched with impatience, rubbing the pale patch of her arm that had been removed from its cast earlier in the day. She eyed Emilia as she tended to her mother.

Nearly every day either the nurse or Dr. Petrovsky would check on her mom, and then they would talk for a while. She didn't always understand what they were talking about, and often drifted in and out of the conversation as she tried to find ways to amuse herself. Other times she would tune in and listen as long as she could before boredom sat in. This usually happened when they were talking about her friend Haruka. Today's conversation was on a much more boring subject, and Gabi found herself hard pressed to occupy her time.

Why isn't Mama done yet?

"Mama, I'm bored."

Gabi threw her arms across her chest and curled her lip into a pout. Her mother regarded her with a terse, blank glance over the shoulder.

"Not now, Mija." She went back to her hushed conversation with Emilia.

"But you promised," Gabi whined.

Her mother snapped back, "I said not now."

The stern glower that stared back at Gabi cut into her, mixing fear and deep disappointment. Her lip began to tremble, and a feeble cry rose up from inside her. She turned away and dropped onto her lumpy bed of leaves, burying her face in the verdant weave. Her sorrowful wail grew in volume as she unleashed her tears.

Gabi waited for her mom to comfort her. The warm, soft touch that silenced the fearful questions within was all she wanted. She cast hopeful glances at her mother as she sobbed, but got no reaction; only Emilia paid her any mind. The nurse glanced up every time Gabi unburied her face to look, and after a few minutes, came over to her.

Emilia curled her arm around Gabi's shoulder and knelt next to her on the bed. "Gabi, honey, can you play by yourself for a few more minutes? I'm almost done with your mom."

"But Mama promised she'd play a game with me!"

"I know. I'm sorry." Emilia flashed a kind smile, but Gabi knew that this particular smile was one that Emilia used when she was trying to change the subject. "It'll be just a moment."

Gabi jerked her shoulder free from the embrace and bolted to her feet. She lashed her hand out as she pulled away, raking a weak slap across Emilia's face. Emilia's eyes and jaw widened in shock and horror.

"Leave me alone. I hate you," she blurted. In an instant, Gabi's mom rose up and spun to face her.

"Gabi!" she shouted, covering the ground between them before Gabi could do any more than flinch. Her mother's face was disfigured with anger, and Gabi realized too late the degree to which she had upset her mom.

One arm arced high and swung downward, connecting with Gabi's behind with a muffled smack. The sharp pain was followed almost immediately by another blow by her mother's hand, and she burst out crying again, half from terror and half from pain.

"Mama, stop!" she howled.

"You don't hit people like that, Mija!" The words spilled from her mother's mouth even as she brought her hand down on Gabi's bottom a third time.

"Maria, stop." Emilia grabbed Gabi's mom by the arm and gently pushed her back two steps.

With her assailant out of arm's reach, Gabi wheeled around and darted toward the exit from the clinic.

"You get back here, right now!" her mother snarled. "Gabi!"

She didn't slow down, and nearly tumbled to the ground as she hit the storm curtain and spilled forth into the street. Gabi staggered and rubbed her tear-blurred eyes as she took a moment to adjust to the light of day. She could still hear her mother cursing and yelling at her to return to the clinic, and her voice grew louder. Gabi knew it would be only a moment before her mom burst through the curtain after her.

In a moment of panic, she ran. She didn't pick a direction; she followed where her feet carried her. Gabi streaked past the entrance to the Palm Palace and crashed headlong into the jungle foliage beyond the edge of the village. As she stumbled through the undergrowth beneath a wide vinewood, she took a bad step, and tumbled about ten feet down the side of the hill, landing on her back in a thick tuft of long-bladed grass.

Gabi could hear her mom's voice echo from far in the distance, calling her back. Though the message was nearly drowned out by the rustling of the grass and the leaves above, the anger was still clear. Gabi climbed to her feet and brushed a couple impacted clumps of dirt from her already filthy clothing, then took a short look around to find something familiar in the landscape. She found the ivory sands of the beach in the distance, in a gap where trees had been cleared by tall men with big axes.

She took one glance up the hill before carefully parting grass with her hands and stepping over gnarled roots. Her nerves tingled as she moved forward, unsure if she would be able to find her way to the beach as it slipped in and out of view. She picked her way around the shoulder of the heights and found the path that ran between the village and the beach. With a grin and a sigh of relief, she began the trek down to the shore.

However, her relief was short-lived. She could hear her mother's voice coming from up the hill, arguing loudly with someone about what she would do to Gabi once she found her. The other voice was Haruka's, but Gabi could not hear what she said. All that was certain was that her mom was furious with both Gabi and Haruka. She did not want to feel any more of her mother's wrath, so she ran as quickly as she could away from the village.

Minutes later she reached the beach. Many other children played in the warm sunshine, including the older kids; their schooling for the day was over. Games of tag unfolded over the broad beach, and several boys playfully fought with sticks. The clacking noises reminded Gabi of the beating she had received at the hands of Marya weeks earlier. Her skin shivered despite the sun, and the urge to play with the others quickly passed. Instead she headed for the river mouth, where a variety of fish and animals could be found.

While still in the open, Gabi found this place to be secluded. None of the other children were present, and the village fishing boats worked far off shore at this time of day. She found a low, wide boulder jutting out from the sand, and crawled on top of it in search of the tide pools that she knew would be on this particular rock, filling the wide bowls etched in its top by nature.

The pools were indeed present, and she sat at the edge of one, watching a pair of three inch crabs fighting over a tiny fish that drifted belly-up at the surface. They danced and skittered under the surface, jabbing at each other with their long, jagged claws, and a pair of pointed leg-like appendages under their shells that Earth crabs did not have.

"I want this one to win," she said to herself softly as she locked her eyes on the one that had a long, purple strip along the ridge of its shell.

As the fight over their meal continued, it looked to Gabi as if her champion would lose. She looked around and quickly found a narrow piece of driftwood about five inches in length. She retrieved it, and jabbed it weakly at the other crab. It snapped a claw and caught the wood in the blink of an eye. Gabi squealed and jerked back, flinging the wood – and the attached crab – several feet down the beach. Her chosen crustacean took full advantage of its adversary's disappearance, and proceeded to eat the prize it claimed.

She smiled, satisfied with the results of her intervention. Slipping from the rock, she padded over to where the stick lay in the sand. The tiny crab, despite being half as long as the piece of wood, raised its pincers and spike-legs at Gabi as she approached. It lunged, surprising her, and forced her to leap to her left. She snatched the wood from the sand, which gave the creature a chance to strike.

Gabi screeched as one of the spike-legs punctured the skin on the back of her hand. She yanked it back, sending the crab spinning into the sand nearby, and sending shooting pains up her arm. Blood slowly seeped to the surface of her skin. She looked down and clutched at it, fighting back the urge to cry. Something else welled within her – something dark – and she was unable to control both emotions at the same time.

She brought the small stick down on top of the crab, hitting its shell soundly. It backed up and raised all four of its weapons. Gabi swung again, and this time the small crustacean wrapped a pincer around the wood.

"Let go!" she shouted at it, and pulled hard.

The stick wrenched free of the crab's grip, so she then jabbed at it. It danced back side to side with its many legs. Its tiny appendages splayed out in front as if its increased size and threatening posture would deter its attacker. Instead Gabi intensified her thrusting assaults, and inch by inch started to back the animal toward the sea. She was vaguely aware of someone talking to her as she worked, but her singular focus was on making the crab pay for stabbing her. The defense that the miniscule beast put up was beginning to irritate her, and she decided to take another heavy swing from above. This time the crab could not deflect the blow in time, and she crushed one of its pincer arms.

There was a brief moment of satisfaction as she watched it struggle to scurry away with the useless appendage hanging limply at its side. Then a harsh voice snapped her attention away from the hapless crustacean.

"I said leave it alone!" Marya repeated as she took two steps closer to Gabi, putting herself between Gabi and her victim. When she stopped, she deliberately flicked sand at Gabi with her toes. Gabi turned her face to keep the abrasive grains from getting in her eyes and mouth, and felt them rake her arm, hair, and ear.

Memories flooded through her mind in an instant as Gabi recalled the beating that the older girl had delivered to her weeks earlier. She felt a twinge of fear that Marya would come after her again. Gabi rose to her feet with her head lowered.

"Why did you hurt that poor thing?" Marya berated. "That was really mean."

Gabi's head slowly rose, and she took in the snarl that the older girl had on her lips. Marya's glare was piercing, striking fear anew in Gabi's heart.

She's going to hit me again.

Gabi could feel her muscles tense and her hands ball up. Her breathing shallowed, and rage began to build up, mixing with the fear. The furious beating of her heart and the tingling of her nerves scared and confused Gabi. Then the fear flushed all at once, and Gabi lunged at Marya, shrieking at the top of her lungs.

Before she bowled into the older girl, Gabi could see her eyes widen in shock. Marya splashed into the surf on her back, and Gabi landed right on top. She straddled Marya's chest and began hitting her over and over again, all while uttering a sound that was half a scream and half a cry.

"Leave. Me. Alone!" she bellowed as she drove her fists into Marya, who flung her arms up over her face in defense. A wave washed in, drenching both of the girls. Marya bucked and thrashed, but Gabi did not relent. "Don't touch me again!"

Her fists rained down on Marya. Another wave rushed in, more powerful than the last, which submerged Marya's face. Gabi had to pause for a second to gain her balance, and in that moment, Marya threw her arms out and tried to push against Gabi. One hand pressed into her face, further enraging her. Without a thought, she clamped down on one of the offending fingers with her teeth. Marya started to scream, but it ended up as more of a cough as a third wave slammed them and again covered the older girl from head to toe.

Gabi slapped away the hands that clawed at her from below and raised her fist to deliver another blow, but then found herself lifted up and away from her victim by a strong set of arms.

"Gabi, stop it!" Kelly commanded. "You're going to kill her!"

Kelly's younger sister Kristen rushed to aid Marya. As Kelly dragged Gabi away kicking and screaming she was forced to hold her tight enough that Gabi found it difficult to breathe. The older Vandemark sister carried Gabi all the way up the beach to where the old sleeper pod took its crooked rest in the dunes. She then sat Gabi down less than gently, and knelt down to look her square in the eyes.

"You're in deep trouble, little miss," Kelly said sternly. "Now tell me why you were trying to drown Marya."

"Because she was angry at me and I didn't want her to hit me again," Gabi pouted.

"What was she angry at you about?"

"I don't know."

"Gabi, this isn't the time to lie to me. I need to know."

"I'm not lying," she insisted. "I was off playing with some crabs and when I was done she was yelling at me."

"And you didn't do anything to her to start this?"

"No!"

Kelly shook her head and sighed. "What's wrong with you? This isn't like you."

"I didn't do anything!"

"Yes you did. Come on, let's go tell your mom what happened." Kelly stood up and offered her hand.

Gabi curled her knees to her chest and shook her head. "No. Mama will just yell at me some more. She hates me."

For the first time, Gabi saw Kelly lose her temper. She jerked Gabi to her feet roughly by the elbow and dragged her along the path toward the village. No matter how hard Gabi dug her heels in, she could not stand against the strength of the Vandemark girl. "I don't have time to argue with you. You're in trouble anyway, so you don't get a say."

As the outlines of the village structures came into view, fear gripped Gabrielle once more.

Mama's going to hit me again.

He shuddered as the familiar grove of trees loomed in front of him as he walked. Though the stiff breeze and overcast skies had cooled the air, Cal knew that the shivers that ran down his spine were not those of chills, but a visceral reaction to stepping foot on the ground where his friend died just days earlier. He paused at a dark stain on the ground a few feet from the boulder that provided him protection as the bullets flew during the fatal conflict.

He heard an almost imperceptible gasp come from next to him, and Alexis pulled his arm close as she drew her other hand to her mouth and looked away.

"Sorry," Cal said. "I shouldn't have shown you this. I should have warned you. I just... I just had to see it one more time. Just to know the sacrifice was real."

"I know. I can't imagine what all you've been going through. I... I still can't believe he's gone."

Cal sighed and his shoulders slumped. "Just when I'm starting to get used to the idea, I find out that the place he was killed is going to become the colony's cemetery. It's kind of a slap in the face."

Alexis squeezed his arm gently. "I don't think they meant it that way when they decided on it. And besides, today is about honoring him."

"And the others."

She nodded silently and drew him away to where a small crowd gathered at the base of the hill. Many were dressed in flight suits, with about two dozen others in civilian clothes. A few had managed to find something resembling formal wear, but most were underdressed for the occasion. Cal glanced up the hill where Lieutenant Hunter Ceretti had gathered seven other officers from the crew, to serve as an Honor Guard. Hunter himself carried the flag that he had scrounged up from storage on *Michael*; the red and white stripes flowed and swayed, and every single star on the blue field was visible as the breeze kept the banner from sagging.

Alexis selected a spot at the end of the human arc, where they had a clear view of four fresh graves, each marked with a carefully stacked cairn at the head. Cal closed his eyes and recalled the order in which he watched the first three bodies be interred, the day after the massacre. Alexis had begged Cal not to go, to take the time to heal and wait for the formal funeral, but he had wanted to see Cameron's burial.

First to be placed in the ground was Major Holden Kintney. The first officer of *Gabriel* had been shot multiple times with his own weapon by Darius Owens after the two had a fierce struggle on the very spot that was now his grave. Cal had not broached with Darius the subject of what happened, as he had seemed quite distraught about taking a life, but rumors from other colonists painted the picture of Kintney as being a blindly loyal officer with a brutal streak a mile wide.

I shouldn't speak ill of the dead, but if half of what I've heard is true, we're better off without that guy. Cal shuddered.

The next victim of the massacre to be buried was Lieutenant Brandon Reid. The young man's execution started the exchange of gunfire between Eriksen's men and Captain Quinn. The devastation that Reid's family endured was unimaginably deep, he thought. He cast his gaze across the circle to Saika Reid. The widow had been provided a black dress by some soul in the colony; Cal was not entirely sure whom. She dabbed her eye with a handkerchief as an older woman – her mother, he presumed – comforted her. Cal's eyes couldn't help but drift to her belly, knowing that she carried Lieutenant Reid's unborn child.

So unfair. He won't ever know his father, thanks to Eriksen.

Then the image of his friend's burial flashed through his mind. Sergeant Cameron Drisko was the last to be laid to rest the day after the slaughter. As the sorrowful sight of the grim task passed from his psyche, he conjured other memories, the most bittersweet of which was the night that *Michael* had landed, and the mix of joyous and melancholy songs his friend had played on the guitar. Cameron had a knack for knowing just how to pluck the strings of the heart just as easily as those on his instrument.

Cal's lip quivered for a moment and he took a deep breath in a bid to force aside the profound pain of loss. He had been a mess for a couple days afterward, and yet he still forced himself during that time to watch and try to comprehend. He wasn't sure he could, even on this day, when the fallen would be properly acknowledged in their repose.

His eyes opened and fell to the fourth grave in the newly dedicated cemetery. Beneath the mound of dirt lay Colonel Charles Eriksen. *Gabriel's* commanding officer had succumbed to his injuries three days after the shootout. In what Cal believed to be another outburst of callous venom, Traci Josephson had speculated that the colonel had willed his own death so that he "wouldn't have to give Colonel Dayton the satisfaction of winning." It was a truly odd statement, as Cal could neither wrap his head around the concept of willing one's own end, nor that said end would be considered a victory.

I just hope someone found out what the hell this was all about before he died. Like he said something on his death bed or something.

Not all who sustained wounds in the battle perished, however. Ex-Captain Quinn was proof of that, as his leg wound would not prevent him from delivering Lieutenant Reid's eulogy in a few more minutes. There were also two civilians who had suffered trampling injuries when the crowd panicked during the fracas. Both were lucky to be alive, but were also expected to recover fully.

Bravo emerged from its hiding spot behind a slate-colored cloud, casting a warm glow first on the hill, then slowly down the slope as it cleared the fringe into the open. As it did so, Colonel Dayton marched slowly from behind the crowd, followed by the rhythmic click of Quinn and his crutches, then Darius Owens, whose eyes were sullen. The rear was brought up by a rather rotund fellow with a receding hair line and a black cassock, adorned with a long red stole with a single crucifix. He carried a thick, black Bible in one hand, and a pair of glasses was folded neatly in the other.

They took their places in a neat row just a few feet from the headstone-cairns. Dayton craned his neck up the hill and nodded, which then prompted Hunter to execute his duty.

"Flight, shoulder… *arms!*" he barked, and each member of the detail crisply brought their M4 carbine to the precise position against their bodies. Hunter gripped the flag staff firmly and brought it to his center, holding it high and straight. "Right… *face!*" The maneuver was carried out with impeccable precision.

Cal watched as the flag masked and revealed Hunter's face as it rippled. The lieutenant paused a brief moment, and for a second Cal thought that his friend might have frozen in the middle of his duty. Instead, he delivered order after order to bring the Honor Guard to its position, off to the right of Dayton and the graves. With one final command, they halted.

The silence that spanned the next minute made it feel like the planet itself had stopped. The wind died, and with it the rustle of the grove. The buzz of insects vanished. Even the birds seemed to stop calling out, as if they knew the solemnity of the occasion.

Colonel Dayton took a step forward and cleared his throat, breaking through the veil of silence.

"We are here today to honor the memory and service of four members of the sleeper ship crews. These men dedicated their lives to the safety of the men, women, and children entrusted to their care." He paused for a moment. "It's hard to reconcile the fact that they lost their lives fighting against each other, when their mission was the same. Whatever the investigation into the incident finds, it should not diminish what these men did for the people of Demeter."

Dayton stepped back in line and nodded to Tyler Quinn, who then hobbled forward on his crutches. His voice wavered as he spoke. "First Lieutenant Brandon Reid was born into one of the First Families of Project Columbus. His father, Major James Reid, was the chief computer analyst for the Project from 1982 until his retirement in 2000. Brandon dreamed of serving aboard one of the ships his entire life, and the minute he was eligible to enlist in the Air Force, he did so."

Quinn tried to smile, but it was contorted by his obvious pain. "I met him four years before launch, when he was assigned to the Project after a number of senior officers resigned. As we filled voids in our upper ranks through promotions, these fresh replacements were just coming out of their respective schools. Brandon... he stood out because of just how excited he was to be there. How determined he was to absorb knowledge and spend time in the simulators. That enthusiasm carried over into his personal life, and it was just plain impossible not to like him. And you got this feeling, when hanging around him, that everything was going to be great, no matter how dark life got.

"He finally got to live his dream of piloting one of the ships, even if it wasn't for very long." He turned his head slowly and looked at Saika Reid, addressing both the widow and a young, fair, blonde woman who clutched her shoulders. "Kayla, Saika... I am so sorry for your loss."

The women broke down into tears as Quinn returned to the line. Colonel Dayton stepped out of rank again.

"Major Holden Kintney served as the first officer of *Gabriel*. His career with the Air Force spanned decades, and he was a decorated combat pilot before his assignment to Project Columbus," noted Dayton. "His transfer to the Project was requested by the research staff because of his fearlessness behind the stick, and his willingness to push the envelope of aircraft capabilities. His tenacity in the simulators paved the way for the development program that trained the navigation staff of every ship in the fleet."

The colonel returned to his place in line again. As Darius Owens prepared to deliver the next speech, Cal compared the previous two eulogies.

Weird. A friend of Reid's gave his, and said what a great guy he was. Then Dayton steps up and lists service records for this Kintney guy? Did the guy have any friends when he was off duty?

Cal's focus returned to Owens, who took an uncomfortably long pause before he started in.

"Colonel Charles Eriksen was the kind of man who inspired both determination and discipline," Darius started. "Whether it was a staff briefing or taking the chair of *Gabriel*, he had this presence about him that just made you listen. He never shied away from commending a job well done, or providing support for a task if an extra hand was needed. His expectations were never out of line, and if you needed correction, he gave it more like a father than a drill instructor. You could always count on his vision and determination; he was possibly one of the most dependable people I know. Though we had our disagreements toward the end, I still held tremendous respect for him, and he was true to himself to the very end."

Kind words from someone who the colonel had turned on, Cal thought. *I don't think I could have stood up there and delivered a speech like that.*

Cal's throat felt tight and he clutched Alexis a little tighter as Dayton's emergence at the head of the line signaled the final speech. His fingers went numb, and he had to check to make sure he still had a hold on his girlfriend's hand.

"I was a bit conflicted as to who should deliver this last eulogy," Dayton admitted. "But in keeping with the current theme, I felt it best if a crew member took care of it. I made the mistake of offering the eulogy to Lieutenant Ceretti *after* requesting that he lead the Honor Guard, which he had already accepted. Ceretti takes his duties seriously, and as much as I know it pains him, he has chosen not to shirk his original assignment.

"Staff Sergeant Cameron Drisko served as the lead information technology officer on *Michael*. His rank and role do absolutely nothing to describe the kind of man that Drisko was, both personally and professionally. He was as talented with a guitar as he was with a computer, and he entertained his comrades both before and after the launch. He was the soul of *Michael's* crew, and as much of an ambassador of goodwill around camp as anyone else I have seen. Sergeant Drisko held himself to a standard that I could only hope to match someday. And it is because of this standard that he died in the line of duty, executing his orders dutifully until his last breath. His early and tragic death is being felt deeply not only among the crew, but the colonists with whom he interacted on a daily basis."

Cal choked back his welling emotions and wiped dry the corners of his eyes.

"Let us now honor the service of these four men," Dayton continued. "Let us reflect and pray." He motioned to the minister with one arm. "Reverend, if you please."

The minister placed his glasses on his nose and opened the Bible. Cal closed his eyes and bowed his head, letting the preacher's words sink into his soul. The prayer of final rites left him feeling oddly at ease, and he felt his anxiety and sorrow ebb from him. He relaxed somewhat, no longer constantly on guard against his emotions. When the prayer finished, he muttered a single "Amen" with the rest of the crowd, and opened his eyes.

"Flight… present, *arms!*" barked Hunter.

Cal stepped behind Alexis and wrapped his arms around her midsection, then turned to face the Honor Guard.

The fallen received their final salute.

Gabrielle Serrano
1 May, Year of Landing, midday
Camp Eight
>|

James Vandemark parted the thick storm curtain at the front of the clinic. "Go," he commanded sternly.

Gabi dragged her feet as she stepped inside the dark and humid building. Her eyes took a moment to adjust to the darkness. Gabi's mother looked up slowly from the vibrant green tangle of palm fronds that was laid out in front of her. Her hands froze in midair, putting a momentary end to the task of knitting together whatever it was that she was making.

James clasped Gabi gently on the shoulders and nudged her closer in front of her mother, whose face hardened into a scowl. Gabi cast her eyes into the dirt, hoping that would somehow allow her to slip away without facing the judgment she knew was coming.

"What did she do this time?" her mom asked in a cold voice.

"Go ahead, tell her," James prompted as he let go.

Gabi shook her head and threw her arms across her chest.

James sighed. "She pushed down Caleb and took his pepperine."

"He wasn't going to eat it," Gabi protested, looking up at him.

James looked to Gabi's mom for a moment, but she just shook her head and resumed her work. He cleared his throat. "That doesn't mean you can take it without asking. And it's not nice to push people over."

"But…"

"No buts, Gabi." He looked again at her mother. "Maria?"

She did not raise her head or acknowledge his request for attention; her right hand continued to move in patterns as she edged a long blade of vegetation into the weave. James shook his head and knelt in front of Gabi, and she was left to face his serious countenance and piercing brown eyes.

"You don't hit or push anyone, okay?" he scolded.

Gabi sighed. "Okay."

He pointed to the partition wall at the back of the clinic. "Can you wait back there while I have a talk with your mom?"

"Okay," she growled and stomped off around the corner, trying to convey her frustration through the tantrum. She waited for one of the adults to come around the corner and give her a tongue lashing, but to her surprise, neither did.

She could hear them talking on the other side of the partition, though the low volume and the intervening structure made it difficult for her to discern much of anything.

Probably silly adult talk anyway, she guessed.

Gabi took in her surroundings. Since she and her mother had moved into their own small hut, there was little left in the clinic for her to play with. She knew better than to play with any of Dr. Petrovsky's medical supplies; that would earn her trouble from several people, not just her mother. Pelusina was back at their home, and as much as she wanted to walk out of the clinic to go get her or find something else to do, she didn't want to disobey James.

She curled up on the stiff bed, turned her back to the wall that separated her from the main room, and let her mind drift away. She began to daydream of Pelusina, only the stuffed toy was a real cat in her vision, stalking the jungle at the outskirts of the village with Gabi as they played a game of "pounce" with the other children. The black and white cat's skill at sneaking up on the young kids was phenomenal, despite her rotund frame. Older kids weren't fooled by either of them, but Gabi decided that they would not be fun to play this game with anyway, since Gina, Kelly, and Kristin were all too big to pounce on.

Next she imagined taking a long journey through the island's thick jungle in search of supply pods from the ship that carried them to the planet. The image she conjured was fraught with peril, and they had to use their wits to escape from a furious long-tusked Demeter hog. Her mother later stared down a jaguar until it ran away in fear. In the end of her short-lived dream, they found a cache of food and water, as well as magical machines that Troy could use to build new houses for everyone in the village.

The dream was interrupted just before Gabi and her mom received coronations with circlets of flowers and vines. She sat up and looked around as she could hear the conversation between James and her mother escalate.

"I know you've been dealt a shit hand," she could hear James say in an irritated voice. "I know you'd rather mope around all day and do nothing instead of facing the fact that life goes on and you need to participate in it. She's part of that life."

"I know that," her mom growled back. "Don't you think I know that?"

"Frankly, the way you've been acting lately, no."

"Oh come on. She's doing fine. She's eating, playing, and social-izing. Hell, she's even sat in on a couple of Charlotte's classes, even though she's a little young for that."

"When's the last time you hugged her?"

Silence followed. Gabi began to realize that they were talking about her. She thought back over the past few days, trying to recall the last time her mother had held her. The answer eluded her.

"When's the last time you told her you love her?"

"How dare you. You know I love her."

"Do you? Because it's like night and day, watching the way you act around her now as compared to before…"

"Don't say it," her mother warned.

Gabi peeked around the side of the partition. Her mother was standing only inches from James. In her balled fists were blades of palm, crumpled from the crushing grasp of her fingers. Her nostrils flared and her eyes burned intensely as she stared him down.

James sighed. "I'd love to give you all the time you need to sort out your issues, but we can't afford it. Gabi can't either."

"I can't what?" she asked softly, taking a step out from the bedroom.

"Go back to the back room for just another minute, alright?" he replied as he glanced quickly at her.

"I wanna know!"

"Gabi, now please," he affirmed.

Grumbling, Gabi shuffled back behind the wall, just out of sight. She slid down to a sitting position and listened intently to the adults' conversation. It took a moment for them to begin again.

"Look, if you need some space or some help, just say the word," James continued. There was a significant pause before he spoke again. "What would help you deal with Gabi's problems?"

Her mother scoffed. "Maybe getting rid of her for a day or two, so she's someone else's problem for a bit."

"So that's it?" he asked, the disappointment in his voice clear. "If that's what it takes, then."

A few moments later James rounded the corner and dropped to his knees in front of Gabi. He clasped her shoulders, smiled, and gave her a quick, unexpected hug.

"Gabi, honey, do you want to come spend the night with us? Kris and Kelly would love to sing with you, and Will should be back tonight as well."

She shook her head. "No thank you."

He stood up and reached down to offer his hand. "Come on. It'll be fun. Your mom said it's alright."

"No." Her response was firmer this time. She felt a twinge of anxiety at the idea that she would be taken from her mom.

"Come on, your mom needs some time to herself. Let's go."

As he reached for her hand she slapped it as hard as she could and screamed.

"No! I want to stay with Mama!"

"Gabi…"

"No!"

James sighed and shook his head, then walked back to the front part of the clinic.

"Told you so," her mother snorted.

"And yet I don't see you lifting a finger to correct her behavior."

"Don't tell me how to raise my daughter."

"I'll stop telling you how to raise her once you actually start doing so."

Gabi wasn't quite sure why what James said was hurtful, but she could tell by her mother's explosive reaction that it was. The banshee-like scream made Gabi scurry to the bed and cover her ears until the outburst was over. She stayed frozen on the covers for a minute before cautiously venturing out to the main clinic. James was gone, and her mother was muttering curses. Her hands were weaving green strips into the mat with speed and fury. When her mother calmed down a little bit, Gabi walked up behind her mom and threw her tiny arms around her shoulders. She squeezed down in the hardest embrace that she could muster.

Gabi was about to say how much she loved her mother when her hug was shrugged off, and repaid with a cold voice. "Not now, Mija."

Her lip trembled and she sobbed softly as she made her way to the back of the clinic and collapsed on the bed.

I just want you to love me, Mama. Please, just love me.

Calvin McLaughlin
1 May, Year of Landing, 17:55
Michael
>|

Sleep was not something that Calvin had been well acquainted with for the last week. Yet something about this night's restlessness was different. It was all emotion and thought, he knew, and trying to put a finger on the issue would be as easy as trying to force the two moons to align. He knew what he had been sent to talk to Colonel Dayton about, but something else entirely had occupied his mind.

He paced the lower gallery, circling the aft stairwell that connected the two decks. The lower deck's lighting was extinguished; only the dim glow of the upper gallery's fixtures kept him from stubbing his toes on any of the ship's fixtures.

Did it really all have to break down like this?

There was nothing that could be done to repair the past. Cal knew that, and had learned to accept it. What ate at him was the fact that Colonel Eriksen had never explained his actions in the end. Members of both crews were still clueless as to why a river had to separate the camps, and why blood had to be shed. But Cal had also seen that there was another man just as distraught by the outcome as he.

What the hell was it, anyway? What hasn't he told us?

Cal's hands fell on the ladder up, and without thinking, he began to climb to the upper gallery. His mind still mulled over what could have caused three respected, high-ranking Air Force officers to be so at their throats that they let everything fall apart around them. Even as his strides carried him down the long corridor toward the bridge he tried to contemplate this, but the more he thought, the less he seemed to be able to understand.

None of it makes sense. It might as well have been Cam's sandwich theory.

He passed through the airlock at the end of the gallery and passed through. Only when his left hand gripped the cold, steel railing standing silently beside the stairs to the bridge did he pause for a moment. He looked back into the seemingly unending hallway he had trod, realizing only now that he was about to intrude completely unannounced on the only man who could answer his questions. Cal turned to walk away from the bridge, but stopped himself.

No, he thought. *He has to tell us. I can't let him keep the crew in the*

J.C. Rainier

dark any more.

Cal turned back to the bridge. His nerves rose as he mounted each tread, but he steeled his resolve and pressed on. He quickly reached the command platform on the dark bridge. The strip lighting built into the bulkhead at the rear of the bridge was not illuminated, and it took Cal a moment to realize that the command chair was facing him and vacant, contrary to his expectations. He sighed and padded toward the chair, while craning his neck upward to view the brilliant glittering trail of stars in the black void beyond the world.

He reached the chair and ran his fingers along the worn padded armrests. The temptation to take a place on the seat of authority was too much to resist, and he lowered his body onto it. He curled the tips of his fingers over the forward edges of the rests, feeling the vinyl covering give way to brushed aluminum. Cal leaned his weight all the way back into the chair and turned it around to look again at the night sky.

The dark silhouette of Arion had already peaked and was beginning its slow plunge to the horizon, while Persephone's brilliant globe emerged from behind the thousands of needle-like trees in the distance. He smiled and sighed deeply.

It almost makes me not miss Earth. Almost.

Cal's heart jumped into his throat and he nearly leaped out of his skin when he heard Colonel Dayton's voice from the darkness of the bridge.

"Quite a sight there, isn't it, Mr. McLaughlin?" the commander asked.

He stumbled and wheeled around, trying to find where the colonel was. After a full rotation, he finally found him, sitting at one of the forward nav stations. His legs were resting on the inactive terminal in front of him, and he was leaning back for a full view through the canopy. His dark uniform concealed him well; it was only the light of Persephone that allowed Cal to finally perceive his presence.

"It is," Cal replied, trying to pass off his surprise.

"It makes me wonder something, though."

Cal waited for Dayton to continue, but after a few seconds of silence, he prompted, "Yeah? What's that?"

"Years from now, or maybe even decades, do you think that we'll have a new space program on this planet? That our descendants will be shooting for these moons here? And which one would they visit first?"

Cal leaned back in the command chair and considered Dayton's question. He hadn't thought about anything of the sort before; it was all Cal could do to imagine what the colony would look like a year from now. But the question was valid, if not entirely academic. With humans being technologically advanced enough to start an extrasolar colony, it was almost certain that, once humanity had a chance to rebuild, they would start their journey into space again.

"That's a good question. I'd say they're going to go to Persephone first."

"Hmm. Why's that?"

"Well, I guess some people are superstitious, and that's not likely to change in the future. A lot of people are afraid of the dark, so they're not going to want to go to the dark moon."

"Reasonable logic."

Awkward silence spanned several minutes as Cal bounced back and forth between thinking of the future and gathering the courage to confront Dayton. It was hard to want to press the colonel when Cal was looking at him as a man looking to the skies and dreaming of what was yet to come. Cal wished that Dayton had been working; he thought about how much easier it would have been to walk up and demand answers.

Dayton pointed a finger up high and drew a shape in the air with it. "That one looks like a really flat version of the Big Dipper. It's not, of course. All the constellations are different here. They either don't exist from this angle, or their shapes are really screwed up. I guess that means we need to make new constellations, right?"

Just do it. Just stand up and do it.

He heard Dayton sigh. "But you're not here to talk about astronomy." He rose from his seat and climbed to the command platform, then leaned against the railing in front of Cal, crossing his arms. "So what is it, Mr. McLaughlin?"

"It's time you come clean, sir," he replied, making sure to enunciate each syllable to keep from stuttering.

"About what?"

"About you and Eriksen. And Fox, too. Why you three were always fighting. Why it is that we're sitting across the river from the rest of the colonists, fighting instead of working side by side."

Colonel Dayton shrugged. "What do you want me to say? That there was some grand argument between us that caused this rift? That there was something so goddamned important that the three of us knew or felt that meant we couldn't avoid this? No, Mr. McLaughlin, there wasn't."

"But you have to know something. Before we landed, Cameron said that you three had fights back on Earth. What were they about?"

"Hell, I can't remember all of them now. Some of them were over really insignificant shit. There was this one time I swear that Fox and Eriksen were going to gang up and beat the living tar out of me because I didn't ask them if they wanted me to pick up lunch for them from the mess hall on the way to a command briefing. My sandwich ended up all over the floor after Fox slapped it out of my hand."

"Wait, a sandwich?" Cal repeated in disbelief. *There was actually an argument over a sandwich?*

Dayton shoved his hands in to his uniform's pockets and slowly walked to the side of the command chair. He faced toward the rear of the bridge when he stopped, showing Cal only the profile of his face.

"I didn't even care about the thing they argued about the most. Hell, I was ready to quit the project and ask to be transferred to a combat role because that's how little it mattered. But I knew it was too late to train another commander, so I stayed."

"They? So it was really Fox and Eriksen that had a beef with each other?"

"That's right."

"So what was so important, then?"

Dayton sighed and laughed nervously. "Oh, God. It wasn't important to me back then. I was so wrong, looking back. I should have worked harder to help them resolve the quarrel."

"Resolve what?"

"A worst-case scenario. Colonial command structure in case the entire research staff was lost." The thick vinyl back of the chair emitted a woeful groan as Dayton dug his fingers deep into it, clenching the fabric with all his might. "Doctor Benedict and his staff refused to play favorites or choose a leader. David said that it could lead to unnecessary resentment if the staff were to favor one over another. He wanted us to work it out, and we couldn't. All we could do was bicker over whose service record was more illustrious, or who pulled more weight back at the compound. A couple days of arguing till we were seven different colors made me sick. I didn't want it any more. I told them I was out, and they could fight over what was surely never going to happen."

"But it did," Cal added. The sorrow in the commander's voice was evident, and for the first time, Cal felt sympathy for the colonel.

"I should have supported Colonel Fox. I may not have seen eye to eye with her all the time, but I know she had a harder path than any of us to get her command. She wouldn't have failed us. Ol' Charlie Eriksen would have had a fit, but we at least would have had the structure."

"And the same problem. Colonel Fox died with everyone else on *Raphael*."

Colonel Dayton nodded and relaxed his death grip on the chair. "You're too damn wise for such a young kid."

"If I was wise, I wouldn't have let you send me across that river," Cal said sullenly.

"And if I had my wits about me I wouldn't have sent either of you across. Cameron's death was all my fault."

"You didn't pull the trigger. You had no way of knowing."

"I should have known. After Eriksen landed on the far side, I should have known. It was a clear message."

Cal stood up and pushed on the colonel's shoulder, turning him face to face. "Cam's death was as much his fault as yours. He was the one who went against your orders and brought a gun. He was the one who drew it during the shootout. He made himself a target."

"To protect you," the colonel added.

"And how do you think it would have played out if you had sent Hunter instead?" Cal snapped back. "Or Lieutenant Josephson? Cam was the right choice to send with me, and he died doing his duty."

"That he did." Colonel Dayton's jaw seemed to clench after he uttered the bitter words. "Doesn't make it any less bitter of a pill." He sighed heavily, the kind of sigh that weighed down a whole room. "I'm tired, Mr. McLaughlin."

"Of what, sir?"

"Everything. Powdered eggs. Picking bugs out of my crap coffee. The lies and distrust. The death. Nothing has gone right since we got here."

"We're still alive," Cal joked half-heartedly.

"We are," Dayton replied coldly.

Cal walked to the railing just above the nav stations and gripped the cold metal in his hands as he leaned on it. Persephone was well above the horizon, and Arion's form was slowly morphing into the silhouette of a distant mountain peak. He heard the groan of the command chair's upholstery as Dayton slumped down into it.

"I've talked to Darius," Cal blurted as the silence began to weigh on him. "He said that Colonel Eriksen accused him of being a 'sympathizer' before trying to exile him to our camp."

"A sympathizer?"

"That's what he said."

"Sympathizing with whom?"

"He thinks Eriksen meant us."

"That would explain why Ol' Charlie was upset at Mr. Owens, at least."

Cal bit his lip and delved deep into thought. Sympathy for the *Michael* crew might get Owens banished from *Gabriel*, but it didn't explain the division in the first place. Cal knew there was another factor; something that Colonel Dayton did differently than Colonel Eriksen.

"Why didn't you prosecute Major Forrest?" he asked.

"Wouldn't be worth it. He's not going anywhere. I'd rather have him working to better the colony than imprisoned. Or dead."

Cal nodded. He thought it over again, and decided that wouldn't be reason enough for Eriksen to cause such a rift. Then a seed of doubt crept in, and Cal got the worrisome feeling that Dayton was still holding back.

"What's the *real* reason, Colonel?"

Silence answered him.

That's it. There's another reason.

"What are you afraid of, Colonel?" he prodded, turning to face him. "Eriksen is dead. Fox and her first officer are dead. Kintney's gone, too. No one can question that you're now at the top of the chain. Everyone will be looking to you for leadership. So what reason can be so horrible that you can't say it?"

Dayton lowered his head and ran his hands through his thick, brown hair. Cal could tell that he was grabbing at it; the tendons on the backs of his hands strained.

"Because Eriksen was right about being a sympathizer."

"What?" Cal gasped.

The man's hands clasped together in front of his mouth, as if he was praying. He then glanced up at Cal, meeting Cal's stare with his own sad eyes.

"I knew about Doctor Benedict and Doctor Kimura's intentions for most of the year before launch," he confessed. "David didn't think that Tadashi would have the nerves to keep quiet during the whole journey, so he wanted someone up there watching over his interests. Someone who could fade into the background and claim deniability if the shit hit the fan. I was always supposed to take control of the colony if the conspiracy was uncovered or if David, Tadashi, and Jonathan were killed."

"Jonathan?"

"Doctor Fairweather," he corrected. "The problem was that David couldn't just put me directly in command; Charlie and Marissa had huge egos, and they wanted that position. David knew this. He hoped that I could convince them to put me in command as a contingency." Dayton let out a heavy sigh and slumped back into the chair.

"But you couldn't, could you?"

"And now my failure has cost lives. Lives of men better than me."

Cal shook his head. He took five long strides to the command chair and placed his hand on the colonel's shoulder, giving it a slight squeeze with his hand. "No, Eriksen's arrogance did that. And you're a good man, sir. You've done just what Doctor Benedict asked of you, in the best way you could."

The colonel's left hand rose to his shoulder and clamped down lightly on Cal's. "It wasn't all a failure. I got this right."

Cal paused for a moment, confused as to what Dayton might be referring to. "Got what right?"

"Kept my promise to your father," he replied.

"My... my father?" Cal gulped.

"His hands were full with his role in the War. Shortly after I found out about the plan to repopulate the ships with the rightful balance of passengers, I also found out that you were in danger of being drafted. Your number was going to be up not long after you graduated, Mr. Mc-Laughlin. Your father was desperate. He didn't want you to go to war. He knew we were losing, and he couldn't bear the idea of you marching in a column to your death."

"Y-y-you..."

"He didn't even have to ask me," Dayton continued. "I had Jonathan add your name to the passenger manifest. By the time your father knew what I had done for him, you were already on your way to Laramie. His last words to me were 'I can't repay you for this, Tom. Tell him that I love him, and that I'm sorry.' That was the day before he was killed in combat."

Cal's lips began to tremble and a tear streamed down his cheek. He had always felt that his father cared, even under his gruff exterior. The affirmation that Thomas Dayton provided gave him the closure he needed, even if the memory of his loss was painful. He took a moment to reflect on the last time he saw his father, dressed in fatigues and climbing into the back of a personnel carrier. The salute that he gave Cal, he now realized, was a symbol of his love and his willingness to sacrifice everything for his only child.

"I'm sorry," Dayton said as he squeezed Cal's hand again.

Cal wiped the tear away. "No, no. Thank you. I had no idea."

"You have no idea how long I've wanted to tell you. From the moment you woke up from stasis, I wanted to let you know what happened. I just... I couldn't. The stakes were too high."

"I understand."

"Do you?" There was a hint of urgency in the colonel's voice. "You can't tell anyone what I've told you tonight. If someone were to find out..."

"Find out what?" Cal interrupted. "The only person who could really do something nasty to either of us is dead. Your entire crew is completely loyal to you. As for *Gabriel's* crew, I don't think you have to worry about Owens, Quinn, or Miller. When I was talking to Darius I was also approached by a couple civilians from over there."

"About what?"

"Negotiations. For the unification of the colony."

Colonel Dayton's demeanor quickly changed to that of complete surprise. "Unification?"

Cal nodded. "The two guys I talked to were both lawyers. Both the prosecutor and the defender in Doctor Kimura's case. They think this has all been blown way out of hand, and they want to sit down with us and talk it out."

"W-when?" the commander stammered.

"As soon as possible. Tomorrow if you'd like."

"Tomorrow is... that's a bit rushed, I'd like a day to prepare. Can you have them meet with us the day after tomorrow?"

Again Cal nodded. "Just tell me when and where. I know they'll be okay with it."

"The bridge of *Michael*. Zero eight hundred hours."

"I'll go tell them tomorrow." Cal started to walk away, and his

nerves tingled as he took each step away. It had been a very taxing conversation, but the results were beyond anything he could have hoped
for.

"Mr. McLaughlin," Dayton called out as Cal neared the end of the
bridge.

"Yes sir?"

"We write history every day we're here. History that will be passed
down to each generation to come, including those who will reach for
Persephone and land on her surface."

"Sir?" Cal asked, puzzled.

"They're going to write about you, you know that? Everything you
have done for us. It's going to be written down and passed along. The
name McLaughlin is going to be revered."

Cal couldn't form a response. He nodded curtly, which hoped the
colonel could see, before he departed the bridge with his hand over his
mouth. He wasn't sure if he wanted to scream or to throw up.

"You fellas are here right on time," Lieutenant Ceretti remarked cheerfully.

The representative from *Michael* smiled broadly and extended his hand as they approached the crew pod. Don Abernathy was the first to shake it, followed by his colleague Fred Hausner. Darius then took his turn exchanging pleasantries with the lieutenant, leaving Rory Baines as the last of *Gabriel's* contingent to receive his welcome.

"Please, come in. We just got done setting up, and Colonel Dayton is expecting you." Ceretti dismissed the two sergeants that had escorted them onto the ship, then beckoned to the group as he passed through the airlock into the crew pod.

The delegation was led up a set of familiar looking stairs that Darius knew led to the bridge. He drew in a deep breath as they walked.

Identically built ships, yet they smell different, he noted. It took Darius a moment to figure out what the difference was, and determined that *Michael* had a slightly musty smell to it, whereas the ship that carried him across the expanse of space smelled more clinical, more sterile.

As Darius mounted the command platform he found that a pair of small portable tables had been set up and pushed together, and they were ringed with the station chairs from the perimeter of the bridge; Darius could see that all but one had been unbolted and dragged to the command platform.

At least we get to sit in comfy chairs, he mused to himself.

Two of the chairs on the right side were already occupied. Calvin McLaughlin was situated at the far right end of the table. To his left, on the near right end, was an older woman with tightly braided gray hair and small, circular glasses dangling on a plain silver necklace around her neck. It took a moment for Darius to recognize her as Dr. Heidi Taylor, who was part of the training staff that helped the flight crews prepare for zero-G back on Earth.

Lieutenant Ceretti took a seat to the left of the doctor, along the near edge. Opposite him, hovering over the seat next to Calvin, stood Colonel Dayton. He looked as if he had seen better days; his beard was unkempt, his hair was a matted mess, and thick black rings under his eyes were visible from where Darius stood.

"Thank you for coming," the colonel greeted. He swept his arm toward the empty seats. "If you please, we can get started."

Darius escorted his companions to the left side of the table. He selected the chair directly across from Calvin, which put him between the two attorneys from *Gabriel*, and left Rory to sit at the foot of the table next to Ceretti. Dayton went to the command chair for a moment to retrieve a stack of notepads and pens, which he then distributed to all present before joining the table.

Dayton cleared his throat and clicked his pen into the open position. "We're here to discuss the unification of the two autonomous colonies formed when the two ships landed on opposite sides of the river."

Not placing blame. Smart man.

"Each colony has its own ship, crew, and passenger manifest. To prevent further misunderstanding between the colonies, we should agree in the majority on several key points. These include, but are not limited to, resource distribution, workforce composition and distribution, and disposition of colonists who wish to move between the two halves. Before we begin, I just want to be sure that the delegation from *Gabriel* speaks with the authority of their crew and population."

"We speak with the authority of the population," Don replied quickly. "The crew is divided. As Darius Owens, Roger Miller, and Tyler Quinn were officially dismissed from service, they were counted with the populace, not the crew."

"I see. And if their votes were counted as crew?"

"Then we also speak for the crew."

"Very well. We will proceed under the understanding that the delegation from *Michael* will present the resulting recommendations to its crew for consideration."

That won't be a problem. They're just sitting back and watching anyway, since just about all the command rank officers were either relieved or killed.

"Let us first start with resource distribution." Colonel Dayton began to scribble on his pad in shorthand. Several others around the table, including both of the attorneys, did the same. Darius held his pen over the pad, but as he stared at the blank page, realized that he had no clue what he was doing or why.

The group had been sent to negotiate, and he had been approached by several concerned citizens with specific concerns or demands they had for the bargaining table. Many were so minute that, while Darius promised to address them, he dismissed them mentally. Others were rooted in a pervasive fear that seemed to be running through some circles in the *Gabriel* camp that the other side was itching for revenge after the death of one of their officers.

Darius knew that he wouldn't be bringing up a single concern that he had been given prior to the negotiation. He had one agenda that was his singular focus; he would let the other representatives negotiate all of the other details.

With unification we need leadership. There is only one way the people will accept that. Darius chewed at his thumbnail and pretended to listen to Fred Hausner's speech about fair distribution of timber harvest resources. He tried to gauge Colonel Dayton's reaction as the details for this issue were laid out, but the man's expressions gave no hint of emotion at all. *And he's the one who's standing in the way of it all.*

"I think there's a good deal of work to be done before we can simply haul logs from one side of the river to the other like that," Dayton added, interrupting Fred's dissertation. "Namely, a bridge across the river."

"Would you like to make a counter proposal?"

Dayton pursed his lips and paused for a moment. "Moving people and tools is easier right now than moving resources. Perhaps all we need is a way to share the workforce dynamically between sides of the river as needs be."

Rory spoke next. "We know you've got a couple of rafts over there, but those can move what, six people at a time? And what if the rafts get stuck on the wrong side of the river?"

"I'm sure we could work out some sort of ferry system," Ceretti said.

Don nodded in agreement. "That would have other uses besides moving personnel across the river. Communications. Lighter supplies as needed."

"And give citizens a bit of flexibility to travel," Dayton noted as he scribbled on his pad.

Darius leaned back in his chair and drifted off into thought about the prospect of civilians being able to cross the river, even as the negotiations continued around him. The idea of crossing to the *Michael* side without repercussions was satisfying, though he bore a slight hesitation when he considered how members of the two crews might react if they came face to face. While civilians would easily and openly embrace each other, Darius had to wonder if any of Eriksen's remaining loyalists would cause trouble. It was even possible that these men could suffer discrimination at the hands of their *Michael* counterparts.

Too many issues. That's why it all needs to go away.

"Mister Owens?" Dayton's voice called him back to attention.

He cleared his throat and leaned forward. "I'm sorry, what?"

"Do you have a preference as to what we name the river?"

He felt the weight of the delegations' collective stares as he looked around the table. He quickly formed a response that he hoped would cover his absent-mindedness.

"Not really. Maybe we should let the people vote, since this is everyone's home."

The attorneys nodded in agreement and jotted some notes down.

"Very well," Dayton continued. "Let the people decide by a simple vote between the proposed names."

Darius glanced to his right at Don Abernathy's pad. Several names were scribbled near the bottom; three had been scratched out, three had been circled.

Fairweather, Benedict, and Raphael. The destroyed ship and two of the senior research staff, he thought. *Both accused of treason, both dead.*

"If I may bring up the next item, Colonel?" Don asked politely. Dayton nodded and gestured in deference. "I hate to burden you with this, but it seems that colonial management has not gone very… ah… smoothly over here for a while. I was just informed yesterday of some agricultural concerns we have."

The air filled with a brief, awkward pause. "Go on," the colonel prompted.

"It appears there was heavier focus on exploring for mineral and building resources, and I've had reports from some farmers that Colonel Eriksen didn't make time for them or give instructions for where or what to cultivate. Some of the citizens took matters into their own hands and began planting anyway, but we're quite far behind."

Too busy with his crusade to lead, Darius thought bitterly.

"How far behind?"

"Hard to tell, but our best guess is that we've only got about a third of our fields planted. I know it's late in the season and we could only plant short-cycle crops at this point, but we could really use the help."

"I know without needing to be reminded that at this point the whole colony lives and dies as one. You don't even need to ask. Help will be there in the morning."

"Thank you, Colonel," Don said as he rose to shake Dayton's hand. "Thank you very much."

"My pleasure. Are there any other concerns that you wish to address before our delegation brings its issues to the table?"

"I have one, sir," Darius interjected without hesitation. He grabbed the pen in front of him and clicked it nervously.

All in, Darius. All in.

"Very well, Mr. Owens. Go ahead."

He cleared his throat and adjusted the notepad in front of him. He was unsure if this gesture was meant to calm his own nerves or to put on a show of confidence for the other negotiators.

"We're talking about a lot of short term goals here. What about the long term goals that were established in the Operational Guidelines? Specifically about governance."

A confused look crossed Dayton's face for a few seconds before his lines hardened into a scowl. "Under the circumstances, I think that the OG's will have to bend a bit for us. We're down a ship and a few officers, in case you hadn't noticed."

"That's exactly why we need to press forward. Eliminate confusion."

Darius could feel breath in his right ear as Don leaned over and whispered. "What are you doing? What are these guidelines?"

"None of the research staff are here to enact the governance provisions," Dayton grumbled. "So the point is moot."

Doctor Kimura is. Well, if you'd let him out of stasis.

"I propose a change. Let the people decide."

"What?" the colonel gasped.

"Decide what?" Fred asked.

"No," Dayton growled. "You can't possibly think of bringing up governance at this meeting. We're trying to unify, not tear apart."

"Exactly," Darius continued, standing his ground. "Just hear me out, and you'll understand why it will bring the colonies together."

He stared directly in the colonel's eyes. Dayton's jaw clenched, and his stare was as fiery as the sun, but he slowly backed down into his seat. "I'm listening."

"As soon as is feasible, we should hold open elections for new colonial leadership. A governor. Maybe a couple other positions as well. If all parties approve, we can have candidates sorted out within a month or so, and the elections a month or so after."

"Two months?" Cal asked. "That's a short time."

"It's not a big colony," Rory remarked casually. "Four thousand people. Heck, one or two debates will probably be enough for folks to make up their minds."

"And just who are you thinking of putting up there for election, Mr. Owens?"

He shrugged. "Whoever the people want. Civilians only."

The scowl on Dayton's face twisted even further, and his lip curled to reveal his teeth. "And what have I done to you that makes you want me to stand aside so quickly?"

"Nothing. I wasn't finished." He drew in and expelled a deep breath, placing the pen down in front of him. "Though your question brings me to the final condition I want to propose. All officers and crew of both ships are to resign from service effective seventy-two hours from acceptance of this proposal."

Silence descended quickly. Darius locked his stare on Colonel Dayton, who returned the favor in kind. Darius was vaguely aware that the remaining delegates were shifting their focus back and forth between the two of them, apparently waiting for one of the men to blink. Dayton's cheeks flushed, and his lips twitched. Darius's heart beat furiously in his chest, and it took most of his remaining concentration to keep his hands steady.

Without warning, Dayton shot from his chair. The chair scraped along the deck plating with a pained metallic screeching. Dayton stormed from the bridge without a word, his footsteps fading into the distance after a few seconds. The table remained silent, and those present leaned back in their chairs and looked at their papers or each other, save for one; Cal McLaughlin took his leave just a few seconds after Dayton, following him into the body of the ship.

"What the hell were you thinking?" Don whispered in his ear.

He couldn't answer. He was starting to realize that he may have single-handedly destroyed the negotiations.

J.C. Rainier

"Colonel, wait up!"

Cal nearly missed his footing on the last tread as he charged down the stairs. He steadied himself quickly before bolting through the open airlock in pursuit of Dayton.

"Sir, wait!"

The commander had made it a little more than halfway to the first pair of sleeper pods when he stopped and wheeled around. The wild look in his eyes and the twisted sneer on his face were further evidence of his fury.

"Who the hell does he think he is?" Dayton fumed as he took three long strides forward. "Who the hell comes to a negotiation table and demands your resignation? Has he lost his mind?"

Cal put up his hands in a calming gesture. "Take a deep breath, sir."

"Can it, Mr. McLaughlin. I'm not going to sit here and let him insult me like that."

"I don't think he meant it that way."

And if he did, he's a colossal ass.

Dayton shook his head and walked away toward the rear of the ship again, prompting Cal to follow closely behind. "You of all people know just what kind of shit I've been through to get us all this far. Does he really think I'm just going to roll over and hand over the colony to some random Joe that the colonists pick?"

Cal caught up to Dayton and grabbed his wrist, pulling him to a stop. The infuriated commander jerked his hand free and glared at Cal, but stood fast.

"It doesn't have to be random. He said a civilian, right?"

"Right, and I'm not."

"Not yet. But if you resign, you will be."

"And then I'd have to get enough support to run."

"You'd have my support."

"It's still a big risk doing that," Dayton added, "when I don't even have to listen to his demands in the first place. I can keep going the way I am."

"For how long, sir?" Cal replied instantly.

The question seemed to catch the colonel off guard. Cal could tell that he was struggling to find an answer, and several times opened his mouth as if to speak, but after almost a minute, he prompted Cal to continue his explanation.

"Other than the crews and the few Marines that made it onboard from Earth, no one here is used to being under military law," he continued. "How long do you think they'll accept that? The idea is as foreign as this planet is."

"They've accepted the planet. They'll live a while longer under our authority."

"Why make them?" The question again had Dayton at a loss for words. "What would *you* give for just a little something that felt normal? That felt like Earth?"

The commander sighed heavily. "After I did it, I thought I'd sold my soul. Just after we landed I had a couple pigs slaughtered so that we could… so that I could taste something familiar, that wasn't bagged and vacuum sealed decades ago."

"I remember that," Cal nodded.

"I damn near had the rest of them butchered the next day because I wanted it again. I almost gave up bacon and pork chops for the rest of my life just to taste it a second time."

"So what do you think the people would give up for a taste of home? What do you think they'd be capable of, if it came down to it? You know everyone's stressed out here, especially the crews."

Cal could hear the clank of footfalls as someone approached from the bridge. He glanced over his shoulder and found Dr. Taylor approaching them slowly.

"Is everything alright?" she asked, cautiously slowing her pace at about twenty feet.

With a quick jerk of his head Cal invited her to the discussion, and she approached the two men.

"Cal here is trying to convince me that Mr. Owens is right. That we should all resign and have an election," Dayton snorted.

She placed her wrinkled, spotted hand on his shoulder. "Tom, we've known each other a long time, so don't take this the wrong way. Do it. Accept his terms."

He regarded her for a long moment before pinching the bridge of his nose with his fingers and rubbing his eyes. "Et tu, Brute?"

A frown crossed Dr. Taylor's mouth. "I'm not trying to insult you. But you knew that the Operational Guidelines would eventually call for an election. Even the timing of that was supposed to be determined by Doctor Kimura and Doctor Fairweather. How long did you really think that the command staff would be running the colony?"

"I was hoping at least a year."

"Well, I know that Doctor Kimura never intended for it to take that long," she said softly. "He wanted them shortly after landing. Doctor Benedict felt that the first winter would be a good time, and Jon Fairweather never could make up his mind."

"That's not helpful."

"So what would be helpful? And I don't mean what would be helpful to you, I mean what would help the people."

Dayton's brown eyes met Cal's for a brief moment. "Healing. Trust. A sense of home," he replied.

"So what do we do then?" Cal asked.

"I can't say yet, Mr. McLaughlin. I have to think about it. If I say yes, quite a bit of our proposal needs to be rewritten, to say the least."

Of course, he thought. *Because we were going to clarify that you were in command of all crew members, and to give a new command structure that would integrate everyone into one crew.*

"What would you like me to tell them, sir?"

Dayton's mouth disappeared behind his moustache as he pursed his lips. "Tell them that we will take their requests under consideration, and that we are adjourned for today. Tell them we'll send a message when it's time to meet again, and that if they wish, we will do so on-board *Gabriel*."

"Yes, sir."

As Cal turned toward the bridge, Dayton added one last request. "Also have them hold their vote to name the river. Give them something to do in the mean time."

He nodded and left the doctor and colonel to talk further. Cal walked slowly as he returned to the bridge, allowing him time to ponder whether or not Dayton would accept the proposal that Darius had made. As much as Cal admired Colonel Dayton's ability to lead, he personally agreed with Darius; affairs in the colony were already a mess, and an election might help bridge the gap between the two camps.

If he does accept, will he even want to run? Or will this be too deep an injury to his pride?

Cal straightened his posture as he climbed the stairs, hoping to exude a more dignified look. The four delegates from *Gabriel* tracked his every move as he approached his seat, as did Hunter. Cal stopped by his chair, but did not sit.

"Colonel Dayton certainly isn't happy with your proposal, Darius," he said. He watched as the former officer nodded solemnly. "He will take it under consideration, but given that this was a surprise, the colonel wants me to let you all know that we are done for the day."

Don and Fred, the two attorneys from *Gabriel*, leaned in toward each other and exchanged whispers for a moment. Darius cast his eyes down at the table and slouched, while Rory Baines, the last delegate, began to tidy his workspace.

"You're not going to make your proposal today?" Don asked, his high voice registering his surprise.

"Not today. We'll send for you all again when Colonel Dayton is ready to proceed. Though in the mean time he does want you to have the people of *Gabriel* hold a vote on the river's name, if you don't mind."

"Of course." Don rose and extended his hand across the table, which Cal shook firmly. "We'll be waiting for your word."

The remaining men from the delegation shook hands with Cal and took their leave, though Darius avoided eye contact but for a brief moment when his turn came. After they departed the bridge, Cal took his seat and threw his long legs up onto the table.

"So what's gonna happen now?" Hunter asked, slicing through the silence.

Cal rubbed his eyes. "Now we wait and see what the colonel values more."

```
Capt Haruka Kimura
5 May, Year of Landing, late afternoon
Camp Eight
>|
```

All six of the hens in the cage squawked and clucked excitedly at Haruka's presence. They strutted around, keeping two steps ahead of her hand as she ran it over the outside of the enclosure, inspecting its construction. The thin bars made from branches were lashed to the frame using coarse palm rope. Though the coop was slightly crooked, it was solid enough overall to serve its purpose. Several similar and smaller crates lay nearby outside the Palace, each containing a rooster. One particularly agitated bird crowed angrily at Haruka and flapped its russet colored wings.

She lifted the hens' cage slowly. Her muscles strained somewhat at the weight, but she was able to maneuver it around without too much effort. Satisfied, she set it back down.

I'm not as strong as I used to be, but there are plenty of people here that can move these around if we need to, she noted. *Troy does an amazing job given the materials he has to work with.*

The center of the village had grown just a little more; Troy's crews had finished building two more huts, and were hard at work clearing a patch of ground for two more. Haruka had tried to lend a hand the previous day by picking up a pick to dig at tree roots, but Troy had dismissed her within a few minutes. Instead, she had found herself wandering around looking for something productive to do to occupy her time.

This day had started much the same. With Maria joining the workforce and taking over much of the weaving from Haruka, she found that she had far more idle time than she preferred. The villagers knew what they were expected to do and who they were to report to, and for the most part, that wasn't her. Only a handful of people would seek her out for updates and direction.

Troy and James had all but shut her down from any form of physical labor, and there was little else to do. Earlier in the morning she had given the Vandemark girls a break from watching over the young children so they could attend one of Charlotte's classes, but that task ended shortly after midday. None of the children had any interest in Haruka staying around, save for Gabi; they were far more used to having the older children play with them, and Haruka had a hard time keeping up with the kids during the more vigorous games.

So what am I still here for? So the team leaders can pander to me and make me feel useful?

She sighed and chose to seek comfort in one of her tranquility spots, where she knew she would be away from the eyes of the colony. Heading down the narrow road toward the shimmering sea, she chose the tiny jungle trail leading to the river estuary. The veil of trees and pepperine shrubs separated her from the white strand where the fishermen were sure to be at work, and children at play. By contrast, she was greeted by the calls of birds high above and acknowledged as she passed by a long, spear-headed lizard that clung to the gnarled limbs of a vinewood. She snagged two ripe pepperines from a bush, offering one to the lizard, which snatched it from her hand with its maw and disappeared higher into the tree. She sank her teeth deep into the flesh of the remaining fruit and continued on.

Haruka emerged from the foliage at her favorite spot, and she sat cross-legged at the edge of the slow-moving river. After taking the last bite of her snack she discarded its core into the water. Only moments later the core bobbed and was inundated by a mass of fish hungrily picking at the remnants.

She watched the spectacle for a minute before her thoughts drifted to back to the colony. As hard as she tried to find a task that she could do without her subordinates stopping her, she could not think of one that would be significant, or that she would be suited to. Frustration began to mount within her, rising along an increasing sense of uselessness.

Almost mindlessly she began to pick whatever vegetation was close at hand and cast it into the river in clumps, as she used to do as a child. Dirt collected under her fingernails until the tips were almost pitch black, and her hands were stained green and blue by the pulp of grasses and leaves. The activity did little to comfort her, however.

Not more than ten minutes later, James found her. He hustled down the beach to reach her, and she rose to greet him. His face wore an almost flat expression, save for the evidence of fatigue under his eyes.

"Thought I might find you here," he said.

"Who ratted me out?" Haruka asked, equally amused and irritated by the intrusion.

"No one. You're just getting too predictable."

She shrugged. "Not many places I feel both safe and alone."

"There's a whole jungle out there," he remarked nonchalantly.

J.C. Rainier

"Yes, there is."

Silence settled between them for a couple seconds.

"Is it Carney?" he asked quietly.

Haruka shook her head vigorously. "No, Carney's a ghost now. I'm a little more worried about the jaguars."

"Not the other ghosts out there?"

It took her a second to realize that he was referring to Marco and Evans. She narrowed her eyes at him as her amusement quickly gave way to irritation.

"Why are you here?" she snarled.

He scratched at his beard and shuffled one foot along the ground. "It's Maria again."

Again. She's back to working, but that doesn't seem to keep her out of trouble.

"What is it this time?" she asked, releasing a sigh of exasperation.

"She seems to have gone from one extreme to the other. She's gone from doing absolutely nothing to doing nothing but work. And guess who's caught up in her issues again?"

"Gabi," Haruka muttered almost under her breath.

"That's right. She picked yet another fight with Marya, this time in the middle of Charlotte's class. Charlotte went to discipline her, and Maria flew off the handle. At both of them."

"Jesus, James. This is getting out of control. Maybe you should just take Gabi from her for a while, until Maria can sort out her issues.

"Who knows when that will be, Captain," he grumbled. "Besides, Gabi wanted to stay with her mom the last time I tried. I don't think this time will be any different."

"Have you seen how scared she is of her mom now?"

"Doesn't mean a thing. She's still her mom. Gabi's not going to want to leave just because she gets yelled at. Kids aren't like adults, re-member?"

Haruka had to take a moment to adjust her frame of perspective. The image of the girl who had survived alone in the woods overnight and hid from a jaguar well enough to let Haruka save her played in stark contrast to the concept of a terrified little girl with an abusive mother, but was too afraid to leave her mother's side.

"That's not Gabi," she countered.

"It is. When you have kids of your own, you'll see."

The words cut deep into her. Haruka scoffed and bit back a response about how her condition, both medically and matrimonially, would make that impossible. "Whatever. It's time to get Ken or Emilia involved again. Maybe they can help her work through this."

James frowned instantly, and his crossed arms tightened against his chest. "We've been down that road already. Besides, we know that both Ken and Emilia have been talking about removing you from your duties."

"I know that. You're not asking them to play nicely with me. You're asking them to see if there's anything else they can do for Maria. No matter how they feel about me, they can't ignore her, or the pain she must be in."

"Fine. But you owe me one."

"Who's counting at this point?"

"I don't know," he replied as he turned away. "But you're definitely keeping them busy."

Well, at least we know what I'm good at.

Darius Owens
6 May, Year of Landing, 08:05
Gabriel
>|

The bridge of *Gabriel* looked much the way that its sister ship looked just a few days prior. Two folding tables butted up against each other to form the platform over which the negotiations would continue, and chairs from the workstations formed a ring around the tables, one of which was occupied by Rory. One key detail had been changed, and it left Darius feeling somewhat unsettled.

At the head of what was to be the *Michael* delegation's side sat the command chair, unbolted and dragged from its position at the head of the platform. It was a symbolic gesture that his companions wanted to make to Colonel Dayton; that they respected his position of command, and he should feel welcome to take his rightful seat. Darius had objected, as that specific chair had been granted to Colonel Eriksen when he assumed command of *Gabriel* all those years ago on Earth. While he could appreciate the sentiment that Don and Fred wanted to convey, Darius couldn't help but feel that Dayton might take it the wrong way.

The command chair that Dayton earned is across the river. He shook his head, disgusted with himself. *Across the river. Here I've been trying to help with unification, and I think something stupid like that. We're not supposed to be two, we're supposed to be one. Damn it, Darius.*

"Something wrong there, flyboy?" Rory asked, shaking Darius from his selfish thoughts.

Darius took the short walk to the negotiation table and slid into the seat next to his friend, though he dared not make eye contact.

"I don't know. Nothing and everything," he replied. "I'm worried that one thing could mean the difference between reconciliation and isolation. It could be something as big as my demand that the crews resign. Maybe something as little as that chair over there. That reminder of Eriksen."

Rory nodded. "It's all a scary idea, I won't kid you on that. But we're here, right? And he's coming. That's got to count for something."

"He could just be coming to tell us to go to hell."

"I don't think the colonel's a fool, Darius. He's not going to let this whole thing go to hell over a chair."

"But he might over the idea of giving up control."

The silence that answered him only reinforced the doubt that was firmly entrenched in his mind. With every passing minute, the wall built up, and he feared that if it continued to grow, all hope of resolution would slip from reach.

You can't take back what you've done, Darius. Even if you pull the demand off the table, the damage is done. Colonel Dayton can't trust you anymore.

Voices echoing from beyond the bridge heralded the impending arrival of the delegation. Darius straightened up and tried his best to put on a stone front, though underneath it was a mass of nerves tearing at his skin from within. The sweat that slicked his palms was not a pleasant addition to the equation, either.

"Please, take a seat," Don urged as he escorted Colonel Dayton and company onto the bridge.

Dayton walked toward the seat at the head of the table with measured, precise steps. His stride faltered for a moment as his eyes caught sight of the command chair, dragged from its perch up front. He shook his head and instead selected the chair next to it. Dayton motioned for Calvin to sit in Eriksen's former seat, and the two remaining delegates took seats to the right of the colonel.

Yeah, that chair was a bad idea, Darius thought. Another brick joined the already formidable wall in his mind.

Once the *Michael* contingent had settled in, the two attorneys took their seats to the right of Darius. The familiar shuffle of paper and clicking of pens around the circle was accompanied by Don Abernathy clearing his throat.

"Thank you for coming, Colonel," he said. "You as well, Lieutenant, Doctor Taylor, and Mr. McLaughlin. Welcome to *Gabriel.* As we left things after the previous session, your proposal had not yet been submitted, Colonel. Would you care to present it now?"

"Not as such," Dayton replied.

Darius felt his heart skip and then quicken.

No proposal. Shit, I blew it. He's going to walk.

"Very well," Don responded, his voice even despite the colonel's rejection. "How would you like to proceed?"

The colonel's chair emitted a long squeak as he leaned back, tenting his fingers in front of his lips.

"It's a risky proposal to say the least," he began. "We've barely started our work here, and already we've had a major incident that has taken away both the confidence and security from the populace. The cohesiveness between the crews is obviously nonexistent, and from what I can see, almost as bad internally with *Gabriel's* crew."

An understatement, Colonel.

"And yet, through it all, one man comes up with this crazy idea to dissolve the one remaining functional unit, and call for an election from the very people whose confidence has been shaken. I'm not inclined to think that this is a good idea. What I'd like to see is a strong leader that takes the colony into its future."

I knew it. Darius bit his lip but kept from showing any other signs of his disappointment.

"Piled on top is this notion of dismissing the entire service corps from their assignments. This is something that I cannot abide by," Dayton continued, shaking his head vigorously. "I have to ask you, with all due respect, Mr. Owens, what you were thinking when you made that proposal of yours."

He was taken aback by this question. Darius had fully expected Dayton to continue his explanation of Darius's failure. He stuttered for a moment, searching for the answer.

"A fresh slate across the board," he finally replied. "A do-over, if you will."

Dayton nodded. His chair squeaked as he catapulted forward and rose quickly to his feet. "It's that part that I agree with," he added.

What? For a moment Darius thought he had gasped the word aloud, but then realized he had held his surprise in check.

"I had to think long and hard, and listen to my clear consciences," he said as he motioned to his companions. "I had to make sure that I could see past pride and pain to get at the heart of the matter. So at this time, I would like to make the counter proposal, on behalf of *Michael*."

Dayton cleared his throat and picked up the pad in front of him, holding it nearly at arms' length as he read from the page. "We accept the proposal to hold an open colonial election for the position of Governor, based on a vote of all colonists of at least eighteen years of age who wish to participate."

Darius stopped breathing for a moment, and the rhythm of his heart could be felt through every bone in his body. *Wait, what?*

"For this position," he continued, "we do not agree that candidates should be limited to only civilians. However, to avoid a possible junta from arising in the aftermath, and in consideration of Mr. Owens' proposal to disband the military contingent, all service members will be required to resign no later than the inauguration date, to be set at a later time. This includes the Marines that were evacuated from Earth during the skirmish at Laramie.

"We do not, however, agree that there should be a complete void of military service. Any person of legal age and able body and mind may volunteer for a new colonial Militia, to be commanded by an officer appointed by the Governor. We have come up with a list of restrictions of use for the Militia, which we would be more than happy to give the representatives of *Michael* time to review. In a nutshell they will be around only for protection and crisis response."

An election. Disbanding the crews. He... he's giving in?

Dayton glanced up from the paper briefly, seeming to gauge the reactions of those at the table. "In exchange for these concessions, we ask for the following non-negotiable clause. All resource distribution must be equal between both sides of the colony for a period of no less than three years, except in the case where distribution of a specific resource will cause an extreme hardship for the party giving up the resource. This includes, but is not limited to, timber, minerals, human resources, and housing."

A stunned silence descended upon the bridge of the mighty ship. Darius exchanged disbelieving looks with his cohorts. As the seconds passed he waited for Dayton to make some outrageous addition to the negotiation, or to reveal that his words were nothing more than a cruel hoax, but the colonel stood fast and waited.

"I know this is probably a little bit of a shock to you all, and you may need some time to absorb it. There is one last thing I would like to bring to the table, however, and this is directed at Mr. Owens." Dayton placed the pad back on the table in front of him and stared directly into Darius's eyes. The cold, stern demeanor of the colonel melted away in nearly an instant. "I would be honored if you would assist me in planning a memorial for *Raphael*. I think that we still, to this day, haven't come to terms with exactly what the loss of that ship meant to us all, and we need to face that. Sooner rather than later."

Yet another surprise by Dayton left Darius speechless and unable to move for several moments. When his mind finally caught up, he slowly rose and walked around the table to Dayton with his hand extended. It was met in kind, and they shared a firm handshake. "The honor would be mine, Colonel."

Dayton clapped his free hand around Darius's and shook solidly, his smile poking out from behind the shaggy wall of fur that ringed his mouth. "Thank you, Mr. Owens. We'll take our leave so that you can discuss the proposal with your colleagues."

He then stepped back, motioned, and Calvin, Dr. Taylor, and Lieutenant Ceretti all vacated the bridge in a calm, swift order, with Dayton himself bringing up the rear. Darius let out a deep sigh of relief once they disappeared from sight.

"What was that?" Rory asked quietly.

"Victory, I think," Don remarked. "Other than the proposition of the Militia, I don't think he made a change to a single one of our proposals."

"No, no, there's got to be a catch. After that fuss he made last time?"

"No catch," Darius added. "You don't know what honor means to this man. He won't back out."

Fred cleared his throat. "So what are we waiting for? Let's accept the offer. Unless anyone here really has a problem with his militia idea."

This time the silence that followed was a sound that Darius treasured. No awkwardness lingered, only an unspoken agreement that the colonel's plan was not unpalatable, and they could refocus their attention on directing the settlement.

But one question remained for Darius, and it left him with a deep void inside.

What do I do now?

Calvin McLaughlin
13 May, Year of Landing, 12:56
River Islands, 1 mile east of the colony
>|

"Is everyone ready?" Cal asked Hunter.

The lieutenant tugged at Cal's freshly cleaned flight suit, picking at one particular wrinkle near his right shoulder that would not smooth out. "Yeah, man. Everything's in place. As long as you've done your part, we should be good to go. We're just waiting for the signal."

"I planted the seed with Dayton. It's not like I could spell it all out for him, though. He'd definitely take it wrong." Cal tugged at the collar of his suit. The day was unexpectedly hot, and even his Texas roots weren't enough to shrug off the sweltering heat trapped by the long-limbed garment.

"Well, it'll be pretty powerful if we pull it off. Stop fiddling with your neck and hold still."

Hunter brushed down his arms and made a slight adjustment to the right shoulder, grinning when whatever issue was bothering him had finally been resolved. "There. Now you look like one of us. Try to keep up, okay? Dayton wanted you to blend in with us to make the wall of blue look bigger."

Darius snickered and rolled his eyes at the display of the lieutenant fixing Cal's shirt. The staff he bore with the colors of the United States was gripped firmly in his meaty hands.

"Don't worry. I think I know how to fit in by now," Cal joked.

"That you do," Darius added.

Hunter nodded as the other crew members arrived and began to fall in. Other than the trio taking place at the head of the column, there was no order as to how they filled their rank; *Gabriel* crewmen fell in beside their counterparts from *Michael* as they arrived. Even Lieutenant Traci Josephson joined the file around the middle. Her face had healed well, leaving only a couple nasty scars from where deadly claws had narrowly missed tearing her face to shreds. Gone too was the cast on her forearm from where the Montoya's Grizzly bear had landed a fierce blow, cracking her limb as she had fought to protect Elaine.

Montoya's Grizzly. Named for its first victim. And it's had a few more since then. The very thought made Cal want to scream. *Just call it a damned Reaper bear. Don't play down her memory by naming a hor-*

rible, murderous animal after her. She was a good person. Why do we have to hang this curse on her name?

He caught Josephson glaring at him, and he pushed the thought from his mind, turning instead to the front of the column and away from her condemning eyes. He knew that she would take issue with him being allowed to march in file with the other service members. The fact that Colonel Dayton considered Cal to be part of his crew did not matter to Josephson.

Mercifully, it was only another minute before Hunter called the detail to attention and began their march around the grove of trees that obscured them from the waiting crowd of colonists. Cal was overwhelmed for a moment by the number of faces he saw when they emerged into the field. It seemed that every colonist from *Michael* was present, as well as some from *Gabriel* as well. He was aware that some families had chosen to take the ferry across the previous night and take advantage of Colonel Dayton's offer of hospitality for the night if they meant to attend the service. But after surveying the crowd, he figured that many had to have come over throughout the morning as well. His quick estimate put the total of civilians in attendance at over two thousand.

Colonel Dayton had taken effective command of both crews, and he had ordered *Gabriel's* entire crew to attend. With Cal at the head of the column with Hunter, and a few volunteers from the Marines who hitched a ride on *Michael*, the detail numbered exactly eighty, with Dayton included.

The exact number of the combined crews. At least, the exact number before the massacre.

Hunter led the company to a position along the river, slightly offset from where Colonel Dayton stood before the gathered masses, a small gray megaphone sitting at his feet. He ordered them to turn left, bringing them to face the people, and placing the River Islands at their backs. By the vote of the colonists, the meandering river had gained a new moniker: Fairweather River.

Named after Doctor Taylor's friend who was assassinated while in stasis. One of the senior researchers for Project Columbus. Dad's friend.

Cal had expected vocal resistance to the idea of naming the river after men who were accused traitors, but he had only heard of two people that were bothered by the concept. As he polled his fellow settlers in the days leading up to the final negotiation session, he found that there were few questions about the alleged treason, and more about each namesake; it was clear that naming the river after a destroyed ship was not favorable. The vote was very close between Benedict and Fairweather, however. Fairweather had won by just fifteen votes.

From the corner of his eye Cal caught a glimpse of Alexis, standing near the front and center of the gathered citizens. Her beauty captivated him, even at this distance, and he found it hard to keep his head still. He had to concentrate on staying in unison with the uniformed wall around him. Yet he could not help but notice that she did not look at Dayton, but rather the stony, treed islands beyond.

Colonel Dayton had selected this spot for *Raphael's* memorial for the simple reason that the ship's radio beacon had landed on the second, larger island. It was a small gesture, as no one could see or touch the beacon without fording the swirling torrent, but even at that it held meaning for anyone who knew of *Raphael's* fate. For Cal, it held another meaning; it was the place where he and Alexis had their first date on Demeter, and where Darius Owens risked his own life to tell of his plight. Cal had happier plans for this site some day, but that would have to wait. He watched Colonel Dayton pull a few folded pages out of his pocket and unfurl them.

"Friends and citizens," he started, speaking into the megaphone. "Those who traveled on *Gabriel* and *Michael* through the empty void of space, as refugees and servicemen. We all have gathered here for the purpose of honoring the lives lost when our sister ship, *Raphael*, suffered a tragic and catastrophic failure. It is not, nor may it ever be known, what happened to cause such a mighty and proud ship to be destroyed with the loss of over two thousand lives. Lives of mothers and fathers, brothers and sisters, children and officers alike.

"They were innocent, and they were brave. They were strangers, and they were friends. All of them were family, not of blood but of spirit. Like each of us standing here today they embarked on a journey to a new world. A world that was completely unknown to them, a world that may not have existed for all they knew. Yet they still took the path of faith as all of us did, leaving all behind and leaping skyward away from the ravages of war.

"Their faith and their memory should be honored. Though their lives may have been cut short, their spirit and courage will endure in each of you for generations to come. Live your lives in honor of those that were lost before you, both on Earth and Demeter. Keep your loved ones close, look after your neighbors, and live in honor and unity with all around you."

Now!

"Honor and Unity!" Cal's voice rang out over the shrub-dotted field, backed with the power of seventy eight other voices standing by his side, including those of Darius and Hunter.

The chorus seemed to catch Colonel Dayton off guard, and he paused for a minute, regarding his honor detail with bewilderment. Cal suppressed a smile, but inside he felt a moment of elation as his plan to demonstrate the crews' newfound unity had worked. The fact that he was able to pull it off without an order from Dayton made the concept that much sweeter.

That should put an end to any doubts he had about unification working, he thought proudly.

Colonel Dayton turned back to the crowd and spoke once more, though his voice cracked for a brief moment. "May God watch over them in Heaven, and may He watch over the citizens of Concordia. Amen."

As Dayton crossed himself and the crowd muttered an "Amen," Cal's jaw dropped. He had not been aware that the colony had been named. Cal knew that Dayton and the two lawyers from *Gabriel* had met two days earlier, but he had been under the impression that the only business they had to conduct was that of resource distribution.

They named the colony. They had to. My dreams... Concordia. They... how could they... His stunned reaction to the revelation engrossed him so deeply that for several seconds he blocked out another chant that rose from his companions.

Finally when the crowd of settlers joined in, shouting "Concordia!" over and over, throwing their fists into the air, he snapped to his senses. He had to move quickly, as the column of blue uniforms began a slow, deliberate march toward Colonel Dayton. To the cheers and shouts of the crowd they walked, and Lieutenant Hunter Ceretti once again brought them to a precise halt, this time in formation behind the colonel. Dairus kept his feet moving, and broke away from the column to take a place beside Dayton. He lowered the butt of his staff to the ground and unfurled the colors.

On the opposite side, Hunter took an Honor Guard from the remaining wall and marched them to the precipice just above the river. He barked order after order until a textbook twenty-one gun salute had been completed.

"It is time for the next chapter of our history to be written," Dayton said. "It is clear that we're on our own here. What we make of ourselves is up to us." He set the megaphone down and turned to Darius. "Strike the colors, Mr. Owens."

Strike the colors? What?

Without hesitation, Darius Owens unclipped the Star Spangled Banner from the staff. Dayton took one end and Darius the other, and with a series of precise movements, folded the flag into a neat triangle, which Darius handed to a sergeant who stood next to Cal.

What the hell is he up to?

An aging woman, in a long dress, with bobbed, silver hair walked forward from the crowd, carrying a folded blue piece of cloth in her arms. It took Cal a moment to recognize her as Sarah Kimura, the wife of Dr. Tadashi Kimura. When she approached Dayton, he took and unfurled the cloth, which he then clipped to Darius's staff. A slight breeze kicked up, lifting the new flag into the air.

Some in the crowd cheered, some seemed aghast at what Dayton had done, while still others gasped at the sight of their new standard. It was a rather angular and modern silver angel on a field of blue, bearing the names of all three ships, as well as a single Latin phrase on its own tiny banner: DUM VITA EST, SPES EST.

"While there is life, there is hope," Dayton barked into the megaphone. "For all that we have been through so far, I still see hope everywhere I look. It will never go away, and neither shall we!"

Pride in the commander's dignity and optimism, as well as the colony's resilience, swelled within Cal. He could not help but cheer at the end of the rousing speech. He was not alone in this sentiment; it quickly spread through the blue wall, and tore like wildfire through the crowd as it gained momentum.

Concordia had been founded, with the resounding voices of more than two thousand champions.

J.C. Rainier

Short green sprouts poked their way through the broken and cracked ground on the hill's western slope. Haruka knelt next to a patch of the tiny plants, running the palm of her hand gently over their tops, letting them tickle her skin. Her disbelief melted away as soon as she touched the Earth plants.

"Food. Of our own," she remarked. "Growing right here. *Growing.*"

"That's right," Troy confirmed as he loomed above her with his arms folded across his chest and a broad grin on his face.

"What is it again, exactly?"

"That's millet over there. On the other side of the trail they've planted sorghum."

"Two different crops?" she asked as she rose to her feet.

Troy nodded. "Thad wasn't sure if one would grow better than the other, if at all. So he had the fields planted differently just in case."

"And what if one crop fails?"

The smile disappeared from her civil engineer's face. "Well, we'll have a bit of a rougher time I imagine. Good news is we'll know for next season."

A rougher time, huh? She thought for a moment. *Not really comforting, especially when we're placing such a gamble on having two crops grow. If both work out, we still don't have enough to feed everyone. If one fails...*

"Are the Karches at least happy with everything?"

Again Troy nodded in affirmation. "They were tired of sleeping outdoors. Their hut may be cozy, but they appreciate the privacy, not to mention the farm that goes with it."

"Good. What's the next stop on our tour today?"

"Nothing. That's the last of the current projects, so I was hoping to move on to something new."

She smiled and nodded, glad that the weekly inspection was drawing to a close.

"What's next on your plate, then?"

"Better storage. Maybe a warehouse of some sort. I was thinking of setting it up below the village along the river path, and maybe adding some other production buildings there later."

"Show me," she replied.

Troy turned down the winding dirt path away from the farm with Haruka in tow. After a couple minutes they left the exposed slope of the farm and entered the lush, pungent vegetation of the jungle floor. As they crossed over the main road to the colony onto the narrow river path, James Vandemark came rushing down from the village above, waving his arms furiously and calling for their attention. He skidded to a halt in front of them, and took a moment to catch his breath.

"Captain," he huffed. "They're all together. Right now."

She furrowed her brow as she tried to guess what James was referring to. "Who?"

"The conspirators. The ones who want to remove you from power. I saw them all go in the clinic, one at a time."

Damn it, she cursed silently.

"All of them? Torres? The Lerner brothers?" she prodded.

James nodded curtly. "And the Reibers, Maria, and Doctor Petrovsky," he added.

She cursed and spat on the ground. "I'm starting to get sick of all of this. If they want something, they should just come out and say it instead of hiding behind the clinic walls."

"We know what they want."

"And until they can find a suitable replacement to me, they're not going to get it," Haruka scoffed in disdain.

Troy scratched at the stubble on his chin pensively. "So what do we do about it?"

"Make a move. Force their hand." Her hand fell almost instinctively to her belt, resting on the grip of her Beretta.

Her companions exchanged cautious glances, and looked down at their respective weapons.

"No offense, Cap," Troy broke the silence in the softest voice he had ever used to address her. "If you want to storm in there armed, I don't think seven against three are the odds I'd like to have, even if they're unarmed."

"They're not armed," James confirmed.

"And again no offense, but you haven't exactly been at full strength lately."

Haruka's blood began to boil, as much for Troy pointing out that her illness had again sapped her vigor as for the brazen daylight gathering of those who would cast her aside without a plan or vision for the colony.

"Fine," she snapped. "Find a few more guys to bring with us. You have ten minutes."

Both men nodded as they scrambled. James bolted down the path to the river, while Troy took his leave toward the beach.

She took the time of solitude to pace back and forth, wringing her wrists and muttering curses about Maria's manipulation of Torres and the Lerners, and she let loose several choice words about the Reibers' lack of gratitude for what Haruka had done, not only for them, but Camp Eight as a whole.

Yet for a brief moment she considered simply walking into the clinic and handing the reins of the colony over to the treacherous group, just to watch them collapse under the pressure. But the idea passed quickly when she weighed the consequences of what she believed would happen to Gabi. The brilliant and spirited young girl, whom she had met the morning after *Raphael's* disaster, had already met with more than her share of tragedy. Haruka couldn't bear the thought of what burdens she might have to carry if her mother, Maria, were to crack from her already unstable mental state.

No, we have to meet them head on and put this to rest. She took a several deep breaths and steeled herself, even as her legs felt tired and strained from Troy dragging her all over the colony for an inspection earlier in the afternoon.

James returned first, bringing with him a face that was all too familiar: Nicholas Petrovsky, the son of Dr. Petrovsky. He was just nineteen, and still had a baby face under the so-called 'beard' that adorned his cheeks, but weeks of wading into the surf to fish had given him deceptive strength, not to mention a nearly bronze complexion. He was also openly critical of his father's views on how the colony should be run, aligning himself more often with Haruka.

James clapped Haruka on the shoulder and whispered as he passed, "That ought to stick in the old man's craw."

Haruka was less than enthusiastic about using Nick as a pawn. Though he looked less overtly threatening without a firearm, she knew that the machete and knife on his hips were just as deadly. In her mind, she questioned the wisdom of bringing one of the conspirators' children to confront them.

She looked at Nick squarely in his cool blue eyes and asked, "Your father is going to be in there. Are you sure you want to confront him? You're not going to do anything stupid, right?"

Nick shook his head vigorously. "I know you're just going to show him up. I'm just going with you to make sure *they* don't do anything stupid. I don't care if it's because I scare them or because Dad is on their side. I don't think they'll try anything with me there."

She nodded, satisfied with his motives, even if steeped in teenage logic.

Troy returned a couple minutes later with Seth and Jenkins in tow, both sporting their service pistols. Haruka greeted them, not stopping for a moment to question their loyalty, as she knew it to be true. Without hesitation she led them up the road and into the town square, stopping outside the Palm Palace to reaffirm their intentions and orders.

"No one draws unless they do first, got it?" she reiterated at the end of the discussion. A chorus of bobbing heads confirmed the plan.

They marched across the street, and Haruka threw back the clinic's storm curtain loudly, letting Seth and Jenkins lead the way before stepping inside. It took a moment for her eyes to adjust to the darkness inside so that she could see that her opponents were indeed unarmed, but just as soon as they did, gasps arose from both parties within the humid, sweltering edifice.

"Nick?" she heard Dr. Petrovsky ask. "What are you doing here?"

Nearly simultaneously, Troy and James called out the names of their oldest children. Standing in the circle of conspirators were Will Vandemark and Gina Bryant, whose expressions changed quickly from shock at seeing their fathers to anger.

The noise level inside the clinic rose sharply as the parents on either side began lamenting how their children could possibly betray them in such a manner, as well as questioning them as to whether they knew what they were doing, or if they knew what their actions meant. Counter accusations flew from the younger generation about their parents' inability to see what was actually going on, and defiant declarations of their righteousness and capacity to think for themselves.

"Quiet!" Haruka bellowed over the ruckus. A moment later the room fell silent. "I know why you all are meeting here. You think I'm some sort of evil tyrant or slave driver that needs to be replaced." Her glare squarely met Maria as she spoke the words. "I'm here to tell you that I'm not going anywhere. You'd like to think that you know the stakes involved and how to run things here, but the truth is you don't know a fraction of it."

"There are some in the colony who think we'd be better off under someone else," Dr. Petrovsky rebutted. "But you're so stubborn in your ways that you won't even consider it. You're working people until they're physically exhausted, and putting people to task who aren't ready for it."

"I'm sorry that I'm giving consideration to your need to eat, or to have a roof over your head, Doctor. Everyone in this room knows we don't have nearly the manpower, food reserves, or tools that we were supposed to have at our command. If we're going to survive out here we have to buckle down."

"Or else what?" Gina spat defiantly. "What are you going to do if I stop babysitting everyone's kids when Kelly and Kristen need a break? Or if I don't do a load of everyone's laundry at the river?"

"What if I were to slow down like you want, and bring back one less bucket of crabs? Or six fewer sharks?" Nick responded, his voice equally passionate. "I don't care if I have to work sunup to sundown because I'm making sure there's food to go around." He glowered at his father. "And you should know that we're stretched thin already. You've lost what, twenty pounds since we've been out here? How can you say we need to cut back on our duties when we're already so close to starving?"

"We've got fields planted now," Emilia protested.

"Not nearly enough to feed everyone," Troy countered. "And we don't got enough houses for everyone. I don't know about all of you, but I know what happens after the dry season in the tropics on Earth. Hurricane season. Not saying it'll be like that here, but if it is and we're not ready, kiss your sorry asses goodbye."

Mark Reiber narrowed his eyes. "Is that a threat?"

"Nope. A prediction."

"No, the threat is right there," Maria shrieked as she leveled a finger at Haruka. "She comes in here to harass us with all of her armed thugs here, when we're just talking, and don't have a weapon between us. First she forces me to work, and now she forces all of us to accept her ways. With intimidation."

Haruka folded her arms across her chest and snarled, "I'm not threatening you, Maria. Besides, we're not carrying anything we don't have with us any day of the week. If you take a walk outside of these walls, for a few minutes, you'd see that the jaguars are still out there, not to mention other threats."

"Like kids you shoot in the head?" Dr. Petrovsky retorted. "When they're starving and searching for food?"

Haruka's head snapped around to face the slanderous doctor. She gritted her teeth and replied, "Carney was a murderer. He was armed and dangerous, and had stolen from us before. And just what the hell did you expect us to do with him if he *had* been taken alive? Chain him up in the Palace for the kids to watch as Charlotte taught civics lessons? If you think that I'm a barbarous tyrant, look in the mirror sometime and see what your ideals look like in play here."

Silence descended for a moment on the room. Haruka narrowed her eyes and judged every one of the shocked traitors.

"It's going to take a lot more than all of your good intentions to run this village," she continued. "Go on with your plotting and scheming if you want, I won't stop you. But think carefully about the impact of any edict you would hand down. Think hard about the downsides, because they *will* come to bite you in the ass someday."

She spun on her heels and snapped her fingers as she walked out of the clinic, all six of her cohorts following close behind.

A long, soft scraping noise heralded the arrival of the simple flat-bottom raft on the sand-and-silt landing on the north side of the river. Construction crews on both sides of the Fairweather River had been hard at work creating suitable termini for the ferry crossing. On the north side of the river rocks that had been dredged up and stacked to the side near a pile of timbers, materials all destined to become a short quay. A heavy loader stood idly by, mud caked on the claws of its stout scoop. Two men and four women idled by this pile in wait of their turn to board for the return trip to *Gabriel* on the south side.

One of the two oarsmen scrambled off the bow, dragging with him a rope that was attached to the raft. He quickly secured it to a post that had been driven into the ground on shore, then signaled for the passengers to disembark. Darius stood up and nodded at the other oarsman and the tiller, then took his leave of the small craft with the four other workers that Thomas Dayton had requested for the day.

Thomas Dayton. No longer a colonel. Darius paused on the shore for a moment and chewed his lip as he thought. He and the entire crew of Michael resigned the day after the remembrance ceremony. The day after unification was declared.

No one challenged Dayton's authority on the north side of the river despite this move. The south side was a different story. A few of *Gabriel's* crew members were hesitant to relinquish their commissions, most notably Sergeant Marks. Darius couldn't blame him for his apprehension; the man had sided with Colonel Eriksen out of blind loyalty. Marks had also been part of Major Kintney's goon squad, and now he was left in the open without the protection of his superiors. Darius had a hard time separating what Marks did from who he was.

The confusion amongst *Gabriel's* ranks, both current and former, was further fueled by the revelation that Tyler Quinn, the ship's engineer disgraced by Eriksen, had decided to run for governor. This maneuver was followed the next morning by Dayton stating his intention to seek the same office, and two days later by groups of colonists from both sides of the river calling for Calvin McLaughlin to be added to the ballot.

As much as Darius admired the kid for his courage and fervor, the idea of an eighteen year old, who had never held a job in his life, becoming the leader of the colony in such a fragile state just did not settle well with him. When he had been called on by Dayton to inspect *Michael's* computer servers, Darius had jumped on the opportunity. This was not so much to give him something to do as it was a chance to come to the north side of Concordia and find out from Calvin himself what plans he held.

Darius departed from the landing, noting how the construction crew on the north side had already graded a wide, gently sloping path up to the high bank above, making the climb on this side of the river much more pleasant and less treacherous. He paused again at the top of the ascent to look out over the river and watch the raft pivot just off shore so the tiller could steer properly on the return trip.

The walk to the slumbering ship was uneventful. The camp was already awake and its inhabitants either gone to work or performing the chores necessary to keep daily life functioning smoothly. As he passed near to the camp kitchen he received an enthusiastic wave 'hello' from Alexis Decker, which he returned in kind. For a moment he stopped and considered asking her what Calvin intended to do with his nomination, but he knew that subject might be sensitive for her. He thought better of it before making the final turn to the rear cargo ramp of *Michael*.

Now this guy, on the other hand, will not mind talking shop at all, Darius thought as he crowned the ramp and found Hunter Ceretti at work leaning over a pallet of crates and scribbling on a clipboard.

"Good morning," he greeted.

Hunter looked at him and blinked for a moment, then smiled and extended his hand. "Darius, good to see you. You here to look at my lady's fine racks?"

"Only if you don't tell *my* lady that I'm doing so," he jested in return. "She might get jealous and cook a blade or null route something. And wouldn't that just ruin my day?"

"Temperamental girl. It's a wonder she didn't stop in orbit and refuse to land."

"Ah, I know how to get her to bend to my will. Hope your girl here is like her sister."

"Nope. She behaves herself." Hunter sighed heavily, and sadness washed over his face. "Cam saw to that."

"I'm sorry. Sergeant Drisko was a huge loss," Darius replied, placing his hand on the former lieutenant's shoulder in sympathy.

"Yeah, he was," came the short reply as Hunter turned back to his work. "But he was doing his duty. Protecting Cal. Can't complain about that."

Darius knew there was nothing more to say about Drisko, but he could almost feel the air chill as Ceretti concentrated once again on his clipboard. As Darius considered the approach to his quandary, he walked silently to the crates and inspected the labels, which revealed the contents to be conduit, circuit breakers, and other supplies for tapping a building into the power grid and wiring it for electricity.

"I heard something about Calvin that got my attention," Darius said, breaking the tension.

"Oh? What's that?" The reply was almost immediate, and was accompanied by an upward glance under a cocked eyebrow.

"That he's been handed a nomination for governor by the people."

"He was," Hunter confirmed. "But that lasted all of five seconds before Cal shot them down. He doesn't want the responsibility. Good on him, too. He's not ready to take on anything like that, not by a long shot."

Darius nodded and put on a stone face, quashing any outward sign of the relief that he felt with this bit of news. "He's got a good head on his shoulders, but I agree that's not the path for him. Not yet, anyway."

"Well, some people out there are hell-bent on making sure we have three candidates. From what I've heard, they've picked a new darling to take on Dayton and Quinn."

"Who?" Darius asked, equally surprised and curious. "Abernathy? Hausner?"

"You."

"M-me?" he stammered, barely able to get the words out as the shock left him almost breathless.

"Yup."

"W-why?"

Ceretti slipped his pencil under the board's clip and set it down gently on the pile. His gaze swiveled to meet Darius head-on.

"If there's going to be a third candidate – which is frankly something I'd love to see – it needs to be someone who has integrity, honor, and morality. You have that in spades, Darius."

"But… but I was insubordinate," he protested. "I disobeyed Eriksen at every turn when I found out what he was planning on doing to

Reid and Doctor Kimura. You could make the argument that I was drummed out of the service if you wanted, though I see it a bit differently."

"You were insubordinate, yes. But no one here disputes that Colonel Eriksen's orders were wrong. Of all the men and women in his crew, *you* were the one to stand up. The cost for you grew the more you stood your ground, but that didn't stop you."

"I got people beaten up. I… got people killed."

Ceretti shook his head. "We know you saved Dr. Kimura's life."

"He's in prison. The worst kind of prison he could possibly be in," Darius lamented. "If the reactor holds, he'll wake up and find his grandchildren to be as old as him. If not, he'll die in his sleep."

"Have faith. There are things that can be done."

"Like what?" he scoffed.

"Governors can pardon criminals, can they not?"

Those words silenced Darius. He hadn't considered the power that the position wielded. For a moment the thought of freeing Dr. Kimura encompassed him, driving nearly every synaptic impulse. Somewhere in the deep recesses, his conscience reminded him that there would be more to the position than simply freeing one man, and the lives of four thousand people would be forever influenced by any decisions made by him as a governor.

"It's still so much. I mean, can you imagine the pressure?" he asked.

"No," Hunter replied bluntly. "I don't want to. I'm actually glad we could resign from the service. I would have shit myself if I made captain. Never wanted that kind of responsibility; I'm happy where I am. But you've proven that you can take heat and come through it with your wits intact. That's why I was one of the people to nominate you."

Darius simply blinked, unable to come up with a response.

"You may not know it," Hunter continued. "But you've got the right stuff in you. That much is clear."

"I… I should probably go look at the servers now," Darius stuttered is a voice barely louder than a mouse's squeak. He started down the long lower gallery.

"Don't dismiss it. Give it some serious thought, Darius," Hunter called from the bright, gaping maw.

I have to at least consider it. For the doctor's sake.

Calvin McLaughlin
25 May, Year of Landing, 17:41
River Islands
>|

A pair of sinister, glowing eyes pierced the dark, staring back at Cal from beyond the faint ring of illumination cast by the lantern, almost obscured by the tall grasses. He stopped at once, throwing his arm out in front of Alexis to keep her from taking another step, then dropped his free hand to the holster on his belt. The eyes blinked at him twice, then disappeared into the darkness, accompanied by a rapid chattering noise. Cal relaxed and let out his breath, not realizing until then that he had been holding it.

"What was it?" Alexis whispered.

"Might have been a brush dog," he replied in an equally hushed tone. "Whatever it was, it took off in a hurry."

Classification of the native life had started almost the day the ships had landed. For the most part it took the form of calling animals by familiar Earth families and species. Something that confounded the scientists, on the other hand, was the people's insistence on naming foods based on what they looked or tasted like, not on the familial characteristics established centuries earlier by the scientific community. The local fauna was often less tricky to classify. The brush dog was a species that looked somewhat like a cross between a greyhound and a wolf, and was mostly nocturnal; hence they had been designated as canines. Several aggressive and hostile species had been identified, though this was not one of them. It wanted little to do with humans except to scavenge from the camp's waste.

Cal took Alexis's hand and pressed forward. After a minute the landscape cut off abruptly ahead of them, giving the illusion that their flashlight could penetrate not penetrate an invisible wall in the night. The rushing water of the rapids that tumbled between the River Islands could be clearly heard ahead of them, though not seen. Cal knew that they were only a few feet from the river's banks, so he stopped. He shone the beam on the ground near them to select a suitable spot, then unrolled a sleeping bag from his pack and laid it on the long, flowing grass, which matted easily. He then guided Alexis to a seated position on the bag, and then took his place next to her, shrugging the pack off to the side.

"You sure picked a beautiful night," she remarked as she lay back to gaze at the heavens.

"I just wanted to get away for a bit."

A brief pause was followed by a simple question from his girlfriend. "Do you want to talk about it?"

Yes. No. I don't know.

Cal simply shrugged and then rummaged through the top compartment of the pack. He produced a few Demeter pears and a small bundled handkerchief. The piece of cloth was stowed immediately in the pocket of his jeans, and he handed two of the fruits to Alexis before switching off the lantern.

In an instant they were plunged into near darkness, though some features of the islands could be seen as faint silhouettes, and the bright sphere of Persephone illuminated the nearby vegetation in a ghostly wash. The bright moon's small, shadowlike companion followed behind by what looked like only a couple inches in the sky. Cal knew that Arion would overtake its orbital partner within the hour, and he had heard that the resulting darkness from the partial eclipse would let them see ribbons of stars that could not be seen in the otherwise crowded sea of pin-like lights.

Moments later, a faint flash of blue streaked through the sky, followed by the shrill call of a raptor. The bird was known as a glow hawk, and Cal had first seen it during his short stint with the Expeditionary Forces. It instantly became Alexis's favorite native animal when Cal pointed one out a few days after he returned. He had to admit, it was quite an intriguing creature. An able hunter in its own right by day, the glow hawk could also hunt small nocturnal creatures with alarming accuracy. Flaps along the side of its body could open for brief periods, casting light from bioluminescent strips of skin underneath. The resultant glow allowed their keen eyes to pick out prey, even in the dead of night.

"Ooh, did you see the glow hawk?" she asked, her excitement clear in her voice.

"Yep."

If tonight's not the night, I don't know when the right time would be.

Cal sunk his teeth into his pear, feeling the flesh give way and sweet juices burst forth. Though it was vaguely reminiscent of a pear in both consistency and taste, the native fruit was a little smaller, had slightly thicker, papery skin, and at its core sat a single large pit. It also grew far quicker than its equivalent from Earth; only a few weeks into the growing season, small trees laden with this fruit were plentiful.

"Ooh, these are good," Alexis chirped.

Cal nodded and slurped on a puddle of juice that was pooling between his thumb and the pear. It took him a few bites more than he expected to finish the dessert, which he flung over the river bank to discard of the pit. Though the food sated his hunger, it did nothing to quell the tingling in his nerves. The day had been a rough one for him, and Cal was hoping that his plans for the night would wash away the world. Yet, as he shoved his hands in his pockets and traced his fingers over the hard lump within the handkerchief, his excitement and his fears rose up anew.

It took him a minute to figure out that Alexis had been talking, and he hadn't heard a word that she had uttered.

"Are you okay?" she asked again.

"Sorry, Lexi. Just lost in thought."

"Was it about lunch today?"

Cal bit his lip and fought the urge to crawl inside a silent wall. Lunchtime should not have been as big of an issue as today's had been. He just wanted to grab a bite from the mess tent and inform Alexis that they would have the night off rotation. But then his supporters showed up in force.

Somewhere along the way the stories of what Cal had said after the execution and ensuing slaughter had been embellished. His role in the unification negotiations had been given a status of near legend, putting him somewhere above Darius and Dayton, as far as his contribution to bringing the two halves of the colony together and making them whole. Cal got the feeling that volunteering to march behind Darius at the Unification ceremony did not help dispel this myth that people held of him.

"I don't get it," he said, both upset and confused as he replayed the earlier incident in his mind. "I've told everyone I can think of that I don't want to be governor. I've told Dayton. I've told Darius and Quinn. I've told every supporter that has ever come up to me. Why do those kids want me so badly that they're almost willing to trample me and drag me around?"

"It's cause you're so damn cute," Alexis quipped. "I mean, all those teenage girls parading around, trying to convince their parents that you're the one."

"Not funny," Cal snapped back. "And their parents know I'm not the right guy for the job. At least most of them."

"Sorry…"

Cal tried to push back the memory of one man in particular that made him shake with anger and fear, and his hands nearly tremble enough to drop his lunch on the ground. The wild look in the man's eyes as he got in Cal's face, passionately demanding that Cal at least meet with his three children to explain why he refused to look after their future, was not a memory easily shaken. Cal was almost certain that he was going to face the man's fury as he tried to shy away and leave the situation. Alternating insults and pleas followed him from the camp kitchen all the way to *Michael*. Only Hunter Ceretti acted as his saving grace. His friend had sternly turned back the small but persistent mob, then given him shelter on the upper deck of the ship.

"Look, it'll all be over after tomorrow." Her words were meant to comfort him, but they did little.

"The election's over a week away. I really don't want to have to hide on the ship the whole time."

Her hand found his in the darkness, and her warm fingers curled into a gentle squeeze. Cal looked to his side and could barely make out her pale silhouette in the moonlight, yet he could still distinguish the upturned corners of her smiling mouth.

"Trust me, it'll be sooner than you think. When you don't join the debate tomorrow it will change. When you don't give a speech with the other candidates, your adoring flock will know it's really over. They'll leave you alone then."

"Are you sure?" he asked, hoping that her optimism would somehow rub off and light the path through his doubt.

"I promise. Besides, if Mr. Pushy comes after you again, I'll kick his ass for you."

An impish grin crossed his face. "If you must. I mean, who am I to stop you?"

He knew that Alexis was joking about the last part, but the image did hold a certain amusing allure. And in that moment he felt that she would truly stand by him, no matter what. Though she had chastised him harshly when he continued to work for Dayton, she had bawled her eyes out when she had learned that Cameron had sacrificed his life for Cal. No rebuke had followed. None was necessary, either. Besides negotiation work and marching for the Unification ceremony, Cal had freed himself of the former colonel's service.

Cal turned around and lay on his back next to her, letting the crisp night's air wash over him. The pungent smells of earth and flowering shrubs filled his nose. Spectral ribbons of white glittered with hundreds of tiny stars as they wove through the night sky, contrasting the surrounding inky void with fewer, though much brighter, points of light from distant supergiants.

In this moment, he felt insignificant and foolish, and the token inside the handkerchief stuffed in his pants' pocket seemed silly. He knew from movies and stories told by friends on Earth that breathtaking sights often accompanied the type of goal he intended to achieve, but he wasn't sure if it seemed more cliché or minute. As he reached into his pocket his nerves rose and threatened to make him lose his dessert, or at the very least his voice.

"L-Lexi?" he stammered after a couple minutes. "I, ah… I…"

She turned on her side, masking her face in darkness as the moons were now behind her. "Something wrong?"

Cal closed his eyes and took a deep breath to settle himself. He slipped the salvaged aluminum spacer ring out of the cloth, feeling along the circumference to make sure the braided leather cord was still attached.

"You know that it bugs me how uncertain things are for me around here, right?" The question he posed was rhetorical, but he waited for her to affirm before he continued. "Through everything that's happened since we landed, you're the one thing that I can count on every day to keep me sane. When I went out on the expedition with Neil, Traci, and…" he paused for a second to fight back another bitter memory.

"Shhh, it's okay."

Cal's chest heaved with another loud sigh. "Look, I've almost died a couple times. I've come close to losing my shit a couple times, too. Every time I go to the edge you bring me back again. Telling you that I love you just doesn't do justice to what you mean to me."

"I… I love you too, Cal," she replied.

Now or never, numbnuts, a voice inside him eerily similar to his long-quiet doppelganger called out.

He took her hand in a way that made her cup it upwards, exposed. With his other hand he slipped the necklace into her palm and gently closed her grip.

"I know it's not what a guy's supposed to give a girl when he says this, but it's all I've got."

"Says what?" she asked, clearly confused, with her voice hinting at slight apprehension.

"I never want there to be a doubt about us being there for each other, ever. Alexis Hailey Decker, would you do me the honor of being my wife?"

Cal heard a loud gasp and then silence. The seconds ground away without a response, and he had a moment of panic mixed with shame and rejection. Just as he was about to bite his lip and hang his head in shame, she threw her arms around his neck and tackled him into the grass, planting a long, sweet kiss on his lip.

"Yes," she cried out. "Of course, yes!"

She sat upright as she straddled him. The left side of her face was lit again by the pale glow of Persephone, and he could see her wide smile as a single tear rolled down her cheek. Alexis raised the necklace over her flowing locks, settling it on her neck. The single ring glinted and faded as it twisted and swung in and out of the shadows. Alexis looked down for a moment, biting her lip as she admired the adornment.

He rose up to meet her in a kiss under the double full moons. The sounds of Demeter seemed to melt away as the lovers united for the first time, watched by the millions of sentinels in the night sky.

Capt Haruka Kimura
1 June, Year of Landing, late morning
Camp Eight
>|

"Are you ready to fire her up?" James asked, tapping on the lifeless radio console inside the wreck of pod eleven.

Only if it actually works this time. Haruka managed a weak smile. "Of course. Always ready to see if we can contact the other ships."

"Alright. Let me remove the battery bypass and we should be in business." He slipped out of the cockpit and she could hear him grunt as he climbed up the precariously tilted ladder to the upper berth hallways.

"I'll believe it when I see it," she muttered once he was out of earshot. A greasy knot tied in her stomach, and she closed her eyes to reflect on the situation.

The first two attempts to revive the radio had been miserable disasters. James had been mystified after the radio failed to power up the first time, and swore that he had just miscalculated how long it would take to charge the batteries. The second failure alarmed the former technician, and he had spent the rest of the day and a sleepless night tracing the problem to a leak in the pod's electrical system that drained the batteries as quickly as they could be charged.

The process of setup, troubleshooting and repair took over a month of his spare time. In the meantime, farming had started in the colony, the dissidents grew louder in their calls for Haruka to be removed, and every survivor had been stressed to their limits. Haruka held little hope that the third attempt at reviving the radio would work, and that she could contact one of the other ships to mount a rescue. It was a Hail Mary at best; assuming the radio worked, they would have to be able to convey their position to another crew, and hope that they were in a position to build seaworthy ships to sweep the survivors of Camp Eight away.

If by some miracle it happens, I'll need to send word to Marsolek's camp and get them over here too. I can't leave them behind to fend for themselves.

She shook aside the thought as folly. There were too many variables, and a barrier at any one would derail the entire plan. The best she could hope for was to simply be able to relay a message to her family and notify the other ships that they had survived.

James returned and took the left hand seat in the pod, deferring the right hand seat – and radio – to Haruka. "We're good to go. I checked and there's power flowing out of the batteries."

"Here goes nothing."

She flipped the main switch on the computer followed by the radio power. The small LED screen that indicated the frequency flickered for a moment and then went dead. Haruka grimaced and flicked her hand in disgust at the console.

"No go, James," she said as she wiped the sweat from her brow.

He muttered a curse under his breath, then pulled open the center console and crawled inside until the upper half of his body disappeared.

"Fuck," he grunted, his voice sounding hollow from the dampening of the enclosure.

Haruka was forced to bite back her sarcasm. "Bad news?"

James withdrew from the cramped console and immediately mounted the chair. His fingers ran along the seam of the window, where the woven frond patch covered the gaping hole left by the vacated glass. He cursed again as he poked his finger through the panel near the front edge, then traced a line down to the forward fittings of the compartment, where he flaked off some rust with his finger.

"Water," he grumbled. "The whole thing's ruined. No way to fix it without cannibalizing another pod."

Haruka remained silent, grinding her teeth together. This revelation should not have shocked her, as their luck had been almost nonexistent since *Raphael* was destroyed. However, the pill was no less bitter to swallow.

"I can go back to pod eight and be back…"

"No," she cut him off.

"Captain?"

"No more of this nonsense, James. This pod's a wreck. Pod eight's a wreck. They're all useless, and you've had more than enough chances to get this thing working. Just give it up."

"But if we can contact the other…"

"We can't," she shot back. "Marsolek has a better chance than we do at this point. It's time to stop wasting your time and face the facts. This project is done."

He was about to protest, but a wave of nausea washed over her and she bolted from the pod. Haruka barely made it to the end of the ramp before she vomited and collapsed to her knees. James was only a few steps behind, and knelt beside her, patting her back.

"Getting sick again?"

"I'll be fine."

"When was the last time you threw up?"

"Last night."

"Weakness? Dizziness?"

"I'm fine," she protested.

"Tell me," he insisted. His tone was the same that he used to shame his children into telling the truth.

"Two days ago."

"You want to go to the doctor?"

"No, I'll be fine."

Haruka took three steps toward the tree line, which began to blur before her, before throwing up again.

"I'm taking you," James said firmly. She did not protest.

James hooked her arm over his shoulder to keep her steady as they walked. At first Haruka attributed her wobbliness to her vertigo combined with the shifting sands, but the situation was no better once they were on the path up the hill to the clinic. In fact the incline exaggerated the issue, and she found herself having a hard time standing up, much less walking in a straight line. She threw up again, this time in the middle of the road. James let her slip to her knees to retch out the last of her stomach's contents.

Haruka was aware during this process that Troy had joined them on the path, and her civil engineer had a brief conversation with James about her condition. They helped her back to her feet and carried her the remaining quarter mile to the village clinic. By the time they arrived, her vision was one blur of light brown that trailed into dark brown, with blue and green fuzz along the top where the jungle canopy should be. When they crossed through the doorway it all faded into a dark gray and black blur.

Haruka's stomach complained as she was laid on one of the beds. The coarse mat of fibrous leaves was icy cold against her skin, and she immediately curled up into the tightest ball she could. In the background she could hear James arguing with Maria, but she blocked out their words to concentrate on finding the most comfortable position she could find on the low slab.

"I'm not a monster, Maria. I'm still a doctor above all else," she heard Dr. Petrovsky say as he moved to her side. "Captain, can you hear me?"

"Yeah," she mumbled.

A meaty, clammy hand clamped on her forehead. "You've got a fever, Captain. You're going to have to stay here a bit so I can keep an eye on it."

Haruka nodded weakly. The motion caused the dizziness to flare up again, so she again became as still as she could.

"James, I'll need some rags from the back. Troy, get me water please. Distilled if you can get it. River water if you can't. It needs to be as cool as possible, too."

"Yeah, Doc," Troy said.

A couple minutes passed as Dr. Petrovsky checked her pulse and respiration, and took a hand-off of supplies from James, whom he promptly sent out of the clinic to retrieve his son Will. Not more than a couple seconds after the storm curtain closed, she felt the presence of another person at her side.

"Look at you," Maria hissed. "You bitch at me to get to work, and what have you done for the village except take up Ken's time and boss people around, huh? Where do you get off on that?"

"That's enough, Maria," Petrovsky warned sternly.

Haruka swallowed hard. She wanted to respond, but in her haze, her mind could not come up with a response quickly enough.

"Well let me tell you; your days of sitting on your throne are over, and I'm going to sit here and watch you fall into obscurity." The tone Maria's voice took on was chilling and ominous. "If you thought you were useless before, you haven't seen anything yet. No one will remember why they ever let you push us around."

"I said that's enough!"

Dr. Petrovsky burst into argument with Maria over her conduct. It seemed to rage on for minutes, with the doctor repeatedly commanding the furious widow to leave the clinic. The voices slowly faded, and Haruka drifted into dreams as her heavy eyelids closed and the spinning of the world subsided.

The fever induced scene had her once again in the engine control room of the doomed sleeper ship. Maynard's corpse was strapped in its seat, exactly as she had remembered, shredded by the shrapnel from the destroyed turbine. Though his body was limp and weeping with blood, Haruka could hear an evil laugh echo from his mouth. She screamed and covered her ears, shrinking back against the wall and away from the countenance of death.

"No!" she screamed through her dream. Sound faded away again, and when she dared to open her eyes again, she looked into the bright, brown eyes and wicked smile of a familiar and friendly face. One that she had dearly missed.

Marco...

"This is my favorite time of day," Kristin Vandemark said with a toothy grin. "I love all the colors in the sky and how the sun melts into the ocean."

"Yeah, me too," Gabi agreed.

The wind blew in a strong gust off of the water, rustling the palms above and eliciting an irritated call from the tropical gulls as they drifted in the sky above like dozens of colorful kites. Strong men from the village hefted loads of split logs down the strand and dumped them in a chaotic pile in the sand a few hundred feet to the side of the village path. There was to be a bonfire tonight, and some sort of celebration for Haruka. This confused Gabi greatly, since James had told Gabi that Haruka wasn't coming back ever again.

I don't want a party if it means Haruka won't be back.

Will and his girlfriend Gina joined Gabi and Kristin under the swaying palm tree. The couple held hands, but their expressions were grim, without even the slightest hint of the warmth that Gabi usually felt when she saw them.

"It's time, Kris." Will uttered solemnly.

The smile disappeared from Kristin's face and she nodded, then stood up and beckoned to Gabi with her outstretched hand. Gabi remained seated and drew her knees to her chest, resting her head on crossed arms.

"No," she pouted.

"C'mon, Gabi. We don't want to be late. Your mom's already down there."

Gabi raised her voice to her teenaged caretakers. "No! I don't want to go if Haruka won't come back."

Kristin squatted down and lifted Gabi's chin softly with her finger. "Gabi, sweetie, we've been through this before. Haruka isn't coming back at all. She's in Heaven now, remember?" Gabi nodded, even as her nerves tingled and her lip quaked. "We're all really sad about it, and that's why we're having this party. We're all getting together to remember her."

Gabi sniffed and nodded. Reluctantly, she took Kristin's hand and walked with her and her companions to the beach, where hundreds of colonists were now milling about, finding seats in the sand and talking amongst each other. A few of the men who had carried the firewood now set to work arranging logs in the center of the human circle. Gabi knew that the bonfire would be ignited in mere minutes.

"Let's try to find your mom," Will said as he looked around.

Gabi nodded. Will lifted her onto his shoulders so she could get a better view of the crowd. Though the occasion was somber, she looked forward to the opportunity to sit next to the fire with her mother, which had not happened once since her father was killed. She scanned the gathering crowd but could not find her.

"See her?" Will asked.

"No. She's not here," she replied with growing disappointment.

"I'm sure she's here somewhere," Gina added.

The acrid smell of smoke mixed with the salty tang of the sea air as the fire grew from a tiny flicker to a steady flame, fueled by the wood and stoked by its tenders. Gabi's attention was captured by the smoky tendrils and crimson flares as they hissed and danced in the dying light. Then three women began to dig at lumps in the sand on the far side of the fire, a couple dozen feet away. They revealed dark green and brown pods of leaves that they retrieved. When opened they revealed cooked fish, roots, and tropical fruits, adding to the symphony of smells in the air. Gabi's mouth watered as she took in the tantalizing smells of the feast.

"We get to eat all that?" she asked Will.

"That and more. I heard there'll be buckets of crabs to eat, too," he replied.

"Yummy!"

She continued to watch the preparations with interest and anticipation. She had almost forgotten about finding her mother when she spotted her just beyond the crowd, talking with James and Dr. Petrovsky. She was clearly upset, as she shook her head and gestured wildly with her arms as the conversation progressed.

"Mama's over there, Will," she pointed.

He walked briskly with Gabi on his shoulders around the edge of the crowd, but stopped short as they came around the side of the circle and the conversation suddenly erupted over the din.

"That's not what happened," Gabi's mom shrieked, clutching her hair in her hands. Her mouth was twisted by her anguish and her eyes were swollen with tears.

James returned a calming gesture that was mostly unheeded. "I know that. Jesus, Maria. Now's not the time for this."

"No. It has to be now. You have to tell them. You have to get them to understand."

"Take it easy, Maria," Dr. Petrovsky urged.

"Why is Mama angry?" Gabi whispered in Will's ear.

He took Gabi off his shoulders and set her down, then turned her away from the argument. "We should go now."

"I won't," her mother cried out again. "They need to know. I can't stand the whispers. The accusations behind my back."

"You're worried about shadows that aren't there," James replied. "Come on, let's go before you make a scene."

Gabi glanced over her shoulder. Her mother had a wild look in her eyes and was pushing back against James, who tried to restrain her and keep her from the crowd. By this time the people had stopped talking amongst each other, and every pair of eyes was fixated on her mother.

"Do I have your attention now?" her mom cried out, pushing James aside and taking a few steps toward them, then shrugging off Dr. Petrovsky. "See what you're doing to me? See what your judging has done to an innocent woman?"

"Maria," James pled, but she shoved him back again.

"I didn't kill Haruka. You all think that because I hated her that I killed her, that I'm no better than the pinche cabrón who murdered my husband. You all think that because I wanted to protect you all from her tyranny that I'm the reason she's dead. Well, chingate. Fuck you all." There was a moment's dead pause as she caught her breath and steadied her shaky voice. "You're the ones that are killing *me*."

She glared intently at the crowd before storming off, with the two men giving chase close behind. The pit of Gabi's stomach fell out as her mother's fierce temper and terrible insults echoed in her mind. She fell to her knees and began to cry. Will and Gina knelt next to her, rubbing her back in comfort.

"It's okay, Gabi," Gina soothed.

"No it's not. Mama's mad at me again and I didn't even do anything."

"No, no, sweetie. She wasn't angry with you. I don't even think she knew you were here."

"She was so mad," she sobbed.

"She was tired and upset," Will corrected. "She's been under a lot of stress for a long time. Sometimes grown-ups can't handle everything, and we throw tantrums like that."

Gabi sniffed and looked up at her older friends through bleary eyes. "Mama's not mad at me?"

"No, not at all."

"Then why did she say all those things? Are people being mean to her?"

Will sighed and shifted from his crouch to a sitting position. "I'll be honest, Gabi. There are a couple people who have said mean things about her over the past few days. They think that your mom killed Haruka."

"But she didn't." She looked up at him, desperately hoping that she was right about her mother, but dreading that Haruka might have borne her wrath. "Did she?"

Gina wrapped her arms around Gabi and gave her a tight hug. "No. Doctor Petrovsky said that her old wound from the jaguar got infected again, and her body was too weak to fight it off this time. Haruka got really sick saving everyone from the ship when it blew up, and that's why her body couldn't handle it."

"Then why do people think Mama killed her?"

Will gave a halfhearted laugh. "Because sometimes people think stupid things when they're overworked and stressed. All of us adults are overworked right now, and some of us have made some bad choices lately." Gina's head turned, avoiding her boyfriend's eyes. "I know I have, and I'm going to have to live with them."

Gabi thought for a moment about all of the adults going crazy. She did not like this prospect one bit.

"So why don't you work less?"

"Because we can't afford to rest. Not yet, anyway. We work or we die."

Will's haunting words ended Gabi's line of questioning. She did not want to know more. The evening's celebration had given way to a terrible lesson that she was only starting to understand.

The world is a terrible place.

Calvin McLaughlin
8 June, Year of Landing, 16:40
North Concordia
>|

Hundreds of faces, both young and old, were illuminated by the faint glow of dozens of lanterns. A single crawler sat to the side of *Michael's* cargo ramp, shining a single flood light at the cavernous archway of the rear airlock. The audience waited for the emergence of two men from within the ship, charged with the most important task of the election: certifying the election. Though there were a half dozen men and women from each side of the river counting the ballots that had been returned from as far as the mining camps in the hills beyond, the two attorneys were charged with the final determination of the results.

The three would-be governors stood atop the deck. Tyler Quinn leaned against the bulkhead with his arms crossed, staring out into the night. Thomas Dayton paced the span from one side of the airlock to the other with his fist raised to his mouth in thought, while Darius Owens sat cross-legged at the edge of the ramp, splitting his attention between his two competitors. For one man, tomorrow would be the dawn of his reign as the most powerful man in the colony.

For Calvin, this meant finally putting to rest the misguided attempt by some colonists to put him in that position. Alexis had been right, for the most part; after he had failed to make a showing at the debate, his supporters had all but vanished. He still wanted to hear the results of the election with his own ears, just to set his mind at ease.

All day, as boxes of votes were carried into the ship from both sides of the river, rumors had been growing about the speculated outcome. By the time the last box had arrived from the mining community of Rust Creek, the speculation had reached a fever pitch, and not tapered off much since. It was only when some of the families with smaller children opted to retire for the evening that the momentum began to wane.

As it was, Cal believed the election was going to be very close. He had heard from many other colonists, and it seemed that Dayton and Darius were neck and neck, with the former colonel holding a slight edge. Cal could only conclude from how rarely he heard the name Quinn that the engineer from *Gabriel* was not likely to win.

Alexis found her way to him in the crowd, having just finished her shift at the kitchen. She carried a cup of steaming coffee in each hand, passing one down to Cal before taking a seat on the ground next to him.

"I didn't miss the show, did I?" she asked as she took a swig of her drink.

"Nope. Still watching paint dry."

"I'm confused. Is it Quinn who's the paint, or Darius?"

"Hard to tell. Quinn makes a hell of a mural though."

"I don't know. I think he's more of a sculpture. Modern realism at its finest, right?"

Cal chuckled and took a gulp of the coffee. It was plenty hot, but both bitter and stale, like most of the food stores on the ships. He was still searching for a drink on Demeter that suited him other than water, but the plants that the botanists had thus far cleared for consumption didn't have the same kick, or were too exotic for his tastes. Tea had never been his thing on Earth, and Demeter's equivalents were no different.

"I wonder how long it's going to take," Alexis remarked as she snuggled closer to him.

He shrugged and put his arm around her, downed the rest of his coffee, and set the cup down. "I'm hoping that it's sometime before midnight. I'm getting too old to stay up like this," he smirked.

"Poor old Cal. Can't keep up with the cool kids or the politicians."

"I take that as a compliment. At least the last part."

"There's a lot less shaking hands and kissing babies going on here than I remember."

"That's cause we cut through all the bullshit. Guess all it took was hitching a ride on a few trillion dollars' worth of stolen hardware and leaving the rest of humanity to die. Oh, and that thing of not having any babies to kiss. That helps too."

"I see your optimism's still unchecked there, buddy," she grinned.

"Shh," he interrupted. "Something's going on."

The crowd quickly hushed as Fred Hausner and Don Abernathy emerged from the belly of *Michael*. Don stopped at the top of the ramp after handing Fred a powerful lantern. Hausner proceeded down the gangway, where he was joined at the bottom by a ferry crew. The four men headed directly for the river.

They're going to Gabriel to announce the election results.

As Abernathy lingered at the mouth of the ship, the three candidates formed a line behind him, constantly looking between the attorney and the crowd. Darius's lips moved as he uttered something to the other men around him. Each reacted with a nod, and the men all shook hands.

The silence in the crowd lasted only a few minutes. Then the restlessness started. Muttered questions began to leap from circle to circle in the crowd, and soon after chants of "Tell us" began to rise from the gathered citizens and they stood in unison with their fists in the air.

Abernathy stood firm in his position, motioning to the crowd to be quiet. "It will be a few minutes, my friends. Look to the south, where the kitchen stands. Our friend and neighbor Gail will shine a light to us when Counselor Hausner has safely reached the people of South Concordia. Only then may I give the results, per our agreement."

Groans and shouts permeated the crowd, but Abernathy shook his head and stood firm, reiterating the importance of his colleague's mission. Cal grinned and shook his head in disbelief of his fellow citizens.

"So who did you vote for?" Alexis's question was unexpectedly blunt.

It took him a moment to realize that the question wasn't a joke. They had discussed the topic many times, and Cal had expressed his uneasiness in choosing between the man that relied on him as a crew member and the man who had single-handedly questioned the corruption of a commanding officer.

"I couldn't do it," he admitted. "I couldn't pick between Darius and Dayton."

Alexis drew away from his body and looked at him in shock. "Why?"

"I just couldn't do it. I mean, I owe so much to Colonel Dayton…"

"Tom," she corrected.

"Sorry, Tom. But would this election have even happened without Darius? I mean, I was there at the table. He was the one who brought it up. And even if he hadn't, the whole discussion wouldn't have happened if he hadn't taken down Eriksen. I mean, he really placed his life above everyone else's. How can that be ignored?"

"By the fact that he was never responsible for anything other than *Gabriel's* computers before all that happened. It's pretty clear to me who should be leading the colony; the only person left who actually *led* something."

Her argument was *déjà vu* of their discussions over the past few nights. It aggravated Cal that he couldn't make a decision either way, despite Lexi's arguments for Dayton. He had been apathetic about

J.C. Rainier

many things as a teenager, mostly dealing with couture or where to go to dinner, but he had never believed that he would pass up making a decision in an election.

Until the first one he had ever been involved in, four point three light years from where he had first registered to vote and never gotten a chance to. The debate between the three candidates had not helped him either, except to affirm that Tyler Quinn was not going to receive his vote. After all, if he could not choose between his commanding officer and the Hero of Concordia, why would he pick the man who stood in their shadows?

"I just don't think anyone said anything meaningful," he deflected. "I mean, they all sound the same when they're up there."

She shrugged and sighed. "I don't know if that's because they all sound like politicians or if it's because they all have the same vision for us. It wouldn't surprise me either way. There's just a few thousand of us, it's not like managing the colony will be that huge of a task. There were mayors back on Earth that had easier jobs than our next governor."

"Easier?" Cal scoffed. "Name me one mayor that you know from Earth that had to feed four thousand mouths with no phones, no roads, no steel, barely any electricity, and a fucking scary-ass breed of bears running around wild. Easy isn't anywhere in this game, sister."

Good. Swear at and demean your fiancée, the double within him shouted. *That's helpful.*

Cal closed his eyes and gritted his teeth. *Go see Doc Taylor tomorrow morning, you idiot. You can take a day off work and no one will miss it.*

Not even the new governor?

Only Quinn would, and I'll be damned if he's elected.

Oh good, you've given me something to hope for.

Cal growled even as he forced aside the inconvenient captive of his mind that needled at him. The absence of anti-psychotic medication was beginning to take its toll, and at times Cal had pondered the wisdom of consuming unknown native plants just to see if it would shut up the 'Twin Cal' he kept locked inside and hidden from the world.

Alexis remained silent, choosing to drown her words in what little coffee was left in her cup. He knew at once that he had screwed up again, and wrapped his arms around her.

"You're probably right. Dayton has years of command experience, and Darius has none. I just couldn't figure it all out, that's all."

"Every vote counts, you know," she replied sullenly.

He wanted to reply with a statistical rebuke that his vote was statistically insignificant, but he knew that was false; of the four thousand or so colonists that made up Concordia and the outlying communities, only a hair more than two thousand were of legal age to vote. One individual ballot could sway the entire election, especially given the fact that there were three candidates, not two.

Cal waited in silence wishing for another cup of coffee, or even a shot of the doctor's whiskey to pass the time and ease the crushing silence between himself, Lexi, and the world beyond them. He resigned himself to wait on edge with the rest of the populace until Don Abernathy returned the results of the election, which would allow him the peace of mind to return to the tent he shared with his soon-to-be bride. The fifteen minutes that intervened were almost pure torture.

"Counselor Hausner has arrived at *Gabriel*," the attorney announced almost giddily. "And with that, I am proud to announce the results of the election."

Cal was not entirely sure, but he believed that he could hear a resounding cheer echo through the hills and across the valley from the south side of the river just a split second before Don Abernathy announced that Darius Owens was the newly elected Governor of Concordia.

The crowd was too hard for the attorney to tame. Darius stumbled to the forefront, urged on by both Quinn and Dayton. Nervously, he delivered his speech in a tone that surely could not be heard by those farther back in the mass than Cal.

"I… I thank you for the honor, and for your support in this process," the once disgraced lieutenant said. "The coming days are going to be hard for everyone. This isn't news to anyone here. It will be my duty to ease the transition from colony to a functioning nation in the coming years. This isn't something that is going to happen by some miraculous intervention on my part, but rather the cooperation and communal spirit of each and every citizen.

"I may be your governor, but I am not above you. Without you, I don't exist. Without you, the citizen to your left or to your right does not exist. I may ask things of you in the coming days, and you may disagree with them, but I do not, in my heart, believe that I will ever do anything to betray you. Please keep that in mind, and do not betray your brothers and sisters in Concordia either. We walk the road together in Honor and Unity."

"Honor and Unity!" shouted Cal. He was joined in unison by the former crew members, as well as a good portion of the civilians, including Lexi.

"And it is in the spirit of Unity that I make my first decision," Darius continued.

First decision? Doesn't he start in the morning?

"I don't want a chasm between those who voted for me and those who voted for another man who stands before you. Whoever was certified in second place by the election board will be my deputy governor," he boomed. "And my other worthy opponent will also hold an office, which will be determined at a later date by myself and my deputy."

A few gasps in the crowd were muffled out by the thunderous applause that followed.

I should have voted for him, Cal thought as he joined in the praise.

Darius glanced up as his deputy slid a green enameled plate in front of him, stacked with grilled and spiced trout, a Demeter pear, and a salad made from native greens recently cleared for consumption by the botanists.

"Thank you, Tom," he said as he leaned back and stretched his taut joints.

It still felt awkward addressing Thomas Dayton by his first name, though he had quickly trained himself to do so. There were times that he wondered if he would ever get used to the informal greetings that etiquette allowed him to use, while many of the colonists would feel compelled to address Darius by his title rather than by his name.

He collected the myriad reports laid out in front of them and placed them in a stack to his right before starting in on his lunch. Tom took the seat at the former negotiating table directly across from Darius. He commandeered the stack of reports and began to flip through them, sorting them into four piles.

"Is that all we get for today?" Darius asked.

Tom nodded. "Don't expect a report from Rust Creek yet. It'll probably be a week or so before they respond. Looks like we finally got the grid reports from your friend Novak today."

"Nice to see he got off his butt."

"Some people are more suited to trade work than paperwork."

"I know. That's why I don't need to read that particular report. I already know he's finished running power from both ships to the river and got the first five buildings prewired on each side."

"Alright, then why did you force him to send an update if you weren't going to read it?"

Darius gestured his intent to reply with one finger as he chewed on a bite of his salad. The native greens were a tad on the bitter side, but the nutritional values that the scientists had reported were impressive. They were relatively poor sources of iron and vitamin C compared to their Earth equivalents, but their other mineral and vitamin contents were unusually high, particularly potassium, pyridoxine, and niacin.

"I want to make sure he doesn't get in the habit of slacking when we need an update from him," he replied after he swallowed the bite. "He's going to have to start working with other teams here soon and we can't have him be a roadblock."

"Fair enough."

Dayton finished sorting the reports as Darius devoured his meal and slid the plate aside. He stretched out his hand, accepting a stack from his subordinate. The pages included detailed reports from South Concordia regarding their stockpiles of timber, stone, and gathered native foods, as well as the progress on establishing three more farms on the outskirts of the town.

"It's the eleventh today, right?"

"It is."

Darius shook his head and picked up a pen. He scribbled some quick math on the page, and the results weren't pleasing. They were running out of time in the predicted growing season, and pulling resources from the tilling of these fields and the construction of farmhouses would allow him to concentrate on other projects such as the industrial sector on the riverfront. On the other hand, food was essential, and industry could be built later.

"Have you looked at this one yet, Tom?"

"I have. I was afraid something like that might happen when I got the first status reports from this side of the river."

Darius sunk deeper into his chair as he reviewed the sketched map drawn on the second page of the report and his own math, verifying it once again in his head. He then reached for his clipboard and paged through the ship's inventory until he got to the seed bank.

"Have them plant as much alfalfa and grass as they can." He traced his finger down the page to an entry with multiple quantities hand written and then scribbled out. "Do we have any more millet?"

"Not on *Michael*. We moved our last crate of cereal grain seeds to *Gabriel* two days ago."

"Alright. Who's on standby today?"

Tom paused slightly. His reply came in a soft, subdued voice. "Dan Forrest."

The one remaining officer who conspired with Doctor K to steal the ships.

The first act Darius took after his inauguration was actually Tom's idea, first voiced well before the elections. He had unilaterally pardoned everyone in the colony who was accused of a crime. This not only cleared Forrest of the charges that Tom had not acted upon, but it also allowed him to order Doctor Kimura's release from stasis. But Darius was careful to make sure it was understood that while Eriksen's supporters such as Doug Garza were also free of culpability, crimes that occurred after the edict would be treated as normal. Thus the criminal slate was wiped clean, and singular focus could return to the task of colonization.

"Have him take a look through the seed bank for that crate. If he can find it, get it in the ground ASAP. I want those structures built to the point where the weather won't rot them out over the winter, then everyone needs to be reassigned to the mill projects on this side."

"Are we assigning those farms to anyone?"

"Not yet. I want the Porters and the Lopezes to work out tending the crops. It'll be a bit more work for them now, but I don't see another good alternative."

Tom nodded and took down notes for the orders. "We've got sixteen people working those farm projects right now. We don't need that many on the mill projects. Ten, tops."

"Send the other six to the north bank to work on the smelter and foundry."

Darius heard the click of crutches approaching, and looked up to find Roger Miller standing at the rear of the bridge. His wounds had healed for the most part, though he still wore a cast on his shattered leg. The doctors had done what they could to mend the damage inflicted by Kintney, but they believed that the former lieutenant would at the very least walk with a limp for the rest of his life. His ability to perform the kind of hard labor so desperately needed had been nearly annihilated, so Darius had given him clerical duties under his office, answering both to Darius and Tom.

"Sorry to bug you, Governor," he said. "But you have a visitor."

"You don't have to call me Governor," he sighed. "Who is it?"

"Doctor Kimura."

Darius froze for a moment in surprise. He had no expected business with the doctor, and it was out of character for him to disturb those who were at work.

"Send him in, Roger."

Miller nodded and hobbled his way to the stairs, then used the hand railing to hop down the flight.

"What's this about?" Tom asked.

"I don't know."

A minute later the doctor emerged from below. His clothes were disheveled and stained, and his hair was a tangled mess. He looked as if he hadn't slept in days, and moved by shuffling one foot in front of the other, as if he didn't have the strength to walk. His eyes were sullen, and he acted as if his soul had been torn from his body.

"Darius," he said in a voice barely above a whisper. "I must speak with you."

"What's wrong, Doc?"

"Please, it is a… personal matter."

Darius nodded to Dayton, who collected his reports and took his leave. He nodded at Dr. Kimura on his way off the bridge. Kimura stumbled over to the vacant seat and let his frail body sink into it.

"I have lost everything, Darius."

He blinked in response, unable to pose an appropriate counter question.

"I brought my family along because I could not bear to be alone. I feared for them, yes, but not as much as I feared for myself. Not as much as I feared the thought of being an old man wasting away amongst strangers."

"You did the right thing by…"

"Did I?" he snapped. It was the first time he knew of that Dr. Kimura had ever interrupted anyone. "My son-in-law is dead. Saika blames me for that. She blames me for the loss of their child, as well. My grandchild."

Darius gasped audibly. At once his heart began to ache with the pain that his friend was enduring. "I'm so sorry, Doctor. I had no idea."

He nodded with trembling lips, tears streaming down his face. "Saika miscarried two days ago. It probably *is* my fault. We never tested the stasis to see if it was safe for pregnant women. We didn't know it could do this."

"That's right. You didn't know whether it could or not. And Saika didn't tell you she was pregnant before the launch, so how could you have known anything would be wrong?"

"I cannot blame my own child for what happened. What kind of monster would I be? She couldn't have known what would happen."

"Exactly," Darius replied. "Neither of you could have known. Don't beat yourself up for what you couldn't have stopped."

Dr. Kimura turned his chair to the side and stared out of the canopy. "It will make no difference, Darius. Saika will not talk to me, nor will she see me. I have one daughter who is dead, that I never got to say goodbye to. I have another who I am dead to, and she will not allow me to say a word. She will barely even talk to Sarah, and then only to speak ill of me. I am lost, and Sarah is breaking under the pressure. I am the reason for that as well."

"I am very sorry, Doctor. Please, what can I do to help you?"

"You must make her see, Darius. Make her see that she is hurting me. Make her see that I never meant for any harm to come to her. I was the one who was supposed to die if we were discovered. Brandon made the same choice, but she will not listen."

A twinge of apprehension picked at him. Darius had promised to help the doctor bear the weight of his sins, but convincing Saika to accept something she viewed so contemptuously was not something he considered to be in the realm of possibility.

"I'll talk to her, Doc. It will be a while, though. Saika's too hurt right now to see that it's not your fault. It was all Eriksen. He could have avoided this if he had just let the past go, like Tom did with Major Forrest."

Kimura forced a smile. "Thank you, Darius. You are true to your word, as always."

"It's the least I can do. If you need to give her some space, please feel free to sleep aboard *Gabriel*. The ship is open for you, except the support section."

"Again, thank you."

As Dr. Kimura departed from the bridge, Darius found himself wondering whether the harder part of his job was going to be planning the development of the city or playing peacemaker for the conflicts that were sure to rise. Though heated, the schism between Dr. Kimura and his daughter would not be the last, and they were not likely to be personal.

The next time I intervene on someone's behalf, I'm going to be changing the course of everyone's lives forever. He held that thought for a moment. *Like when I stood up to Eriksen. Hopefully less costly in the end.*

Gabrielle Serrano
12 June, Year of Landing, early evening
Camp Eight
>|

"Can you go get Pelusina, honey?" Jeanette Vandemark asked, smiling softly.

Behind her, Gabi's mother screamed and wailed as she pounded her fists on Dr. Petrovky's chest wildly. James was barely able to restrain her. Gabi whimpered in the corner, fearing that her mother would break free and start beating on everyone in the room.

"You can't do this, you bastard," her mother screamed hysterically.

"Calm down, Maria. You're not helping anything," James growled as he tightened his arms around her chest and dragged her backward away from the doctor.

"You can't take my baby away from me! You're even worse than Haruka, you son of a bitch!"

The pure hatred in her mother's voice cut into Gabi's soul, and she could no longer hold back the flow of tears. Jeanette knelt next to her, rubbing her back and talking to her in a soothing voice.

James grunted and smirked. "Should have thought about that if you were so desperate to get rid of her. Who did you think the villagers would put in charge, you?"

"James, that's not helpful," Dr. Petrovsky retorted. "This is going to be hard enough for her as it is."

"Shut up, you asshole," her mother hissed. "You're doing this to me. You're letting him take her from me."

"You need to rest. You're not well."

"First you want me to work, now you don't. Make up your minds, but don't take Gabi from me."

Jeanette picked up Gabi and held her tight to her chest. She placed her warm hand over Gabi's ear, drowning out much of the angry rhetoric that filled the room. Jeanette took Gabi around the rear partition wall and found the dirty stuffed cat that had become Gabi's last remaining positive memory of Earth. She then carried Gabi from the clinic and down to the beach. Gabi cried nearly the entire way. Her eyes burned with her tears and she choked as she breathed in the mass of saliva in her mouth.

"I'm so sorry you had to see that, dear," Jeanette said when she finally placed Gabi under a tree, looking out over the sparkling water.

She clutched Pelusina tightly. "Why are you taking me from Mama?"

"You need somewhere safe to stay while she gets better. Doctor Petrovsky says she's really sick, and she can't be around you right now."

Terror rushed through her. "Is she going to die like Haruka?" she squeaked.

"No, honey. She's not going to die."

"Then why can't I be with her?"

Jeanette was always kind to Gabi, though when she sighed and looked away, her sadness was clear. "Because Doctor Petrovsky thinks she might hurt you."

Gabi wanted to refute this, but she had been the target of her mother's anger several times since her father died. On more than one occasion her mother had lashed out and struck her with no warning.

"It's only for a little while. We want you to be with your mom, but she needs to get better. You can stay with us; the girls would love to have you over. They want to sing with you, and Will promised to take you to class every morning."

"But I want my mama!"

Jeanette wrapped her arms around Gabi's shoulders. "I know. As soon as the doctor says she's better. We won't keep you from her one minute longer, I promise."

Gabi leaned forward against her knees, crushing her stuffed animal between her legs and body. She rested her head on the tops of her knees and watched the fishermen as they paddled their canoes in to shore for the day and unloaded their catch. One had to fend off a particularly bold gull that tried to steal a meal from the basket at the prow of the boat.

"Mama said that James is worse than Haruka. Why did she say that?"

"She didn't mean it. Your mom is really sick, and one of the things this sickness does is make her say funny things."

"So she didn't want the people to vote for her?"

"Not if she had any sense."

"And she's not angry that they picked James?"

Jeanette paused for just a second. "Maybe a little bit, but it's not because she thinks he's a bad person. You know your mom has had a really rough time since we've been here, right?" Gabi nodded. "You have too. We really want things to get better for both of you and this is part of it."

"Okay, I guess."

Gabi turned back to the sea and watched everyday life unfold in front of her. She had a moment of sadness at the realization that her life was harder than the other kids on the beach, but that sentiment passed as she made a new set of plans for when her mother was better.

The first thing we'll do is watch a sunset together. Just me and Mama.

The weight of a thousand stares threatened to suffocate Cal, but his tongue was tied and made lame by the beautiful young woman standing before him with joyous tears in her emerald-green eyes and a smile on her trembling red lips.

No bridal gown was available for Alexis; formalwear was not something that any of the colonists had packed for their hasty evacuation, nor was it on the project team's list of necessary supplies for the colony. He had no idea what she would be wearing when she walked down the aisle, and the one wedding tradition that wasn't complicated by either logistics or supplies was the one where he could not see the bride beforehand. Cal had no argument with that, and had kept his distance.

When she had finally emerged from the neatly split crowd he froze for a moment, then his head spun and he thought he was going to pass out. This was the first time he had ever seen her dressed up, and though it was a simple short-sleeve red dress borrowed from another colonist, the way it flowed with her fluid movements gave him teases of her curves. She wore a circlet of native flowers which rested just above her brow, and the aluminum ring flashed in the sun as the leather necklace danced in the slight breeze. Even though a casual onlooker might have mistaken Alexis for a bridesmaid, Cal thought with absolute certainty that she carried the crowd's rapt attention.

Cal also had to borrow his attire for the day. His ill-fitting slacks were too wide in the waist and a hair short in the leg, and the blue button-down shirt he sported was made for a larger man; it flapped and waved with every variation of the wind. If he had been given a choice he would have avoided the necktie altogether, but Hunter had insisted, tying the double Windsor knot so tightly that it almost choked Cal.

He couldn't take his eyes off of her, not even as Reverend Malson gave his speech about marriage and union. Cal's love for Alexis stood firmly as a wall against the waves of terror and doubt that wracked him as he stood before her. He had never looked in her eyes for this long, and he wondered if she could see through his countenance and into his soul.

Then her smile twitched just a hair wider, and she mouthed the words "I love you." All he could do was swallow and nod as all his sensibilities seemed to fail him at once. For a fleeting moment he believed that she might have done that just to see if he would pass out. Then he remembered that, despite how well she could read him, she wasn't actually in his head.

He had just enough time to take a deep breath before the preacher finished his speech and went straight into the vows. Cal managed to get them out without stumbling over his tongue, and also somehow kept upright as Alexis delivered the same vows in return.

The exchange of rings took on a very different form since no gold had yet been sourced on Demeter. Instead, Cal untied the leather band that hung from Alexis's neck and slid a second aluminum spacer ring – sourced from a failed hard drive from one of the ships – into place next to the existing one, then joined the two pieces of metal together with a thin strip of leather before adorning his wife with the jewelry once more. She then slipped another identically crafted necklace over his head. In an instance the symbolism of union sunk in, and even before Reverend Malson declared it before the crowd, Cal knew that they were married.

He leaned in and kissed her tenderly, apprehensive of the mass of onlookers. As she pressed back against him with rising passion, his tension melted away, and the whoops and cheers from the crowd faded into the background of the moment. Only the warmth of her skin and the gentle tickle of her breath on his skin as she finally pulled away lingered in his senses.

The moment was all too short, and Cal found himself and his wife ushered away by Hunter. They made the short trek from the outskirts of Concordia to a spot overlooking the ferry landing on the river's bank, where Hunter placed them to receive congratulations from the wedding's attendees. The stream of well-wishers came and went in a blur; after a few minutes he could hardly remember who had already greeted them, and friendly faces in the crowd faded into the background as they mixed with the vaguely familiar acquaintances that made up the hundreds who came to exchange pleasantries with the newlyweds. The smells of grilled fish and roasted vegetables taunted Cal as he stood in line with his stomach grumbling.

The jubilant sentiment of the colonists was overwhelming, and after nearly an hour Hunter had to pry Cal and Alexis away for the wedding feast; this was actually equal parts buffet and picnic, thanks to the lack of formal dining area and catering facilities. The evening air was cool enough to be pleasant, and the shadows crept into the east valley as the sun sank into the western mountains. The newlyweds enjoyed their dinner parked on the back side of the hill watching the river, surrounded loosely by close friends who kept the guests at bay while they could eat.

"This is delicious," Alexis whispered as she took a bite of the river trout.

"I could get used to it. Or I have to get used to it. I haven't decided yet."

"Oh come on," she teased as she pushed his shoulder gently. "I know you love it when Gail grills it over the wood we have here."

"Of course I do. Just wish I had a steak right about now."

"Can't butcher any cattle yet, and you know it."

"I know," he grinned impishly. "But if I go much longer, I might forget what one tastes like. Then what would I do?"

"Hmm," she pondered mockingly. "Go crazy and live life as a hermit in the woods, I guess. Or stay here with your wife."

"Tough decision. I've always loved the woods."

He chuckled as she slapped him across his shoulder in mock indignation. As Cal looked around he saw the wedding guests settled into their social circles, scattered like pebbles over the landscape. Hunter made eye contact with Cal and made a swift bob of his head and snapped his fingers, a gesture he made whenever he forgot something. He placed his plate on the ground and disappeared down the hill.

Hmm. Wonder what he missed.

Cal set his plate well to the side as he finished up the meal, leaving only a scrap of flatbread made from the flour ground from a local tuber, which he relished as he lay back in the crisp brown-and-green grass. Wispy clouds passed far overhead, tinted pink and orange by the fading sunlight. The smell of searing fish gave way to the sweet smoke of campfires, and even the din of the dozens of conversations lowered, giving an air of relaxation to the otherwise festive day.

"How long do you think before we can make our getaway?" Alexis asked.

"Well, let's see. There hasn't been a toast yet. Hunter hasn't given whatever philosophical or embarrassing speech he has planned. Doctor Taylor said she has a surprise for us later, and the Porters haven't shown up with our rides."

"So we ditch the horses and sneak out early. I don't think anyone will notice."

"Alright, let's do it. I'll be right behind you, sneaking right through the middle of everyone in the middle of the reception," he grinned.

"Spoil my fun, why don't you."

Cal's smile cracked slightly as he caught Traci Josephson approaching them. The grievous wounds delivered by the reaper bear had nearly healed. Only a single bandage on her forearm and wrist remained, and in that hand she bore two cups. Grasped in her other hand was a dark green bottle. Her ever present scowl was oddly absent, replaced by a hollow look that Cal couldn't quite read. He scrambled to his feet to greet her, taking a half step in front of his bride in the process.

"Traci," he nodded, his smile evaporating in her presence.

She stretched out her bandaged hand and passed the enameled cups to Cal, then offered the bottle. "Ceretti forgot this back at camp. It's yours for the toast, a little something from his private stash. You can call everyone together when you're ready."

"Thank you," he replied curtly as he took the offering.

Traci's mouth twitched into a fleeting smile, and she turned away. After only four steps she stopped and slowly turned to face them again.

"I'm sorry, Calvin," she uttered in an eerily soft voice.

"For what?"

"For everything I've done to you. For everything I've put you through since we've been here, and every snarky comment I made to you on *Michael*. For threatening and bullying you. I was wrong. I couldn't see how wrong I was about you until it was almost too late."

"Traci, it's okay."

"No, it's not," she cut him off. Tears began to stream down her face, though Cal could tell she was fighting off a complete breakdown. "Jesus, I had the gun in my hand and I was going to shoot myself. I failed my mission, and only you and Neil were left. You should have hated me. But you stopped me."

Cal felt Alexis wrap her fingers into his forearm, almost digging her nails into his skin. "Traci, please. This isn't the time for this."

"I know, Alexis. I'm sorry." Traci wiped her eyes with her bandage and fixed her attention on Cal once again. "I just thought you should know that you saved my life. I know that I'm supposed to give you guys a gift on your wedding day, but I don't really have anything. All I can give is my deepest thanks, and my sincerest wishes for the best. For both of you."

Cal was struck speechless. After a moment's hesitation and dozens of responses rattling through his head at the same time, he stepped forth and hugged Traci and whispered, "Thank you. That's the only thing I could wish for."

The embrace ended, and Traci nodded before walking away, just as distraught as during her confession. Cal looked numbly down at the bottle of Irish whiskey in his hands.

Every day, work is our reality. But I guess it's not just tilling fields, building homes, or cutting trees. At least not for all of us. Traci's wounds may have healed on the outside, but she's still wounded on the inside.

Cal closed his eyes and remembered the small, private burial ceremony for Elaine Montoya, and the utter grief that her family wore that day. The dead silence that engulfed *Michael's* bridge as Cal broke the news of Cameron's death to the crew haunted him, even weeks later. And even though he had never seen the face of a single refugee or crew member of *Raphael*, he could feel the sorrow echoing subtly through the colony every day.

The wounds we all bear are deeper and wider than the Fairweather. So I guess healing is our reality, too. We still have a long way to go with that.

He opened his eyes and looked again over the revelers. Among those gathered closest were familiar faces from both sides of the river, engrossed in conversation and laughter.

But it's a start, he thought, and his bright smile again broke through.

"Is everything alright, Cal?" Alexis asked.

"It is. And it will be," he replied as he removed the stopper from the bottle.

He raised the bottle in the air and whistled loudly for the crowd's attention.

```
Gov. Darius Owens
15 August, Year of Landing, 09:42
Gabriel
>|
```

Darius tried to concentrate on the stack of reports in front of him on the table, but the air had become insufferably hot and stagnant over the course of the morning. Bravo lingered in the sky at its apex, turning the bridge into a greenhouse and much of the upper gallery into a sauna. As the first beads of sweat dripped from his brow onto the crinkled pages he decided to collect his work and relocate to just inside the cargo door on the lower floor. The temperature was considerably cooler, and the shape of the open tail allowed the wind to form small eddies just inside.

The first summer on Demeter had been quite warm, and though there had been rain through much of June, the skies had been fair for weeks on end. The landscape around Concordia had taken on a sepia color, broken only by the green of hardier trees and farms, the murky blue of the river, and the gray hulks of the sleeper ships. Earth-based crops only grew modestly when planted away from the river due to the lack of available irrigation. Native plants grew much better, but Darius knew it would be some time before the farmers of the fledgling colony fully understood their growth patterns and requirements. As Darius dangled his legs off the end of the cargo platform he cast his gaze out to one of the fields at the very edge of the encroaching town boundary.

It's going to be tight, that's for sure, he thought.

Early projections from the farms were less than stellar. There would be plenty of food for everyone at harvest time, but supplies were sure to be stressed during the winter, especially if it was harsh, as the livestock would likely need to share the grain supply with the humans.

Darius worried far less about supplies of protein since a small group of intrepid colonists had become trappers, as had their ancestors two hundred years earlier on Earth. He was thankful for the food that this venture provided for both Concordia and Rust Creek. New businesses had also spawned that processed the hides of these animals into new clothing and blankets to replace articles that were wearing out across the colony, further evidence of the populace's understanding that waste was as big of an enemy as any other factor on Demeter.

As he flipped through several pages of detailed reports, he heard Tom approach from inside the ship. Roger was with him, evident from the limp that he walked with, though he at least no longer needed crutches.

"Done with the inventory?" Darius asked.

"Indeed," the reply came from Tom.

"How much is left?"

"Almost three months' worth, evenly divided between the two ships."

"Three? That's more than I thought we'd have."

His deputy grimaced as he sat on the deck next to him. "It's less than I'd hoped for. I don't think Colonel Eriksen was thinking that far forward. Either that or his botanists weren't as sharp as ours."

"In any case, it might just make the difference in getting through the winter. If we have to burn through our stores keeping the livestock alive, we'll be thankful for those ration packs later on. Even if they do taste like rubber and hot sauce."

"Nothing like a little home cooking to put perspective on things," Roger added.

"After harvest, you can kiss that goodbye for a while. Or at least the kind of cooking we get right now. We're going to pull up stakes on the camp kitchen as soon as the weather turns."

"So only the lucky few with homes will be able to cook with fire," Tom finished the thought.

"That reminds me," Darius said as he snapped his fingers and rose to his feet. "I haven't talked to Calvin yet about his situation. Has he had any success in making biodiesel?"

"So-so. His last batch didn't gel up, which is a good thing. I still wouldn't put it in anything that we want to keep running, though. Give him time and I bet he'll come up with usable fuel. He's been experimenting with other stuff, though."

"Oh?"

"He's figured out how to make soap from his waste and errors."

Darius chortled. Though the ships still had plenty of soaps and detergents in their stores, it was somehow comforting to know that the townsfolk could still wash themselves once these supplies ran out. It also seemed that every week someone figured out how to produce something that filled either an immediate or short-term need. As everyone fell into their niche, Darius found himself spending less time micromanaging the labor force and freer to look to the future.

"Go get him, Tom. I want to talk to him."

"Alright."

Tom descended the ramp and made his way toward the river. Cal McLaughlin resided on the north side of the river, and it would be some time before Deputy Governor Dayton would return with the young man.

Darius occupied his time by reviewing construction reports with Roger, all the while trying to shove aside the feeling that his boon for Calvin might spark resentment in a few families that he knew of. He had decided not to back down from his decision, though that didn't quell his uneasiness at all.

The two men finished their work over the course of the next hour, culminating with an order that would pave the way for an ambitious construction project for the next spring. Darius had visions of a bustling market square in Concordia, with residences above shops allowing for a smaller metropolitan footprint. He selected the site of *Michael's* current camp kitchen, as it would be a familiar location for all, at least on the north side. In turn, he envisioned that this would allow the existing farms to stay in place longer while the town grew out of its canvas infancy.

Maybe next winter we won't all be cooped up inside the ships for protection. Maybe our home will actually look like one.

Just as Darius was contemplating lunch, Dayton returned with Calvin, whom he greeted with a firm handshake. Calvin wore a patched and threadbare flight suit, marred along the arms and lower legs with oil stains of varying sizes and colors. Dark smudges adorned both cheeks, and his hair was a greasy mess. Despite this, Calvin had taken the time to wash his hands, a courtesy that Darius appreciated at once upon clasping the younger man's hand.

"Thank you for coming to see me."

Cal shot a timid sideways glance at the other men in his presence. "Sure. Is something wrong? Dayton wouldn't tell me anything; he just dragged me away from what I was doing. I barely had time to take off my apron and clean up."

Darius's smile evaporated. "I hope it wasn't something important. I didn't mean for him to disturb you like that."

"It's okay. I had just finished up anyway."

"That's good to hear." Darius paused and began pacing the width of the deck. "I know you've been making progress on your diesel project. Would it make things easier if I could manage some better equipment and a more consistent work space for you?"

"That would probably make a huge difference."

"Roger has an inventory of what's left on the ships, and knows what's already been allocated. Go over what you need with him. Hopefully we can scrounge up something that would help you out."

Cal smiled broadly. "Thanks. I appreciate it."

Darius moved directly in front of Cal, just about an arm's width away. The sense of apprehension he carried suddenly melted away, replaced by muted pride. He mirrored Cal's facial expression.

"It's we who appreciate you, my friend. From your efforts to produce fuel for our equipment to your role in unification, we all owe you something. Perhaps more than we can repay. I'm willing to try, though."

Calvin's grin was swept away as confusion washed over him. "What are you talking about?"

"Solving your workspace problem and giving you something that we all believe you deserve. Your own home."

His eyes shot wide open and his jaw slacked as he stammered. "W-what?"

"There's a shop and home just a little upriver from the smelter on the north bank that we think will suit the needs of your project, and give you and your wife privacy at the same time," Darius replied, fighting back the urge to show anything other than polite gratitude.

"N-no," Cal stuttered after a moment. "No, I don't deserve that. There are so many others who I know would want a home like that. I just… no, I couldn't take that."

"The shop is well suited to your needs," Roger jumped in. "It's got a storage room and a small reception area on the main floor, and the workspace is under cover out back. You can do your dirty work without getting wet, and keep the fire hazard down also.

"There's a small apartment on the second floor," added Dayton. "Well, apartment might be a generous word. It's a converted loft. But it's much bigger than the inside of a tent or sleeper berth, I can tell you that. For the two of you, it's perfect."

"No," Cal protested. "I mean, I appreciate the thought, but I just can't. Someone else deserves it. We can wait our turn."

"It *is* your turn, Calvin," Darius extended his hand again. "Now don't make me tell your wife that you're turning down a house. I get the feeling I know what she'd have to say about it, and where you'd end up sleeping tonight."

Cal gulped and froze for a moment. Then the smile crept back onto his face, growing wider than ever. He gripped Darius's hand and clapped him on the shoulder. "Thank you. Thank you so much," were the only words he could muster. He repeated them over and over as he shook the hands of Dayton and Miller.

"Go tell her the good news," Darius beamed. "Come back later when you're ready to talk about what supplies you need."

"Thank you," Calvin hollered back as he tore down the ramp like a frenzied brush dog.

Darius crossed his arms across his chest and leaned against the outer airlock bulkhead. For a moment, in his mind, he could see the elation on Alexis McLaughlin's face as her husband delivered word of their fortune.

"Ready to make more people jump for joy?" Tom asked, bringing his attention back to the task at hand.

"I wish I could make them all that happy today."

"Soon enough, Governor. Soon enough."

"Not soon enough," he replied. With that, his smile faded into nothing. "Two houses north of the river and four small apartments on this side, right?"

"Right. Who's up first?"

Darius pursed his lips and breathed deeply to clear his thoughts.

"Bring me the Montoya family," he said as he eyed the continuous activity in the camp beyond.

God knows, if the McLaughlins deserve a home for what they've given us, the Montoyas deserve one for what this planet has taken from them.

>END PLAYBACK|

Credits and Acknowledgements
28 July 2013
The real Earth, somewhere in Washington State

This is the third book in the Project Columbus series. That's such a simple statement, but it doesn't do any justice to the amount of time and effort that goes into a book, much less an entire series to this point. I've been very fortunate to have a strong core of help throughout this series, and I hope to continue working with each and every one of them in the future.

Thanks to my test readers Rob, Karie, and Sarah. Without their insight, I would miss many crucial details during editing. After all, what makes sense in my head doesn't always make sense to the reader, right? I'd also like to thank Mathew Reuther for his continued help in self-publishing, and Bridgette Reuther for creating the wonderful covers and layouts for the entire series.

To my wife and children, thank you for your continued patience and love. It means more than the world to me.

To the readers who picked me up for *Flight* or *Ashes*, I am honored, and welcome you back. To those who are new to my works, welcome!

I will see you all in a few months for the next installment of Project Columbus.

. . .

About the Author:

J.C. Rainier is product of the Pacific Northwest, born in the Seattle area in 1978, and living in the Puget Sound area his whole life. He is the younger of two children in his family, and his older brother proved to be a giant pest up through his teenage years (as siblings tend to be).

J.C.'s parents were both educators working at the middle school level, and he married into another family of educators. In his family, counting in-laws, there are now two retired principals, two retired teachers, a retired school counselor, and an active science teacher.

In his youth, J.C. read quite a lot. The Call of the Wild was one of his early favorites, and into middle school he began to devour other books such as Anne McCaffrey's Dragonriders of Pern series. Unfortunately, J.C. developed a form of dylexia that made reading from the page of a book difficult. It was later discovered that the curvature of the page itself caused the issue, and the advent of the eReader (with its perfectly flat screen) has allowed him to once again enjoy reading as he used to.

He enjoys both indoor and outdoor pursuits including computers, cars, and camping. J.C. and his wife enjoy hockey, and set aside time several times each season to watch the local WHL franchise.

J.C. and his wife are raising three boys, including a set of twins. If his blog ever fails to make sense, he's probably had a very long night just prior to writing it. If said writing is just a random set of characters similar to "adsk,wr3.1", then one of the children has managed a surprise attack on his laptop.

. . .